HIDDEN
IN
MEMORIES

ALSO BY VIVECA STEN

HIDDEN
IN
MEMORIES

TRANSLATED BY
MARLAINE DELARGY

VIVECA STEN

AMAZON **CROSSING**

Previously published as *Botgöraren* by Forum in Sweden in 2022. Translated from Swedish by Marlaine Delargy. First published in English by Amazon Crossing in 2025.

Published by Amazon Crossing, Seattle

www.apub.com

Amazon, the Amazon logo, and Amazon Crossing are trademarks of Amazon.com, Inc., or its affiliates.

EU product safety contact:
Amazon Media EU S. à r.l.
38, avenue John F. Kennedy, L-1855 Luxembourg
amazonpublishing-gpsr@amazon.com

ISBN-13: 9781662529825 (paperback)
ISBN-13: 9781662529818 (digital)

Cover design by Ploy Siripant
Cover image: © Edmund Lowe Photography / Getty; © Maridav / Shutterstock

Printed in the United States of America

For Mischa, the whole family's little Easter darling

NORGE

SVERIGE

Ideråker

STORLIEN

Storvallen

Tjäl

Enafors

Handöl

Snasahögarna

Tångböle

Ånn

Staa

DUVED

ÅRE

Björnänge

Undersåker

JÄRPEN

Kall

ÅRE

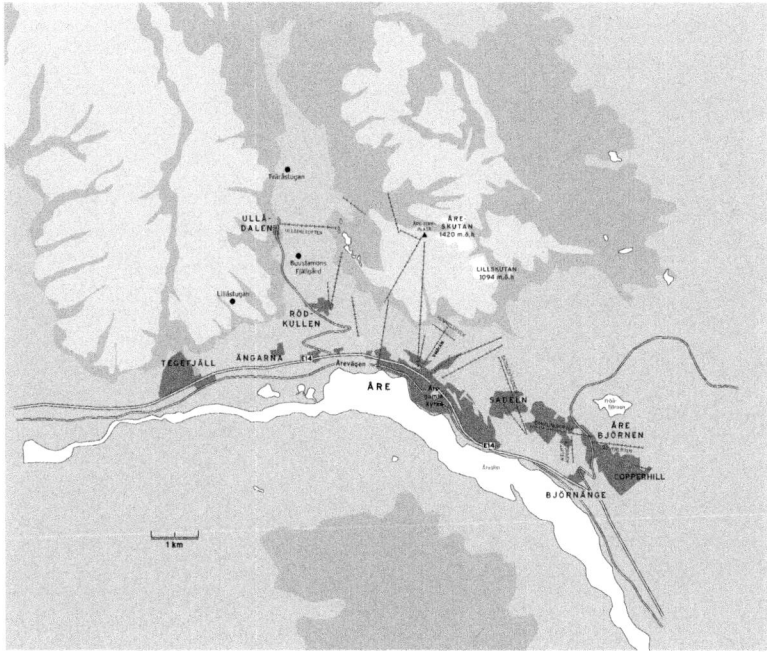

TRÄCKSTUGAN

ULLÅ-
DALEN

BUSSTÄRANS
FJÄLLGÅRD

Lilládugen

RÖD-
KULLEN

ÅRE-
SKUTAN
1420 m.ö.h.

LILLSKUTAN
1094 m.ö.h.

TEGEFJÄLL   ÄNGARNA   E14   Årevägen

ÅRE

SADELN

ÅRE
BJÖRNEN

COPPERHILL

E14

Åreälven

BJÖRNÄNGE

1 km

PROLOGUE

Aada Kuus, the cleaner, is standing in the bathroom of room 633 at Copperhill Mountain Lodge in Åre. She has just hung up two towels when she hears a noise from the Silver Suite next door.

Was that someone groaning . . . ?

It is late, after midnight. She was just about to finish her shift when she noticed that 633 needed clean towels. She had to sort it out before she went home—guests are due to check in first thing tomorrow morning.

Now she is standing there as if she has been turned to stone, her eyes fixed on the bathroom wall adjoining the large suite.

A woman screams, her desperate cry slicing through the night. Then comes a curse from a deep voice, followed by a muted thud, almost as if a lamp has been knocked onto the floor.

What is going on?

Aada hears a whimpering sound, and something within her reacts. A paralyzing horror takes over, as it had in the past when her stepfather was drunk and used his fists to beat her mother black and blue.

She is seven years old again.

Fear floods her body. Her blood turns to ice.

Aada meets her own terrified gaze in the mirror above the washbasin. There is silence next door now, but she has adopted a defensive stance—shoulders up, body hunched. Her nerves are exposed, on the outside of her skin.

Her breathing is jerky, her mouth open. Should she go and knock on the door? Call reception?

Raise the alarm?

She doesn't know what to do, it is becoming increasingly difficult to breathe. It is as if the oxygen is getting jammed in her throat; her tongue is sticking to the roof of her mouth. Her brain is telling her to do one thing, but her body wants her to hide. Nobody must find out you are here, *a voice yells inside her head.* Something bad might happen to you too.

Aada stares at a fixed point on the tiles until her eyes sting.

The feeling that she has to get away picks up speed like an avalanche; in the end it is so strong that her muscles actually cooperate. Legs trembling, she edges into the hallway and fumbles for the black door handle.

That is when she catches a glimpse of him.

Just as he is on his way out.

She has opened the door a tiny fraction, her hand is still on the latch, but she instinctively recoils when a man rushes out of the Silver Suite clutching a shiny, bloodstained object.

His cap is pulled well down over his forehead, and he is wearing a black mask over his mouth and nose. Aada can see only his burning eyes.

A second later she closes the door for her own protection.

Her mind whirling, she stands there frozen to the spot. She is so frightened she cannot move. In the end she drops to her knees and puts her head in her hands. Tries to suppress the nausea as she rocks back and forth in shock.

Something terrible must have happened in the Silver Suite.

The man was covered in blood.

Is he still out there?

What if he tries to get into this room to attack her too?

SATURDAY, MARCH 27, 2021

1

It looks like the place that God forgot.

Charlotte Wretlind knows that she ought to be horrified, standing here in front of the Storlien mountain hotel. It is Easter season, but the sky is overcast. The afternoon light is gray. The whole area is enveloped in a desolate mist.

And yet Charlotte sees something else. She doesn't care about the shabbiness or the general decay, the sense that time has left the hotel behind. Instead she sees it as it used to be during its golden age, when she was a child and her family spent every Christmas holiday here.

When she was a little girl, her body tingling with excitement and anticipation.

She remembers the almost ceremonial atmosphere as the night train from Stockholm pulled into the station on December 23 and they were collected by a horse-drawn sleigh. There was a huge Christmas tree in the elegant foyer when they arrived, and sparkling garlands hung from the ceiling.

Charlotte recalls the feeling on Christmas Eve as they walked up the imposing staircase to the restaurant. How the hem of her mother's full-length velvet gown brushed each step, how beautiful she was with her red lips and her dark back-combed hair.

In Charlotte's memory those Christmases at Storlien are still surrounded by a magical glow. For many years she has dreamed of building a new exclusive mountain hotel here, just like her father always talked about.

And now it is going to happen.

It took a great deal of persuasion to convince her business associate, Henry, to come on board with the project, but at long last she has a partner who is prepared to supply the necessary capital. For decades she has worked on realizing others' projects in the property and financial sector, but now it is time to carry through her own plans. She is fifty-six years old, and she wants to build something that she will be remembered for.

Daddy would have been so proud, if only he could have been here.

She can see it now: the new main building, the wing housing a luxury spa, the panorama windows. The footprint will be twice as big. There will be exclusive suites and specialist restaurants offering top-class gastronomic experiences.

Storlien will spring back to life, and the guests will come flocking, just as they had when she was a child. When she is done, the mountain hotel will be the destination of choice for premium international visitors. Tourists from the Arab countries, from China—she has already begun sketching out a marketing strategy to attract them all.

She smiles to herself and heads for the car to return to Åre. She is spending the whole of Easter week at Copperhill Mountain Lodge, with the intention of doing some skiing when she isn't working. It is only a forty-five minute drive from Storlien to Åre.

She has been preparing herself for so long; she has dreamed of this for years and years. It has taken countless hours of planning, meeting after meeting. She has had to cajole and threaten in order to secure all the necessary permissions. On Monday she has one last important meeting with the local council to finalize things, followed by a press conference at five o'clock in the afternoon.

Bengt Hedin, the council's representative, will be there too, and Henry is flying up. Charlotte frowns. She must remember to call him this evening—she needs to keep him sweet.

As she slides in behind the wheel, she can't help taking one last look at the building on the mountainside. If only Daddy were here to share her triumph, but he passed away some years ago, and her mother is in a home, suffering from advanced dementia.

Daddy will never be able to rejoice in Charlotte's greatest success, even though she has spent her whole life proving her capability to him.

However, she is looking forward to showing the plans to Filip, her beloved son, who has promised to come to Åre next week.

She can't wait to see him.

Darling Filip.

She is doing this for his sake too. He is her only child, and she has raised him on her own since she divorced his father, Mats, when Filip was little.

Secretly she dreams of working with Filip, so that one day he can take over. Admittedly they have fought quite a lot over his failure to stick to any kind of study program, but she is hoping that a few days together in the mountains will make everything better.

He has just dropped out of yet another course, this time at the Royal Institute of Technology in Stockholm, and the news made Charlotte both angry and upset. They had a huge quarrel a couple of weeks ago, and she said things that she deeply regrets.

Since then he has barely responded to her text messages.

All she wants is to support her son, but she finds it so hard to understand why he doesn't make more of an effort.

Charlotte rests her hands on the wheel.

She hates to see Filip wasting his talents. He is intelligent and quick thinking. He could achieve so much if he would just take things seriously. Which is why she can't keep quiet when she sees him playing computer games twenty-four seven.

At the same time, she hates the tension between them. She has never been afraid of conflict, but being at odds with your only child is another matter.

Filip means the world to her, she can't bear his silent remoteness.

When he comes to Åre, she must try to fix their relationship. She has already made an attempt to compensate by inviting his sweet girlfriend, Emily, but that's not enough to salve her guilty conscience.

It is warm inside the car, and Charlotte lowers the temperature. Her phone on the passenger seat buzzes, the display glowing in the darkness. It is a message from Bengt Hedin, the chair of the town council's planning committee.

We need to talk about the land purchase. The opposition is asking questions and I don't know if it's going to go through.

Charlotte manages to hold back an angry exclamation. She has paid a great deal to secure Hedin's support. He must realize it's too late to back out now. He can't change his mind just a few days before they go public.

The entire project in Storlien depends on Charlotte being able to buy the land for the expansion. Releasing the necessary acreage has been a complicated process, and some council officials have fought her every step of the way. First of all they insisted that she renovate the dilapidated existing hotel; then they refused to approve the new architectural drawings. They had the nerve to claim that the design didn't fit in with the general ambience of Storlien.

After many lengthy and fruitless discussions, when it finally became clear that the council did not share her vision, she realized she was going to have to use more unorthodox methods to achieve her aim.

She glances at her phone again. Everything is due to be signed on Monday, then the project will be revealed at a press conference. No way is she going to allow Hedin to sabotage things at the last minute. Obviously she has meticulously documented all the payments he has received from her.

That is her insurance, in case he gets cold feet.

Slowly she types a response that leaves no room for misunderstanding.

That is not my problem, it's yours. The press conference is on Monday and it is too late to postpone.

She presses send. That will have to do. She puts down her phone and is about to drive off when it buzzes once more.

What does he want now?

She picks up the phone and sees that she has received a text message from an unknown number.

Get out of here, or you'll regret it.

She sighs wearily.

This isn't the first threatening message she has had since her plans became known in the area. And it probably won't be the last. There are reactionaries everywhere who don't like change, who want things to remain the same as they have always been. A Facebook group has also been set up, where people spew their hatred of her and the hotel project.

She will have to call Stefan over the weekend and ask him to sort this out. He is one of Sweden's most skilled lobbyists, a former agriculture minister with contacts throughout the community. That's the advantage of being a well-known ex-politician. He has worked on the project from the very beginning, and has helped to smooth the way for the new hotel.

And that isn't his only talent.

Charlotte smiles at the memory of their most recent night together.

With a shrug she decides to ignore the troll, then pulls out onto the slush-covered road. Her phone buzzes again, but she takes no notice. She has no intention of letting herself be scared by cowards who refuse to reveal their identity.

SUNDAY, MARCH 28

2

Detective Inspector Hanna Ahlander is having an early dinner with her older sister, Lydia, at the restaurant known simply as the Wine Bar; the place is packed. It is just after seven, and they have ordered coffee and dessert. Both have had a mild dose of COVID; otherwise they wouldn't have dared venture out to this kind of environment.

They are sitting at a round table in the corner. At the long bar a few yards away, the bartender is busy preparing a tray of liqueur coffees for another party.

Lydia pushes back her blond hair and picks up her glass of Italian Ripasso. The large diamond in her wedding ring sparkles in the candlelight. She is a successful lawyer and owns a huge house in Sadeln, an area a few miles outside Åre. That was where Hanna sought refuge the Christmas before last, when she was dumped by her partner Christian and sacked from her job with the Stockholm City Police on the same day.

Lydia, who is ten years older, has always been Hanna's rock. She and her family have arrived in Åre to celebrate the Easter break, and the sisters have sneaked away to spend some time on their own.

"How's work going?" Lydia asks, taking a sip of her wine. "I guess it's been pretty quiet lately."

Hanna nods. During the winter she has been mostly investigating narcotics crimes, and one or two cases of extortion. She is usually in Åre for a couple of days each week, and works from Östersund the rest of the time, where she is attached to the Serious Crimes Unit—just like her colleague Daniel.

As usual she feels a stab of pain in her heart when she thinks of him.

As usual she ignores it.

Right now he is probably at home with Ida and their daughter, Alice, preparing Sunday dinner. That's how it should be. He is with his family. That's where he belongs.

She and Daniel are workmates, nothing more.

Hanna wipes her mouth with her napkin and pushes aside the forbidden thoughts. It has been more than a year since she realized she had deeper feelings for Daniel, and every day, she tries to make them go away.

Back then they were working together on the murder of the skier Johan Andersson, and grew very close. Daniel has been a great support over the past year. Hanna still wakes in the middle of the night after a terrible dream about the traumatic resolution of the case. It has taken her a very long time to process what happened, and the burden of guilt because she didn't manage to intervene quickly enough is always with her.

"What's wrong?" Lydia asks.

Her sister is very good at picking up on small signals, but Hanna can't tell her how she feels. Lydia gives her a searching look.

"Nothing," Hanna replies dismissively.

Fortunately the waitress arrives with their desserts, distracting Lydia's attention. Hanna tucks into her crisp apple pie with Marcona almonds, beautifully served on a bed of vanilla sauce. Lydia has chosen a chocolate mousse with cherries and meringue.

"Is it about a guy?" Lydia persists. "Have you met someone new?"

Hanna's sister didn't only take care of her when Christian broke up with her out of the blue—she also made sure that he shared the money from the sale of the apartment they had lived in together. Without her, Hanna would have received nothing, and she wouldn't have been able to buy a place of her own.

"I'm afraid not," Hanna mumbles with her mouth full. "This is delicious," she adds. "How's yours?"

Lydia has no intention of dropping the subject, despite Hanna's best efforts.

"Just because Christian behaved like a pig, it doesn't mean all men are the same," she points out gently.

Hanna sees Daniel's face in her mind's eye. The hazel eyes that can switch between warmth and gravity in a second, the short beard, the way his cheeks move when he smiles.

He is the one who has made her feel at home in Åre. They often travel to Östersund together, and those are the best times in the whole week as far as Hanna is concerned.

Daniel would never have an affair behind Ida's back, or try to con her out of money. He is totally different from Christian, a much better person.

But he is taken, Hanna reminds herself.

The music from the loudspeakers has been turned up, and the hum of conversation increases accordingly.

"It's time to move on," Lydia says. "Time to meet someone who really cares about you."

"I know. I know."

The problem is, Hanna has no idea how that is going to happen.

Not when she can't stop thinking about Daniel.

3

The airy foyer at Copperhill Mountain Lodge is crowded with guests at seven o'clock in the evening. Paul Lehto is on duty at reception, working as fast as he can to deal with the long line. People are also waiting in the seating areas, and there are suitcases everywhere.

Paul has worked at the hotel for many years, but he has never had a worse day.

He is fighting to maintain a professional smile in spite of the stress in his body. A blizzard in central Sweden has meant that every train and flight to Jämtland has been significantly delayed. Now it feels like every single guest for the Easter break has arrived at exactly the same time.

Everyone is running out of patience. It doesn't help that the huge open fire is crackling away merrily, or that there are lanterns with candles and Easter eggs piled high with candy in every corner. Nor that the décor, in tones of burnt reds and oranges with hints of copper, has been carefully chosen to create the right atmosphere.

People just want to check in.

They also want a scapegoat to take out their frustration on.

Paul can feel himself getting more and more irritated as they all crowd around the reception desk. No one is waiting their turn or showing the least scrap of understanding. And they are standing much too close, bearing in mind the social-distancing requirements.

It's not our fault that the blizzard caused chaos, he wants to yell, but he bites his tongue, takes a deep breath, and reminds himself that his shift will soon be over and he will be able to get away from these spoiled fuckers. He can hardly breathe behind his mask. The guests don't have to wear them, but they are compulsory for all members of staff as soon as they set foot on the premises.

"Next," he says quietly, without looking anyone in the eye.

A well-built man in his mid-thirties moves forward, followed by an attractive blond clutching a two-year-old by the hand.

"Aavik," says the man, tilting his chin upward. "We've been waiting for over half an hour."

Paul instinctively dislikes the guy, but he pushes back his dark hair and consults his computer screen. Out of the corner of his eye, he sees someone else approaching the desk—a woman in her fifties, marching toward him with confidence. She is wearing leisure gear, but Paul can see that her purse costs more than he earns in a month.

He knows exactly who she is. Her name is Charlotte Wretlind, and she has stayed at the hotel many times over the past year. She stays in Silver Suite on the top floor, one of their most expensive and most elegant suites, with triple-aspect windows.

"Excuse me," she says angrily, ignoring the other guests. "I've been calling housekeeping for the last fifteen minutes, but no one is answering!"

"I'll be with you in a moment," Paul says. "I just need to finish checking in this family."

Perhaps he ought to be more apologetic, but her attitude is too much. Can't she see that he's doing his best?

"I've been out all day, and yet the waste bin in my bathroom hasn't been emptied," she complains. "And there's no toilet tissue!"

She doesn't seem to have heard a word that Paul said. And she is standing way too close. When he instinctively steps back, she leans forward instead of taking the hint.

He manages to control himself, but herr Aavik is clearly annoyed with Charlotte Wretlind.

"You need to wait your turn!"

She ignores him and continues to harangue Paul. "Didn't you hear what I said?"

She has raised her voice, and a few of the other guests are looking in her direction. Paul's colleague Iris glances up from her screen, where she is entering someone's details.

Paul hesitates, he doesn't want a scene when they're so busy, but he can see that herr Aavik is frowning. In Sweden people wait in line, and he clearly thinks that Charlotte shouldn't be pushing in.

And it is Paul's job to make sure she doesn't do that.

He grits his teeth and finishes registering the family's key card. The two-year-old is grizzling now. The mother picks up the child and tries to console her, while giving her husband an inquiring look.

"If you're not capable of sorting this out, then I want to speak to your line manager," Charlotte demands. "And I'll take the opportunity to discuss your behavior with him."

There is no mistaking the threat. And Paul needs to keep this job, despite the fact that he is surrounded by idiots. The pandemic took a harsh toll on the hotel industry, and he knows he's been lucky not to fall victim to the cutbacks.

"Give me a couple of minutes," he murmurs apologetically.

Charlotte's expression is icy. Paul sees Iris roll her eyes at his inability to handle the situation better. She is from Stockholm, a dyed-in-the-wool know-it-all. He is in no doubt that she is enjoying seeing him struggle.

"Are you deaf?" Charlotte raises her voice even more. "I have no toilet tissue in my room! Can you please sort this out?"

Herr Aavik has had enough. "I was here first!" he snaps.

Charlotte waves her hand impatiently. She might have plenty of money, but she clearly has no manners.

"How long are you going to keep me waiting?" she barks at Paul.

He hears a howl as the two-year-old begins to cry in her mother's arms. She twists and turns, determined to escape, and flings both arms wide. Unfortunately she makes contact with a tall vase filled with pussy willow and apricot-colored feathers that is standing in the middle of the reception desk.

Before Paul can react, the vase wobbles and crashes to the floor.

The mother just manages to jump out of the way, clutching her little girl.

"For God's sake!" she yells at Paul. "How can you have something so dangerous on display? What if it had fallen on my daughter?"

"She could have died!" the child's father pipes up. "What is wrong with you people?"

Paul feels the sweat break out on his forehead. He can't breathe behind his mask. He stares at the shattered vase, unable to decide whether to deal with it immediately or to complete the check-in.

Needless to say, Iris doesn't lift a finger to help.

Everyone is staring at Paul.

"I've had enough," Charlotte says. "I have never been treated so unprofessionally. Is this your first day in the job?"

Paul's ears are filled with a rushing sound. Iris's scornful smirk doesn't improve matters. Suddenly his patience runs out.

"I'm doing my best!" he bellows. "Look around—you need to wait your fucking turn like everybody else!" He rips off his mask and slams it down on the desk. "Can't you see we're working as fast as we can?"

There is absolute silence, apart from the little girl's sobbing. The guests are staring at him in shock. Paul knows perfectly well that he has stepped over the line, but he is so angry that his entire body is shaking. Out of the corner of his eye, he sees Erik from the concierge department hurrying over. Erik looks shaken, but he slips behind the desk and places a calming hand on Paul's arm.

"Pull yourself together," he whispers. "You'll get a formal warning if the boss hears you shouting like that."

At that moment, the key cards are finally ready. Paul hands them over to herr Aavik, who snatches them without a word.

"I'll take care of your bags," Erik offers quickly. "Don't forget to put your mask back on," he says to Paul before heading off toward the elevators with a heavy suitcase in each hand.

When Paul looks up, Charlotte Wretlind is still standing there, looking absolutely furious.

"This will have consequences," she hisses, before turning on her heel and storming off.

4

It is dark outside the panorama window in the Silver Suite. Charlotte is sitting on the rust-colored sofa with a glass of red wine in her hand, trying to sort out the thoughts whirling around in her head.

She frowns; the way that guy at reception behaved was totally unacceptable. She might have gone a little too far, but you can't lose your temper like that with a guest. It's not okay. He must have serious issues with aggression, and Charlotte intends to pass her concerns on to his line manager as soon as she has time.

He really ought to be fired.

Restlessly she twirls the glass around in her fingers. The blood-red wine matches her nail polish. An unpleasant receptionist is the last thing she wants to waste her energy on right now; tomorrow is a big day. She doesn't usually get nervous before public appearances, but presenting the Storlien project to the press is a big deal. Her PR team has established that there is considerable interest—all the significant media players will be there, either in person or via video link.

And tomorrow Henry arrives in Åre, and she will need to take care of him.

She groans to herself. Henry is a brilliant business partner, but something of a diva. She had to summon up all her powers of persuasion in order to get him on board with the project. Without his financial resources, the plans would never have gone through. Henry is a superstar in the Swedish property market, and his support has opened doors that would otherwise have remained closed.

Charlotte would like Stefan to be here too, but he is away with the family—two kids and his snippy wife, Ulrika. Charlotte pulls a face at the thought of Stefan's wife, the high-court judge. They have met in social situations on a few occasions and greeted each other politely, but nothing more. Charlotte has never understood how Stefan, who is so powerful and charismatic, could possibly have fallen for her.

She hasn't asked him, of course. Their discreet arrangement has suited Charlotte very well for many years, but recently she has begun to long for more. She is tired of sneaking around, of never being able to appear in public together.

As long as Filip was living at home, it was practical to keep her two worlds apart, but now that the apartment is empty in the evenings, she misses having someone there.

She leans back on the sofa, snorts derisively at her own feelings.

Stefan is never going to divorce his wife; he made that clear right from the start. Especially as it's Ulrika's family money that pays for their generous apartment and luxury vacations.

Charlotte takes another sip. She wonders what Filip is doing now. He still hasn't replied to her text asking whether he is coming to Åre. It stresses her out. She hopes he won't leave it until the last minute. She really wants him here when the world hears about her Storlien project for the first time.

She would never say it aloud, but she hopes he is proud of his mother's successes.

Her phone buzzes with a text from Bengt Hedin. She hasn't heard from him since yesterday, when he tried to back out. What now?

The message makes her furious.

The purchase of the land will have to be postponed. I can't make tomorrow's press conference.

Charlotte digs her nails into the palm of her hand with such force that she almost breaks the skin. He can't do this to her. Not now. Quickly she types a response.

It's too late to back out.

She remains still for a moment, then continues:

Everything you have accepted is documented. If you ruin this for me, I will ruin you.

The answer comes immediately.

Are you threatening me?

Charlotte considers; then her fingers fly across the screen.

You can interpret it however you like. I will see you tomorrow.

She is interrupted by a sharp knock on the door. She looks up. She isn't expecting anyone. With a sigh she puts down her phone and gets up. Outside the door is the tall man from reception, the one who was so rude earlier.

She doesn't have time for him at the moment, and she is still angry about his behavior.

"Yes?"

"I'm sorry to disturb you," begins the man, who, according to the name badge on his chest, is called Paul. "I just wanted to . . . apologize for what happened this afternoon."

Charlotte raises her eyebrows. So now it suits him to apologize.

"I didn't mean to lose my temper," he adds.

"Maybe you should have thought of that before you were so rude to me in front of all the other guests."

In spite of the dim lighting, she can see that he isn't happy. He is surrounded by an aura of frustration. She doesn't believe he's sorry at all—one of his colleagues has probably persuaded him to come and apologize because the way he acted was unforgivable.

"I really am sorry," he says stiffly. His expression is challenging, as if he is trying to force her to accept his apology.

"I heard what you said." If he thinks that a few empty phrases are going to fix things, then he's wrong. With such poor self-control, he shouldn't be allowed to keep his job.

In *her* hotel he would be out on his ear immediately.

The silence between them is oppressive.

"Was there anything else?" Charlotte says, keen to bring the conversation to an end. She wants to close the door; she has to prepare for tomorrow's press conference. She suddenly spots the fabric bag of dirty laundry she has put out, ready for housekeeping to collect.

She reaches for the bag and holds it out to Paul.

"Could you take my laundry, as you're here anyway?"

He looks vaguely offended. "That's not my job."

Charlotte's irritation flares up again. "You work here, don't you?"

Paul takes a step closer, opening and closing his fists as if he is about to lose control again. "Be careful," he says quietly.

Charlotte stares at him. "What do you mean by that?"

"You know exactly what I mean."

Even though she is determined not to show weakness, she steps back. Her suite is at the far end of the corridor, no one else can see what is going on.

"I don't have time for this," she says, grabbing the handle to pull the door shut.

Paul sticks his foot in the way, preventing her from closing it.

"You think you can treat people however you like, just because you've got money. But you can't tell me what to do."

Charlotte swallows. His face is only inches away from hers. He is tall and strong, with a thick neck. His shirt collar looks too tight.

"If you don't leave immediately, I will be speaking to your boss," she says, straightening her shoulders. She wants to sound powerful, make him back off.

It takes a moment, but eventually he turns away. Charlotte is about to close the door when she hears him mumble something.

"Fucking upper-class bitch."

"What did you say?"

She can't help reacting, although she immediately regrets it. The situation is already uncomfortable. She shouldn't have said anything, she should have simply let him go.

Paul doesn't answer. He just keeps walking down the corridor. Then he slowly looks over his shoulder. His expression is so full of contempt that she physically recoils. Rage sweeps away her self-control—this guy needs to be put in his place.

"Don't think you'll be keeping your job after this!" she shouts.

She closes the door, feeling more shaken than angry.

Countless stars are twinkling above Åre as Hanna walks the last few steps up the hill to her little house in Solbringen, the area diagonally above the village, north of the E14. The sky changed to a deep, velvety blue while she was having dinner with Lydia at the Wine Bar, and afterward Hanna went back to the house in Sadeln with her sister for a cup of coffee.

That's typical of Åre, she thinks. *The weather changes so fast.* In the same day it can snow then clear up half a dozen times. No matter how many apps you check, the forecast is never correct.

She fumbles for her front door key.

Her new home isn't very big—one bedroom, living room, kitchen, and bathroom—but Hanna loves it. At long last she has a place of her own after almost a year in Lydia's luxurious lodge. She is grateful for her sister's generous hospitality, but it feels like a special kind of freedom to be standing on her own two feet. There is also a compact sauna, and a decent hearth, where she often lights a fire.

Just as she turns the key, she hears meowing around her feet. A gray-and-white cat rubs its body against Hanna's legs. When she bends down to stroke it, she sees that it resembles a Norwegian forest cat. Its coat is long and fluffy, and it has tufts of fur between its toes.

"Hello, sweetheart," she says, rubbing behind its ears. "What are you doing out and about at this time of night?"

The cat begins to purr loudly. On closer examination she discovers that it is a large male, but he isn't wearing a collar. Hanna looks around for any sign of his owner. It's way too cold for a pet to be outside all night.

"Where are your mom and dad?"

She straightens up, still scanning the neighborhood.

The cat purrs even louder.

Hanna opens the door. "Time you went home, sweetheart."

Before she can do anything about it, the cat slips between her legs and into the house. Hanna hurries after him and catches up with him in the living room. She picks him up and heads back toward the front door, then hesitates.

She doesn't like the thought of throwing the cat out into the cold if he doesn't have anywhere to go. Plus he seems hungry.

She places him on the floor, goes into the kitchen, and opens the refrigerator. She finds some cooked ham, which she chops up and puts on a plate.

It's as she thought—the cat falls on the food; he seems to be starving. She gives him a bowl of water, which he eagerly laps up.

Since he doesn't have a collar, she has no idea what his name is, but somehow he looks like a Morris.

"Okay, I guess you can stay the night. We'll try to find your owner tomorrow."

Morris gazes up at her, and Hanna could swear that there is gratitude in those beautiful eyes.

The suite is in darkness when Charlotte wakes up. It takes her a few seconds to orient herself. She was deeply asleep, and it is pitch black outside, so it must still be night.

She is lying on her back in the double bed, and blinks in an attempt to see better.

What has woken her?

She usually sleeps like a log, which is a welcome ability during intense periods. She rarely has a disturbed night, whatever is going on.

She shuffles up into a half-sitting position.

Even though there is silence all around her, she has a strong feeling that all is not as it should be.

She is not alone. There is someone else in the suite.

A shudder of fear runs through her body, starting at her ribs and coursing down through her belly. She stares at the walls, but sees nothing. She has goosebumps all over her skin.

Pull yourself together, she thinks. *There can't be anyone here.*

The door is locked, and she pressed the security button before she went to bed.

Or did she?

She reaches out to switch on the bedside lamp, but the thought of being bathed in light and discovering the presence of an intruder makes her draw back her hand. The darkness feels safer. As if this is nothing more than a nightmare from which she will wake at any second.

This isn't real. Tomorrow she will laugh at the memory.

Charlotte listens intently for another minute, then takes a deep breath to calm herself. There is no point in getting agitated—she needs to sleep. She can't appear in front of the press with red-rimmed eyes.

She is about to slide down under the duvet when she hears it again. A sound, barely audible, but it definitely came from the living room. As if a foot had been placed down on the rust-colored rug.

There *is* someone here.

Has that bad-tempered receptionist entered her room? Is he planning on punishing her because she didn't accept his apology?

She begins to panic.

She pulls the sheet tight to her body. She always sleeps in only her panties, but right now she wishes she had something, anything, with which to cover herself. Her nakedness makes her feel even more vulnerable, but her robe is on the floor at the foot of the bed.

Where's her phone?

Her throat constricts when she remembers that it is charging in the living room, along with her laptop, which she left on the sofa when she finished dealing with her emails.

An acrid smell reaches her nostrils, and she realizes that she has broken out in a cold sweat. She tries to breathe silently, even though her heart is pounding.

She hears the sound again, a heavy footstep, then another. The intruder is heading for her bedroom.

Then the door flies open, and before she has time to react, she is completely dazzled by the glare of a flashlight. The figure behind the light is a shapeless shadow, impossible to identify.

She is paralyzed with fear. She knows she ought to scream, yell at the uninvited guest, tell him to get out, but she is incapable of making a sound. Instead she lies there as if she has turned to stone as the shadow comes closer.

She can't move, she can't shout for help.

She wants to whisper *Please don't hurt me,* but all that comes out is a groan.

For a few seconds the figure stands motionless in front of her. Even though she can't really see anything, she is aware of an aggressive rage, so strong that she can almost touch it.

Now she can smell alcohol.

She stares at the flashlight as if she were under hypnosis, tries to focus on its beam in order to keep some kind of composure.

Suddenly the paralysis is gone. She flings her hand to the side and knocks over the bedside lamp. It lands on the floor with a thud, and mortal fear makes her scream.

There is a flash of silver.

Why? she thinks before the sharp blade of the knife pierces her throat, as easily as if her neck were made of soft clay.

Her mouth is filled with a metallic taste. Something warm and sticky is bubbling up from inside her, and she can't breathe.

She wants to call out to Filip, but cannot form the words.

Then everything goes black.

MONDAY, MARCH 29

7

The therapist's practice is on the corner, in the red-brick house where the psychologist lives with her family. There is a light glowing through the lavender-colored curtains when Detective Inspector Daniel Lindskog parks his car early on Monday morning.

He is in Järpen—he deliberately chose a psychologist who doesn't work in Åre.

No doubt there is a good explanation for that, Daniel thinks as he switches off the engine. His partner, Ida, is the only one who knows about these visits; he hasn't told anyone else.

Not even Hanna, despite the fact that they see each other every day.

She knows him almost as well as Ida does; he can talk to her about more or less anything.

But not this.

This is private.

As always Daniel feels a certain measure of reluctance before he gets out of the car, even though he has been seeing Jovanka Horvat regularly over the past year. He's not sure if it's down to shame or distaste. It shouldn't be either. He doesn't want to be ashamed of needing therapy, not when his aim is to become a better person, a better father to little Alice, the child he had longed for.

It's hardly surprising that digging into his past is hard work, given his own father's betrayal when Daniel was a child. The fact is that he has more or less regarded himself as an orphan since his mother, Francesca, died in a car accident in Sundsvall almost a decade ago. His father is still alive, but Daniel hasn't seen him for twenty-eight years. After Daniel's tenth birthday, the sporadic visits to his father's new family in Umeå stopped completely.

Nor has he seen his half siblings since then—a sister and a brother who are eight and five years younger than him.

He knows it is good for him to see Jovanka. She has helped him to acquire the tools to deal with his volatile temperament and the recurring outbursts of rage that have plagued him all his life. Over the past twelve months, he hasn't lost control once, which is a huge relief.

If he hadn't decided to try therapy, his relationship with Ida would probably have been over by now. He doesn't want to think about what would have happened to his relationship with Alice. His daughter is just eighteen months old now, and Daniel's greatest worry is that she will be as afraid of him as his own mother was of her bad-tempered father. Daniel has inherited that aspect of his grandfather's nature, even though they have never met.

He has promised himself that he will never be like that, which is why he continues to see Jovanka.

But it is so difficult to bring to the surface things that have been buried for so long. He is not used to talking about his innermost feelings; it makes him feel alone and exposed.

Sometimes he has been on the verge of tears, making it difficult to get the words out. Sometimes he has broken out into a sweat with the unpleasantness of it all. He has always hated it when his emotions get the better of him.

On many occasions he has been on the brink of calling Jovanka to cancel his appointment, but at the last minute, he has forced himself to go.

It is only in the last few weeks that they have begun to talk about his complex relationship with his father, who walked out on Francesca and his child when Daniel was just two years old. If he wants to be a better father to Alice, then he has to sort this out too.

That is Jovanka's clear perception.

Intellectually, Daniel realizes that she is right, but it's so hard to process the past. It brings up far too many unhappy memories. He used to think that therapy would be somehow redemptive, but it has often been agonizingly painful, and has demanded far more of him than he could ever have imagined.

After an hour with Jovanka, he is tired and depressed, and often drives back to Åre the long way round in order to compose himself. He has been known to park in a lay-by for a while before he is ready to see his family or colleagues.

The clock on the dashboard shows one minute to seven. Jovanka allows him to come early because of his job.

Daniel takes a deep breath, unfastens his seatbelt, and gets out of the car.

8

When Tiina Nilsson goes down to the basement on Monday morning, the door of the laundry room is ajar. She pushes it open with her foot and places the basket of dirty laundry on the worn stone floor. She has to be at the school in Duved in an hour, and wants to set the machine going before she leaves.

She rubs her right shoulder with her left hand. The pain comes and goes, but she can't seem to get rid of it completely. She has worked as a teaching assistant in the elementary school for many years, and shouldn't be lifting the smaller children. However, she loves her job, the kids, and her colleagues.

She flicks the switch, and the cold fluorescent light reveals the piles on the counter. Every time Tiina sees the chaos down here, she promises herself that she will fix it at the weekend, but then something else gets in the way. It's not as if Ogge would think of doing it. They have lived together for fifteen years, since Tiina was thirty-five and her girls, Anna and Andrea, were five and eight, but he has never done much around the house.

The only thing he cares about is Zelda, their dog—he loves her more than anything.

Tiina reaches for the basket to start loading the machine; then she realizes that there are already clothes in the drum. That's weird—she doesn't remember putting on a wash yesterday evening.

As she begins to pull out the contents, she sees that this is Ogge's stuff. He has shoved everything in together—pants, T-shirt, underwear, even though they are different colors and should be separated. As a result his white tee now has a grayish tinge. One of his sport socks is missing, but the one that remains is no longer white either.

Tiina stands there holding his damp vest. Ogge must have put a wash on overnight, even though he got home so late. She was already asleep; she was too tired to sit up and wait for him.

It's very odd—Ogge doesn't usually deal with his own laundry. Why would he start now?

It doesn't matter. She hasn't got time to stand here wondering. Not if she's going to have breakfast before she leaves. Quickly she hangs his clothes in the drying cupboard and gets the next load underway.

Then she switches off the light and hurries back up the stairs.

9

Something warm and heavy is pushing Hanna down into the mattress when the alarm clock wakes her. She is lying on her stomach with one leg drawn up beneath her, and it feels as if someone has placed a great big, warm sack of cement on the small of her back.

Her muscles are aching because of the uncomfortable position, and she is covered in sweat.

She tries to switch off the alarm while struggling to free herself from the unfamiliar weight. The ringing stops, and she hears a loud and reproachful meow as she rolls over and tips Morris onto the bed. She peers out from beneath the covers to find that the cat is now standing so close that his nose is almost touching her face. As soon as they make eye contact, he begins to purr loudly. He turns around and marches back and forth, clearly delighted that she is finally awake.

Slowly Hanna drags herself out of bed and heads for the kitchen, where she gives Morris a tin of liver pâté and refills his water bowl. She fixes up a provisional litter tray with shredded newspaper so that he will be okay while she is at work.

This afternoon she must find out who owns him. He can't live here. This is not the right home for a cat, not by a long way.

She makes herself a sandwich and a cup of tea and sits down at the kitchen table. This is a short working week because of the Easter holiday, which is why she has allowed herself a bit of a lie-in. She has no meetings today, and intends to devote herself to a pile of ongoing cases. From Thursday she will be free for five days so that she can spend time with Lydia and her family—her husband, Richard; thirteen-year-old Fabian; and eleven-year-old Linnéa. Hanna adores her nephew and niece, and is looking forward to celebrating Easter Saturday with them.

Morris has finished eating, and is rubbing contentedly around Hanna's legs. Suddenly she has what feels like fifteen pounds of cat on her lap. He is purring with such joy that she doesn't have the heart to put him down on the floor, even though she is covered in cat hairs.

She sits there for almost ten minutes before she finally decides it's time to get ready for work.

The coffee machine in the small kitchen by the door has just finished gurgling when Hanna sees Daniel arrive at the station a little while later.

As usual her heart flips when he is standing right there in front of her. Today he is wearing a moss-green sweater that brings out the color in his hazel eyes. The sun shining in through the window sprinkles specks of gold in his dark-brown hair.

"Coffee?" she says, handing him the cup to cover her confusion.

"Excellent service." Daniel gives her a warm smile as he takes it. "But wasn't this meant for you?"

"I can easily make another."

They chat about this and that as the machine grinds fresh beans. They are both planning to work from Åre over the next few days. It's nice not to face the journey to and from Östersund; the round trip takes a good two and a half hours.

"What does your week look like?" Daniel asks as the machine finishes its task. "Have you got a lot to do before the long weekend?"

Hanna takes a sip of her coffee. "Not too bad. Today I'm going to try to check out some witness statements from that narcotics arrest in Staa back in January, if you remember?"

Daniel nods as they set off toward their offices, which are on the right-hand side of the corridor three doors apart.

"How about lunch at Broken later?" Daniel suggests. "I didn't bring anything today."

Hanna usually loves eating at the popular restaurant, but Daniel must have forgotten how busy everywhere gets during the Easter break.

"What—like, you, me, and a thousand tourists?" she says, raising an eyebrow. "We'll have to wait forever for a table."

Daniel laughs and sips his coffee. "I never thought of that."

"I think you're going to have to settle for a hot dog from the OKQ8 kiosk, unless you want to stand in line for an hour," Hanna says with a smile. "But I'm happy to go along with you if you like?"

10

The corridor leading to the Silver Suite is silent when Ivar from maintenance knocks tentatively on the door. It is ten thirty, so it should be okay to go in and check the thermostat that the guest complained about. It is a sunny day, and by this time most people are out on the slopes.

There is no **DO NOT DISTURB** sign on the door, so the room is probably empty. Ivar uses his key card to open up, and just to be on the safe side, he calls out, "Hello? May I come in?"

No reply. Good, that must mean he can get on with the job, even though he can see a cell phone charging on one of the side tables.

He is about to walk in when he notices something odd about the carpet. It is covered in dark-red patches. It looks as if someone has splashed red wine all over the place, then trampled around in the mess.

Although there is something else . . . a weird smell that stops him in his tracks. It is unpleasant, acrid, almost like . . . blood.

He gazes at the marks on the carpet, then glances toward the bedroom. The door is ajar, and the room is in darkness—it seems like the blinds are still closed.

The silence grows, becomes oppressive and frightening.

Cautiously he moves forward, pushes open the bedroom door with one foot. It takes a few seconds for his eyes to adjust to the gloom.

Then he sees the body on the floor next to the double bed.

The unseeing, dead eyes are staring up at the ceiling. There is a gaping wound in the throat, the skin is peeled back around the edges. The rest of the body is covered in stab wounds, and the sheets are drenched in blood that has dripped from the bed and formed puddles on the floor.

There is sticky redness wherever he looks.

It takes a moment for Ivar to process what is in front of him. Then he staggers into the corridor and vomits.

11

Daniel appears in the doorway of Hanna's office, his phone pressed to his ear.

"We have to go up to Copperhill right away." His expression is both alert and serious. "There seems to have been a fatal stabbing at the hotel during the night. One of the guests has been found dead in their room."

Hanna grabs her jacket and runs to catch up with Daniel on the way to the parking lot. As he reverses the car, he summarizes the information that has come through from regional dispatch in Umeå, via the Serious Crimes Unit in Östersund.

"The alarm was raised at ten fifty-three."

"Who called it in?"

"The hotel manager. A maintenance engineer found a dead woman with multiple stab wounds in one of the suites."

Hanna is lost for words. A murdered woman lying in her own blood is one of the worst sights anyone can see. She has attended this kind of crime scene before, when she worked with victims of domestic violence in Stockholm.

It gave her nightmares.

"The poor guy must have been badly shocked," she murmurs.

In her head she has already begun to go through everything that will need to be done. She can forget about having any time off over Easter. Daniel puts his foot down. The speed limit on the highway is fifty miles per hour, but there is no other traffic in sight.

"Are the CSIs on the way?" Hanna wonders.

"Yes, but it will take at least an hour for them to drive up from Östersund."

In Norrland most police officers have to spend many hours in their cars simply to attend a crime scene, and the district of Jämtland also includes Härjedalen.

Hanna hopes that the lead CSI will be Carina Grankvist. They worked together on the case of the dead skier, and she is direct and approachable. Carina is also formally attached to Östersund, just like Daniel and Hanna, but she lives in Mattmar, which is closer to Åre— only fifty miles away.

"Do we know any more about the victim? Do we have a name?"

Daniel shakes his head. "We'll find out when we get there."

The dark-brown building housing the chocolate factory appears on the right. It is directly opposite the turning for Copperhill on the road to Sadeln, where Lydia's impressive home is located.

Hanna knows the route by heart; she has driven this way many, many times, both in darkness and in daylight.

As they leave the E14, the road becomes steep and narrow. It winds up the mountain, more like an Alpine track in Switzerland than something you would expect to find in rural Sweden. On one side there are amazing frozen waterfalls, while on the other, the view is open and dizzying.

When they reach the center of Björnen, Daniel takes a sharp right. A small sign points them in the right direction, with COPPERHILL MOUNTAIN LODGE printed in black letters.

After several more twists and turns, the spectacular building appears before them. The hotel is right at the top of Förberget. Hanna has been here for dinner with Lydia and her family, but has never stayed the night. That would be out of the question on a detective's salary.

The milky morning mist makes her screw up her eyes. The lump in her stomach grows as they approach the crime scene.

Way down below she can just make out Lake Åre like a white strip of ice on the way to the mountains in the west, while on the other side of the lake, the mountain known as Renfjället is in shadow.

Daniel finds a space and quickly reverses in. Two patrol cars are already there, parked a little farther away. The parking lot is almost full; Easter is one of the busiest weekends of the season.

"Crap timing," Hanna comments. "The first day of the school break—the place must be packed."

Daniel's expression is grim as he opens the car door. "It's a tragedy. For the victim, the hotel, and the whole area."

THEN

DECEMBER 21, 1973

The black-and-white uniform is laid out on the bed in front of Monica in her bedroom, so clean and freshly starched that she can hardly believe it's hers. It is three days to Christmas Eve, and time for her first shift at the mountain hotel in Storlien.

She still can't get her head around the fact that she has secured a job as a waitress in the area's most sparkling establishment, where the guests look like the movie stars in the magazines she secretly reads.

Even the king comes here sometimes!

Monica gets shivers down her spine at the thought that she might one day catch a glimpse of him. He is twenty-seven years old, unmarried, and the most attractive royal in Europe. It is well known that he often calls in at the hotel when he is staying in his cabin nearby.

With trembling fingers she gets dressed and inspects the result in the mirror. The uniform fits her neat figure to perfection. She is only just over five feet tall, but her new bra works wonders. She has put up her brown hair to make her look older, and she has applied extra eyeliner for the same reason.

When she is ready, she goes downstairs to show her mom, who is listening to the radio in the living room.

"What do you think?" Monica asks nervously.

Her mother is clearly unimpressed. "Are you supposed to wear such a short skirt for work?"

Monica has turned up the hem so that she will look better. More grown up.

"Yes, this is how it's meant to be," she says airily, putting on her coat.

It takes twenty minutes to walk to the hotel. Monica is breathless with excitement by the time she arrives. The building is beautifully illuminated, richly decorated with bunches of fir and dark-red velvet rosettes above the entrance. There are tall Christmas trees on either side of the staircase, and burning torches in cast-iron holders line the path to the impressive double doors.

She has dreamed of this for years, as well as the chance to become independent and earn her own money.

This is a way out, a portal to another world.

Maybe she will meet her future husband among the guests? Someone from Stockholm who will take her away from here, offer her a different life.

She longs to escape from the darkness and the cold, the suffocating atmosphere at home with all the rules and regulations that govern her parents' lives, and therefore hers.

She will soon be eighteen, it is time to start living for real.

Dreams can come true, *she thinks, smiling happily as she makes for the staff entrance.*

12

The unexpected turn of events forces Daniel to readjust. The therapy session with Jovanka has taken its toll, and he had been hoping for a quiet morning concentrating on paperwork.

Things have changed dramatically.

As soon as Daniel and Hanna walk in through the automatic glass doors, a man in his fifties hurries toward them. He has a ponytail and is wearing jeans and a black jacket.

"Are you from the police?" he asks with a Norwegian accent. "My name is Espen Lund and I'm the hotel manager. I was the one who called when we discovered what had happened."

Daniel shows his ID. He can see the panic in Espen's eyes. A crime of this magnitude would frighten most people. For the manager, who is responsible for the whole place, it is a disaster. He is constantly looking around, presumably worried in case a guest overhears what he is saying, even though the huge foyer is comparatively empty. However, since all the rooms open onto walkways surrounding the expansive atrium, it's not that difficult to work out what is happening on the ground floor.

Another man is standing at the reception desk, watching them with a tense expression. When he realizes that Daniel has noticed him, he leans toward his computer screen as if to indicate that he is busy and is definitely not eavesdropping.

"It's terrible," Espen Lund says. "Incomprehensible."

Behind him there is a copper wall almost a hundred feet high, toning perfectly with the wood paneling on the other walls. An enormous open fire is crackling away.

Daniel's gaze is drawn to a bright-red lamp, or maybe it's a work of art, right in the middle of the foyer. On another occasion he would probably have found it beautiful, but right now the color makes him think of bloodshed. They will soon see the scene around the deceased for themselves, but his own body has already begun to steel itself. His shoulders are tense, his stomach feels heavier than usual.

No one can be unaffected by this type of homicide.

"Shall we take a look?" Hanna says before turning to the manager. "Could you show us the room where the body was discovered?"

Espen leads the way to a black stone staircase on the left of the fireplace. At close quarters Daniel realizes how enormous it actually is, with various shelves and a tall chimney, also covered in copper.

They reach the sixth floor and follow the corridor right to the end, where the Silver Suite is located. Uniformed officers are already on the scene, and the characteristic blue-and-white tape is in place.

Hanna is a few steps ahead. Espen looks anxiously at Daniel.

"Does that tape have to be so visible? It's going to frighten the guests."

"Where can we find you when we're done here?" Daniel says without answering the question. It will be a long time before the tape can be removed.

"If you come down to reception, they'll call me." Espen makes his way back toward the stairs.

"No damage to the door," Hanna comments when he is out of earshot. "It doesn't look as if anyone broke in."

Daniel nods. This is an important observation that could mean a number of things. The victim might have known the killer and let him or her in voluntarily. Another possibility is that the perpetrator works at the hotel, and therefore has access to a key card.

"I wish the CSIs were here," Hanna says. "We'll have to wait for them."

The rules regarding a crime scene are very clear. No one goes in until the technicians have done their job, unless it is a matter of life and death. All too often biological traces have been contaminated by careless officers or emergency personnel who have destroyed the chances of a thorough crime scene investigation.

Daniel cranes his neck. The hallway leads into what looks like a living room, with a sofa, armchair, and glass walls, but he can't see anything more. The deceased was found in the bedroom, which is out of sight.

He'd hoped to get a glimpse of what it looks like in there, but Hanna is right. They have to wait until the CSIs arrive.

"Have you seen that?" he says, pointing to the hallway.

Dark-red patches are spread across the floor in an irregular pattern, with a possible shoe print just inside the door.

When he bends down to take a closer look, the smell of blood hits him.

13

It is dark in the storage area where Aada Kuus is sitting on the hard concrete floor, weeping. She is below the hotel's ground floor, where spare equipment is usually kept. At the moment it is almost empty, and Aada has hidden herself in the far corner. She ran down here when she saw the police officer cordoning off the Silver Suite, she had to find a safe space.

Her mind is whirling. She can't stop shaking after the shock of hearing about last night's murder.

Someone said it was Ivar from maintenance who found the body, and the police are going to question him. Then they will probably want to speak to all the staff. That means they will come looking for Aada too, ask her if she saw anything.

She clasps her hands tightly together in an attempt to stop them shaking. It doesn't work.

Aada knows she should have raised the alarm last night when she realized that something terrible must have happened. Instead she rushed away as quickly as she dared.

She is so afraid, and doesn't trust her memory. Did she really see a masked man holding a bloodstained knife emerge from the Silver Suite?

And did he see her?

He must have done. She remembers those burning eyes.

She lay awake all night, tossing and turning. When she came into work today, it was worse than she could have imagined. There were police officers everywhere. Her colleagues were deeply shaken when they explained what had gone on.

The guest in the Silver Suite, a woman, has been stabbed to death.

Aada lets out a sob. She is ashamed of herself for doing nothing, and at the same time, she is terrified that the murderer will come after her too.

The hairs on her arms stand up at the very thought.

A little voice says that she ought to go to her line manager and tell her what she saw, but she is scared to come forward. She is a foreigner and hardly speaks the language, why should they listen to her?

She knows from bitter experience that the police in her homeland cannot be trusted.

What if the police in Sweden are the same?

Who will protect her then?

14

Hanna and Daniel have been allowed to use a conference room on the first floor, with windows overlooking the dense fir forest outside the hotel. Here too the décor is in burnt tones: The chairs are upholstered in rust-colored fabric, and the carpet is a shade of dark mustard.

Daniel notices that the sun has gone behind the clouds, and it looks dark out there even though it is the middle of the day. No doubt it will start snowing soon.

The gloomy weather matches his mood perfectly. He is finding it hard to shake off the nauseating stench from the Silver Suite, the knowledge that there is a dead woman just along the corridor.

Espen Lund is sitting opposite them. He can't keep still, and is constantly moving his hands. First of all he adjusts his dark jacket, then fiddles with his leather belt. Finally he concentrates on scratching the back of one hand. His expression says that he has a thousand things to take care of, but no idea where to begin.

Hanna is next to Daniel, with her notepad on the table.

"How long will the Silver Suite be cordoned off?" Espen asks. "It's not very nice for our guests. We'd like to get in there and clean the place as soon as possible."

"I can't tell you that," Daniel replies.

A crime scene of this caliber will need to be examined many times. The last thing the police want is for someone to go in there and clear up.

"We'll be in touch as soon as we know more," Hanna adds.

The manager doesn't look reassured.

"We need all the information you have about the guest who was staying in the Silver Suite," Daniel continues. "Her name, how long she was staying—everything you have."

Espen sweeps his fingertips over the iPad in front of him.

"Charlotte Wretlind," he begins, his eyes fixed on the screen. "She arrived last Friday and was staying for the whole of the Easter break. The booking was made in the name of her company, SEG—Swedish Establishment Group. They're property developers, I believe."

"Was she a regular guest?"

"She's stayed here quite a lot. I'd say seven or eight times over the past fifteen months. Her last visit was in February."

"Why so often?" Hanna wonders.

"She was behind the new Storlien project," Espen explains. "Refurbishing the old mountain hotel. You might have seen the article in *Östersunds-Posten* a few weeks ago? Apparently the plan was to put Storlien back on the map, make it as renowned as it was all those years ago, in the 1960s and '70s."

Daniel searches his memory. He probably read about it but didn't give it another thought. He exchanges a glance with Hanna. Storlien's glory days are long gone.

"I'm not sure how much you know about the development since then," Espen goes on, "but in those days Åre was just a small village, and Storlien was the center for skiing and tourism in the area. The king has a mountain cabin nearby, which no doubt contributed to its reputation."

"I believe the king and queen usually spend Easter there," Hanna says. "So they should be there now?"

"That's right."

Espen scrolls down and Daniel leans forward.

"Can you tell us more about the victim's stay here at Copperhill?"

"Like I said, Charlotte Wretlind was supposed to be with us for just over a week. She had also booked one of our finest conference rooms for a press conference this afternoon. She was going to reveal her ambitious plans for a new mountain hotel."

Daniel sees that Hanna is frowning. Something about the way Espen said "ambitious plans" doesn't sit well.

He almost sounded contemptuous.

It puts him in a new light.

"Was there something controversial about the project?" Hanna asks.

"I don't quite know how to put this." Espen looks uncomfortable. "Many people in Storlien have been worried about the consequences, with regard to both the execution of such a large build and what the final result will look like. They don't want a 'new Åre.'"

"Why not?"

"It's no secret that Åre is widely believed to have been overexploited. A lot of new houses have been built, and the number of tourists has increased significantly. Those of us involved in the hotel industry are pleased about that, of course, but it's clear that the infrastructure hasn't really kept up. During high season there are long traffic jams, and the ski lift system needs improvement. It's often closed due to technical reasons, which leads to complaints from the guests."

Espen looks away and scratches his neck, leaving red marks.

Daniel wonders whether it's the competition that really concerns him.

"People move here because they want a different life," the manager goes on. "Calmer, less hectic. If you flood the area with hundreds of tourists, it affects everyone. Particularly in view of the clientele I believe Charlotte Wretlind was hoping to target—the luxury sector. It creates tensions."

"What do the owners of Copperhill think about the development?" Hanna asks. "Were they—and you—worried about a rival?"

Daniel had exactly the same question in his mind. Hanna is very good at putting things into words without sounding harsh or judgmental, which makes people lower their guard. He gives her an encouraging nod, and she smiles back almost imperceptibly.

"Why do you say that?" Espen mumbles.

"A great big luxury hotel in Storlien, no more than an hour from here—surely they'll be looking to occupy the same market position as Copperhill? Is there room for two high-profile establishments so close together?"

"I would never think along those lines." Espen looks at Hanna with more than a touch of arrogance. "Especially not now, when Charlotte Wretlind has met such a terrible fate."

Hanna is not giving up.

"Are you absolutely certain about that? Surely the thought must have occurred to you?"

Espen refuses to look her in the eye.

"Not at all," he says, his attention fixed on the iPad.

Motive, Daniel jots down discreetly. *Check out Espen Lund's alibi.*

15

Hanna turns her head and feels the vertebrae in her neck crack.

"Shouldn't the CSIs be finished soon?" she says to Daniel, who is sitting opposite her. "Carina and her team arrived at about one, didn't they?"

They have spent several hours in the conference room. After the conversation with Espen Lund, they spoke to the maintenance guy who found the body. In a shaky voice he explained how he had gone up to the suite in the morning and discovered Charlotte Wretlind's remains drenched in blood.

They have begun to gather information about the deceased, and the police in Stockholm have been tasked with informing her relatives. Apparently her business partner, Henry Sylvester, is already on his way to Åre. They are now waiting for the staff lists that the manager promised to supply. Hanna is particularly interested to see which employees had anything to do with the murdered woman during her stay.

On the table is a pot of freshly brewed coffee and a plate of sandwiches that some kind soul brought in. Hanna pours herself a cup and takes a sip, even though it's too hot. Then she reaches for a cheese sandwich and eats, without really being aware of the taste. She would really like to move, the air in here is beginning to feel stuffy, and restlessness is tearing at her body. She wants to get back to the Silver Suite, go through the crime scene.

She needs to see the scene and the victim with her own eyes.

Daniel holds up his phone, showing her the screen.

"Have you seen the headlines in the evening papers? They've already dubbed it 'The Hotel Murder in Åre.'"

Hanna frowns. "I don't understand how it's gotten out so quick—we've only been here for a few hours."

"It's impossible to keep something like this a secret. You know how they operate."

Daniel is right. A violent homicide in a well-known hotel in the middle of Easter week is unlikely to escape the attention of the press. Besides which, the media had already been invited to the venue because of the planned press conference.

"How do you feel about not getting any time off over Easter?" Hanna asks.

Daniel looks tormented. Hanna can tell that he is worried about Ida's reaction. His partner doesn't like it when he has to work overtime, and they often quarrel about how much he is away from home, especially during major investigations. It has taken its toll on their relationship, and on several occasions Daniel has asked Hanna for her advice.

"Ida won't be happy," he admits. "I'd promised to spend the whole of the long weekend with her and Alice."

That's life with a cop, Hanna thinks. It's not always fun, but it can't be helped. They make an important contribution to society, and Ida should be pleased that Daniel is doing something that makes a difference.

She would never say that out loud, of course.

"Shall we go and talk to Carina?" she suggests, finishing her sandwich.

The Silver Suite is at the other end of the building, toward the northwest. From the walkway, Hanna can see a number of people gathered around the reception desk. Despite the distance, the gravity of the situation is clear. It looks as if several guests are in the process of checking out.

Who wants to celebrate Easter at the scene of a homicide?

For the sake of the investigation, she would have preferred people to stick around so that they could be interviewed, but the police have no right to stop anyone from leaving. However, those occupying the rooms closest to the Silver Suite have been asked to stay. Hanna can only hope they understand how important this is.

"I guess there won't be so many people in the hotel over the next few days," she says.

The fire down in the foyer is still crackling away cheerfully, with brightly colored Easter eggs displayed on the mantelpiece. Somehow the coziness and festive atmosphere feel kind of creepy under the circumstances.

"You're probably right," Daniel agrees.

The door of the Silver Suite is wide open, and the uniformed officers have disappeared. Carina and some of her colleagues are busy in the living room. The chief technician is wearing a full-body suit, with a white hood covering her blond hair. They make eye contact, and she comes over to them.

"Do you want to come in? If so, take a deep breath."

Without waiting for an answer, she hands them blue overshoes and disposable protective suits to put on before they are allowed in.

By this stage Hanna and Daniel have acquired several photographs of Charlotte Wretlind, but the scene that meets them has very little to do with the stylish businesswoman in the dark jacket, perfectly applied makeup, and well-cut, highlighted hair that they saw on their screens a little while ago.

As soon as Hanna sees the half-naked body and the blood-soaked sheets, she knows that the image will stay in her mind for a very long time.

Charlotte Wretlind looks like a rag doll. Her entire body is covered in knife wounds; someone had stabbed her over and over again, as if unable to stop themselves. Her face looks like a mask made of wax. The dead eyes stare into nothingness, her hair is messy, the ends dark with dried blood.

"Jesus," Daniel says quietly by her side.

"It's not a pretty sight," Carina agrees.

Hanna instinctively clamps her lips tightly shut. The smell in the room is overwhelming, a mixture of blood and other unpleasant odors that are excreted by dead bodies. She is grateful that the mask covering the lower part of her face keeps out the worst of it, but she can still feel her stomach muscles contract as a wave of nausea wells up.

The violence of men against women, she thinks automatically, even though they have no evidence that the killer is male. But Hanna saw so many abused women during her time with the City Police in Stockholm, and she cannot avoid the immediate association.

It is also hard to imagine a woman losing control and stabbing another person to death like this. Such extreme violence is virtually unknown among female perpetrators.

Men are killed by men, and women are also killed by men.

The statistics tell a clear story.

In addition, the victim isn't particularly short. Hanna guesses that she is perhaps five eight. She also looks pretty fit, judging by the muscles in her upper arms.

This also suggests a male attacker; it must have taken a certain amount of strength to overpower her.

"Any idea of the course of events?" Daniel asks Carina as he takes a step back, presumably to avoid the stench.

"Bearing in mind what she's wearing and the location, I would assume that she had gone to bed before the attack. That should give us some kind of timeline. There's also a phone and laptop in the living room, so you can see when they were last used."

Hanna nods. It's good to know that they won't have to search for the victim's phone and laptop.

"Cause of death?"

The question is superfluous, but Hanna asks it anyway.

"Loss of blood due to multiple stab wounds," Carina replies in a matter-of-fact tone of voice.

She points to the gaping wound in Charlotte's throat. The skin has peeled back, revealing both muscles and sinews.

"That alone must have been enough to end her life. Obviously the forensic pathologist will examine her in detail, but I would assume that she died pretty quickly when her windpipe was severed with such brutality."

In spite of the smell, Hanna leans forward to look at the victim's palms. They are smooth and white, with no visible signs of damage.

"I can't see any defensive injuries," she says. "Could she have been asleep when she was attacked?"

"If she was lucky," Carina replies. "Although the bedside lamp ended up on the floor, which might indicate some form of struggle."

"Or maybe the perpetrator knocked it over," Daniel says.

"Possibly. Or perhaps the victim woke up when the attacker came into the room and fumbled for the switch, but knocked the lamp onto the floor instead."

Hanna notices that Charlotte is lying on her back, wearing only a pair of lacy panties. She looks for a nightdress or T-shirt that may have been torn off, but finds nothing.

The blood-soaked panties haven't been pulled down.

"Is there anything to indicate a sexual assault?" she wonders.

Carina grimaces. "Nothing that's visible to the naked eye—you'll need to take that up with the pathologist."

Daniel nods. "Have you found any trace of the perpetrator? Or is that too much to ask?"

"We've gathered material as usual. It's too early to say where it comes from."

"This really is dreadful," Daniel says.

Hanna can hear his heavy breathing behind the mask, and knows they both share the same feelings of horror and frustration.

He looks away, shakes his head. "I've never seen anything like it."

THEN

December 23, 1973

Her feet are aching after the first few days at work, but Monica has never felt so excited.

The hotel is like a fairy tale, with a hair salon, its own bakery, bowling hall, and swimming pool. It can accommodate five hundred guests, and there are so many members of staff that Monica can't possibly remember all their names. One guy, Leffe, is employed purely to change light bulbs. He is even younger than her, only fifteen.

In the Loft, where there is dancing to live music every night, seventeen waitresses work each shift, serving coffee and cognac.

By the time Monica gets home in the evenings, her head is spinning with all the new impressions.

As soon as she wakes up, she can't wait to get back there.

Today is December 23, and she is with Stina, an experienced waitress who has seen most things, folding napkins for the first dinner service.

In Monica's eyes Stina is old, over forty, and many years of smoking have made her voice hoarse and rasping. She shows Monica how to shape the big linen napkins into something called the fleur-de-lis.

It is complicated, but Monica is getting there.

She really loves her job. Her eyes widen every single time she enters the extravagant dining room. Shimmering baubles hang from the chandeliers, lighted candles adorn each table. The lavish buffet isn't like anything she has seen before—tray after tray of exciting delicacies that make her mouth water.

For the first time in her life, she has tasted a green fruit called an avocado.

To think that she gets to experience all this—Monica, who grew up on meat and potatoes. It is like being in a Hollywood movie. It doesn't matter that her shifts can last for ten hours, or that she barely gets time to eat. She is the youngest of the waitresses, the only novice, but almost everyone is kind and answers her questions.

"This is when it really starts," Stina says, putting down yet another perfectly folded linen napkin.

"What do you mean?"

"Today the train arrives, bringing the upper-class families from Stockholm. You'll see." Stina winks at her. "If you do well, there will be plenty of tips when they leave. Give the gentlemen a special smile, be polite to their wives, and you'll reap the rewards."

She looks Monica up and down.

"You're so cute—you won't have any problems!"

16

Daniel is facing the window in the conference room at Copperhill. Hanna has gone to the bathroom, so he is alone. Images of the murdered woman flicker through his mind following the visit to the Silver Suite.

He rubs his hand over his short beard.

A terrible crime has been committed, and they now have to do their best to solve it, even though resources are as limited as they were a year ago. He hopes their boss, Birgitta Grip, will have a plan to fix the staffing issue; otherwise he doesn't know how they are going to manage yet another demanding investigation.

His gloomy thoughts are interrupted as the door is flung open and a man aged about fifty appears. He is wearing an elegant camel-hair coat and a dark suit, and has an air of authority and gravitas.

He runs his right hand over his thick silvery-gray hair.

"Are you the officer in charge?" he says before Daniel has time to react. "I came as soon as I heard about Charlotte. I can't get my head around it. Who would do such a thing? Here, at a top hotel?"

The questions come so fast that Daniel has no chance of answering them. He gets up and stands opposite the man, who is about the same height as him—around six feet.

He manages to hide his irritation. "And you are . . . ?"

He doesn't want to be unpleasant, but would have appreciated it if the man had knocked before bursting in. What if there had been a sensitive interview going on?

"My apologies." The stranger takes a deep breath. "I'm so shaken up. My name is Henry Sylvester—I'm Charlotte's business partner."

Daniel remembers that the victim's associate was on his way to Åre from Stockholm. Good—that means they can start looking into her business affairs.

"Please take a seat."

"I flew up to attend the press conference this afternoon." Henry puts down his briefcase. "I got a newsflash on the way from the airport, and then I heard what had happened." He falls silent, takes a deep breath. "It's terrible."

At that moment Hanna returns. She looks at Henry, who is still standing. Clearly agitated, he introduces himself to her.

"It's good that you're here," she says immediately. "Can we ask you some questions right away?"

"Of course—ask whatever you like."

Daniel studies Henry as he sits down on the opposite side of the table. His face is pale, and he runs a hand over his hair once again, as if he needs to keep his hands occupied.

"Can I see Charlotte?" His voice is unsteady.

Daniel would like to explain that this would be a bad idea. Seeing Charlotte's body was difficult even for experienced police officers like him and Hanna. He would prefer to spare Henry that ordeal.

"Not at the moment, I'm afraid. The technicians are still working on the scene."

Hanna pours Henry a glass of water. "How close were you and Charlotte?"

"We've known each other all our lives. Our fathers were good friends, and our families spent time together. For example we all celebrated Christmas in Storlien together for many years."

Storlien, Daniel thinks. That word keeps on coming up.

"Could you tell us about your project? We've heard that a great deal of money is going to be plowed into the new mountain hotel. Have you been on board from the start?"

"To be honest, I don't usually get involved in that kind of property project, but Charlotte was very keen and managed to convince me in the end. She's wanted to do this for years, but had problems securing the finance. In the end she persuaded my company to provide capital."

Daniel notices the expensive watch Henry is wearing. A Patek Philippe—of course a man like him will have a wristwatch worth a small fortune.

It is tempting to judge, but he wants to be careful. After all these years, he has learned that people are not one dimensional, they are neither black nor white. In fact most exist in a gray zone, with layer upon layer of character attributes that are not always obvious at first glance.

Even a brutal abuser of women can be nice to small children. A cold-blooded gang member can go and visit his mom on Mother's Day.

"It wasn't easy to say no to Charlotte," Henry continues. "Not when she'd decided on something. If you'd met her, you'd understand." He falls silent and looks away, as if the agonizing reality of the situation is sinking in. "Oh God, I can't believe she's been stabbed."

Daniel notes that Henry knows how the murder was committed. Then again, it's hard to keep something like that under wraps. No doubt the poor maintenance guy who found the body told other people as well as the hotel manager, and the news would have spread like wildfire.

Hanna leans forward. "So why was the hotel in Storlien so important to your partner? What was so special about it?"

Henry doesn't answer immediately. He presses his fingertips together, forming an inverted V shape with his hands.

"Well, it might not look like much today, but years ago it was different. It was like celebrating Christmas in the Snow Queen's palace. When I was little it was a magical place that I dreamed of for the rest of the year. A winter's tale full of snow, sparkling garlands, and the aromas of saffron, cloves, and cinnamon."

Henry's eyes are filled with nostalgia. He seems to be overcome by his childhood memories. For a moment his face softens, and Daniel can almost see the little boy happily racing toward the Christmas tree with all the beautifully wrapped presents underneath.

"I don't think I've ever loved Christmas as much as during those years when we went to Storlien," he goes on. "Charlotte was an important part of that experience."

His voice is thick with tears.

"I understand," Hanna says gently. "But where did the idea of building a completely new hotel on the site come from? I believe it's been empty for a long time, and it's decades since it was a famous ski resort."

"I think Charlotte wanted to fulfill a dream. Or maybe it was her father's dream."

"Why was it so important to her?"

Henry takes off his camel-hair coat and places it on the chair beside him.

"Charlotte was her daddy's girl." He sounds deeply sad. "She constantly sought his approval. Curt—that was his name—often urged her to make something of her own, something that would last. He was an entrepreneur in the restaurant industry and had a lot of opinions on how things should be done. At some point during all those visits to Storlien, I guess he began to think that he might take over the hotel. Gradually, as time went by, it became about creating a magnificent new establishment in the mountains. He never succeeded himself, but he passed on the idea to the next generation."

"What was the relationship like between father and daughter?" Hanna wonders.

Henry reaches for the glass of water and takes a sip. Daniel notices that he doesn't answer right away.

"I don't want to speak ill of the dead, but Curt was . . . a hard character. He regarded his children as an extension of himself rather than as independent individuals. It had a lasting effect on his daughter, if I can put it that way."

"You can put it however you like," Hanna replies.

Daniel makes a note, then meets the businessman's gaze again.

"Can you give us an example of what you said about Charlotte's father?"

"Where do I begin?" Henry's expression is resigned. "Charlotte and I studied at the Stockholm School of Economics together. She almost didn't get in—she wasn't quite up to the standards they set. Eventually it worked out, she was accepted as the last reserve candidate, but until then she was devastated. Curt would never have approved of anywhere else. Reading economics at an ordinary university wasn't good enough—only the elite institution would do. Charlotte placed high demands on herself, and that came from her father."

He shakes his head at the memory.

"I have to say that he could be very entertaining, and he was an excellent businessman. He helped me at the start of my career. But he wouldn't have won a prize as daddy of the year. He was more like the patriarch in *Succession*, if you know what I mean?"

Daniel gives a brief nod. He hasn't seen the TV series, but he's heard that it's about four siblings fighting to gain the approval of their ice-cold father.

He is also well aware that the nuclear family isn't the answer to everything. If it were, then his relationship with Ida shouldn't be so complicated.

Henry rubs his forehead and sighs. "This is so difficult to take in."

"How about brothers and sisters?" Daniel asks.

"She had a younger brother, but he passed away a few years ago. He developed problems with alcohol at a young age, and eventually his liver gave up. There wasn't exactly a supportive atmosphere in that family . . ."

He doesn't elaborate, but the meaning is clear. Growing up in the Wretlind family seems to have been quite difficult, in spite of those magical Christmases in the mountains.

Hanna glances at Daniel, as if to indicate that she would like to change the subject. He nods—he trusts her intuition.

"How come you decided to invest in Charlotte's project?"

"To be honest, I was her last resort. I know she'd tried other investors, but they'd turned her down. She swore it would be profitable and I wouldn't be disappointed."

Henry breaks off and clears his throat.

"I said no to begin with. During the course of the journey, there have been times when I've wished I'd stuck to my guns, bearing in mind how much money we're talking about. The costs have already increased considerably, and we haven't even started demolishing the old complex."

"And yet you provided the capital," Hanna points out.

"Like I said, Charlotte didn't take no for an answer, and I guess I got a little sentimental, remembering our childhood Christmases. And she was stubborn—once she'd made a decision, there was no stopping her. Whatever the cost."

"And how did people react? It sounds like a recipe for making enemies."

The ringtone of Henry's phone interrupts them. He takes it out of his jacket pocket, glances at the screen, and rejects the call before placing it on the table.

"Enemies?" he repeats.

Most people have enemies, Daniel thinks. Especially if they work in a tough industry, like Charlotte. However, it rarely leads to murder, especially not in such a brutal way.

He gazes at Henry across the table. The financier is lost in thought, it's impossible to guess what's going on in his mind. Despite the shocking situation, he seems composed now. Maybe he is used to keeping his emotions in check after years working in business.

"Obviously Charlotte had her differences with some people," Henry says. "She wasn't exactly the kind of person who panders to anyone."

Hanna frowns. "Could you be a little more specific? Do you know individuals she'd fallen out with?"

"Unfortunately that would be a very long list."

"Are you thinking of anyone in particular?"

Henry gives a half smile. "I don't really want to name names—isn't that something the police should be looking into?"

Daniel glances at his watch; it is almost six o'clock in the evening. They need to go back to the station to run through the day, and to link up with Östersund. Grip has messaged to say that she wants a debrief as soon as possible.

"What happens with the Storlien project now?" Hanna asks Henry. "Will you be taking it forward now that Charlotte is gone?"

Henry picks up his phone and puts it in his pocket.

"It was all built on Charlotte's driving force," he says with a certain weariness in his voice. "She was the engine. Her vision was key."

"So does that mean the plans will be canceled now she's dead?" Hanna persists.

"I can't answer that. It's way too soon."

Daniel isn't letting go either. "But if the scheme were to be ditched, then doesn't that mean you wouldn't have to invest all those millions?"

Henry is clearly irritated. "I don't understand where you're going with this." His tone is suddenly razor sharp. "Are you insinuating that I stand to gain from Charlotte's death?"

17

A camera flash goes off as Daniel and Hanna make their way down the stairs to the hotel foyer a little while later.

Daniel gives a start and stops on the bottom step. Hanna is a short distance ahead of him. When he looks around, he sees a gaggle of photographers by the reception desk.

Charlotte's press conference. The journalists have a completely different sensation to write about.

Someone points to Daniel, and a man in his early thirties with short blond hair comes hurrying over, full of self-importance. He is holding a microphone bearing the logo of one of the big TV stations. The mic is on the end of a long boom, which he holds out toward Daniel.

"What can you tell us about the homicide?" he says challengingly.

Daniel holds up one hand. "We have no comment at this stage."

The TV journalist ignores the rebuff—in fact, it seems to spur him on.

"A woman has been found stabbed to death in one of the hotel rooms," he continues in the same hectoring tone. "What can you tell us about the situation we're facing?"

"I'm sorry, I can't comment on that right now."

The other man comes closer. "Do you have any suspects?"

Meanwhile, most of the other reporters have realized that they have a senior police officer in front of them. They too hurry over and surround Daniel, holding up their microphones.

There are too many of them, and they are too close. Daniel tries to back away, but there is nowhere to go.

There are people everywhere.

The blond guy is so close that Daniel can smell his breath.

"Are any hotel employees involved?"

It is suffocatingly hot, Daniel can hardly breathe. It is becoming harder and harder not to lose control.

"Enough!" he yells. "I've already said I can't comment!"

Without thinking he lashes out with one hand. The movement is more violent than he had intended. He catches the arm of the microphone and knocks it over the banister onto the stone floor. The volume in the foyer immediately shoots up, there are horrified exclamations from the pack of journalists.

"What are you doing?" the reporter shouts.

Suddenly Hanna pushes her way through. She grabs Daniel by the arm and drags him through the crowd.

"There will be a press conference later, when you will be given more information," she calls over her shoulder. "Right now you'll have to excuse us."

She manages to get Daniel out into the fresh air, and doesn't stop until they are at least ten yards from the entrance.

It is such a relief to get out of there. Daniel takes several deep breaths. He is so angry that his entire body is shaking. He can't understand why he had such a strong reaction. After many months of therapy, he thought he had his emotions in check. Over the past year he hasn't lost his temper once, either at home or at work.

"Are you okay?" Hanna asks sympathetically.

"I'm fine."

She waves a hand in the direction of the reporter, who is still standing in the foyer.

"I don't understand how he can behave so disrespectfully. We're talking about a murdered woman here, not some sleazy celebrity scandal."

Daniel turns and sees the guy staring at them. The anger that was beginning to subside comes back like a tsunami.

His blood is boiling.

That's when he realizes. That journalist reminds him of his father.

18

The parking lot outside Åre police station on Kurortsvägen is empty. As they get out of the car, Hanna sees Carina Grankvist's white Volkswagen turn in off the main road. The crime scene investigation must be finished.

Daniel locks the car, and they make their way with Carina up to the meeting room, where Anton Lundgren is waiting with Rafael Herrera— or Raffe, as everyone calls him.

Both men are based in Åre as general investigators. They are really supposed to deal with crimes such as robbery, abuse, and criminal damage, but in a homicide case like this, every available resource is needed.

Anton and Raffe are sitting at the rectangular wooden table on bright-red chairs. The colorful upholstery forms a stark contrast to the otherwise white room. Only a few years ago the local hospital was housed in this building, and its legacy still lingers in the décor.

As Hanna walks in, Raffe is busy setting up the link to Östersund. A second later their boss, Birgitta Grip, appears on the screen. She is accompanied by several colleagues from the Serious Crimes Unit, much to Hanna's relief. Both she and Daniel have been worried about the lack of resources. This means that the case is being prioritized, even if that means that other matters have to be set aside.

Grip, who is in her sixties, strokes her chin and looks from Daniel to Hanna.

"Which of you would like to begin?"

Hanna can't help feeling a sense of satisfaction that Grip included her in the question. Daniel has been with the unit for a lot longer than her, and he was the one who helped her to secure the post in Åre. He is regarded as more experienced, although he is only two years older. However, they have worked together for almost fifteen months now, and it seems as if Grip regards her as a reliable member of the team.

Hanna sits up a little straighter. She has the utmost respect for Grip, who leads the unit with a firm hand. Grip grew up in Östersund, and is well aware of the challenges of working in a rural community. She is also wise and fair, and extremely practical.

Hanna has never had a female boss before, and she likes it.

Manfred, her former superior who gave her no choice but to leave her post in the Domestic Violence Unit with the City Police in Stockholm, was completely different. He had his favorites, and didn't like it when anyone opposed him or asked difficult questions.

In complete contrast, Grip encourages different points of view. She likes it when her officers look at things from another angle.

In the past, Hanna didn't give much thought to the need for female role models—she would simply shrug if the issue arose. Now she realizes what it's about. Grip makes Hanna stronger as a police officer. She feels more secure in her own role with a competent woman as head of the unit.

In a case like this, involving extreme violence against a woman, that feels especially good.

Daniel glances at Hanna. "You or me?"

"Go for it."

There is no power play here. They are equals, and she knows that he would never show off at her expense.

Daniel summarizes the situation they encountered when they arrived at the hotel in the morning. He gives their first impressions of the crime scene, the brutality of the attack, the shock among the staff.

"Anything you'd like to add?" he asks Hanna.

She studies her notes. Daniel has already given an overview of the interviews conducted during the day, and the people they met. He hasn't said anything about motive or possible perpetrators, but that will come later. They don't know enough at this stage.

"I think you've covered most things," she says.

"Okay." Grip turns her attention to Carina, who is sitting opposite Hanna. "What can you tell us?"

Carina shares a number of photographs from the scene. The first, a close-up of Charlotte Wretlind from the waist upward, makes Anton cover his mouth with his hand. Hanna can see that their colleagues in Östersund are also affected.

Raffe gasps. "My God."

"Indeed," Carina agrees. "I've never seen anything like it. The body is on its way to the National Forensic Center in Umeå, but we can state that Charlotte Wretlind suffered several dozen knife wounds over her entire body. The one to the throat would have been enough to kill her."

Carina shows more pictures of the body and the hotel room—all equally difficult to look at.

"So let's talk about the perpetrator," Grip says. "What's your view, Carina? Man or woman?"

"We've managed to secure a partial shoe print. It seems as if the murderer stepped in the victim's blood on the way out, then trod on the carpet. According to our measurements, we are looking for someone who wears a size forty-five shoe, which suggests it's a man. The strength behind the blows with the knife also leads me in that direction, because there are so many and they're so deep, but I'd like to hear what the forensic pathologists have to say."

Hanna doesn't think there can be any doubt about the killer's gender. As soon as she saw the victim's mutilated body, she was certain they were looking for a man. They have already established that there don't seem to be any defensive wounds. That could be down to either the murderer's physical superiority or that the victim was simply unable to defend herself in the face of acute danger. This is known as the freeze response, when a person is so afraid that they can't move a muscle. It often happens to women, especially in assault cases. Hanna has come across it frequently in the past.

Grip nods. "Okay, so it sounds like a man with size forty-five shoes. That suggests someone who is quite tall, and presumably pretty strong. What else can we say?"

"He must have been covered in blood," Carina says. "It went everywhere, all over the room. With the kind of close contact required to stab someone in this way, it would have been impossible for the perpetrator to avoid getting blood on his clothes."

"So little chance of a discreet exit." Daniel leans back on his chair. "If anyone saw him after he left the Silver Suite, it must have been obvious that he'd committed a crime."

"It's a big hotel," Hanna points out. "They have over four hundred beds and one hundred and twenty members of staff in the high season. There should be witnesses who noticed him leaving the scene."

"What about CCTV?" Raffe asks. "Could we be lucky enough to find that he was caught on film?"

"They're gathering everything up and will send it over as soon as possible," Hanna replies. "We mentioned it to the manager."

"Carina, what can you tell us about the murder weapon?" Grip says.

"Obviously it's a knife, probably an ordinary hunting knife, given the number and size of the wounds."

"A hunting knife," Raffe echoes. "Where do we even start?"

The question is rhetorical. Everyone knows that a large percentage of the population of Jämtland go hunting. If you hunt, you have a hunting knife as part of your basic equipment.

"That's your problem," Carina says dryly. "I just answered the question."

"Thank you, Carina—that's a good start," Grip says.

Daniel folds his arms and looks around the table and at the screen. "It doesn't seem like a very professional job. It's too messy. If the main aim was to kill the victim, then the single blow to the throat would have been enough. Instead he seems to have stabbed her repeatedly, in a frenzy."

Hanna agrees. There is something deeply aggressive about the whole thing, from the multiple stab wounds to the fact that Charlotte was attacked in bed.

"I don't think it was just about taking her life," she says. "It almost feels as if Charlotte Wretlind was being made to pay for something."

A punishment.

Grip pushes back a strand of her steel-gray hair, which tones with her deep-set eyes. "I agree. Let's take a look at the victim's background. What do we know about her?"

Anton has looked into Charlotte's life while Daniel and Hanna were at Copperhill. He has his laptop open in front of him.

"I ran a multiple inquiry and searched all our databases," he begins. "She doesn't appear anywhere."

A model citizen, in other words, Hanna thinks.

"She renewed her passport six months ago—this is what she looked like then."

A passport photo of Charlotte appears on the screen. She looks cool and professional, wearing a dark jacket and a blouse with a pussycat bow.

"Born in 1965," Anton continues, "which means she was fifty-six at the time of her death. Her mother lives in a care home for dementia sufferers. Her father is dead. She was married to a man called Mats Rutberg for a few years in the late nineties—the divorce went through in 2000. Since then she has been single, and is registered at an expensive address in the Östermalm district of Stockholm—Tysta Gatan 7."

"Children?" Raffe wonders, adjusting the dark ponytail that his is signature. Hanna has never seen him with his hair loose, and only once with a different style, when he went for a man bun on top of his head.

"One son, born in 1997. His name is Filip Rutberg Wretlind, and he lives not far away from his mother, on Banérgatan in the same district. He has embarked on several education courses, including at the Royal Institute of Technology in Stockholm, but he hasn't completed any of them. At the moment he seems to be mostly drifting around."

"Has he been informed?"

"Yes. The Stockholm police took care of it."

"And the ex-husband?"

"They're trying to track him down—apparently he lives abroad."

"What do we know about the victim's finances and work situation before the Storlien project?" Daniel asks.

"For many years Charlotte was a partner in a well-known risk capital company, IQP. By any standards, her personal financial situation was very comfortable. Her apartment is pretty large, and is in one of Stockholm's most desirable areas. She also has a summer cottage on the island of Ingarö in the Stockholm archipelago, and an apartment on Majorca. Three years ago she left the company and started her own business known as SEG—Swedish Establishment Group—where she is the director and chair of the board."

"SEG are behind the Storlien project," Hanna adds. "Charlotte's business partner, Henry Sylvester, told us."

"Exactly," Anton says. "They have five employees, and the office is also in Östermalm."

"What shape are the company finances in?" Daniel wants to know.

"I can look into that," Raffe offers.

Hanna remembers that he took care of the financial aspect of their previous investigation, when the skier Johan Andersson was murdered. Apparently Raffe has completed some courses in business finance over the past year; personally she can't think of anything more boring.

She also knows that Raffe and his partner, Nilla, are trying to have a baby, but it's not going too well. Hanna has met Nilla a few times; she's a sweet person in her early thirties who enjoys baking and works as a preschool teacher in Kall, where they live.

Maybe Raffe's online courses are a form of distraction? Or maybe he's just ambitious.

She glances at Daniel. He told her quite early on that Ida had unexpectedly found herself pregnant with Alice when they had been together for only a few months. At the time, they weren't even sure they wanted to keep the child. It somehow seems unfair that Raffe and Nilla, who have been together forever, are struggling to have a family when it's so easy for others.

Life, she thinks. It rarely turns out the way we expect. She is thirty-six years old and single, something that her mother often points out. It seems increasingly unlikely that she will ever meet someone and have children of her own.

The thought is unexpectedly painful.

Daniel's voice interrupts her gloomy reverie.

"It's interesting that the door of the suite shows no sign of forced entry, suggesting that the victim herself might have let the perpetrator in—but then again she was wearing nothing but panties when she was found, which contradicts that idea."

Hanna thinks about Henry Sylvester, the business partner who has known Charlotte since they were children, and now seems likely to be able to drop out of a multimillion kronor investment he'd been talked into.

If he'd knocked on her door late at night, no doubt Charlotte would have let him in. Could he be involved? He said he flew up to Åre this afternoon—yesterday he was in Stockholm. Hanna makes a note to check out his alibi. She can't really see the elegant businessman wielding the knife himself, but neither can she rule it out.

"Take a look at Sylvester too," she says to Raffe. "See what shape his company finances are in."

Grip steps in. "A member of staff could have opened the door with a master key."

"That's definitely a possibility," Daniel says. "We need to check which key cards were used for the victim's suite yesterday, and we also need to map all the hotel employees."

Daniel's final words make Grip sigh in a way that says it all. Background checks take time. She begins to allocate tasks. Two younger investigators from Östersund will question individually everyone who was on duty the previous day. In addition, background checks must be carried out on every employee. Hanna is disappointed when that job goes to an older colleague, Nisse Sundbom, who has failed to impress her. He is one of the veterans in the unit, someone who rarely overexerts himself.

"Is there anything to indicate that this could happen again?" Grip asks. "Should we be afraid that the killer might intend to harm other guests? If so, we might need to consider closing the place down."

Hanna meets her boss's worried gaze. Once again the image of Charlotte's body comes into her mind. The idea that they could be dealing with a crazed killer is terrifying.

"I'm inclined to think this was personal," Daniel says. "It doesn't feel like she was chosen by chance, even if we don't have any evidence to the contrary."

Hanna agrees. Her gut instinct tells her that Charlotte's death wasn't a horrific random act.

Then something else occurs to her.

What if the aim of the brutal murder was to create a smoke screen, a facade to send her and her colleagues in the wrong direction? What if someone out there wants them to start looking for a madman, when in fact it's a contract killing?

In which case, what appears to be frenzied violence could be something else.

A plan to mislead the police.

19

Anton is in his parents' kitchen, and puts down his knife and fork. Their house, where he grew up, is only ten minutes away from his apartment in Duved. Today is his father's sixty-seventh birthday, which is why he has dragged himself away from work to join them for dinner.

He can't help feeling guilty. After what happened today, work ought to come before his personal life.

"Time for coffee and cake," his mother, Susanne, announces. She points toward the cake stand waiting on the counter. They have just eaten moose stew with rice. Anton's father, Åke, likes hearty food; it's a legacy of a career in the army and his role as lieutenant colonel, from which he stepped down two years ago.

"Sounds delicious," Anton says, getting to his feet.

He helps to load the dishwasher, then gets out three mugs. As usual Åke remains seated at the table, straight-backed as befits a soldier, without lifting a finger. His mother always says that you can't teach an old dog new tricks when Anton questions the fact that she works full time as a dental hygienist and still does all the cooking and cleaning. Now that his father has retired, Anton thinks he could make more of a contribution at home.

However, there is no point in bringing it up this evening and spoiling the atmosphere. After all, it is his father's birthday, and Anton knows how much it means to his mother that they should get along. She hates it when there are arguments over family dinners, which unfortunately happens all too often.

It infuriates Anton when his father treats him like one of his subordinates, while Åke doesn't think Anton shows sufficient respect.

They are very similar in appearance, both short and muscular with cropped hair, but they are totally different on the inside. Where Anton is meticulous and cautious, even reserved, his father is domineering and utterly sure of himself.

Anton waits his turn to speak, while his father interrupts without a second thought.

Susanne fetches the freshly brewed coffee and the cake. They chat about this and that, about Anton's sister, Karro, and her two children—Wilda is almost eleven, Emil is eight. Wilda has a cold; that's why they're not here this evening. Anton misses them; he is very fond of his niece and nephew.

The new case means he won't be able to hang out with them over Easter.

"Isn't it time you thought about a family of your own?" his father says, adjusting the collar of his checked flannel shirt. "You're not getting any younger. Think of the fun Karro has with her kids. The clock is ticking!"

Anton stiffens. This is precisely the kind of conversation he tries to avoid having with his parents. Even though he is thirty-four years old, he hasn't come out to them. Nor to anyone else; as far as he knows, no one at work is aware that he prefers guys.

That's the way he wants to keep it.

He has wrestled with the issue many times, and always reaches the same conclusion. It's better to keep quiet and pretend that everything is fine than to tell the truth. He doesn't want to be "the gay" at the station, the guy who makes his colleagues feel uncomfortable in the changing room or is responsible for an awkward atmosphere in the sauna.

HR can talk until they're blue in the face about basic values and everyone's right to equal treatment, but the reality is considerably tougher. Old attitudes still exist within the Swedish police. Not many officers are openly gay, whatever the leadership might say in its policies.

Especially not outside the big cities.

"You can't spend all your time working, training, and playing the saxophone," his father goes on. "You need to think about the future—do you really want to live alone for the rest of your life?"

Anton swallows an angry response. It's typical of his father to bring up the saxophone too. Åke is tone deaf; all the hours Anton spent practicing in his room when he was growing up were a source of conflict. Fortunately his father served in Boden for many years, so he was often away for weeks.

Anton is about to speak when his mother holds up her hand.

"Leave him alone," she says sharply. "He'll find the right person eventually. We have no right to nag him—he's an adult and he can make his own decisions."

Anton gives her a grateful look. He can't work out whether she is deliberately trying to save him from a difficult topic or whether she is simply irritated by Åke's pompous comments.

He can't have this discussion again, especially not tonight. It has been a long and demanding day. He intends to go in early tomorrow to make up for his absence.

He decides to change the subject. "Delicious cake."

For some reason his thoughts turn to Carl, the man he met at the night club known as Bygget last year. Anton still hasn't gotten over him. They spent a few unforgettable nights together, moments that shook him to the core. It was new and inexplicable, and for the first time he could imagine openly being with another guy.

It all went wrong of course, and it was his own fault.

First the investigation got in the way; then time simply passed. He doesn't know whether he avoided contact because he was afraid of rejection, or whether he was too cowardly to stand up for who he is.

Over the past year, he has seen Carl in the village now and again, but has never gone over to say hi. His courage has failed him on every occasion.

"I need to make a move," he says, pushing back his chair. He can't sit here any longer. He needs fresh air.

"Now look what you've done!" his mother snaps at Åke. "You frighten him away with your stupid questions!"

His father grunts something incomprehensible and reaches for another slice of cake. It is clear that he doesn't enjoy life as a retiree. He complains constantly and gets irritated by small things. Having nothing to do doesn't suit him, but that isn't Anton's problem.

He can't deal with any of that, not today.

Right now he just wants to go home, play his saxophone, and try to obliterate all his memories of Carl with the help of the music.

20

The sound of a key in the lock makes Ida look up from her tablet.

She is sitting on the sofa, the TV is on, but most of her attention is on an intense online discussion about the fatal stabbing at Copperhill. There are hundreds of contributions in the comments field. Emotions are running high. Some people are even claiming that it was a ritual killing.

It's so awful.

Daniel appears in the doorway. He looks terrible; his eyes are tired; his brown hair is all over the place. He messaged about the new case earlier in the day, and Ida has read the rest for herself.

"Hi," she says with a smile. "How are things?"

Daniel runs a hand over his beard. He steps forward and kisses her on the forehead.

"Sorry I'm late. Is Alice asleep?"

It's almost nine o'clock. Of course she is.

"Yes," Ida says, trying not to snap. "She went down at seven thirty as usual."

Daniel glances toward the kitchen. "Any food left?"

"Half a jar of baby stew."

Daniel looks disappointed, as if he were hoping for leftovers from dinner to warm up. "What did you have?"

"I couldn't be bothered to cook when you said you were going to be late. I just had a cup of tea and a sandwich."

Ida is slightly ashamed of herself; it sounds as if she's lazy. But she had to leave work in a hurry to pick up Alice from preschool, as Daniel wasn't going to be able to do it. It was all very stressful.

When they first met she was a guide and ski instructor, and loved every minute. Now she is an administrator with a local company. Not exactly her dream job, but the hours are regular and mean she can make life as the parent of a small child work.

Although sometimes the boredom gets to her. She has never been a fan of routine.

"Okay, I'll make myself something," Daniel says, heading for the kitchen. "Back in a few minutes."

Ida feels guilty when he has left the room. She could of course have made something that would be enough for Daniel when he got home. But she hadn't. She had had neither the desire nor the energy.

Sometimes she wonders what is happening between them.

She still remembers the feeling at the beginning, how much in love they were. Her whole body tingled as soon as she saw him, even if he'd only been gone for a few minutes. They made love several times every day.

That was fewer than three years ago—not very long.

Today she doesn't feel like that at all when he walks in. Nothing happens inside her, and when they talk it is mostly about Alice, or practical matters. Who is going to pick her up from preschool, whether they should go somewhere at the weekend.

Once or twice Daniel has mentioned the possibility of a brother or sister for Alice, but Ida has dismissed the idea.

She feels trapped in a way she can't really explain, never mind acknowledge out loud.

She often reminds herself that she is lucky to have a beautiful daughter and such a sweet partner. He has even started seeing a therapist for her sake. He is determined to make their relationship work, and Ida knows why. He has told her about his upbringing and his absent father, how important it is for him to give Alice a different childhood.

Ida stares down at her tablet.

It can't just be about Alice all the time, she thinks, absentmindedly scrolling through the ever-increasing barrage of comments.

She is only twenty-seven.

Is this it for the rest of her life?

21

A glowing full moon surprises Hanna when she finally emerges from the police station after a fourteen-hour day.

The mountaintops beyond Lake Åre are sparkling, the moonlight is so bright that she can see her own shadow in the snow, and everything around her is in silvery tones.

In spite of the ongoing investigation, she is transfixed. Thoughts of the horrific homicide fade away. It is almost ten o'clock, Hanna is exhausted, but the cold, fresh air chases away her tiredness.

She stands there with her face turned up to the sky for a few seconds before reality catches up. It is time to go home; she wants to make an early start tomorrow. At least she knows that Henry Sylvester has an unshakable alibi for Sunday evening—that was the last thing she checked out before leaving the station. Several witnesses have confirmed that he had dinner with them in Stockholm.

The moonlight accompanies her on the short walk to Solbringen. The snow crunches beneath her feet as she walks up the hills. After the last bend, her little house appears, bathed in a magical, luminous shimmer against the background of the dense forest, a brown gingerbread house that is hers and hers alone.

She takes her keys out of her pocket, and as soon as she opens the door, she is met by Morris's meowing. He winds himself back and forth between her legs, even though Lydia has been over to feed him. He is so thrilled that she feels like a queen making her grand entrance.

Before she goes to bed, she must check on the local Facebook groups to see if anyone is missing a fluffy gray-and-white cat. Part of her hopes not. She posted on the noticeboard of the Åre police home page asking if anyone had inquired about lost pets, but so far there has been no response.

Hanna kneels down in the dark hallway, and Morris rubs his body against hers. He is purring like a tractor. When she strokes his head, he stretches his neck and closes his eyes; there is no mistaking his intense enjoyment.

She is covered in cat hairs, but it doesn't matter.

It is so nice not to come home to an empty house.

22

The pain in her right shoulder is keeping Tiina awake, even though it is after eleven and she needs to sleep.

She turns over, tries lying on her side, glances at Ogge's sleeping form next to her. He is on his back; in the darkness she can see a few black hairs protruding from his wide nose. From time to time, he lets out a snore; it starts in his throat, continues to the roof of his mouth, and emerges as a rasping sound from his open mouth.

In sleep his face is calm and peaceful; he almost looks kind. His hands are resting on top of the covers. His eyes, which can narrow with anger when he is drunk, are closed.

Tiny movements beneath his eyelids suggest that he is dreaming.

Sometimes he has terrible nightmares, when the memories from his childhood catch up with him. He is rarely willing to talk about those days, but occasionally, dreadful stories have slipped out.

At the beginning of their relationship, Tiina tried to persuade him to see a therapist, talk to a psychologist to process his experiences, but he got so angry that she dropped the idea. Over time she has abandoned her efforts, despite the fact that he seems to be increasingly tormented by his difficult childhood.

Recently his outbursts of rage have become more frequent, and he has also started drinking more. Sometimes she finds him in the living room late at night, sitting up and brooding with a grim look on his face.

Tiina shudders and draws the covers more tightly around her. Ogge groans and inhales deeply. It sounds like the final rattle of a dying man. There is silence for several seconds, then he exhales.

To be on the safe side, she shuffles toward the edge of the mattress in order to give him space, even though he is already taking up more than half the bed.

Then she lies perfectly still. Tries to make herself relax so that the pain will go away and she can finally get to sleep.

TUESDAY, MARCH 30

23

Hanna's eyes are stinging as she heads for the small kitchen at the station on Tuesday morning to pour herself a large cup of coffee. Six hours' sleep is not enough; a yawn gets the better of her on the way. It is seven thirty, and they are due to hold a briefing with everyone involved in the special unit that has been put together to investigate the murder of Charlotte Wretlind.

She says good morning to a couple of colleagues who are heading out on patrol, then makes her way to the conference room. Daniel is already seated at the table. His face lights up when she comes in, and as usual her mood improves as soon as she sees him. Today he is wearing jeans and a crewneck sweater with a white shirt underneath—his standard attire. His hair is tousled, as if he simply ran his fingers through it this morning instead of looking for a comb.

Hanna is seized by an impulse to lean forward and smooth it down, but quickly pulls herself together.

Daniel also seems to be suffering from a lack of sleep, but he no longer looks as desperately tired as he did during Alice's first year. Hanna pictures Daniel and Ida smiling with their arms around each other, holding their baby daughter.

The unattainable nuclear family.

Which is not hers.

Maybe she's acquired a cat instead.

The thought provides some consolation, even though she was woken at least ten times during the night because Morris seems to have decided that the only acceptable place to sleep is on Hanna's bed, preferably on her chest.

For the first time, she understands why Daniel looks so worn out when Alice has had a bad night.

"How long did you stay yesterday?" he asks.

"I think I got to bed around midnight. By the way, I checked out Henry Sylvester's alibi, and several witnesses confirm that he was in Stockholm on Sunday evening."

The door opens, and Raffe and Anton join them. Anton is carrying a pile of printouts, which he places on the table, while Raffe's contribution is a plate of brownies baked by Nilla.

"Okay, let's go," Daniel says, opening the link to Östersund, where the rest of the group are assembled with Birgitta Grip and the prosecutor.

They have several matters to deal with today. After lunch they are meeting the victim's son, who is due to arrive in Åre this morning. Before that they plan to go through the printouts of the interviews with hotel staff conducted so far. Hanna also wants to speak to Carina to get the lowdown on the examination of the crime scene, and she hopes to find time to dig deeper into Charlotte's background and private life.

She glances at the wall, where the photographs of Charlotte's mutilated body have been put up.

The red blood against the white skin, the wide-open eyes staring into eternity.

Hanna shudders. Who does that to another person?

24

The lump in Aada's stomach grows as soon as she leaves the staff accommodation and sets off for the hotel. It is only a few hundred yards, but every step is an effort.

Last night she dreamed of a dark figure who flung open the door and attacked her in her sleep. She would prefer to stay in her room and hide, but she dare not miss work.

With her head bowed against the wind, she heads for the parking garage and the staff entrance. The cold nips at her cheeks; she shivers all the way.

After a great deal of thought, she has decided to keep quiet.

The police are bound to catch the murderer without her help; there's no point in getting involved. She speaks Swedish very poorly, and her English isn't much better. She doesn't know how to describe what she saw on Sunday, let alone explain how frightened she is that they won't be able to protect her.

Aada remembers all the times her mother tried to get help back home in Maardu. No one was prepared to intervene, because her stepfather was a police officer. The odd argument at home should be dealt with behind closed doors; they ignored the fact that her mother was regularly beaten black and blue. Aada's stepfather's colleagues refused to get involved, even though her mother eventually suffered such a serious assault that she was left with permanent brain damage.

The police in little Maardu had one another's backs.

What if the Swedish police are the same, protecting men who hurt women?

There is nothing to suggest that the forces of law and order in Sweden are any different. And what if they don't believe her, and rumors start?

She could lose her job.

Or even worse, the murderer might find out and regard her as a threat.

As she approaches the parking garage, she takes out the key card that hangs around her neck. The staff entrance is next door. She swipes the card and lets herself into the desolate area. There are only a few cars today. The lighting is sparse, and fights a losing battle against the black concrete floor.

The dark-red walls remind her of blood.

She shudders and glances over her shoulder. She can't see anyone, but that doesn't calm her nerves. As she hurries toward the changing room, a noise stops her in her tracks.

It sounded as if the door opened again, right behind her.

She looks around anxiously, but there is no one in sight. She peers at the dark corner, but can't make out any movement.

The murderer can't have seen her clearly on Sunday, she tells herself. Everything happened so fast, and the door was only open a little bit.

He can't possibly know who she is.

But as she sets off again, she hears something behind her. Footsteps following her—she is no longer alone in the parking garage.

She stops dead, too scared to look around.

Has he come after her? Is he determined to silence her?

Her heartbeat is pounding in her ears, her palms are sticky with sweat.

At that moment the changing room door opens. Two girls emerge, chatting and laughing. Aada hurries forward and slips in behind them.

When she turns her head, she catches a glimpse of a dark jacket disappearing in the direction of the exit.

She is absolutely certain now.

There *was* someone there.

Someone who had followed her.

25

Daniel hurries across the square with Hanna. They have just grabbed a quick hot dog for lunch, and now they are on the way to Åregården Hotel, where Charlotte's son, Filip, has checked in. He flew up this morning, but preferred not to stay at Copperhill, where his mother was murdered.

The snow sparkles as they approach the hotel. The daylight is so bright that Daniel wishes he hadn't left his sunglasses in the car. The square is full of relaxed skiers, taking a lunch break in the spring sunshine. Most food outlets have moved their operations outside because of the COVID restrictions, and a long line has formed at a pop-up bar. In the middle is a guy wearing a bright-yellow chicken costume; his helmet is adorned with yellow Easter feathers sticking out from the top of his head. Next to him is a girl in a white furry helmet with bunny ears.

Yesterday's brutal murder doesn't seem to have impacted the atmosphere around here.

Nor does the pandemic.

"Idiots," he says, waving an arm in the direction of the crowd.

"They're young and think they're invincible," Hanna points out.

"And presumably they're from Stockholm," Daniel replies with a grin.

As someone who was born and brought up in Sundsvall, he likes to remind Hanna that she is a blow-in from the capital. In return she calls him a country hick. They both love living in Åre, but they're not quite so fond of the tourists.

As soon as they reach the hotel, the automatic glass doors slide open. They are more or less the only modern feature on the facade. The rest—the dark-brown wood paneling, the pillars on either side of the entrance, and the leaded windows in white and English red—look exactly the same as they have done for 125 years.

"Did you know that this place was built by a woman at the end of the nineteenth century?" Hanna says. "Imagine embarking on a project like that—in those days."

Daniel did know. Kristina Hansson, who came from Skåne in the south, didn't even have the right to vote when she started the construction of Åre's first hotel.

"I guess she and Charlotte Wretlind would have had a lot to talk about," Hanna goes on. "They both seem to have had tremendous drive."

From what Daniel has heard about Charlotte so far, there seems little doubt that she was equipped with both stubbornness and a strong will. The question is—was it those qualities that led to her tragic death?

They walk into the foyer, and Daniel looks around for Filip; they have arranged to meet him here. He can't imagine what the young man is going through right now. How do you even function after hearing news like that?

The responsibility for finding the killer feels like a heavy weight on his shoulders. He stares at the stuffed moose, which has stood in the entrance for as long as he can remember.

It stares back with sorrowful eyes, almost as if it is offering its heartfelt sympathy.

26

A young man with fair hair and a pale complexion gets up from one of the club armchairs and comes toward them.

Hanna immediately assumes he is Filip Wretlind. According to the records, he is supposed to be twenty-three, but he looks younger with his rounded cheeks. He has tucked his longish hair with its center parting behind his ears.

"Are you the police?" he asks.

Hanna and Daniel say hello and shake hands.

A pretty girl of about the same age appears behind Filip and tucks her arm through his.

"This is Emily, my girlfriend," he explains. "She came up with me when I heard . . . that Mom . . ."

He doesn't finish the sentence; he seems stunned, as if he can't quite take in what has happened. His eyes are red-rimmed, the skin beneath them is thin, with a bluish tinge.

Hanna notices some kind of tic as he quickly shuts his eyes and opens them again.

She pats him on the shoulder. "Shall we sit down?" She leads the way to the Malmsten Room, the hotel's most beautiful lounge area, with wooden paneling and beams on the ceiling. Hanna and Daniel have arranged to interview Filip in there, hoping that the cozy atmosphere might make him feel better.

Daniel turns to Emily. "Would you mind waiting in the foyer? We'd like to speak to your boyfriend alone."

Filip looks panic stricken. His fingers find Emily's; he squeezes her hand so tightly that she visibly winces.

"I want her there," he says breathlessly.

"No problem," Daniel concedes after a quick glance at Hanna, who nods. This is not a formal interview. If having Emily there is easier for Filip, then that's fine.

She is surprised to see that he is wearing ordinary sneakers, even though it's well below freezing outside, with snow on the ground.

They settle in a corner of the Malmsten Room, where they can be in peace. A pleasant waiter brings a tray with four glasses and a carafe of water.

"We're so sorry for your loss," Hanna begins. "This can't be easy for you."

At first Filip says nothing, his eyes flitting between the police officers and his girlfriend.

"I can't get my head around it." He looks up at the ceiling, swallows hard. "I can't believe that Mom is . . . gone. The whole thing feels unreal. I keep waiting for a text message from her." He sighs deeply. "It's easier if I just imagine she's away . . . Maybe that sounds stupid. Sorry."

Hanna wants to tell him that he doesn't need to apologize, but Daniel has already started to explain where they are in the investigation, without going into the most upsetting details.

Filip doesn't let go of Emily's hand. They are sitting close together on the sofa, opposite Daniel and Hanna in wing-back armchairs.

"We need to ask you a few questions about your mom," Hanna says. "Tell us if it gets too difficult."

"Yes. Absolutely. Of course. I'll do anything if it helps you find . . . the murderer."

Filip nods resolutely, as if he is determined to be strong for his mother's sake. It is a way of finding meaning in total chaos. He is clearly struggling, and Hanna feels a new respect for him. After all, he is only twenty-three. Someone so young shouldn't have to lose a parent, especially not through a brutal murder.

"When did you last speak to her?"

Filip rubs one hand on his thigh as he thinks.

"A while ago—two weeks, maybe?"

"That sounds like a long time?"

"We mostly texted." He takes out his phone and clicks on the messaging app. "The last one arrived on Saturday." He shows them the screen so they can read it for themselves.

Shall I book tickets to Åre for you and Emily on Monday? And have you sent in your application for the fall semester? Love Mom

"What's that about?" Daniel asks.

"She thought I should get my act together and start studying again." Filip sounds embarrassed. "I dropped out of the Royal Institute of Technology in February, and Mom wanted me to go back. Or at least apply for a different course."

"What have you been doing since then?"

"Not much. Gaming, training. Hanging out with Emily and my friends." He looks apologetic and lowers his eyes. "You kind of flip the day around when you're playing, then it's hard to readjust."

"So why did you drop out?"

Filip looks up. "I had no motivation."

He says it as if it's obvious. Hanna can't help wondering if it's because of his age. She is only about twelve years older than him, yet it's as if they live in different worlds. She was brought up to grit her teeth and get on with things, even when she doesn't want to.

Gen Z has a different attitude.

"It was Mom who insisted I should study civil engineering," Filip goes on. "I applied to the institute to stop her nagging. Before that I did a semester of economics, but that was even worse. I didn't fit in. And she wasn't happy, because she'd wanted me to go to the Stockholm School of Economics, just like she and my grandfather did."

"What did your dad think?" Hanna asks.

Filip shrugs. "I've no idea. We haven't been in touch since Christmas."

"You haven't spoken to your father for three months?" Daniel is astonished.

Filip looks away, as if he is embarrassed. He quickly continues. "My dad doesn't live in Sweden anymore. It's over ten years since he moved to France with his new wife. They have a house in Antibes."

"This might sound strange," Hanna says, "but I have to ask if you know whether your mom had any . . . adversaries."

At the last moment she decides to avoid the word *enemies*. It sounds too dramatic, she doesn't want to scare Filip. Not when he is so devastated and has just lost the only parent who was present in his life.

"You mean people who hated her?"

His lips are trembling. His grief pierces Hanna's heart. Charlotte's son might have been born with a silver spoon in his mouth, but he doesn't seem to have had a particularly easy time.

"Mom could be . . . difficult to like," he says quietly. "It was way too important for her to achieve her goals, even if she upset people."

The word *upset* sounds strange in the context. Presumably it's more representative of how Filip felt in relation to his mother, rather than the perception of those around her.

"I understand," Hanna says. "Can you think of anyone who might have been so upset that they didn't want her to live?" Once again she chooses her words carefully. There is something about Filip that triggers her protective instincts.

"I've no idea. I didn't have anything to do with her business associates. The only one I know is Henry."

"You mean Henry Sylvester?"

"Yes—he's my godfather."

The news takes Hanna by surprise. She exchanges a glance with Daniel; they knew Charlotte and Henry were childhood friends, but not that they were close enough for him to be Filip's godfather.

Why hadn't he mentioned it yesterday?

Filip checks his phone, then notices Hanna's inquiring look.

"Henry is coming here to meet me and Emily in a little while," he explains. "We're going to have dinner together."

They ask a few more questions, but Filip doesn't have much more to give them. It is time to round things off.

"Will you be staying in Åre for the next few days?" Daniel wants to know.

"That's the plan." Filip looks at Emily, who seems to be his rock.

"Are you okay for money?" Hanna asks on an impulse. "This place doesn't exactly have the cheapest rooms in the area."

"We're fine."

Filip smiles faintly for the first time. He has a lovely smile, open and honest. He seems to be a decent young man.

"Mom had her faults, but she wasn't mean. The credit card she gave me still works, and Henry will help out if necessary. He was the one who fixed the room here, even though they were fully booked. He was worried that it would be too hard for me to stay in the hotel where . . . where my mom . . ."

He swallows. He doesn't need to say any more. Hanna understands perfectly.

"That was kind of him," she says to help out.

She wouldn't necessarily have associated that sort of consideration with the successful financier.

They are about to get to their feet when Filip makes eye contact.

"I was wondering if I could . . . see her?"

He looks up at the ceiling as if he is struggling to hold back the tears.

Hanna realizes that he doesn't know the body has been sent to Umeå, where it will remain. It could be several weeks, even months before it is released for burial.

For his sake it is best if he remembers his mother as she was.

"I'm so sorry, your mom isn't in Åre any longer."

"There has to be a forensic examination," Daniel explains. "That takes place in Umeå."

"Okay."

Filip's voice sounds small. Emily edges even closer. Hanna is more moved than she should be. She takes out her card and hands it to Charlotte's son.

"My number is on there. Call me anytime."

THEN

The hotel dining room is filled with a festive hum of conversation when Monica walks in at about seven o'clock in the evening, carrying a tray of cocktails for the round table with a view over the extensive mountain landscape.

The group consists of eight people, four children and two sets of parents. Children are usually served earlier, but because it is Christmas Eve, they are allowed to stay up and eat with the adults.

Monica sets out the tall V-shaped cocktail glasses. Dry martinis with green olives for the gentlemen; rusty nails mixed from Drambuie and whiskey for the ladies.

"At last!" exclaims the nearest woman with a coquettish smile as she reaches for her glass. "I'm dying of thirst!"

Her hair is up, and she is wearing a moss-green silk dress that looks ridiculously expensive. Her long, pointed nails are dark red, and the eternity ring on her left ring finger is sparkling.

"Chin-chin," she says, toasting her friends. "Here's to a wonderful vacation together!"

Her husband smiles contentedly and takes out a slim gold lighter, which he uses to light a Marlboro cigarette.

Monica stares at him in fascination. In his elegant smoking jacket, he looks just like the actor Sean Connery. He must be twenty years older than her, but Monica has never seen such an attractive man before.

As if he is aware of her silent admiration, he glances up and gives her a warm, almost flirtatious look.

"Are the other drinks for our friends?" he asks in a jocular tone of voice. "Or are they staying on the tray?"

Monica tugs at her dress in embarrassment and quickly serves the other couple. The children each get a bottle of Christmas soda.

"Are you new here?" the stylish gentleman asks when she has finished.

Monica blushes. "This is my first week," she mumbles. Her cheeks are burning; she can't look him in the eye.

He blows a perfect smoke ring. "How charming. Everybody here is like one big family."

27

No one on Facebook seems to be missing a long-haired gray-and-white cat.

Hanna is standing at her adjustable desk in the police station. She has checked all the groups in the area, and posted a message of her own saying where Morris is.

He has been with her for only a few days, but she already knows she would be happy for him to stay. The warm feelings have come as a surprise. She hadn't realized how lonely she was.

She moves the mouse. She has spent the last hour surfing the net, looking for more information about Charlotte Wretlind and her private life. It is now after two o'clock; she has a meeting with her colleagues in just over twenty minutes. Before that she wants to see if people have written anything about Storlien online.

She starts searching on Facebook, and immediately gets a hit.

The group is called Preserve Storlien. It has several hundred followers, and the banner shows an image of the hotel complex. The photo seems relatively recent—the buildings look dilapidated and very much the worse for wear.

Hanna scrolls down through the plethora of comments. It quickly becomes clear that the group is opposed to the plans for a new luxury hotel. They don't like the idea of international tourists, or that a well-used area of common land will be taken over in order to extend the complex. They are also concerned that some of the most popular ski slopes will be reserved for the exclusive use of hotel guests.

The project doesn't seem to have much support. The tone of the comments is bitter, and unexpectedly strong language is used. In several places Hanna reads that the environment is being "raped," and that the judgment of future generations will be harsh. The expenditure involved is mocked and derided. Many ask why the council doesn't put its foot down and stop the plans before it's too late.

"We don't want to become a new Åre!" someone insists.

One post refers to a newspaper article where a former minister for rural affairs, Stefan Forsberg, had only positive things to say. Apparently he is attached to the project as an adviser, which leads a number of people to complain about superannuated politicians who accept lucrative roles as lobbyists.

Prejudice and swear words abound, the use of language is anything but sophisticated. And the most explicit posts have attracted the highest number of likes.

The nasty comments make Hanna uneasy.

People have become so careless in the way they direct threats and hatred toward their fellow human beings online. It's as if they think the recipient doesn't really exist, as if it's all pretend, even though the words are frightening and hurtful.

Hanna reads a few more posts, then decides she has had enough. Presumably these idiots don't even realize that the majority of what they write would be punishable by law if anyone chose to take action.

She leaves the Storlien group and searches for an image of Stefan Forsberg instead. A photo of a man with short gray hair appears on the screen. He has a firm chin and is looking straight into the camera. It isn't hard to picture him in a political debate—or as a convincing and well-paid lobbyist.

He would definitely have connected through the TV screen when he was a minister.

As she carries on googling, the screen is filled with headlines about Forsberg's time as an active politician, and his new career as a lobbyist. He seems to work for a communication company called Excellence. According to its home page, the aim is to support businesses that want to "establish and maintain good relations with the community and decision-makers."

A glance at her watch tells Hanna she has five minutes before the meeting begins.

She opens a new window and goes into Flashback. The site is certainly one of Sweden's most visited, but it has no responsible publisher and therefore allows wild and sometimes unethical speculation.

She types in Charlotte Wretlind's name, and is confronted with a number of contributions, all critical of the dead woman. Then she tries Stefan Forsberg. Most of what is written concerns his political activities, but there is one thread claiming that he is a ladies' man who regularly cheats on his wife, a high-ranking judge.

Hanna thinks for a moment, then enters both names together. She immediately finds several comments claiming that Charlotte Wretlind and Stefan Forsberg were more than business associates.

They were allegedly in a relationship.

28

A few minutes later Hanna hurries along to the conference room. It is time for the special unit to meet again. She sits down with Daniel, Anton, and Raffe at two thirty, and they link up with Östersund.

Birgitta Grip begins by reporting on the press conference that took place earlier.

"Just so you know, the media is going crazy. The murder has also been picked up by the international press, and our communications department has its hands full."

Hanna shakes her head as she thinks about the journalists in the hotel foyer yesterday, crowding around Daniel on the stairs. She tries to catch his eye, but his attention is on Grip, who has moved on to the current situation. They discuss the conversation with Filip Wretlind and the interviews with hotel guests and employees. Unfortunately not much has emerged from this process; no one staying on the same floor saw or heard anything from the victim's suite on Sunday night. Their colleagues are now speaking to those staying on the floor below.

Hanna prepares to share what she found on Flashback.

She does a quick mental recap on the information they have gathered so far on Charlotte's private life. Since the divorce in 1999, she doesn't seem to have had any long-term relationships in the public eye, focusing instead on her job and her son. A secret boyfriend would explain why details of her love life are so sparse. If she was having an affair with a public figure who was married and therefore worried about their reputations, they would of course want to stay under the radar.

Maybe Henry Sylvester knows something about that.

Or Filip.

"I found a couple of pointers about Charlotte Wretlind's private life on Flashback," she begins, and runs through the posts on Stefan and Charlotte's relationship.

"Well done," Grip says. "We'll ask our colleagues in Stockholm to check out his alibi right away."

Then she turns to Raffe.

"Did you get anywhere with the Storlien project and its finances?"

"We've only just started, but we have found some interesting things about the deceased and her business partner, Henry Sylvester." He jerks his head toward Anton, who has also spent the day looking into the finances surrounding Storlien. After a brief pause, Raffe continues. "Charlotte Wretlind's company, SEG, has taken out substantial loans in order to build the new hotel in Storlien; the project is being run by a separate company. If anything went wrong, she stood to lose a great deal of money."

"So she must have been desperate to push it through," Daniel comments.

Anton nods. "Exactly. The fact that she was prepared to take such a huge personal financial risk says a great deal about her commitment."

"The question is, how far was she prepared to go in order to succeed?" Hanna wonders. "With such high stakes?"

"Are you thinking it might be a motive for murder?" Grip says.

"I am. It doesn't sound like you'd want to get in Charlotte's way."

Hanna looks at her boss on the screen. When Hanna first came to Åre, it took her a while to get used to the digital meetings, which were essential because the team is so far apart. After a year of working at home, it has become the norm all over the world.

Everyone is following the example of the Norrland police, she thinks with a faint smile.

"Have you had time to take a look at Henry Sylvester's company?" Daniel asks.

"We have, and that's interesting too," Raffe replies. "It's called Pecunium AB, and they've been investing in various commercial property projects throughout Scandinavia for a long time, but they've never put capital into a hotel before."

Hanna nods. This fits with what Henry told them yesterday. He admitted he'd never had anything to do with the hotel industry. What was it he'd said when they asked why he'd gone along with Charlotte's plans?

That it wasn't easy to say no to her.

Which still doesn't explain why he got involved with a high-risk project that contradicts his usual business strategy.

Hanna wonders if Charlotte had some kind of hold over him, something that meant he was more or less forced into the investment.

From the little she has read about him, she knows that Henry is a year or so younger than the victim, fifty-five, and single. He has three grown-up sons from a previous marriage. During the last decade he seems to have made a habit of going out with significantly younger women who all look the same. He is very rich, and has an apartment on Strandvägen in Stockholm, one of the capital's most desirable addresses.

The description of Henry is something of a cliché, but one thing stands out. He has publicly stated that after his death, the lion's share of his fortune will go to a foundation he has started in order to keep the Baltic Sea clean, and to combat the destruction of the environment.

A wealthy man with a conscience, in other words. Someone who wants to use his millions to make a difference.

To be honest, Hanna is finding it difficult to form a clear perception of Henry Sylvester. He seems to be a man with contradictory qualities. On the one hand he is a philanthropist, on the other a hardheaded businessman. He comes across as willing to cooperate, but it is impossible to penetrate beneath the surface.

He also seems to be a thoughtful godfather to Filip, although he failed to mention their relationship yesterday.

What else has he chosen to keep to himself?

"Anyway," Raffe continues, "Henry Sylvester's company owns thirty percent of the Storlien company, Charlotte twenty-five, and the rest is divided between various investors."

"How much money are we talking about?" Grip wants to know.

"In total we're looking at between three and five hundred million kronor."

A collective gasp sweeps through the meeting.

"Are you kidding?" Hanna says. "That's unbelievable—for a hotel in a place like Storlien."

Raffe looks pleased, as if he was looking forward to their reaction.

"There was a piece about the sale in the local paper," Anton says. "The owners had been trying to sell for quite a while, although at the time it sounded as if they were only asking twenty million."

Grip joins in. "I think it was sold for over three hundred million ten years ago."

"That's right," Raffe confirms. "But then the complex was bought back after three years because the buyer at the time hadn't secured the investments that had been agreed to in the contract."

"And then it was put on the market for a pathetic twenty million?" Hanna says.

"Correct. But the problem isn't the purchase price; it's all the rest that burns money. It's a huge construction project, and the demolition costs alone are astronomical," Anton explains.

"Demolition? Won't there be anything left?" Daniel asks.

Raffe holds up a photograph of the mountain hotel, showing five rectangular buildings in a snowy landscape. Hanna recognizes it from the Facebook page she visited earlier. The picture was taken in brilliant sunshine against a clear blue sky, but even though the image was obviously intended to show the hotel to its best advantage, it looks dated. There is a kind of tired 1960s vibe about the place.

"The current hotel consists of a main building and four attached annexes," Raffe explains. "I spoke to the site supervisor, who told me that most of it is very run down, with seventies or eighties standards. You can imagine—dirty carpets, peeling wallpaper, bathrooms that would need replacing, and so on. It would need a huge amount of renovation."

Hanna is impressed by the amount of information Raffe and Anton have come up with in such a short time.

"So the plan is to flatten the whole lot?" Daniel says.

Anton nods. "Seems that way. It would cost far more to renovate than to demolish, if I've understood correctly. And they have soaring ambitions. Charlotte had engaged an overseas architect who is known for his spectacular buildings."

"You should see the drawings in the planning application we got from the council," Raffe adds. "Enormous windows, dramatic lines. I've never seen anything like it. With that kind of vision, you'd have to start again from square one."

Anton reaches into his bag and gets out a bottle containing something green. He is a fitness fanatic, and often brings in protein drinks and homemade smoothies. The smell of raw spinach and broccoli spreads through the room when he unscrews the cap.

"I don't understand how they got permission," Daniel says.

"They seem to have had good contacts on the council," Anton replies, taking a swig. "Apparently Bengt Hedin, the chair of the planning committee, gave the project his personal backing."

Hanna remembers that Hedin was supposed to have been participating in Monday's press conference—she'd read about it earlier.

"I was thinking of checking him out," Anton adds, putting down the bottle. "I'll go over to Järpen first thing tomorrow and have a chat with him."

Time to change the subject. Grip flicks through her papers and looks up.

"How about the CCTV cameras at the hotel? Any luck there?"

A younger colleague in Östersund shakes his head. "I'm afraid not. It turns out they have hardly any cameras. The few they do have aren't working. They wanted to put up cameras by the staff exit a couple of years ago, but they weren't allowed for reasons of integrity."

Hanna groans silently. She understands that there are arguments in favor of regulation, but in this case a single functioning camera would have been a big help. She holds up her hand to indicate that she has something to say, and tells the team about the Facebook group she found.

"We need to look into that," Grip says. "I'll ask IT to track down the administrator, see what they can find out."

It is almost four o'clock and Hanna is getting hungry. She wishes she'd brought a snack, like Anton. The hot dog she had for lunch didn't really cut it.

"Anything else before we finish?" Grip asks.

"We've checked Espen Lund's alibi for Sunday," says one of the investigators in Östersund. "There are witnesses who can confirm that he was at home in Undersåker from 5:00 p.m. that day. His brother-in-law and sister-in-law were visiting, and it was a late night—they didn't leave until after midnight."

At least we can eliminate him from our inquiries, Hanna thinks. Which is something at least.

Grip looks around.

"So to summarize: We have a hugely expensive hotel project, the profitability of which is dubious. We have the murder of the individual who was most passionate about the project, a reluctant fellow investor, and possibly a secret lover. And there may be questions regarding the planning permission." She pauses. "Have I missed anything?"

No one has any suggestions.

The meeting comes to an end, and Hanna stays where she is as Anton and Raffe leave the room. She is still brooding over Henry Sylvester's involvement in Storlien.

Daniel has stood up, but notices that she hasn't moved. "What is it?"

She weighs her pen in her hand while she works out what to say.

"I just don't understand why Henry agreed to invest. The amount of money is staggering. If he owned thirty percent of the company, we're talking about huge sums, even if the majority should have been financed through loans."

Daniel leans on the table while Hanna continues her train of thought.

"A commitment of three to five hundred million is a hell of a lot, even for a businessman on his level."

Daniel seems to understand.

"So why don't we go back to the hotel and have another chat with Henry Sylvester?" he suggests.

29

When Hanna and Daniel walk into the foyer at Copperhill, a woman in her early thirties is at reception. Daniel goes over to ask about Henry, and Hanna notices that she asks to see his police ID before she answers.

Sharp lady.

It seems that the receptionist needs permission from her boss before she can give out the information, which will take a few minutes. Hanna sits down on one of the sofas by the fireplace.

While she is waiting she can't help glancing up at the sixth floor, where Charlotte's body was found. From here it's impossible to see anything except the colossal copper wall reflecting the sun. Even from this angle, diagonally below, the corridor leading to the Silver Suite is well hidden.

A hotel employee would have known that.

A man wearing a shirt with the hotel logo approaches Hanna, looking hesitant. According to his badge his name is Erik, and he works in the concierge department.

"Excuse me, but aren't you one of the detectives?"

Hanna sits up a little straighter. "I am."

The man looks around, as if he's afraid that someone will hear what he is saying.

"I probably shouldn't tell you this, but . . ." Again he scans the area. "Something happened on Sunday that you ought to know about."

Hanna stands up so they are face-to-face. His forehead is shiny with sweat.

What's this about?

"I'm listening," she says encouragingly.

Erik swallows, composes himself. "One of my colleagues who works at reception . . . There was a huge row between him and the woman who was murdered in the Silver Suite."

Hanna is immediately on full alert. Nobody has mentioned a quarrel between Charlotte and an employee—she would definitely have remembered if they had.

"Who was it? Do you know his name?"

Erik is clearly uncomfortable, as if he is torn between a desire to help the police and loyalty to a coworker. "Paul Lehto. He's worked here for a long time." Sounding hopeful, he adds, "But maybe you already know about this?"

Hanna shakes her head as she searches her memory. Paul Lehto? She's read the transcripts of the interviews that have been conducted so far, and he didn't feature.

"So what happened? Can you tell me more?"

Erik shifts from foot to foot, he seems reluctant to continue. "Well . . . it was really busy in the foyer on Sunday, lots of guests had been delayed because of the blizzard, and check-in was pretty chaotic. The woman who was killed tried to push in front of people, and there was an argument. I don't remember exactly what it was all about, but it was really unpleasant. She and Paul stood there yelling at each other in front of the other guests. You can ask Iris—she was on duty that evening."

He lets out a long breath; he seems relieved. He's done his duty and he doesn't need to say any more.

From the corner of her eye, Hanna sees Daniel approaching. Erik notices too, and steps back.

"I have to go. Please don't tell anyone it was me who spoke to you. I don't want problems. At least now you know the situation."

Before Hanna has the chance to ask him to stay, he disappears through a side door that closes behind him.

Daniel joins her. "We need to go over to the Villa—that's where Henry Sylvester is staying."

Hanna is still staring at the door through which Erik vanished. "Did you see that guy I was talking to? His name is Erik, and he claims that Charlotte had a huge row with one of the receptionists on Sunday—a Paul Lehto."

Daniel raises his eyebrows. "First I've heard of it. Who is he?"

"I don't think Erik was making it up. The way he spoke, very quietly so that only the two of us could hear, suggests the opposite. It sounded as if he found it quite difficult to pass on the information."

Daniel takes out his phone. "Worth following up. I'll text Anton, ask him to check out this Paul Lehto right away." He quickly types a message. "Lucky you were on your own, so he felt able to come over and speak to you."

Hanna glances at him. Was that a compliment?

"So what are we doing now?" She didn't understand what Daniel had said about Henry.

"Going to the Villa where Henry Sylvester is staying."

"What's that?"

"A separate building for VIP guests. We have to go outside—it's a few hundred yards down the hill."

On the way they pass a life-size illuminated reindeer woven from twigs, guarding the entrance. A family is busy loading luggage into their car in the nearest parking lot. They seem to have just checked out, and Hanna picks up fragments of their conversation.

The parents are talking about the murder; she can hear the anxiety in the mother's voice.

Daniel and Hanna hurry past a long row of cars in the guest parking lot alongside the building. Suddenly Daniel slips on the ice; Hanna's arm shoots out to catch him before he falls.

"Thanks," he says with a warm smile.

They are up at the top of Förberget. The afternoon sun is bathing the Åre valley in a golden light, and the mountainsides are shimmering in warm tones.

The air is almost mild, even though it's only the end of March.

Hanna could stand here with Daniel forever.

"Let's go," he says.

As they make their way down the hill, they see a huge gray-painted wooden building on the left.

This is where Henry is staying.

They have reached the Villa.

30

The VIP accommodation has an unimpeded view across the valley. Daniel has heard about the place, but until now he hadn't realized the scale of the magnificent building hidden behind exclusive slate walls.

"Wow," Hanna says, rolling her eyes. "This makes Lydia's house look like a dog kennel."

Daniel visited Hanna several times when she was living in her sister's home in Sadeln. Lydia's place outshines many houses in the area, but it can't hold a candle to the Villa.

They walk up the stone steps and knock on the front door. There is some kind of Japanese flower arrangement outside, a collection of tall white birch twigs in a slim gray vase.

Daniel isn't easily impressed, but he can't help being taken aback when they walk in.

The entire ground floor is open plan, dominated by a nine-foot-high slate fireplace. Modern chandeliers are suspended above a generous dark-brown sofa and armchairs, and farther in there is a dining area with space for a dozen people.

"How can I help you?" Henry asks when they have said hello and taken off their coats.

Yesterday's dark suit has been replaced by faded jeans and a pale cashmere polo shirt. He seems to have been working, because a laptop is open on the exclusive dining table, with piles of papers spread out beside it. Daniel sees the logo of something called Save the Baltic, that must be the foundation Hanna mentioned.

"We have a few more questions," he explains.

Henry points to the wine refrigerator to one side of the kitchen, which has an industrial look; almost everything is made of glass and stainless steel. It is clearly equipped for a significant number of guests, with double ovens and dishwashers.

"Can I get you anything? There's an excellent espresso machine, or how about a glass of wine? A Bordeaux, perhaps?"

"Thanks, but we're on duty."

It is an unnecessary comment; both Henry and Daniel are well aware of that fact. Daniel interprets the offer of a glass of wine as a demonstration of power, but he tries to suppress his irritation. He can't allow the conversation to be derailed by his own prejudices.

"Shall we sit down?" Henry suggests, leading the way.

Daniel chooses the nearest sofa, at an angle from Henry. Hanna sits down beside him.

"Can you tell us more about your friend Charlotte?" she begins. "What kind of person was she?"

The financier looks around the room before he answers, his gaze settling on the panorama window with its stunning view of Åre's snow-covered mountains in the northwest.

"To be honest, I'm not sure how well I knew her," he replies. "Sometimes I don't think anyone did."

"I believe you're godfather to her son?" Hanna points out.

Henry's face softens. "I'm very fond of Filip."

"Why didn't you tell us he's your godson?"

"You didn't ask."

The evasive response bothers Daniel. They don't have time for Henry Sylvester's Stockholm ways.

"You and Charlotte had known each other for over fifty years," he says. "Plus you're Filip's godfather. Surely that means you must have had a close relationship."

"Certainly, but at the same time, Charlotte was a complex person who kept her cards close to her chest. I don't think many people really got close to her. She had high standards, and found it difficult to trust those around her."

"How come?" Hanna asks.

Henry crosses his legs. The open fire is crackling away, with logs piled up decoratively on either side of the hearth.

"I guess it was a survival strategy. Women of her generation who've gotten involved in the venture capital industry have had an incredibly tough time. This was long before the #MeToo debate, the jargon was brutal and ruthless. To be honest, it was sometimes flat-out misogynistic. The competition was fierce; it can't have been easy to stand your ground. Charlotte had to fight hard to be respected. The only way to do it was to become the same as her male colleagues—or even worse."

"It doesn't sound like a particularly pleasant working environment," Hanna remarks.

"It wasn't. Ask anyone who's fought their way up in those companies. On the other hand, when you do make it to the top, the world is your oyster, so to speak. As a partner in the big venture capital companies, you earn a vast amount of money—much, much more than most people could ever dream of. But like I said, it's a matter of surviving until you reach that level. Many fall by the wayside."

"So Charlotte learned to stick at nothing in order to get what she wanted? Is that what you're saying?" Daniel asks.

"That's one way of looking at it."

"And how about you?" Hanna says. "Have you become like that too?"

"Touché." Henry winks. "I'm not saying I've been an angel when it comes to my business dealings, but I hope I've gotten better with age. And maybe I've managed to atone for past sins to a certain extent by giving away what I don't need."

Daniel gives him a searching look, but Henry seems genuine. There is nothing to suggest that he is having fun at their expense.

Hanna takes a different tack. "What can you tell us about Charlotte's relationship with Stefan Forsberg?"

"They've known each other for a long time. Stefan was an adviser on the Storlien project—he has a lot of useful contacts in the political world."

There is nothing wrong with Henry's answer, but Daniel can see that Hanna is not satisfied.

"Did they have a more intimate relationship? An affair?"

"You're very direct," Henry says.

"Was he her lover?"

"I couldn't possibly say."

He gets up and goes over to the kitchen area. "Are you sure you wouldn't like a coffee, or something else?"

Daniel shakes his head. In fact he would love a decent cup of coffee now he has the chance, but there is something about Henry's attitude that irritates him. He seems so convinced that he is part of the elite, a more elevated circle. The fact that he doesn't sound remotely humble gets under Daniel's skin.

Henry presses a button, and the espresso machine gurgles. Then he returns to the sofa with a small silvery cup, and takes a sip before putting it down on the table.

Judging by the aroma, the beans are high quality. Daniel knows his coffee; the Italian tastebuds are part of his DNA.

"Do you really have no idea about Charlotte's personal relationship with Forsberg?" Hanna persists.

"I would prefer not to speculate on the matter."

They're not going to get any further. Daniel signals to Hanna to drop the subject, and she leans back on the sofa.

Daniel moves on.

"We'd like to hear more about your involvement in the company behind the Storlien project. When we spoke before, it sounded as if you were a pretty reluctant investor, and we're not exactly talking about small sums of money. Why did you really agree to be a partner?"

"As I said, it wasn't easy to say no to Charlotte."

"I find it difficult to believe that an experienced businessman like you would invest millions just because you can't say no to a woman," Hanna says. Her tone is challenging, and there is a flash of irritation in Henry's eyes—but it disappears instantly.

"Sometimes we do things for . . . old times' sake."

"Oh, please—I don't believe that. Did she have some kind of hold over you?"

Daniel studies Henry's reaction. Hanna doesn't pull her punches; she has a particular ability to find the weak point in the person she is questioning. She knows when to play nice, and when it's worth taking a tougher approach.

However, this question is borderline. Even if Charlotte did have something over her business partner, or was exercising some kind of blackmail, there is no reason for him to admit it now. Not when Charlotte is dead.

Henry looks somewhat taken aback. "Now you're just guessing," he says eventually.

"Look at it this way," Hanna explains. "If you cooperate with the police, we can eliminate you from our inquiry. If we understand why you were on board, why you invested so much money, and that there was no element of blackmail involved, then we can dismiss the theory that you had a motive for getting rid of your partner."

"You don't pussyfoot around, do you?" Henry gives Hanna a look that is hard to interpret, and takes another sip of his espresso. His voice hardens as he continues. "If any of my employees spoke to me like that in the office, they would be out on their ear—just so you know."

"But we're not in your office."

Hanna refuses to give way, which makes Daniel a little tense. She knows from past experience that her persistence can have consequences. It has often been very useful in her work as a police officer, but sometimes it has led to catastrophic results.

Once, she almost died.

It doesn't seem to matter. Hanna is like a terrier that sinks its teeth in and refuses to let go. Maybe there is something about her personality that appeals to Henry, because his expression softens, almost as if he recognizes himself in her.

Or as if he is charmed by her.

Daniel suddenly sees his colleague from Henry's perspective. Her expressive brown eyes capture the attention. That curious gaze, which can switch between empathy and intellectual analysis in a second, is hard to resist. She has the ability to captivate those around her, and her laugh is infectious when she allows it to come out.

At the beginning of their working relationship, she rarely laughed, but over the past year, she has settled into the job. When she secured a permanent post and a place to live, it was as if her sense of security came back.

Henry puts down his cup, and the sound makes Daniel realize how long he has been lost in thought. However, Henry is fully focused on Hanna. Daniel might as well be on another planet.

"Speaking purely hypothetically," Henry says, stroking his chin, "if we accept that Charlotte was in fact blackmailing me in order to make me go along with the project, what would the basis for that blackmail be? Do you have a theory?"

Hanna meets his gaze with a smile. In another context Daniel would have called it inviting. He doesn't like it, but Hanna can use whatever tactics she wants. It's none of his business as long as she gets the information that will help them move forward.

"I can think of plenty of possibilities," she replies.

"Name one."

"Tax evasion?"

Henry laughs. "No chance—I pay far too many conscientious accountants and lawyers to go down for tax-related offenses."

"How about intimate relationships? For money, maybe?"

"At my age? Don't insult me. Do I look as if I need to pay for company?"

He sounds more amused than annoyed—in fact he almost seems to be enjoying the cut and thrust. Daniel gets the feeling that something is playing out right in front of him, something he doesn't really understand, as if he is watching a color movie being shown in black and white.

The action is clear, but the nuances are lost.

It's frustrating; why can't Henry Sylvester just get to the point? If he has important information to contribute, he needs to talk.

"What about mutual favors?" Hanna continues. "Did Charlotte have something you wanted, and vice versa?"

"I'm afraid not." Henry smiles; his teeth are white and even. He leans back on the sofa, and now it's his turn to give Hanna a challenging look, as if he wants to test her.

This irritates Daniel even more. Time is passing; they can't sit here all evening playing stupid games.

Hanna also seems to have had enough. Daniel suspects that she is about to change tactics again.

"Then let me ask you this," she says firmly. "Do you know of any aspect of your joint hotel project that could have led to personal danger for Charlotte? That could be linked to her death?"

Henry stops smiling.

The atmosphere in the room changes.

"This is a murder investigation," Daniel adds to emphasize the gravity of the situation. "We need all the information we can get, and I hope you realize that."

"I realize perfectly well that this is not a game." Henry's tone is ice cold. "One of my oldest friends has been murdered, and I'm trying to take care of her son. This will also have serious consequences for our mutual business project. Who do you take me for?" He gets to his feet, clearly moved. "I have to get back to work. Thank you for coming."

Hanna seems confused by the abrupt dismissal. She turns to Daniel as if to say, *What happened?*

"If you know something, you must cooperate with us," Daniel stresses.

Henry is already heading for the door to see them out.

"I'm sorry," he says over his shoulder. "I have an important Teams meeting shortly."

"We can't force him to carry on," Hanna whispers so that only Daniel can hear.

"I know." Reluctantly he stands up. "But right now I wish we could." He gives Henry Sylvester a long look before they leave. He can't shake the feeling that Henry is hiding something from the police.

31

Time to go home, Hanna thinks, yawning. It is past eight o'clock, she is the only one left in the station, and Morris must be wondering where she is.

She has spent the last hour reading incoming emails and typing up the interview with Henry Sylvester. She'd thought she was getting somewhere with him, and hadn't expected him to bring the conversation to such an abrupt end when she felt they were establishing a kind of understanding.

She can't get her head around the guy, and it was very clear that Daniel doesn't like him at all.

After checking her notes one last time, she shuts down the computer and fetches her jacket. When her phone rings she answers automatically, without looking to see who it is.

"Hanna Ahlander."

"Hi, it's Filip."

She stands there holding her jacket. Charlotte's son sounds very down, and just as heartrendingly young as when they met him earlier. Why is he calling her so late? Has something else happened? Shouldn't he contact his godfather if he needs to talk?

"Hi—how are you?"

"Not great."

Hanna really does feel sorry for him. He needs to see a psychologist as soon as possible in order to help him process his mother's death. A murdered relative causes severe trauma. She wishes there were something she could do to make him feel better, but that's not her job.

"Have you spoken to your father?" she says tentatively.

"No."

His tone is weary and dismissive. Hanna makes a mental note to double-check that the Stockholm police have been in touch with Mats Rutberg so that at least he's aware of Charlotte's death.

Surely he ought to be there for his son in some way.

Filip remains silent.

"Was there something in particular?" Hanna says. "Can I help you?"

"There's . . . I wanted to ask a question."

"Ask away."

"A journalist called me a few minutes ago—from one of the tabloids. She wants to interview me. About Mom."

Hanna looks up at the ceiling. That sounds like a seriously bad idea. Filip has just lost his mother, and now the papers want to expose his misery to the whole population of Sweden.

"I don't know what to do," Filip continues. "The reporter said it would be great if I got to describe Mom in my own words—it would help me to say goodbye."

Hanna wants to tell him that there is only one reason why the press is chasing him—to sell hard copies of their papers and boost the number of clicks online.

But pointing that out feels too brutal.

"So how do you feel about that?" she says, adopting a more diplomatic approach. "Are you comfortable with the idea of talking publicly about your mom?"

"I think so, but what if I say something stupid? I want to . . . honor her memory."

"It's lovely that you're thinking along those lines."

Silence again.

"I know Mom loved me," Filip says eventually, his voice thick with tears. "She just wasn't very good at . . . showing it."

"How do you mean?"

"We argued about my future all the time. She wanted me to study, like she'd done. To pursue a career in finance or something equally prestigious, where I could earn a lot of money and have a fancy title."

Filip's description of his relationship with his mother sounds all too familiar—an echo of Hanna's own frustrating discussions with her parents. They have always stressed the importance of getting a "good" job, as a lawyer or a doctor. They have never fully accepted her decision to join the police.

But at least she has Lydia, who always supported her.

Filip seems so alone.

"And what do you want?" Hanna asks. "What do you dream of?"

"Certainly not being like Mom."

The answer is so raw and honest that Hanna gets a lump in her throat. She sits back down and moves her phone to the other hand.

"I don't want to seem ungrateful. Mom made a career for herself and earned a lot of money, but she was never around when I was growing up. I was looked after by a string of childminders, and by the time Mom came home, she was tired and wanted to be left in peace. I played basketball, and I don't think she saw more than two or three matches during all those years at high school."

Filip takes a deep breath. His voice is steadier when he goes on.

"If Emily and I ever have kids, I want to be at home with them. Have a job where I finish at five o'clock so we can all have dinner together. It might sound terrible, but I don't want to be like Mom, even if she was hugely successful."

"And you argued about that?"

"Mm."

Filip sounds eager now, as if he is desperate to explain why things were so difficult between him and his mother.

"The thing is, it was so important for her to follow in her father's footsteps. She talked about him all the time. Even after he died she was still determined to prove herself in his eyes, and as far as she was concerned, it was obvious that I would do the same. Third generation and all that, if you know what I mean." He gives a humorless laugh. "It all went wrong, of course."

Hanna pictures her own mother. That constantly reproachful expression. All the reprimands over the years. The feeling of never really being able to live up to her parents' expectations.

"Everyone has to make their own choices," she says. "Your parents don't get to determine what you do. It's your life, not theirs."

In a way it feels as if she's talking to herself as much as to Filip. You can't shape your life according to what other people want. That won't make anyone happy.

She hears a young woman's voice in the background. It sounds like Emily—she says they have to go because they've booked a table.

"So what do you think I should tell the journalist?" Filip wonders.

Hanna hesitates; she would really like to advise him not to do it. The reporter is probably after a sob story. If Filip does the interview then regrets it, he will feel even worse.

Then again, he's an adult. He has to make up his own mind.

"Maybe you should wait a little while until you've processed what's happened?" she says with some trepidation. "It can't be that urgent. But it's your decision, of course."

32

The temperature is unexpectedly mild when Tiina takes Zelda out for an afternoon walk. The dog skips along happily as they head for the forest trail that is their usual route.

The thought that the girls don't want to come home for Easter brings tears to Tiina's eyes. She has just spoken to Andrea, and her daughter's words are still ringing in her ears.

We just can't handle it anymore.

They won't come as long as Ogge is there. They can't cope with his drinking and mood swings. Tiina is only fooling herself when she hopes it will pass. That the relationship between her husband and the girls will one day be warm and loving.

He hasn't had an easy life, she reminds herself—as so many times before. Ogge didn't grow up in a calm, safe home like her daughters did. His father was never in the picture, and they have no contact. In fact Ogge has never met him—not once.

In the foster home where he spent his teenage years, he was treated in ways that would be regarded as child abuse these days.

Tiina takes the narrow path that winds through the trees. The snow sinks beneath her feet. At the beginning of March, the higher temperatures consumed the snow cover, but over the last couple of weeks, it has both snowed and frozen hard again.

And today it is thawing.

She really misses her girls. Maybe she could compromise, catch the train to go and see them on Easter Sunday? What would happen if she told Ogge she wanted to spend a few days with them?

Tiina isn't sure why she's so nervous about bringing it up, but the fear kicks in as soon as they have different views on anything. It makes her feel anxious and insecure.

Last night he didn't even need to raise his voice for her stomach to flip.

She buries her chin in her scarf and plods along to catch up with Zelda, who is busy investigating interesting smells.

Tiina has never been able to put into words what it is that frightens her so much when Ogge gets mad. Why the fear races through her belly like a stream of cold water when he becomes argumentative and gets that expression in his eyes.

He has never hit her. Ogge has never been violent, never so much as raised a hand to her or the girls. He is kind to children, and loves his dog more than anything in the world.

And yet it only takes a look for Tiina to fall silent.

Sometimes she wonders if that's what used to happen in his terrible foster home. If that was where he learned to shut up after a single glance, because he knew that otherwise he would be punished with a hard leather belt against his skin.

Is he repeating the same pattern as an adult, but without the physical violence?

Tiina can't really explain how they've ended up here, but as soon as Ogge becomes the least bit quarrelsome, she is petrified. The aggression is just below the surface; it feels as if he could explode at any moment, and when he drinks it's even worse. Then it's like living with a human pressure cooker, with the feeling that disaster is lurking only seconds away. It's as if the dreadful events of his childhood are just waiting to be let out.

Now, after fifteen years together, she wishes she had behaved differently when they first got together. She should have given him an ultimatum, insisted that he had counseling to deal with his mood swings. Not allowed him to self-medicate with booze.

Back then she was in love and naive; she believed that her love could heal him. Instead things have gotten worse, he has become more introverted and brooding.

Bitter.

Zelda comes running with a stick in her mouth. Ogge would do anything for that dog. Sometimes, when the situation is particularly bad, Tiina wonders if her husband prefers Zelda to her.

She pats the dog's head and praises her, then Zelda scampers away again.

Tiina wishes she were stronger. She has tried to set boundaries before, but it doesn't work. The words refuse to come out; they stick in her throat.

The fear that Ogge will lose control always holds her back.

33

The open fire is blazing away hypnotically before Hanna's eyes. The orange-and-yellow flames dance as she lies on her newly purchased gray sofa, relaxing with her phone in her hand.

She curls up on her side. It is nine thirty in the evening, and it has been a long day. She still feels down after the conversation with Filip, and the images of Charlotte's mutilated body won't leave her. She is just about to check out the evening papers' websites to see what they're saying about the murder when Morris starts meowing loudly from the floor. A second later he lands on Hanna.

"Ouf," she groans as the cat settles down on top of her ribs. The only things Morris seems to want to do in life are eat and cuddle. He is a big cat with an even bigger personality, and he has clearly decided that Hanna is his person.

Her view on this seems largely irrelevant. She has to deploy a limited amount of force in order to move him so that she can actually breathe.

"Seriously, Morris," she murmurs, shifting slightly so that she can see her phone screen.

Morris doesn't care; he just purrs even more loudly. After a few days together, there are gray and white cat hairs all over the house—and Hanna's clothes. Then again, Morris is probably the only live-in partner she will ever have. Her relationship with Christian ended in disaster, and as long as she feels the way she does about Daniel, she's not likely to meet anyone else.

Her phone rings, and Hanna tries to sit up to answer. Morris gives her a reproachful look.

The display says, "Mom." Even though she knows better, at first Hanna thinks that maybe Ulla is calling because she senses that her daughter is feeling lonely and low—but her mother has never provided that kind of emotional security.

Reluctantly Hanna accepts the call.

"Hi," says a cheerful voice. "You haven't been in touch for a long time."

It has been three weeks since they spoke, and if it were up to Hanna, it would be a lot longer.

The constant criticism, the insistence that she needs to find a new boyfriend, the reminder that it will soon be too late to have children of her own—all this makes her want to avoid conversations with her parents. They live in the Costa del Sol in Spain, enjoying a carefree life as retirees.

"Sorry," she mumbles, immediately on the defensive. "Work has been kind of busy."

"Lydia said you went out for dinner together the day before yesterday."

The subtext is clear—*So you have time to hang out with your sister.*

Hanna is very well acquainted with Ulla's ability to allocate blame; she almost admires her mother's skill in unfailingly making her feel guilty.

"Are you and Dad okay?" she says, changing the subject. "How are the lemons?"

It works. Ulla embarks on a colorful account of the lemon trees in big pots on the terrace. Hanna tunes out. They have never had an easy relationship. Hanna has always been the difficult child who has failed in her mother's eyes.

Maybe that's why she can't stop thinking about Filip? It struck a chord when he talked about Charlotte—the experience of having a parent who is constantly disappointed in you. Hanna knows exactly how it feels when you can't live up to their expectations. The fact that Filip and his mother had clearly argued a great deal before her death must be very hard for him right now.

Suddenly Morris stands up, waving his fluffy tail in her face. She starts to sneeze.

"What are you doing?" her mother demands.

"Sorry, it's just the cat."

"Cat? Have you bought a cat?"

"Not exactly."

Hanna tries to explain that it was Morris who adopted her rather than the reverse.

"Oh, Hanna, it's no good getting a cat instead of building a family of your own. I don't understand you at all."

The misinterpretation is absolutely typical. Hanna has neither the patience nor the energy to continue the conversation. However, she does manage to end the call without starting a quarrel.

She pushes Morris away so she can breathe again.

"I was here first," she informs him. He couldn't care less.

She feels better when he rubs his nose against her cheek, as if he understands that she needs consolation.

WEDNESDAY, MARCH 31

34

It has been only two days since the murder of Charlotte Wretlind, but Daniel is already exhausted. The first forty-eight hours are the most important. The time has been filled with short and long interviews, background checks, and the mapping of various people linked to the victim.

An intense search for the murder weapon is ongoing.

It's always like this at the beginning of a homicide investigation, and he is starting to feel it. The first wave of adrenaline is ebbing away; the lack of sleep is taking its toll. It is hard for the body to be in a constant state of readiness, and to try to keep a thousand things in his mind at once.

Always with the nagging feeling that they should be doing more, should be in several places at the same time.

Daniel would really prefer to move into the station in order to get everything done, but that's out of the question when he has Ida and Alice to consider. Yesterday he didn't get home until nine, and Ida's cool greeting made it very clear that she wasn't happy.

It is now seven thirty in the morning, and they have gathered in the conference room again. Today the prosecutor will also be participating in the digital briefing, as will the forensic pathologist in Umeå, who against all the odds has managed to conduct the autopsy in record time.

An hour later the pathologist, a clean-shaven young locum, has gone through the results. He has confirmed that the primary cause of death was the violent blow that severed Charlotte Wretlind's windpipe. If that hadn't killed her, then the many stab wounds to the rest of her body definitely would have ended her life. There was no possibility of the victim surviving her injuries, and the perpetrator must have had a clear intention to murder her.

Such extreme violence cannot be explained away.

Finally the pathologist described the other injuries in detail, and showed a number of photographs that made everyone in the room politely decline the buns that Raffe has brought along.

The time of death was probably sometime after midnight on Sunday.

The pathologist leaves the meeting. The National Forensic Center is very busy, and the fact that the autopsy was carried out so quickly is nothing short of a miracle.

Birgitta Grip must have put them under a great deal of pressure to prioritize this case.

Daniel glances at the clock. As soon as they're done here, he wants to go to Copperhill and track down Paul Lehto. The information about the argument between him and Charlotte could be critical.

Yesterday evening after speaking to Henry Sylvester, they had asked about Lehto in reception, but had been told that he was off sick. They have to get a hold of him today, however ill he is.

"We found out something very interesting," Hanna says, as if she knows exactly what Daniel is thinking. She tells the group about the quarrel.

"We need to follow up on that," Grip says. "Someone from reception could definitely have accessed the suite."

"Do we know any more about how the attacker got in?" Daniel asks. "The door wasn't damaged, and we don't know whether Charlotte let him in."

He's given this a great deal of thought, and they have discussed it more than once.

"We've checked everyone who went in and out," Anton says. "The information came from the hotel. They log every card that is issued, which means they can see who was there. According to their data, no one apart from Charlotte and members of the housekeeping team were in the suite before the murder."

Carina looks up from her papers. Today she is in Östersund. She looks tired. She is usually positive and energetic, but right now her expression is strained. Presumably she was as adversely affected by the pathologist's photos as everyone else in the meeting.

"We found fingerprints on the card reader on the wall," she says. "Where you insert the key card. Prints that don't belong to the victim."

Daniel tries to picture the suite.

When you open the door, the card reader is on the left, about three feet up from the floor. A key card is required to make the lights work. This is standard in most hotels, with the aim of protecting the environment and not wasting electricity.

"Can you expand on that, Carina?"

"There were fingerprints from someone other than the cleaners who, according to the information we were given, had been inside the Silver Suite," she clarifies. "This could of course be because the cleaners didn't wipe down the surface after previous guests . . ."

"Or because the perpetrator touched it," Hanna interrupts.

"Exactly."

"Maybe he stole the card earlier?" Hanna seems to be thinking out loud. "If there was already a card in the holder, and he managed to grab it when Charlotte wasn't there . . ."

Daniel understands where she's going. "We'll check it out with the hotel."

There's a whole series of questions he wants answers to when they return to Copperhill. Apart from the key card, he also wants to investigate possible escape routes, how the killer got away from the scene of the crime without being noticed.

He shuffles uncomfortably on his chair.

The meeting has been going on for an hour and a half. He has things to do; he needs to get on. Anton also seems restless; he is sitting with his arms folded, jiggling his knee up and down. He has already said that he intends to go to the council offices in Järpen to speak to Bengt Hedin as soon as they're done.

"One last thing," Raffe says. "We've heard from a guest who was staying in the suite on the fifth floor, directly below Charlotte. He has a small child, and happened to be awake late. He says he heard a thud from the room above at around midnight, maybe also a faint scream, but he couldn't swear to that. He thought the guest must have dropped something heavy on the floor. Then there was silence, and he fell asleep soon after."

Grip nods. "That fits in with the pathologist's estimated time of death."

Midnight. Daniel suppresses a shudder. So the attack happened when the victim was presumably already sleeping.

She went to bed in the belief that she was safe.

Then along came the intruder.

35

There are significantly fewer cars in the parking lot today when Hanna pulls up by the entrance.

Hardly surprising, she thinks. No doubt there have been plenty of cancelations in the wake of the murder. People in the area are afraid, and the murder in Åre has made the national news.

She pushes aside the thought, she doesn't want to lose focus. As a police officer it is easy to feel the pressure to solve the crime right away. That's their responsibility. But one thing at a time—they can't simply conjure up a perpetrator.

Only a few guests are sitting on the chocolate-brown velvet sofas in the foyer when Hanna and Daniel walk in. Espen Lund is waiting at reception. He is talking to a female member of staff, but breaks off as soon as he sees them.

Hanna takes the lead. "We have a few questions about your key cards. We need to double-check a couple of things, and we also need to speak to one of your receptionists."

Espen looks around anxiously. He pushes back his hair from his forehead, and says quietly, "Maybe we could go somewhere more private? I'd appreciate it if you could be discreet."

He beckons a tall man who is busy piling suitcases onto a luggage trolley. Hanna recognizes him—he's the guy who told her about Paul Lehto yesterday. She tries to catch his eye, but he won't look at her. Presumably he is uneasy at having revealed sensitive information about a colleague. She assumes he doesn't want to risk being questioned again in front of his boss.

She can respect that.

"Erik, do you know if anyone is using conference room C4?" Espen asks.

"No, it's supposed to be empty all morning."

"Thanks—that's where I'll be if anyone needs me."

The manager leads the way up a wide staircase and into an airy room on the western side of the building. There is a podium at the front, with rows of chairs set out.

"This is where Charlotte was supposed to be holding her press conference on Monday," he explains.

Hanna understands why she chose this particular room. The view from the windows captures the Jämtland mountains perfectly. It's like a painting in different nuances of white, a composition of snow, ice, and frozen moments.

The early spring sunshine is so bright that it creates a sparkling halo around the Åre valley. The view seems to go on forever.

"Isn't it odd that Charlotte wanted to meet the press in your hotel?" Hanna asks, leaning against the wall with her arms folded. "Isn't that"— she pauses briefly—"fraternizing with the enemy?"

She tried to ask Espen about this when they first met, but he avoided answering. Now he frowns, as if he finds the allegation insulting.

"Are you suggesting that Charlotte's plans constituted some kind of threat to us?"

He lets out a small snort. Hanna chooses to interpret this as supercilious rather than scornful.

154

"Have you been to Storlien?" he continues.

"Not yet."

Daniel sits down on a chair with his back to the window. "We haven't had time."

"When you get around to it, you'll understand why Charlotte chose to hold her press conference here. The state of the place is off-putting to say the least; in her shoes I would have done exactly the same. Better to bring the media here to show them what a fantastic establishment you can build with quality and care, rather than inviting them to somewhere that looks as if it should be in a horror movie."

Espen is clearly proud of his own hotel.

"So you didn't mind Charlotte using your facilities to spread the message about her plans?" Daniel asks.

For the first time Espen gives a small smile. "I chose to regard it as pure marketing. Even if the journalists left here with her words ringing in their ears, I thought it was the impression made by *our* hotel that would last." He sounds almost calculating as he continues. "No one can beat us when it comes to offering a world-class mountain experience."

It's convincing, but Hanna can't help wondering if he really is so unconcerned. If Charlotte had realized her plans, then surely it would have involved a considerable risk to Copperhill's income stream. The manager must have been worried about the increased competition, whatever he says.

Then again, maybe they shouldn't be putting their energy into him. Espen has a solid alibi, confirmed by their colleagues in Östersund yesterday. He is not a suspect, even if he sometimes comes across as not particularly likable.

Their focus must be on Paul Lehto right now—the receptionist who had access to all the key cards, and who also seems to have had an altercation with the dead woman.

36

Filip is five minutes late and distinctly ill at ease as he goes downstairs to meet the reporter who requested an interview. She was so keen when they spoke on the phone yesterday; she said so many nice things about his mom that it was impossible to say no.

And yet his stomach is churning as he looks around the foyer. He has never met a journalist before; he really wants this to turn out well.

He is doing it for his mother's sake.

It might have been a good idea to ask Henry what he thought, but Filip didn't want to bother him. His godfather has such a lot to do now that Mom is gone; he has his hands full sorting out business matters and the plans for the hotel.

He would probably think that Filip can make up his own mind whether or not he wants to be interviewed. And Henry has already taken care of so much—surely Filip can do some things for himself.

A blond woman is approaching him.

"Hi, I'm Bella. Thank you so much for agreeing to talk to me."

Filip gives a faint smile, and the journalist keeps chatting as she steers him toward a table on the glass veranda beyond reception. Two cups of coffee and a carafe of water are waiting. She sits down and places her phone on the table.

"I assume it's okay if I record our conversation?" she says in passing, as if it is self-evident.

It makes Filip uncomfortable, but he assumes this is how things are done in the newspaper industry. "Of course," he mumbles.

Right now he is most worried about losing control when they discuss Mom and how she died. He only has to think about it and he gets a lump in his throat.

He hopes he won't cry in front of the reporter.

All he wants is to do his mom proud; that's why he's here. She might not be around anymore, but at least he'll be able to tell everyone about the wonderful things she did, despite the fact that people saw her as a hardheaded businesswoman.

She loved him, he has never doubted that, even when they argued.

"I want to hear all about your mom," Bella says gently, leaning forward and placing a hand on Filip's knee. Her long pink nails glisten in the glow of the overhead light. "Don't worry. All I want is to write a fantastic article about you and her. You can trust me."

37

After twenty minutes in the spacious conference room, Espen Lund has described in detail how the key cards in the hotel are used by the staff.

Hanna has made notes. According to Espen, it is only the leadership team who have access to all areas; everyone else has different levels of eligibility depending on their individual duties. The security system makes it possible to see who has entered which room. In addition, each hotel guest is given a card when they check in—one for every family member in multiple-occupancy rooms.

Hanna glances over to the window where the sun is high in the sky above the mountain known as Renfjället. It is going to be a beautiful day, as it usually is during the Easter break. The temperature is only a few degrees below freezing, and she can see that the drag lift is running. A family with two small children is getting ready to hit the slopes. The youngest girl is so small that she can barely stand up in her ski suit, but she hurls herself enthusiastically toward her daddy, arms outstretched.

Hanna reads through her notes.

"If you're staying alone in a suite, like Charlotte, do you just get one key?"

"Hmm." Espen strokes his double chin. "You can request two."

"So theoretically she could have left one key in the holder so that she wouldn't have to keep getting her own out and putting it away again? Even when she wasn't in the room?"

Espen nods. "Absolutely. A lot of people do that—it's more practical."

Hanna turns to Daniel to explain what she's thinking. The cleaners have confirmed that the Silver Suite was empty when they were there on Sunday.

"We know that Charlotte was out when the room was cleaned. When I've stayed in hotels, the doors are sometimes left open as the cleaners go back and forth. I'm wondering if someone took the opportunity to steal the card then?"

That would also mean that if the murderer was a hotel employee, he wouldn't need to use his own card, and it wouldn't be possible to trace the crime back to him.

Daniel nods. "Espen, could you check if more than two cards were issued to the Silver Suite?"

Espen takes out his phone and calls an internal number. His nails are bitten to the quick, his fingertips are red and swollen.

He finishes the conversation.

"You're right. Charlotte Wretlind came down to reception on Sunday and said that the card she'd left in the holder was missing. She asked for another, which was issued. No one gave the matter any thought."

Hanna and Daniel are thinking along the same lines—they seem to have found out how the murderer got into the suite.

"In other words, the perpetrator could be absolutely anyone who was in the hotel over the weekend," Daniel says.

The color drains from Espen's face. Once again Hanna wonders about Paul Lehto. They really must get a hold of him.

"We need to speak to one of your colleagues who works at reception," she says. "It's urgent."

38

Wednesday's roster means that Aada is due to clean on the fourth floor. She is relieved that it's not the sixth, where the Silver Suite is located. She doesn't want to go up there again if she can avoid it. Quickly she changes into her work clothes and takes the staff elevator.

Each floor has a special room where all the equipment is stored—cleaning trollies, and boxes of soap, shampoo, and so on for guests' bathrooms.

Aada glances around before she opens the door. She is on high alert; she feels as if she is being followed all the time, although she hasn't actually seen anyone since she sensed that horrible shadow in the parking garage.

Her shift ends in three hours. She longs for the security of her own accommodation, a place where she can lock herself in.

She takes a few steps into the narrow space and reaches up to the shelf of clean towels.

Suddenly the door slams shut. The light goes out; it is pitch black. Time stands still.

Aada wants to scream, but dare not. *He* must have found her, and now she is trapped in here. There is no way out, and no one will hear her cries for help.

She should never have come here.

The darkness is making her panic. When she takes a step forward, she bangs her forehead so hard that she sees stars. She wobbles, but grabs a hold of a shelf and manages to keep her balance.

It is impossible to orient herself, but she thinks she can hear another person breathing.

Only a few feet away.

There is no air, and a terrified whimper escapes between her lips. Then the light comes on, and her colleague Sussie is standing in the doorway, looking surprised.

Aada stares at her, openmouthed. She is holding her hands up in front of her chest in a defensive position; she is so scared she can't move.

Her throat is constricted; she can't make a sound.

"Did I scare you?" Sussie says. "Sorry, I didn't mean to. I hit the switch by mistake and happened to close the door at the same time."

Sussie is ten years older, and has worked at the hotel for years. She is responsible for the rosters.

Aada shakes her head and tries to find the words in her broken Swedish. She gives up and chooses English instead.

"It's okay. I thought . . . after what happened . . ."

"I understand," Sussie reassures her. "Everyone is shaken up—hardly surprising under the circumstances."

Aada manages a weak smile. "Exactly."

"By the way, have the police interviewed you yet? They spent a whole hour questioning me, and I wasn't even working over the weekend."

Aada doesn't know what to say. She dare not admit that she has deliberately stayed out of the way. If her bosses find out, they might be angry.

"I have to get to work," she mumbles, lowering her head and grabbing the rest of the items she needs to add to her trolley.

Tears are scalding her eyes as she scurries away.

39

While the manager tries to track down Paul Lehto, Hanna and Daniel have gone up to the Silver Suite.

Daniel positions himself with his back to the suite so that he has an overview. The fire door is directly in front of him, separating the walkway from the last three rooms, located in their own corridor. The number of the suite is 632, next door are two more rooms—633 and 631—to the left. All have been vacated while the technical investigation is ongoing.

It's like a world of its own in here, he thinks. The rust-colored wooden walls create a cozy, cave-like atmosphere. Warm light spills from the wall lamps; the sound of footsteps is silenced by a graphite-gray carpet.

The perpetrator left a bloody shoeprint in the hallway, but the traces ended after only about three feet. It has been impossible to establish which way he went.

Hanna is frowning. She adjusts her ponytail, then slowly runs her fingers down the smooth wooden wall while she ponders.

"He fled after the murder. But where did he go?"

Daniel joins her, and they go through the fire door and continue along the walkway. He looks around carefully when they stop. On the right is the staircase leading down to reception, at the other end, to the south, a wall of glass. He can just see crisscrossing wooden bridges between the rectangular buildings. There are plenty of comfortable chairs and tables of different heights so that guests can chat or work.

From up here they have an excellent view, with the communal areas on the ground floor at their feet.

Hanna points to the guest elevator about twenty yards away—a stainless steel construction that breaks up the row of identical doors. Ten yards farther along is the staff elevator that Espen showed them earlier. You have to have a special key card to use it.

"I can't imagine him taking the elevator," she says. "If he'd used the staff elevator, we'd be able to trace him through the card, and he would have known that. We also know that he must have been covered in blood. No one in that state is going to simply step into an elevator that can stop to pick people up on any floor."

"He can hardly have walked down the main staircase either," Daniel points out.

He looks around again. To the left of the fire door is a plum-colored velvet sofa, then another door with no number on it. It blends into the wall so well that he's only just noticed it. "Have you seen that?"

They go over to the discreet door. A red fire extinguisher hangs next to the frame. Maybe that's what confused them before.

Daniel suddenly realizes something. They are standing on the other side of the tall copper wall in the airy foyer. No one can see them, not from reception or the other walkways. They are well hidden from curious eyes.

"I wonder if it's locked?" Hanna says.

Daniel reaches out and opens the door to discover narrow stairs that appear to go all the way down to the ground floor. His expression is grim.

"How about this for a possible escape route?"

40

There is hardly anyone waiting when Ida reaches VM8, the wide chairlift at the heart of Åre's ski system. With an elegant turn she slows down and skis over to the barrier.

She is surprised at how few tourists are around, given that it's the middle of the Easter week. She can't quite believe how lucky she is. Alice is at preschool, and Ida's mother is picking her up this afternoon— which means a rare opportunity to spend some time on the slopes.

Daniel couldn't have come, of course—there was no point in asking him. This new case of the hotel murder is taking up every waking hour, and as usual it has swallowed him up completely.

He is barely aware that she and Alice exist.

It's fine—she doesn't mind skiing alone. Actually it's nice to be on her own. She can't remember when she last had time to herself. At the weekends she always does something with Daniel and Alice. In spite of her determination not to lose touch with her girlfriends, she has noticed that they are drifting apart.

Today is a rare luxury.

Ida shows the lift pass on her sleeve and slides through the barrier to the embarkation platform. The chairlift sways as she settles down on the far left of the seat.

March and April are the best months in Åre. The weather is nice, and the snow is still good. Today the sun is high in the sky, and it's wonderful to be outdoors.

Before she had a baby, she often used to ski the "eight at eight," like many other enthusiasts. That means you are at the VM8 lift at precisely eight o'clock, an hour before the rest of the system opens. The slopes aren't busy, and with a bit of luck, you might be the first to ski on virgin snow.

It's quite a while since she did that.

Ida can feel the sun on her back, and she turns her head so that the rays touch her left cheek. It is lovely and warm. She closes her eyes and enjoys the sensation. She pulls down the zip of her jacket a little way.

"Ida?" says the guy sitting next to her. "It is you, isn't it?"

She looks in his direction. He's wearing an oversized sand-colored ski jacket and black ski pants. A dark-gray helmet covers his hair. It is impossible to see behind his mirrored goggles.

He pushes them up onto his forehead, and she realizes who he is. "Gustav! Hi!"

He smiles, clearly delighted to see her. "It's been a while! How are you?"

Ida smiles back.

Gustav also used to be a ski instructor; they were colleagues for several years. She's heard that he now works for the Åre Guides, which sounds like an absolute dream job. They take groups of expert skiers out onto the mountain, or skiing on powder snow on the back of Skutan. If she'd been able to juggle the hours with looking after Alice, she would have applied without hesitation.

"I'm fine," she says, shifting her position so that she can see him properly. He's every bit as cool and good looking as he ever was.

"Someone said you had a baby—fantastic!"

Ida nods. "A little girl. Her name is Alice, and she's eighteen months old."

She almost takes out her phone to show him a picture, but stops herself. It seems silly—why would he want to see that? She can't imagine Gustav being interested in looking at photos of a toddler.

He lives in a different world.

"I'd never have believed it," Gustav says with a grin. "You used to love to party!"

Ida isn't sure how to interpret his comment. They are approaching the disembarkation point at the VM plateau, over twenty-five hundred feet above sea level. From there she is intending to take the gondola lift all the way up to Åreskutan.

It is such a long time since she was there. And since she really let go on the slopes.

"Are you on your own?" Gustav asks. "Or are you meeting friends at the top?"

Ida shakes her head. "No, it's just me."

"Would you like some company? I promise to behave myself."

He winks at her, and Ida has to laugh at his mischievous expression. All at once the atmosphere between them is easy, the way it used to be when they worked together. They are the same age and have always had a casually flirtatious relationship; they even made out at a party or two.

Before she met Daniel. Before she got pregnant.

The teasing glint in Gustav's eyes makes her feel more cheerful, younger, less weighed down by responsibilities. Like the girl she used to be before she had a baby.

Carefree.

She is suddenly glad that she didn't put on her old, worn ski jacket today, but chose the new black-and-white one she bought in the Christmas sale. The one Daniel thought was too expensive.

The snow sparkles in the early spring sunshine. Their chair slowly moves up the mountainside. The stately fir trees beside the lift posts are a beautiful shade of dark green, their branches still carrying patches of snow.

In a particularly sunny dip, a narrow stream has come to life, and is burbling cheerfully on its way to freedom.

The chairlift glides over the steep overhang where one of Ida's favorite routes, Lundsrappet, begins. As they continue onto the plateau itself, she sees the embarkation platform for the gondola over to the left.

There aren't too many people waiting in line here either. Ida picks up her ski poles and prepares to get off.

"So what do you say?" Gustav prods her gently in the side. His interested look is irresistible.

"Why not?" Ida beams at him. "Let's go!"

41

The telephone rings in Bengt Hedin's office at the council headquarters in Järpen. When he reaches over to pick up, his chair squeaks loudly. He has gotten used to it by now, but new visitors often react to the unpleasant noise.

It's all about leading by example. Not buying a new chair sends a clear message. It is important to be thrifty with public money.

Bengt glances at the display—it's Musse from customer services. What does he want? It's almost eleven o'clock, and he doesn't have anything in his diary until after lunch.

"Hi." Musse also deals with visitors. "There's a detective here who wants to speak to you."

It takes a few seconds for the words to sink in. Then they hit him hard. He really hopes this isn't about Storlien and Charlotte Wretlind.

"A detective?"

"Can you come down and collect him?"

A thousand thoughts crowd into Bengt's head. He rests his forehead on his hands as he tries to compose himself. They can't possibly have discovered what's gone on—not yet. It's only two days since Charlotte was found dead in her suite, and he has been so careful.

They can't catch him out.

Or can they?

His mouth is so dry that he can barely formulate an answer. Sweat breaks out on the back of his neck as he mentally reviews the latest bank transfers.

How easy would they be to trace? Can the police access his computer, see what he's done?

The thought makes him sweat even more profusely.

Bengt looks around the room, as if the solution were hiding in a corner. His phone feels damp in his hand.

He has to fix this.

Hatred for Charlotte burns intensely within him, even though she is dead. She is fucking haunting him. Will he never be rid of that woman?

"Hello?" Musse says. "Are you there?"

"Sorry," Bengt croaks. "On my way."

42

Hanna's footsteps echo in the narrow stairwell. They are on their way down to the emergency exit, and Daniel is right behind her. From time to time the motion-sensor light goes out, but it comes back on as soon as Hanna waves her arms.

She is annoyed with herself; they should have taken a closer look at possible escape routes on Monday rather than waiting until now. But everything was so chaotic, with people everywhere and hysterical hotel guests running back and forth once the news got out.

Plus Carina almost went crazy when they tried to look around—she just wanted them out of the way. The crime scene had already been contaminated by the guy from maintenance who discovered the body, along with anyone else who had entered the suite before the alarm was raised.

At the time it had felt like the right decision to sit down in the conference room and prioritize interviews with key individuals. They needed to form a clear picture of the situation rather than staying at the scene. Since then time has run away from them, and they have both had their hands full.

It's still poor police work, she thinks, wishing she could turn back the clock.

"We should have done this earlier," Daniel says, echoing Hanna's self-critical thoughts.

"Absolutely. We should."

They have reached the ground floor. Daniel is two steps above her, with his hand on the rail. At that moment the light goes out again. A smell of cedarwood and leather, possibly from his beard oil, reaches Hanna's nostrils, evoking something primitive within her. She doesn't want the light to come back on. She wants to stay here in the darkness with Daniel.

She wants him so much that it hurts.

Then her sense of duty takes over. She waves her hand and the light comes on.

In order to increase the distance between them, she moves forward. She looks around and sees several doors. Daniel joins her and presses down the handle of the closest one to discover a gym with a treadmill and spin bikes. A surprised man in his sixties looks up from a rowing machine.

The next door leads to an open area, which Hanna recognizes as the hotel's lower lounge. There is a large billiard table covered in green baize in the corner.

She goes over to the last door, pushes down the handle, and finds herself in a dimly lit parking garage.

This *must* be the escape route.

This has to be where the perpetrator came rushing along, filled with adrenaline, on Sunday night. Maybe he was still clutching the murder weapon.

Hanna stops, wondering what committing such a heinous crime does to a person? Did he even think about what he'd done, or was he simply hell-bent on getting away?

Meanwhile Daniel has made his way over to the exit, which consists of a wide opening for vehicles and a small side door for pedestrians.

He beckons her over.

"There's no card reader. You just have to push down the handle and walk out."

He opens the door, and Hanna follows him. The fresh air feels good, it's nice to get away from the gloom.

"I think this is it," Daniel says. "Let's bring in the dog handler to go through the stairwell and the entire garage. See if they can trace the perpetrator's route, even though a few days have passed."

"I can take care of that," Hanna offers. She buries her chin in her scarf. They already have a valid theory of how the murderer entered the Silver Suite while Charlotte was sleeping; now it looks as if they know how he escaped afterward.

And yet they are a long way from solving the mystery.

They have no motive, no prime suspect, no murder weapon.

"I really wish there was a functioning CCTV camera," Daniel says, pointing to an empty bracket above the entrance to the parking garage. "It would have been an invaluable help."

Hanna walks forward, and the door closes behind her. When she turns around, it is locked. There is a metal card reader on the outside wall.

So you can get out this way without a key card, but you can't get in.

Would a killer on the way to his victim use the main entrance and risk being seen in the foyer?

Probably not.

"We need to request a list of everyone who passed through here on Sunday," she says to Daniel, and explains why.

She is becoming increasingly certain that it wasn't a guest who murdered Charlotte. Everything she has seen so far convinces her that the risk of being recognized would have been too great.

For a start you have to register, give your name and credit card details. Second, the perpetrator would have either had to check out before the murder or return to his room with blood all over his clothes and shoes.

A huge risk.

Which leaves two alternative scenarios.

Either it is a hotel employee who killed Charlotte, or a member of staff helped the perpetrator to get in.

They need to concentrate on the staff.

That's where they will find their killer.

43

The white snow is dazzling in the sunlight. Ida can't help smiling at the sight spread out before her.

She and Gustav have had to walk quite a distance with their skis over their shoulders in order to reach the highest peak. Now they have arrived, and the view over the mountaintops is exhilarating.

A private universe of powder snow and untouched slopes awaits them.

With every fiber of her body, Ida can feel how much she loves this. How intensely she has longed to stand at the top of the mountain with the adrenaline pumping.

The sense of freedom is monumental. It's a long time since she felt so alive.

Gustav has stopped a few feet away. He adjusts his goggles and looks every bit as happy and excited as Ida.

"Wow," he says. "It's amazing up here!"

Ida laughs out loud.

People who don't ski can never understand the sheer joy that comes from being in a sea of powder snow. But Ida, who grew up in Åre, understands perfectly. She loves the kick you get when you are first on the scene. When you are about to hurl yourself out into all that whiteness.

Few experiences can beat that sensation. It's almost as good as sex. She has always been a powder snow junkie.

She gazes all around. Here and there the snow has piled up in thick, ruffled drifts. The wind, which is almost always blowing up here, has created strange formations in the landscape. The lifts in the high zone are often closed because of the wind, but today the air is perfectly still.

She drives her poles into the snow. At this point the mountain has an even steeper incline than in the Eastern Ravine, another of her favorite challenging runs. When she leans forward, the mountainside appears to be concave, as if it is bellying inward.

If she leans too far in the other direction, she feels as if she might fall.

"Shall we go?" Gustav says.

Ida nods and glides over the edge. She doesn't need to work to get up her speed; it simply happens. Her skis find their own way, effortlessly slicing through the snow cover.

Within seconds she finds her flow. Her body knows exactly what to do, swaying gently from side to side as she rhythmically makes her way down the steep slope. From the waist up she is poised in the dynamic stance, her gaze fixed on the mountainside. Only her legs are working as her hips and her skis change position with each new movement.

The snow is spraying in all directions.

Out of the corner of her eye, she can see that she and Gustav are traveling in parallel lines. He is slightly to her right, and they are maintaining roughly the same speed.

She's still got it!

They are approaching an abrupt stop where the piste becomes a narrow ravine. The mountainside is exposed in several places where the snow cover is thin. They can't carry on here; they will have to turn off and move sideways in order to continue.

Gustav stops first with an elegant parallel turn that throws up a cloud of soft snow. He leans on his poles and nods to her.

"Talk about powder cruising!"

Ida grins at him. Her thigh muscles are trembling with exertion; she can feel the lactic acid in her legs. Her heart is pounding with excitement.

She almost feels drunk.

"So. Fucking. Fantastic," she replies.

Gustav points to the slope farther down to the left. A short section is in shadow, the rest sparkles invitingly in the bright sunshine. It is as untouched as the slope they have just come down.

"Ready for the next one?"

Happily Ida holds up her poles. "Born ready!"

44

Anton feels ill at ease as he walks down the corridor toward the door of the council offices.

The conversation with Bengt Hedin left a nasty taste in his mouth. The man was curt, bordering on unpleasant, and did everything he could to play down his contact with Charlotte Wretlind.

Of course it could be that Hedin is simply afraid of bad publicity, that he doesn't want to be drawn into the sensationalist stories about the murder, but Anton has a feeling that's not the whole picture.

Why else would Hedin deny any involvement in the press conference that Charlotte had arranged? It's a strange thing to lie about. The press release that came out in advance had already publicized his attendance at the event, yet now he is barely prepared to acknowledge his support for the ambitious hotel project.

He had also sweated profusely throughout the conversation. Anton knows that doesn't necessarily mean anything, but he couldn't avoid noticing the beads of perspiration that gathered on the politician's forehead.

There was also something about the way he uttered Charlotte's name, with an undertone of dislike, bordering on loathing.

Experience tells Anton that Hedin is worried about something, and he has no intention of letting it go.

He opens the glass door, lost in his own thoughts, and is about to dig out his car key when someone bumps into him.

Feeling irritated, he looks up.

And there stands . . . Carl.

The shock is so overwhelming that Anton simply stares at him.

Carl recovers first. "What are you doing here?"

"I've been to see Bengt Hedin. So why are you here?"

"This is where I work. I've just had lunch."

Anton's eyes are darting all over the place. Of course. Carl said he was employed as a development coordinator with the council. Anton just hadn't registered that this meant he was based at the council offices in Järpen.

Or had he? Was that why he was so quick to offer to come here? He doesn't know what to do. He tries to compose himself, but without success.

Carl hasn't changed. So good looking, with the same beautiful face and the same thick fair hair, with a little curl over his forehead.

Right now there is nothing Anton would rather do than to reach out and stroke that rebellious curl with his fingertips. Apologize for his clumsy behavior, tell Carl he wants to start over. Explain that he has longed to get in touch all year, but was afraid of being rejected.

Then take Carl in his arms, let his mouth seek out those soft lips.

All he wants is to be with Carl. Cook together, fall asleep together, wake up with a foolish, happy smile.

"How are you?" Carl says in a friendly tone of voice.

The question brings Anton back to the moment. Carl unzips his padded jacket, as if he is feeling warm after his walk in the cold.

Anton has a sudden flashback. It's the same dark-blue jacket that Carl wore when they went home together after an evening at Bygget. That was when they met for the first time, late one February night just over a year ago.

Carl was an important witness in an ongoing investigation into the murder of his best friend. The case was later cleared up—with a tragic outcome—but it was impossible for Anton to go on seeing Carl back then.

The whole thing was so complicated.

"Er, fine," Anton stammers. "Really good."

Carl's phone rings, and he glances at the screen. Anton notices that it is a man's name.

His boyfriend?

Carl has moved on, of course he has.

"Sorry, I have to take this." Carl gives Anton an apologetic smile and walks past him into the building.

The glass door closes behind him.

Anton watches him go with a heavy heart.

45

Hanna is leaning against the highly polished reception desk at Copperhill. Two scented candles in dark glass holders are spreading a pleasing blend of musk and linen, and nearby, Daniel is speaking to Iris, the female receptionist, about Paul Lehto.

They still haven't managed to get a hold of him. Admittedly he has called in sick, but he isn't answering his phone and seems to be unreachable. His mysterious absence doesn't exactly allay Hanna's suspicions.

"I believe you saw your colleague arguing with Charlotte Wretlind on Sunday," Daniel says. "Can you tell me more about that?"

Iris explains what happened, and Hanna recognizes the description from the account given to her by Erik, the concierge.

Iris purses her lips. "Paul was furious. He tore off his mask and yelled at the poor woman. The other guests were shocked—it was incredibly unprofessional."

"Did you report his behavior?"

"I didn't." Iris gives an apologetic shrug. "Maybe I should have done." She tugs at her sleeve; the question seems to bother her. "I felt uncomfortable," she adds. "Paul has such a temper—I didn't want to make an enemy of him. Although I don't know how he's kept his job."

Daniel thanks her, and he and Hanna sit down in armchairs opposite the open fire to discuss their next move.

"It sounds as if there was a real set-to on Sunday," Hanna begins. "What now? Should we bring in Lehto?"

"I think so."

Hanna takes out her phone and calls the station, asking for a patrol car to go to Lehto's home and bring him in for questioning. She has just finished when a message comes through.

"A dog handler is on the way," she tells Daniel. "It's Jarmo—he'll be here in an hour."

Jarmo Mäkinen lives in Järpen, not very far from Åre, which is a distinct advantage. Most of his colleagues are either in Östersund, or even farther away in Strömsund, or even Sveg. Hopefully he will be able to help them secure the escape route.

The fire crackles merrily, its orange-and-violet flames dancing. It is almost two o'clock in the afternoon.

"How about some lunch while we're waiting?" Hanna suggests. She glances around and points to the library, which is also a restaurant. There is an empty table by the window, with a stunning view over the valley. The sun is shining on the dark surface of the table, and the snow outside is sparkling.

"Good idea," Daniel agrees, getting to his feet.

They both order a burger with fries. Hanna is shocked at the price, but it can't be helped.

She is still thinking about what Iris said. The situation sounded really bad, as if Paul had completely lost his temper and she was a little scared of him.

Could it be a coincidence that Charlotte was murdered only a few hours after their very public quarrel?

"I'm wondering if Paul Lehto is the person we're looking for?" she says. "I'd like to compare his fingerprints with the ones Carina found on the card holder in Charlotte's suite."

Daniel nods. "At the moment he's our best lead. His coworker didn't have much that was positive to say about him."

The waitress arrives with their food, interrupting the discussion.

"I'm looking forward to this," Daniel says warmly. He smiles at Hanna, and she notices the laughter lines around his eyes.

For a moment she forgets the investigation and all the terrible things they are dealing with.

And simply smiles back.

THEN

December 25, 1973

The seven-piece band has just finished a live set featuring a series of disco hits that got the whole dance floor bouncing. The Loft, which is on the floor above the dining room, is full of relaxed guests enjoying the music, along with coffee and cognac after Christmas Day dinner.

Monica has never seen so many beautiful dresses in one place. The singer is in a cyclamen-pink sequined outfit that must have come from Paris.

Imagine wearing such a creation! Standing in the center, soaking up everyone's admiring looks.

Monica would give everything she owned to experience that, just once in her life.

This evening she has jumped in and taken a late shift in the bar, which is famous for its Viking-inspired ceiling paintings with bold, stylized figures. It is half a staircase up from the Loft, with endless views over the landscape.

Monica scurries back and forth carrying trays laden with glasses and coffee. The atmosphere is amazing, the ladies' perfumes mingle with cigar and cigarette smoke. It is well below freezing outside, but in here the temperature is soaring.

"Miss!" a voice shouts from one of the round tables. "Miss?"

When she turns around, she sees the stylish gentleman she served on Christmas Eve—the one who looks like Sean Connery. He is with the other man from yesterday, but there is no sign of their wives. Maybe they're taking care of the children.

Monica goes over to the table.

"What can I get you?" she says politely, almost with a little bow.

He gives her a smile, so charming that Monica goes weak at the knees. He really does remind her of the famous movie star. "I'm afraid we have an emergency situation," he says, pointing to his empty brandy balloon.

"You'd like another drink?"

"Indeed we would—Martell for both of us. Doubles."

His eyes sweep over Monica's body, and she can't help blushing.

"I'm wondering if you have any other treats on offer?"

His friend laughs loudly at the joke, but the guest who resembles Sean Connery is looking at her in a way that she has never experienced before.

As if she were beautiful and desirable. As attractive as the singer, sparkling in her sequins at the microphone on the stage.

As if Monica belongs, like the elegant ladies who are guests at the hotel.

"You're very cute," he says in a quiet voice, meant for her ears only.

Monica reaches for the empty glasses to hide her confusion. When she leans forward, she feels his fingertips brush the side of her breast, his touch as light as a feather. It happens so fast that she doesn't realize what's happened until it's over.

"Two Martells," she says, and hurries away.

There aren't many people around when Anton gets back to the station at about two o'clock. Most of the offices are empty, and there are no uniformed colleagues sitting in the kitchen.

He is still confused after the encounter with Carl. All the feelings he has so carefully tried to obliterate over the past year are back with a vengeance.

Why can't he just get over him?

During the entire drive from Järpen, he pictured Carl in his mind's eye. He longed desperately to touch him. He almost turned around and drove back.

Ridiculous idea.

There is no point in brooding over what they once had. Carl has clearly moved on, and Anton should do the same.

It's just so difficult.

He hangs up his jacket and finds Raffe in the conference room, concentrating on a series of printouts spread across the table. He scratches his slightly crooked nose, a legacy from a snowboarding competition when the board hit him hard. Back in the day, Raffe competed at elite level in the national junior team. Even today he can perform in Åre's Snow Park in a way that makes Anton dizzy.

Personally he prefers skis.

"Hi—how's it going?"

"I'm looking at Copperhill's finances—the hotel has struggled over the past year."

"I guess the whole industry has," Anton says. "The question is whether it's been so bad that they can't cope with increased competition. Whether someone was prepared to commit murder in order to put a stop to a luxury hotel in Storlien."

Raffe grins. "Between you and me, I'm not convinced that idea is worth pursuing. It's Hanna who wants us to go through the finances."

He stretches both arms out in front of him and straightens his spine. There is an audible cracking sound as he follows up by linking his fingers to release the air from the joints.

"How did it go at the council?"

The question takes Anton by surprise. Raffe can't possibly know that he happened to bump into Carl. Or is he aware of the situation, even though Anton has been so careful?

Then he realizes that of course Raffe is simply asking about his conversation with Bengt Hedin. He has no idea about Anton's disastrous love life. How paranoid can you get? He tries to marshal his thoughts.

"I don't think Charlotte Wretlind got her planning permission without pulling a few strings," he says slowly. "The whole thing seems pretty mysterious. Hedin wasn't very helpful—in fact I'd say he was uncomfortable."

Raffe pushes away the laptop to concentrate on what Anton is saying.

"How do you mean?"

Anton sits down and focuses on formulating his conclusions. Hedin was defensive from the get-go, and Anton has a lingering feeling that something was wrong.

"It was hard to get clear answers out of him. He came up with a whole lot of platitudes, talked about the future prospects for the area, the importance of creating new jobs in Storlien."

Everything he said had sounded . . . rehearsed. Almost as if he didn't really believe it himself.

"I took a look at what happened the last time the Storlien mountain hotel was sold, back in 2011," he goes on. "The council placed stringent restrictions on what could be done, and was very clear about what had to be preserved. There was no question of demolishing the entire building. I very much doubt if the view of the planning authority has changed so much since then. In fact I'd say the general attitude has gone in the opposite direction—it's seen as more important than ever to hold on to cultural and historical values."

"You mean there's something suspicious about the planning permission?"

"Exactly."

Anton is almost certain that Hedin is hiding something. He was too keen to explain every detail, and yet there was no real substance in anything he said. The tension in his voice, those restless movements, the raised chin, the beads of sweat on his forehead—it all bothered Anton, and it still does.

Call it a police officer's instinct, but Hedin's account didn't ring true.

He looks up at the ceiling while he thinks. A shadow of gray cobwebs adorns one of the fluorescent lights.

Hedin has been a councillor for a long time; he's used to getting his own way. So was Charlotte Wretlind. Everything they have found out about her so far points to a highly goal-oriented individual, a woman who would stick at nothing to achieve success.

"Both Hedin and Wretlind were powerful people," Anton says. "They could have gained from each other, at least in the beginning."

Charlotte wanted to build her hotel at any price. Maybe they reached some kind of agreement?"

Anton is well aware that this is pure speculation; there is no proof for his new theory. However, Hedin's insistence on denying his involvement in the canceled press conference makes him suspicious.

"You think we're looking at bribery and corruption?" Raffe says. "Charlotte paid Hedin for his cooperation, and something went wrong?"

Anton nods. "It's too early to say for sure, but it's a possible scenario."

"Which could mean that Hedin had a motive to murder her," Raffe says.

47

Just over an hour later Jarmo, the dog handler, appears in the hotel foyer, dressed in a thick black jacket and a knitted hat.

Hanna goes over to greet him. His sand-colored Belgian Malinois is on her leash, which seems unnecessary given how well trained Molly is.

"Thank you for coming so quickly," Hanna says as Daniel pats the dog on the head.

They go up to the sixth floor and show Jarmo the Silver Suite and the door to the fire exit. Then he and Molly take over.

Hanna is equally thrilled each time she sees an experienced police dog in action. Even though she knows that a dog's sense of smell is thousands of times more sensitive than hers, with 220 million olfactory receptors compared with a human being's 5 million, it is still fascinating to see it in practice. Molly has learned to seek out traces of blood and objects based on the scent of victims. She sets off with her ears pricked, totally focused on the task at hand. Daniel and Hanna follow on behind, keeping their distance in order not to disturb her, but they have to break into a jog to stay on track.

Molly reaches the ground floor and marks clearly at the door leading to the parking garage. Hanna's pulse rate shoots up, and Daniel nods. It seems as if they were right—this was the perpetrator's escape route after the murder.

They enter the garage, and Molly stops halfway to the exit, then heads for the side door and barks until Jarmo opens it. She then aims for the parking lot, and Hanna wonders what that means. Did the killer return to the hotel after all? But then the dog heads for a different, lower parking lot that stops just before the skiers' entrance on the basement level.

She is very excited now, Jarmo has his work cut out to stay with her, and her leash is at full stretch. Molly passes all the parked cars until she reaches the hill where the ski lift stops.

Hanna is having difficulty catching her breath. "Where do you think she's going?" she asks Daniel.

"No idea."

More frantic barking; then Molly makes for the dense fir trees. She goes around the disembarkation platform for the lift, then carries straight on.

"Daniel, look!"

Hanna can't help yelling. The dog is on her way to what looks like the tracks of a vehicle that has been parked—a snow scooter. Large footprints can also be seen in the snow. Could this have been the perpetrator? Are the prints size forty-five?

The tracks continue into the forest; it looks as if the scooter drove northwest.

The dog is still going, and once again the leash is pulled taut. It becomes harder to follow her through the deep snow.

They plod on, a hundred yards, two hundred. Farther and farther in among the trees. They are careful not to walk in the tracks, nothing must be contaminated.

All at once they hear a bark with a different tone. It almost sounds triumphant to Hanna's ears. The leash is slack now, lying on the ground. Molly is standing motionless next to a thick tree trunk. She is marking, even though the scooter tracks continue.

The snow has been disturbed.

"I wonder what she's found?" Hanna says breathlessly to Daniel.

He drops to his knees and begins to dig with his hands, snow spraying in all directions.

Molly doesn't move. Jarmo's gaze is fixed on Daniel.

"Yes!" Daniel shouts, and immediately stops digging. Carefully he brushes the snow off an object in the hole, making sure he doesn't touch it with his fingers.

Hanna screws up her eyes in the bright sunshine and sees a hunting knife with a sharp, highly polished edge. The silvery blade glints in the sunlight. The leather shaft is discolored with brownish-red marks, contrasting sharply with the white snow.

The stains look like dried blood.

Could it be Charlotte's?

Have they found the murder weapon at last?

48

Two girls are sitting on the bench in the changing room when Aada walks in after her shift.

The relief is immense; it's so good not to be alone in the basement, which is slightly isolated. It feels safer with other people around—it means no one can harm her.

All day she has been looking over her shoulder. Her nerves are jangling; she was on edge every time she went into a different room to start cleaning. The very thought that there could be someone in there, someone who was waiting for her, was enough to make the lump in her stomach as heavy as lead.

Aada greets her colleagues and begins to take off her uniform. She recognizes the girls; they both live in Åre and grew up in Jämtland. She can tell they're old friends—they are chatting away eagerly. Aada can't follow everything they say, but she thinks they might be talking about the murdered woman in the Silver Suite.

A shudder runs through her body. She feels dizzy and has to sit down.

The older girl, Liv, turns to Aada and says something, but she speaks so quickly that Aada doesn't understand. Her colleague repeats the question in English.

"We're talking about the terrible murder. Have you heard that the police think the killer works in the hotel?"

Aada goes cold all over. She remembers the man rushing out of the suite. She is so frightened, so worried that he saw her and is trying to track her down.

"It's horrible, isn't it?" Liv says. "You hardly know whether it's safe to go out at the moment."

"The police were searching with a dog this afternoon," the other girl informs them, speaking quickly and agitatedly. "There were a few of them running after the dog."

The conversation is interrupted by the arrival of Sussie, the supervisor. She glances around the room, and her gaze settles on Aada.

"There you are!"

Aada is confused. She doesn't understand why Sussie has been looking for her, but hopes she hasn't done anything wrong.

"I was wondering if you could take on an extra shift this evening," Sussie goes on. "We have a lot of absentees due to illness. I can't get the roster to work, and I thought of you."

"An extra shift?"

"Yes—the same as the one you did at the weekend, the late shift."

Aada swallows hard. Last Sunday she stood in the bathroom of room 633 and heard that helpless scream.

If only she'd raised the alarm at the time. Instead she did . . . nothing. A woman has been murdered, and Aada fears for her own life.

"It really would help me out—I don't know who else to ask if you can't do it. And you live so close by."

Under normal circumstances Aada is happy to work extra hours. It means more money, and she saves most of what she earns. At some point she wants to get a place of her own. But a late shift means finishing in the early hours of the morning. After midnight. Which means walking home in the dark, all by herself.

She wants to say no, but can't come up with an excuse. She can't explain to Sussie how frightened she is.

"Of course," she says through stiff lips. "No problem."

"You're a diamond, Aada." Sussie claps her hands, looking very relieved. "Thank you so much for stepping in."

49

Anton is on his way to the kitchen to get himself a coffee when he sees the email from the IT department in Östersund. They've finished with Charlotte's phone, and have sent over a list of her text messages.

He quickly scrolls through the file and immediately focuses on the exchanges between her and Bengt Hedin. Anton's vague theory was correct—it's almost too good to be true.

Tucking his laptop under his arm, he goes back to Raffe, who is still in the conference room.

"Look at this," he says, bringing up the data. Incoming messages are marked in gray, her replies in blue. Above each one is the day, date, and time.

Raffe reads the first two, which begin with a text from Hedin.

Saturday, March 27 20:15 (Hedin)

We need to talk about the land purchase. The opposition is asking questions and I don't know if it's going to go through.

Saturday, March 27 20:17 (Charlotte)

That is not my problem, it's yours. The press conference is on Monday and it is too late to postpone.

Raffa inhales sharply. "Wow."

"Keep reading," Anton says, pointing to the exchange that took place on Sunday evening, the day the murder took place.

Sunday March 28 19:32 (Hedin)

The purchase of the land will have to be postponed. I can't make tomorrow's press conference.

Sunday March 28 19:34 (Charlotte)

It's too late to back out.

Sunday March 28 19:35 (Charlotte)

Everything you have accepted is documented. If you ruin this for me, I will ruin you.

Sunday March 28 19:36 (Hedin)

Are you threatening me?

Sunday March 28 19:37 (Charlotte)

You can interpret it however you like. I will see you tomorrow.

Raffe lets out a low whistle, and Anton exhales slowly. So there was nothing wrong with his instincts. He knew something wasn't right about Hedin. If only he'd had access to the text messages before he went to the council offices—the conversation would have been very different, then.

Instead Anton's visit has acted as a warning. Hedin knows the police are interested in him.

"What's the land purchase they refer to?" Raffe wonders.

"I need to check—hold on."

Anton goes back to his office to fetch the documents relating to the planning permission for Storlien. It's a substantial pile.

He spreads everything out on the table in the conference room so they can go through them together.

Raffe sees it first. He points to the architect's drawing of the new hotel complex.

"There. The planned building is significantly larger than the current footprint, and it's facing in a different direction. In order to realize these plans, they needed to secure more land."

"Do you think Charlotte's company paid too low a price?"

"The question is how they managed to buy it at all. The council is usually pretty cautious on these matters, and in a case like this, which has led to so many protests in the area, it would be extra sensitive."

Anton studies the drawings again. Raffe is right. They clearly show the need for more land. If their theory is correct, Charlotte Wretlind managed both to push through a remarkable land purchase and to obtain planning permission that should perhaps never have been granted.

How did she do it?

"Let's see if there were any suspect financial transactions between Charlotte and Bengt Hedin. If she paid him any money, possibly under the table. I think that would be a lot more useful than digging around in Copperhill's accounts."

Raffe has already started making notes.

"The text message exchange is a strong indication that Hedin has been paid for helping Charlotte," Anton continues. "Even if it sounds as if he wanted to pull out."

"I agree." Raffe looks up from the screen. "But how does that fit with the murder?"

Anton pictures various scenarios. Could it be Bengt Hedin who got into the hotel on Sunday in order to attack Charlotte? He didn't exactly give the impression of a man with violent tendencies, although he did seem nervous during their meeting earlier today.

Could more than one person be behind the killing?

"I think he's involved in some way," he replies eventually. "The question is how."

50

The pillars at the entrance to the Timmerstugan restaurant not far from the VM6 lift are adorned with colorful Easter branches. There are tables and benches outside for those who want to enjoy a beer after skiing. Ida feels a little guilty as she sits down opposite Gustav. She ought to go home and relieve her mom. She promised to be back by five at the latest, and it's already quarter to.

But it's wonderful to sit in the afternoon sun with a glass of foaming lager. They've had a fantastic day on the slopes, skiing like crazy people, as if it were the last day of the season.

Her body is exhausted, but her heart is full of joy. She can't remember the last time she had so much fun.

"*Skål,*" Gustav says, raising his glass to her. "I'm so glad we bumped into each other. It must be fate!"

His smile is infectious. He has taken off his helmet, and his curls hang loose over his shoulders. They are like a halo around his head, shimmering in the sunlight. Gustav's hair makes most girls sigh enviously; Ida used to laugh and say it was wasted on a guy.

"You're an amazing skier," he goes on. "So confident, brilliant technique."

Ida feels her cheeks flush red. She competed in the slalom as a child, like many others in the area, but stopped in her teens when other interests—like boys and clothes—took over. She never really had the competitive edge that would have made her willing to sacrifice everything for training, but she still has the technique.

"I guess it's just muscle memory," she mumbles into her glass. The unexpected praise warms her heart. She rarely feels . . . cool.

Or openly admired. There is no doubt that Gustav likes her, she can see it in his eyes.

The sun is still warm, and melting snow drips from the gutters. VM6 is no more than a hundred yards away. It has just closed for the day, and the chairs are on their way down from the top station. Ida can see the last of the skiers skimming down Stjärnbacken, the piste above the restaurant.

The DJ changes the track to "Jump" by Van Halen, the music pumping from the speakers. Ida gets the urge to leap up and dance.

"We should do this again," Gustav says, winking at her like he did on the chairlift when they met a few hours ago. He takes a swig of his beer, and a little of the foam sticks to the corners of his mouth. It's kind of cute.

Something within Ida comes to life.

Gustav puts down his glass and reaches out across the table. He takes her hand between his, gently runs his fingertips over her palm, lingering on the sensitive skin in the center.

His touch burns like fire, and a shiver of excitement runs through Ida's body.

He leans forward until his face is only a couple of inches from hers. His lips are slightly parted, and he doesn't take his eyes off her.

What the hell is she doing?

Ida yanks her hand away. She picks up her phone to check the time, making it impossible for Gustav to misread the gesture.

"I'm sorry, but I'm afraid I have to go," she says a little breathlessly.

"I understand." He looks disappointed, but not annoyed. Maybe curious, as if he's not prepared to give up so easily.

Quickly Ida gathers her things—her helmet, her ski gloves, the back protector she wears for off-piste runs.

She promised Daniel she would never leave it at home.

Once again her guilty conscience kicks in, and she gets to her feet. "Thanks for today."

Just as she is about to leave, Gustav raises his hand as if he wants to ask a question.

"By the way." He gives her his most disarming smile. "Do you still have the same phone number?"

Ida hesitates, she ought to say no. Whatever it was that just happened, it can't happen again. It's been an enjoyable but completely innocent day. That's all. Now she is going home to Alice and her partner.

Nothing happened.

Then she nods.

"I do."

51

Hanna is still filled with relief at having found the murder weapon as she sits at her computer back at the station. The knife has been sent off to forensics. She really hopes they will be able to secure the perpetrator's fingerprints or DNA.

At the same time, she is frustrated because they still haven't got a hold of the mysterious Paul Lehto.

The information about the argument with Charlotte must be followed up as soon as possible, especially now that another witness has confirmed the original tip-off about his volatile temperament and outbursts of rage.

A patrol went to his home earlier and knocked on the door, but no one answered. He is not taking phone calls either. Hanna has tried his wife, but it went straight to voicemail.

It is getting late, after six in the evening, and Daniel has just left. Hanna has decided to stay a while longer. She wants to go through Paul Lehto's background in peace and quiet.

Anton is still here too, digging into Charlotte's finances and trying to find links to Bengt Hedin.

Hanna heard about the councillor's involvement when she got back from Copperhill—it's important. Anton and Raffe's speculation about bribes, plus the incriminating text message exchange, cannot be ignored.

She runs a search on Paul Lehto through PMF, the system where you can ask multiple questions with the individual's personal identification number. In seconds she is looking at a passport photo of a man with dark hair, narrow eyes, and bushy brows. He lives in Krok, he is fifty-three years old and married. There are stepchildren in the equation, and he has worked at the hotel since it opened. He has a license for a Carl Gustaf 1900 .30-06 rifle, one of the most common in Sweden. He also owns a snow scooter.

A further search shows that he was stopped by a traffic patrol outside Undersåker a few years ago, and was fined for drunk driving.

She leans back and opens the top drawer. If she remembers correctly there should be half a bar of chocolate in there, which should keep her going until she gets home and can make herself a proper meal. The chocolate is in worse condition than she recalled, whitish around the edges, but it slips down nicely with a cup of coffee she fetches from the machine.

As she munches she checks out the online articles about the hotel murders. The headlines are as striking as before, but there is no sign of the interview Filip mentioned.

Good—hopefully he said no.

Hanna throws away the chocolate wrapper and brings up the Facebook group called Preserve Storlien. The contributions are crude, and don't seem to have diminished since the murder. As usual it is men who are responsible for the worst comments, several threatening various sexual acts that they think Charlotte "deserves," or in their opinion is "gagging for."

Hanna tries to avoid brooding over the banal suggestions. She is so tired of those who think they have the right to comment on a woman's appearance, or to threaten rape or other forms of assault because they don't like her opinions or plans. Most don't even have the courage to use their own name, but hide behind obviously fake profiles.

She would like to find out who is behind all these aggressive outpourings.

It's late, but the IT team usually works long hours. She calls Nadim in Östersund; he has helped her with other cases.

She is in luck. A deep voice answers, and Hanna quickly explains the situation. Could he check out a few posts while she's on the phone?

"Start with the administrator," she adds.

Nadim taps away on his keyboard as the minutes pass.

"Okay, her name is Annika Wäster. She's sixty years old and lives in Storlien—one of about seventy people who are permanent residents. She has children and grandchildren."

There is nothing in Annika's profile to suggest that she is capable of violence. Nor is she responsible for the worst comments, the ones Hanna has read and reacted to.

"Can you take a look at those who've been the most active in the group?"

"No problem."

Nadim taps away again.

"That's interesting," he says, sounding surprised. "One of the IP addresses seems to come from the council offices in Järpen."

Hanna is so taken aback that she sits bolt upright on her chair. "What did you say?"

"It's an anonymous contributor who calls himself Storlien Man," Nadim goes on. "I'd say it is a man, judging by the way he expresses himself."

Hanna scrolls through the posts to find him. He has written delightful comments such as "That fucking cunt should be shot" and his latest little gem, posted after the murder became public knowledge: "That bitch finally got what she deserved."

Charming.

"Any chance of a name?" she asks Nadim.

"I'll see what I can do—I'll have to speak to the council's IT department."

"Okay—call me as soon as you find anything."

Hanna gets up and goes along to Anton's office. He too is staring at his computer. She sinks down in his turquoise chair and quickly tells him what Nadim has found out—that it looks as if someone at the council has been particularly active in the group called Preserve Storlien.

"Do you think Bengt Hedin could be involved?" she asks her colleague.

Anton ponders for a moment while Hanna glances toward the dark corridor. At this time of day, the lights work on motion sensors. She and Anton are only a few doors apart, but the lights have already gone out following her short walk.

"Of course it could be pure coincidence," she adds.

"You mean Hedin seems suspiciously mixed up in both the land purchase and the planning permission at the same time that aggressive posts emanating from the council offices appear on the Facebook group?" Anton frowns. "Plus Charlotte sent him threatening text messages."

Hanna is also finding it difficult to believe in coincidence in this case.

"Could Hedin have been playing some kind of double game?" she wonders. "Taking money in return for supporting the project, while at the same time working against it by posting vicious comments online?"

"It's not impossible. He didn't sound especially fond of Charlotte when I spoke to him, and given their exchange of text messages, it sounds as if she was definitely threatening to expose him if he didn't do what she wanted."

Hanna tries to process the latest information.

"Do you think Hedin might have resorted to murder in order to protect himself? The message was sent on Saturday evening, and Charlotte was killed two days later. That's enough time to plan an attack."

"You could be right," Anton agrees. "One way or another, Hedin is involved."

During the course of the day Hanna's conviction that the murderer is a hotel employee has grown stronger—but the person who stabbed Charlotte and the person who planned it aren't necessarily one and the same.

Incitement to homicide also counts as homicide. For the right amount of money, there are those who kill on behalf of others.

Paul Lehto could be that man.

Unless he's just a receptionist who happened to have a bad day?

"What about this?" she says, allowing herself free rein. "Charlotte paid Hedin a considerable sum of money to push through the land purchase, and to make sure she won planning permission without any problems. When things went wrong and he felt threatened by her, he used some of that money to get rid of her."

Outside, a car starts up and zooms out of the parking lot, its tires screeching as it disappears.

Hanna pictures the hunting knife, the sharp blade shining in the sunlight when Daniel brushed off the snow.

Maybe they are getting close to a solution.

They could be looking at a serious crime that had to be hidden by an even more serious crime.

52

Aada stumbles as she hurries through the empty parking garage. It is almost half past midnight. She is so tired that her legs are trembling. All she wants is to get home and fall into bed.

She doesn't start work until midday. If she can just get to sleep rather than lying awake tossing and turning, then maybe she will be able to get some proper rest.

The sky is black and cloudy as she sets off for the staff accommodation. It is snowing, a curtain of white flakes falling to the ground. The snowplow hasn't yet cleared the road.

It is horrible being alone on this cold night, but Aada consoles herself with the thought that it is only a short walk. Soon she will be able to lock the door behind her and she will be safe.

In spite of her fears, she managed the late shift. It gives her a little spark of hope—maybe things aren't so bad after all. Maybe there is a way out of her difficulties. She really wants to build a new life in Sweden. Settle down somewhere safe, create a good future. In the best case scenario, meet a kindhearted man who doesn't drink and isn't violent.

Preferably a Swede. Swedish men seem nicer than those back home in Maardu.

She'd love to have children too—well, at least one. A little girl who wouldn't need to go to bed at night feeling terrified because of a drunken, menacing stepfather.

A cold gust of wind comes racing through the night, and Aada pushes her hands in her pockets. She has left her gloves at home, and her fingers are freezing.

The distant echo of an avalanche control blast rolls across the valley and fades to the west. Aada knows they are clearing the snow to prepare the ski runs for the next day, but the dull rumble still makes her shudder. It feels ominous, and it reminds her of home, of her grandmother's heartrending tales of the war and the Russian invasion.

She increases her speed, walking quickly with her head down.

The cold nips at her cheeks.

An unexpected noise makes her look up. It sounds like a push notification, as if someone is nearby.

She glances around, but can't see anyone.

Or is someone standing waiting by the steps?

She is only fifty yards from the staff-accommodation block, but the whirling snow makes it hard to see properly.

Aada screws up her eyes, but it doesn't help.

A shadow peels away from the darkness.

A tall figure, a man with a powerful physique, comes toward her. It is too dark to make out his facial features, but Aada stands there as if she has turned to stone.

She recognizes the way he moves. She knows who is walking quickly toward her.

He has found her.

It is late, after midnight, and Monica is lying in her narrow bed in the room with the faded wallpaper. After another long shift at the hotel, she shouldn't have any problem getting to sleep, but her whole body is fizzing with excitement.

Her heart is pounding so hard that she is aware of every beat.

She can't stop thinking about Sean, as she has started to call him in her mind. At dinner this evening she was allocated to the round table once again. He was sitting there with his wife, their two children, and the other family.

He was every bit as stylish as before, in a dark-blue suit and a silk tie. Just like a movie star.

She felt nervous going over to take their order, she couldn't get the words out, but the candlelight bathed everything in its warm glow and hid the embarrassed blush on her cheeks.

She noticed Sean as soon as he walked into the dining room, the way his attention immediately focused on her. He didn't take his eyes off her as she moved from table to table, his gaze followed her all the time; she could actually feel it burning into her back.

It is still impossible to understand why a man like him, so worldly wise and elegant, would be interested in someone as insignificant as her. However, she doesn't think she's imagining things. It was as if he didn't even see any other women. As if they were two magnets, helplessly drawn toward each other.

When she eventually brought their dessert, a beautiful, freshly browned glace au four, he watched her secretly, almost hungrily. She got a sense of something dangerous yet unbearably exciting, as if they were the only two people in the room.

Her skin was covered in goosebumps, her nipples hardened.

The memory makes her genitals throb in a strange new way.

Monica places her hands firmly on top of the covers. What she is thinking about is forbidden. Plus he is married, and she shouldn't be dreaming of another woman's husband in this way.

And yet it is impossible to stop thinking about Sean.

Her hand slips inside the covers, slides down her body; she can't control her fingers.

She has read about love at first sight in magazines. How you just know it's right, from the very beginning.

Why couldn't that happen to her?

All those romantic stories can't be made up.

She is certain that Sean wouldn't look at her like that if he wasn't serious. He is a gentleman, she has known that from the start.

You can't control your emotions.

He is married, she reminds herself again, but she can't help imagining the two of them together. Sitting beside him in the hotel dining room next Christmas, looked after and cherished, treated like a fine lady instead of working as a waitress.

She really can picture herself in a delightful silk dress, with diamonds in her ears and a shiny wedding ring on her left hand.

He would never deliberately hurt her. Her heart tells her that his intentions are honest.

53

When Alice wakes and starts crying at two o'clock in the morning, it is Daniel's turn to get up. He was lost in a dream, deep in the forest with bloody knives scattered across the snow.

The day's events linger in his subconscious.

With gritty eyes he picks up the little girl from her cot and is greeted by the familiar odor of a dirty diaper. When he has changed her, he goes into the kitchen to make up a bottle. It takes only a couple of minutes to open the packet of formula and measure it out, but the few seconds required in the microwave feel like an eternity.

As soon as Alice's little mouth finds the food, blessed silence reigns once more.

Daniel takes her into the bedroom and gently lays her down on the double bed next to Ida. She is fast asleep; Alice's screams don't seem to have woken her this time.

He lies down beside his daughter, who is clutching the bottle tightly. Her eyes are half closed, all she cares about is assuaging her hunger. A trickle of formula runs down from the corner of her mouth onto her pink pajamas.

In six months she will be the same age as Daniel was when his father walked out on their family.

He still can't get his head around it. He's been seeing a therapist for over a year, and he can neither understand nor forgive his father's behavior.

He was so small back then.

How could his father abandon him and Mom like that? He didn't even come home; he just left a short message on the answering machine to inform them of his decision, then vanished from their lives.

He didn't get in touch again until he was settled in Umeå with his new wife.

Daniel has never been away from Alice for more than twenty-four hours. He can't imagine not seeing her for a week, let alone months or years.

Memories from his visits to Umeå have begun to torment him more and more. The therapy sessions have made him remember events decades after he managed to bury them in a dark corner, deep down inside.

Now it has all come back, just when a homicide investigation is taking up every waking hour.

He needs to focus on the job rather than brooding over his childhood experiences, but they refuse to be ignored. The conversations with Jovanka have upset many things, and sometimes he wishes that the memories had stayed buried.

They don't make him feel better—just worse.

Maybe that was why he reacted so strongly to the journalist who spoke to him in the hotel foyer on Monday. He had treated him as harshly as his own father used to do when Daniel was little.

The feeling of never being really welcome, of always being in the way, comes flooding over him again.

He remembers how his father's new wife divided the children into an A team and a B team.

Her own children, his half siblings, were in the A team. Daniel wasn't, of course. It wasn't his siblings' fault. They were far too young to understand, but the comparison has stayed with him, and maybe that's why he broke off all contact with them too.

He carries with him the sense of not being good enough.

He was only there on sufferance; he was never part of the real family.

He recalls weekends when he was hungry between meals, but didn't dare get himself something to eat. He didn't have the courage to open the refrigerator in case his father's new wife got mad. The solution was to persuade his half brother to go and ask for a sandwich. Then Daniel could offer to make it for her, and make himself one at the same time.

How old was he then? Eight or nine, maybe.

You developed a strategy to deal with a difficult situation, Jovanka has said. *You were forced to come up with survival tools, because no one was taking care of you the way they should have done.*

The rage he feels toward his stepmother has never gone away. He blames her and his father equally for what happened.

I was just a little boy back then, he wants to scream in his stepmother's face. *Just a child. You were an adult, married to my father. It wasn't my fault that I existed when the two of you got together.*

How could you treat me like that?

Daniel forces himself to breathe more slowly. Alice is lying on her back beside him, with a little smile on her face. Her small fingers have released their grip on the bottle, which has rolled down onto the blanket. She is sleeping peacefully once more, at the same time completely secure and utterly helpless.

As far as Daniel is concerned, it is obvious that a parent must protect such a young child. That's why he finds it even harder to understand how his father could be so blind. Why have a child at all if he wasn't prepared to shoulder his responsibility?

Personally, Daniel would give his life for Alice if necessary.

And yet his own father was able to dismiss him and their relationship without a second thought.

He has never made any attempt to contact Daniel in almost twenty-five years, not even when Daniel's mother died.

Daniel clenches his teeth, so hard that his jaws hurt. With a huge effort he manages to calm his breathing.

As an adult he has realized that it probably took all his father's strength to extricate himself from his marriage to Daniel's mother. He couldn't risk the new relationship falling apart too.

Today Daniel can understand how it all played out, but the child within him cannot forgive.

His father hated conflict, and always gave in to his wife. He was weak and let her do whatever she wanted; not once did he take his son's side against her.

Daniel allows his head to sink back on the pillow. Instinctively he reaches for Alice's tiny hand. The skin is soft beneath his fingertips, he gently presses his lips against her forehead and inhales her sweet baby smell.

A sob bursts through, blocking his throat. The sob he holds back when he is sitting with Jovanka.

He still wonders why his father didn't love him more.

Was there something wrong with him?

54

Aada stands rooted to the spot as the man comes toward her in the darkness.

Her greatest fear has come true, the nightmare is real.

He has found her.

He is going to murder her too.

Then her survival instinct kicks in; she has to get away from this stranger who is already reaching for her. He is tall and well built, she is small and skinny, but the conviction that she is going to die lends wings to her heels.

She ducks beneath his arm and flees into the night.

There is no chance of making it back to the hotel before he catches up with her. The staff accommodation is out of the question—he is blocking her way—and she wouldn't be able to get out her key card in time.

In her despair she runs toward the forest instead. Maybe she can escape among the dense fir trees, hide behind the trunks until the complex wakes up in the morning.

Aada is running for her life.

When she casts a terrified glance over her shoulder, she sees that he is no more than ten yards away. It is difficult to negotiate the deep snow, and her footsteps are becoming slow and clumsy. Time and time again her boots get stuck, and she has to pull herself free.

The fear is making it hard to breathe. She already has a stitch; she doesn't know how long she is going to be able to keep running from the man who is chasing her.

He is so close now that she can hear his panting breath right behind her.

She must increase her speed, force her legs to move faster even though he is catching up.

Out of the corner of her eye, she glimpses the snow-covered road. During the day lots of cars travel along this stretch between the hotel and the E14, but tonight there isn't a single vehicle in sight.

No one is coming to her rescue.

Aada screams as she hurls herself in the direction of the dark forest. She is almost there, maybe she will be able to get away.

The swirling snow makes it hard to see properly, and tears are blinding her.

Just as she reaches the first trees, the man grabs a hold of her jacket and pulls hard.

Aada loses her balance and falls, taking him with her. She lands on her stomach, the impact knocks the breath out of her. She remains motionless for a few seconds, vaguely conscious of the icy snow against her cheek.

It smells salty.

Then she comes to her senses, rolls over, and begins to drag herself along on her elbows, pushing with her feet, desperately trying to stand up so she can run.

This is her last chance.

It has to work.

But in seconds he has grabbed her again.

This time Aada fights back, hitting out at his face, attempting to scratch him with her nails, punching and kicking as hard as she can with her hands and feet.

Somehow he gets a hold of her scarf and pulls.

His grip is so strong that Aada feels her neck being squeezed. A burning pain stabs the back of her neck and at the same time, in a second, all the air disappears.

She can't breathe.

There is no oxygen.

Her hands fly up to her throat, and she struggles to relieve the pressure on her windpipe—but her scrabbling fingers achieve nothing. The man simply tightens his hold.

She can't get him off her.

The scarf, knitted for her by her mother back home in Maardu, has metamorphosed into a thick rope that is killing her.

The world spins. Her muscles stop obeying her. She paws feebly at her throat as the life leaves her body.

The darkness is filled with little red dots, hovering before her eyes.

I should have gone to the police, she thinks, *I should have told them everything and asked for their protection.*

She doesn't want to die like this.

The last thing she sees is his face, very close to hers.

This time his eyes are not burning like they did in the hotel corridor, when she was hiding just inside the door.

They are staring at her with an almost pleading expression.

As if he wants to say sorry.

55

It is dark in the bedroom when Tiina wakes up. She needs the bathroom, and gets up quietly. It is only when she comes back that she realizes Ogge isn't lying beside her. She checks the time—almost one thirty. What is he doing up at this hour, when he has work tomorrow?

She hears a humming noise outside. The sound of an engine—as if the snow scooter is being driven into the garage. It doesn't make sense.

She slips out of bed again and pads over to the window. It is north facing, overlooking the freestanding garage. When she cautiously moves the blind aside a fraction, she sees a beam of light. Ogge is sitting on the snow scooter, about to put it away.

Why has he been out in the middle of the night? They went to bed together at about ten o'clock. After dinner he had a cup of coffee while the sports roundup was on. To her relief he'd had only a couple of beers with his meal.

A thud outside tells her that the garage door has closed. Then she hears the front door open. Ogge is heading upstairs, and Tiina hurries back to bed so he won't know she's been awake.

In spite of his weight, he moves quietly and smoothly up the stairs. He has no problems hunting grouse, or traveling long distances during a moose hunt. He is an outdoor person who loves the mountains.

She hears him taking off his clothes and slipping into bed. After a few minutes his breathing slows. He has always been able to fall asleep as soon as his head touches the pillow.

Tiina remains lying on her side. She dare not ask why he has been out at this hour. It's so strange; what on earth can he have been doing?

Suddenly she is wide awake. Could Ogge be having an affair? Did he go off to see someone else behind her back?

The idea is a shock, but in an odd way it seems logical. It would explain why he has been so surly and irritable lately.

He has a mistress.

Tiina squeezes a corner of the sheet between her fingers. Of course. She is stupid, just like Ogge often says when he's drunk.

Her husband doesn't want to be with her any longer; he is dreaming of someone else, someone better than her. Younger and prettier no doubt, someone whose body doesn't bear the signs of childbirth and sweet treats.

She sniffs the air for traces of another woman's perfume, but all she picks up is snow and the smell of petrol from the scooter.

If Ogge is being unfaithful, that would explain the business with the washing machine. Presumably he didn't want the other woman's scent to give him away.

While Tiina was sleeping last Sunday night, he was lying in bed with his new love.

She stares into the darkness as the tears run down her cheeks.

Ogge is going to leave her.

THURSDAY, APRIL 1 MAUNDY THURSDAY

56

Finding the murder weapon is a breakthrough, Daniel thinks as he sits in the conference room listening to Anton's summary of the suspicions surrounding Bengt Hedin.

He tries to console himself with that thought, even though he is feeling inadequate both at work and at home. After all those memories that rose to the surface last night, he is still very low.

It is eight fifteen, and they have gathered for the morning briefing with their colleagues in Östersund. Daniel has just finished his second cup of black coffee from the machine. It took him a long time to doze off after feeding Alice. Maybe the lack of sleep is still affecting him, but for some reason the images of Charlotte Wretlind's mutilated body are even harder to look at.

Daniel and Hanna have already gone over the events of the previous day for the benefit of everyone else, explaining how they found the knife in the forest thanks to Molly and Jarmo. It has been sent off for forensic analysis; Carina and her team have visited the location and examined the scooter tracks and footprints.

He glances out of the window. The sun is shining once more after last night's snowfall. It is Maundy Thursday, which means that Åre is packed with tourists who have come up to celebrate Easter.

What will happen as far as his own celebrations are concerned is unclear.

His mother-in-law, Elisabeth, has invited them for dinner in Järpen on Saturday. He daren't think about Ida's reaction if he can't go because of the case. He's already warned her that he is going to have to work all day on Good Friday.

Although for once she didn't seem annoyed. Actually she was very quiet yesterday evening when he got home. She went to bed early, said she was tired.

Hanna nudges him in the side—she can see that his attention is wandering. He gives her an apologetic look; he didn't mean to let his thoughts drift, or to get caught. She gives him a tiny smile and nods toward the screen, where Grip's serious face can be seen in close-up.

"We've started to go through Charlotte Wretlind's financial links to Bengt Hedin," Raffe begins, reporting on the situation. "We really need permission to look into his other finances and his cell phone traffic, if the prosecutor will go along with that?"

The question is directed to Grip, who nods. "I'll see what I can do when we're done here."

The prosecutor, who makes the formal decision, has been delayed and is not in the meeting.

Today Grip is wearing a black jacket. This usually means there is going to be a press conference; otherwise she prefers knitted sweaters. Daniel is relieved that he doesn't have to get involved in that kind of thing anymore. After his first and only appearance on the podium, when eighteen-year-old Amanda went missing after a Lucia party, he and Grip have agreed that his talents lie elsewhere.

He is hoping that his boss won't find out about the encounter with the TV reporter at Copperhill on Monday.

Anton takes over.

"It's looking like Hedin should be investigated for bribery and corruption. And he could well be mixed up in Charlotte's murder."

Daniel notices Hanna and Anton exchange a brief glance. They have both raised the possibility that there could be more than one person behind the attack on Charlotte—that the perpetrator could be a hired killer who carried out the murder for payment.

It wouldn't be the first time. Daniel is familiar with this kind of scenario from his time in Gothenburg, where he worked on gang crime. Here in Åre it feels like more of a long shot, but the text message exchange Anton showed them is worrying. There also seem to be links between council employees and the Facebook group Preserve Storlien.

However, they need more evidence to establish a connection between Hedin and whoever killed Charlotte, if that is the case.

"How far have you got with the background checks on hotel employees?" Grip asks, turning to Nisse Sundbom.

He scratches the back of his neck as if he needs to think. He and Grip are roughly the same age; they have both turned sixty. The big difference is that Grip still has drive, while Nisse prefers to take things easy.

Daniel knows that Hanna isn't impressed with their gray-haired colleague, who rarely makes more of an effort than he absolutely has to. *He wouldn't have lasted five minutes in Stockholm!* she snapped the last time Nisse infuriated her.

"We are working our way through the entire staff, but we're talking about a hundred and twenty people," he whines. "It takes time—you have to accept that."

Hanna can't keep quiet. "We already said the other day that we're probably looking for a male attacker. It's unlikely that a woman would have the physical strength required to cause those injuries."

"Like I said," Nisse continues, taking no notice whatsoever. "All these checks are very time consuming. So far we haven't found anything out of the ordinary—speeding fines, late tax returns, and so on. Several employees have moved here from other countries, so searching Swedish records is no help at all. If we're going to get any further, we'll need to contact our colleagues overseas."

Hanna isn't giving up. "How about abuse? There might be someone who has a conviction for violence. From a purely statistical point of view, between three and four percent of the adult population are exposed to violence every year. Which means the same is true when it comes to perpetrators. If there are fifty male employees, then there should be two or three with evidence of violent tendencies. Start with them."

Hanna has all the figures at her fingertips, especially when it comes to violence against women. Daniel gives her an encouraging nod, and she responds by discreetly rolling her eyes.

"We'll take a look," Nisse says.

Grip has also had enough of his lackadaisical approach, and gives him an impatient look.

"Come back to us as soon as you find something. This case is top priority."

It is a long time since Daniel saw her so stressed; she usually remains calm and composed. She must be under a lot of pressure from above.

Grip brings the meeting to a close.

"The media are churning out pages and pages about this murder. The phone never stops ringing. It's unfortunate that it's Easter and that we're understaffed, but we have to try to solve this case as quickly as possible."

Daniel knows she is right.

There is a killer on the loose in Åre. And it's their job to find him.

57

As Daniel drives out of the parking lot at the police station, the sun is so bright that Hanna has to flip down the visor to avoid being dazzled. There is a feeling of spring in the air. The snow is gone from the road surface, and here and there patches of brown earth can be seen on the slopes. The winter's frozen streams have begun to flow down the mountainsides, and a constant gurgling can be heard in the shallow ditches.

She ought to be spending an afternoon like this on a sun lounger with a glass of rosé in her hand, Hanna thinks gloomily. Not focusing on a tragic homicide investigation.

She spoke to Lydia a little while ago, and her sister sounded anxious, in spite of the fact that she doesn't tend to worry unnecessarily.

The uncertainty is taking its toll on everyone in the area.

They are on their way to Copperhill to speak to Paul Lehto. Apparently he is in work today and seems fit and well.

Hanna clamps her lips together. They don't know if or how Lehto is involved, but it feels as if he is an important piece of the puzzle. She intends to do all she can to make sure the guilty party doesn't walk free.

She takes out her phone to see what the papers are saying today. Over the past few days, they have wallowed in wild speculation.

The first thing she sees when she brings up the largest evening paper's home page is an image of Filip's grief-stricken face.

Oh no. So he agreed to the interview after all.

If only she'd advised him more strongly against it. He's in a very difficult position, and under those circumstances it's easy to let yourself be exploited.

In the photograph he is standing at the entrance to Åregården, looking so vulnerable. The resemblance to Charlotte is striking—they have the same eyes, the same chiseled facial shape, although his cheeks are rounder, slightly childlike.

The subeditor has done a worse job with the headline than Hanna was prepared for.

Son of Murdered Businesswoman: Who Killed My Mom?

She skims through the article, which sensationalizes the complicated relationship between Filip and Charlotte. The reporter also claims that Filip has come to Åre to bid a final farewell to his mom, but that the police have denied him this opportunity.

They don't know what they're talking about, Hanna thinks. She is angry that the journalist has managed to attack the police while at the same time exposing a young man and his grief.

Filip is a victim too.

The most upsetting thing is the way the writer has managed to present the fact that Filip and Charlotte had quarreled about his studies shortly before she was murdered. It sounds as if Filip has no direction in life. He comes across as weak and spoiled, and Charlotte is portrayed as a harsh parent who placed unreasonable demands on her son.

As if that weren't enough, the piece deep dives into every detail about the murder, and expresses indignation that the police have yet to identify a suspect.

Hanna feels dejected.

Filip said that he wanted to do the interview in order to honor his mom. Instead he has helped the reporter to produce a character assassination of both her and himself.

There is nothing she can do except hope that Filip doesn't read this crap. And that his godfather, Henry Sylvester, will help him through his grief. Filip needs a wise and empathetic adult in his life, someone who can support him. Maybe Henry will be that person. When they met at the Villa, he came across as someone with sound values, in spite of his wealth and status.

On an impulse she sends him a quick message about the article. She hopes he can do something to protect his godson. Filip already has so much to deal with.

They are about to turn off at the chocolate factory when Daniel's phone rings. Hanna has a bad feeling as soon as she realizes it's Grip. The meeting only finished a little while ago—she hopes nothing serious has happened.

"There's been another murder at Copperhill," their boss informs them.

Hanna inhales sharply.

This is the worst possible news.

"We'll be right there," Daniel says, putting his foot down.

58

Ida can't help feeling guilty. It is the Thursday before Easter. She is home alone with Alice. Daniel went off to the station first thing this morning, before she woke up.

She is sitting on the floor in the living room, playing with her daughter and doing her best to concentrate, but her thoughts are all over the place. Distractedly she moves the brightly colored bricks—Alice wants her to stack them up so she can knock them down.

Ida is thinking about Gustav. About yesterday's skiing, and the feeling of being free, of not being tied down. Like in her old life.

But back then she wasn't Alice's mom.

Ida shakes her head. How can she even think like this? She loves her daughter more than anything in the world, and yet she keeps on remembering the two of them sitting outside Timmerstugan. The tingle she felt when Gustav took her hand and gently stroked the palm.

"Stop!" she exclaims.

Alice looks at her in surprise, and her blue eyes fill with tears. Ida hadn't realized she'd shouted. Or sounded so angry.

"Sorry, sweetheart," she says quickly. "Mommy didn't mean it."

She stacks four bricks on top of one another so that Alice can knock them down, which immediately makes the little girl feel better.

The sun is streaming in through the south-facing window. If Ida cranes her neck, she can see Lake Åre. Several cross-country skiers are moving smoothly over the ice, and farther away she can just make out a couple of snow scooters that seem to be heading for Duved.

It must be wonderful up on Skutan today. It snowed overnight, several inches of powder just lying there waiting.

The sensation from yesterday when she sped down the slope still lingers in her body. She would do anything to be there again.

No, she tells herself firmly. This has to stop. It isn't fair on either Alice or Daniel.

But she does need to get out into the fresh air; sitting indoors is driving her crazy. It is quite a project to get Alice into her snowsuit and haul out the stroller, but it will be worth it.

She is just about to get up when her phone buzzes.

A message from Gustav.

Ida's pulse rate shoots up. She feels as if her blood is fizzing when she reads what he has written.

Thanks for yesterday. Fancy a coffee sometime?

59

Daniel drives up the steep, winding road to Copperhill as fast as he dares. As he takes the final bend he sees the police officers and cordons. There is no doubt that they are approaching a crime scene.

Curious and anxious onlookers have gathered behind the blue-and-white tape. Several are holding up their phones and trying to record as much as they can. Daniel sees Hanna frown at this tasteless behavior, but there isn't much they can do. These days unauthorized individuals often film at crime scenes, even when they should be helping out.

That's the way the world looks with social media.

He parks the car, and they hurry down the hill. A short distance away they can just see the roof of Zlatan Ibrahimović's house, a much-talked-about mountain lodge that the famous footballer had built a decade ago.

Today there is no time to admire its bold architecture. Instead they hurry to the area behind the hotel's staff accommodation, a three-story gray building in front of a dense forest of fir trees.

A uniformed colleague whom Daniel recognizes beckons them over.

"Over there," Jocke says, pointing.

Daniel's stomach contracts when he sees the outline of the dead body, right next to a clump of trees.

"Who found her?" Hanna asks.

"The woman with the dog."

She is sitting in one of the police cars. The back door is open, and a dog on a leash is sitting outside, whining impatiently. It's a Samoyed—Daniel recognizes the characteristic fluffy coat that almost blends in with the white snow.

"I asked her to wait until you got here," Jocke explains.

"We'll talk to her in a minute—let's take a look at the victim first."

They make their way over to the spot where the body is lying on the ground. Daniel feels a terrible emptiness inside. They are standing in front of a deceased person who will never speak, laugh, or breathe again.

It's a young woman. She looks very small lying half on her side, with pale cheeks and closed eyes. Her hands are resting on the snow, palms upward. Her fair hair surrounds her head like a frozen halo.

But there is nothing peaceful about this horrific sight.

Her quilted jacket has slipped down, exposing part of her throat. Her scarf is tight around her neck. It is obvious that someone has pulled as hard as they could.

"I don't think there's any doubt about the cause of death," Daniel says, "although of course the pathologist will have to carry out an examination."

"Do we know her name?" Hanna asks.

One cheek is pressed down into the snow. The scarf has dug deep into her skin. Hanna spots a pass card hanging from a lanyard, and crouches down to take a closer look.

"Aada Kuus. It seems she worked at the hotel."

Daniel turns to get an overview. The hotel is a few hundred yards away up to the right, on the same side of the road as the accommodation block. However, this particular area is well hidden. There aren't many windows at the back of the staff building, and you can't be seen from the road. Nor are there any streetlights. The entrance to the block is around the corner, so the exterior lighting is facing in the opposite direction.

He looks at the dead woman again.

No unwelcome eyes would have seen what happened here.

And no one would have heard her scream.

60

When they have finished with the crime scene and spoken to the woman who discovered the body, Hanna and Daniel set off for the hotel. They are meeting Espen Lund to find out more about the latest victim. They have had to postpone their plans to interview Paul Lehto, but are hoping to catch up with him later in the day.

On the way to the entrance, a group of journalists catches up with them. The guy from the major TV company who was so rude the other day more or less pushes Hanna aside and positions himself in front of Daniel. Hanna can see that he thinks he's picked up the scent of something big. She recognizes his behavior from Monday, before Daniel yelled at him.

He has a feverish glow in his eyes.

"Is it the same killer as last time?" he asks loudly. "Has there been another stabbing in Åre?"

Daniel holds up his hand in a defensive gesture and tries to continue toward the door, but the reporter refuses to give up. He blocks Daniel's path so that he has no choice but to stop.

"Come on, you have to give us something!"

"I don't have to give you a damned thing," Daniel replies.

"Is it the same killer? Could the police have foreseen this?"

"Enough!"

Daniel is getting angry. Hanna knows the warning signs—the deep frown, the compressed lips.

"Do you really have no idea what's happened?" the journalist almost shouts in his face.

"No comment."

Daniel moves to the side to go around him, but the journalist steps sideways so that he is still blocking Daniel's route.

"Shouldn't the hotel have been closed after the first murder?"

He persists, ignoring the clear signals that he needs to stop. This could go badly wrong. Hanna realizes that Daniel is going to punch the guy if she doesn't do something.

"Get out of my fucking way!" he bellows. "Can't you see we're working?"

He is about to lash out when Hanna steps between the two of them. She feels as if she is undermining her colleague, he ought to be perfectly capable of handling the situation himself, but she has been here before, she has seen him lose his temper in other contexts.

Although it's been a while.

"Call our press office," she snaps. "If you don't stop this right now, I'll have you removed by our colleagues."

Somehow she manages to edge Daniel away from the journalist before he explodes. They stand outside the main door while he pulls himself together.

"Thanks," he says after several long, silent seconds.

"What happened?" Hanna has to ask. "I thought you were going to hit him."

Daniel looks both tense and resigned. She would like to give him a hug, but contents herself with a cautious pat on the arm.

"I can't really explain it. That guy, he was so disrespectful. There's a dead woman, strangled, only a few hundred yards away. It just sickened me."

Hanna understands—she is shaken too. But she has a feeling there is more to tell. He is holding something back, something that seems even more difficult to talk about.

"He . . ." Daniel pushes his hands deep into his pockets without looking at her. "He reminds me of my father."

"Your father?"

She tries to catch his eye. Daniel has never said much about his father, even though they know each other pretty well by this stage. Of course she knows that his mother died in a road traffic accident, but his father is no more than a vague figure who disappeared from the picture when Daniel was little.

"There's something about the way he acts." Daniel sounds tortured. "It's weird, the anger came from nowhere. I couldn't control it." He kicks out at a pile of snow, sending snow in all directions. "Shit!"

They ought to go inside and get on with the job, but Hanna can see he needs time to calm down first.

"I thought I was more professional than this! A year in therapy, and I haven't learned a fucking thing!"

Hanna can't hide her surprise.

"You've been seeing a psychologist? Why didn't you say anything?" She tries to sound sympathetic, but she is shocked. She had no idea.

Daniel's jaw has never been so tense. Beneath the tightly controlled surface, she senses powerful emotions that he is trying to keep in check. He never wants to appear weak, and yet she catches a glimpse of the unhappy child inside the man she cares about so deeply.

A short distance away they hear the hum of the tow lift, followed by a crack when a skier lets go of the loop, which flies up in the air.

"I guess I was embarrassed," Daniel says eventually. He speaks quietly, his face turned away.

"You have nothing to be embarrassed about. Lots of people have therapy."

237

"It doesn't feel that way."

"I had counseling last year," Hanna points out.

"That's different. It was because of something that happened to you in the line of duty."

This sounds so stupid that Hanna rolls her eyes. "You know what I think you should do?" she says, without giving him time to ponder. "Ask for an emergency appointment with your therapist. Go and see him or her, explain what happened today. Get some help to process it right away."

"I can't do that—we're in the middle of a case, we have a new victim . . ."

"Just do it." Hanna isn't giving up. "If you don't deal with this now, you won't be any use in the investigation."

"I don't have time," Daniel protests, but with less conviction.

"Find the time. What if this happens again, and you really lose it?"

Hanna steps forward and hugs him tightly. Her feelings spill over when he relaxes in her arms.

"Thanks," he murmurs in her ear. "For understanding."

61

There isn't much left of Espen Lund's professional persona as he sits opposite Daniel and Hanna. The hunted look in his eyes reveals a high stress level, and there is a noticeable twitch beneath one eye. He is slumped on his chair, chewing a fingernail.

They are in the same conference room as before, and it is just over an hour since the body was found.

In spite of the difficult situation, Daniel feels calm. It was a relief to tell Hanna about the therapy, and he has taken her advice. He sent a message to Jovanka asking if she can squeeze him in as soon as possible. He has to try to find a window, even though the case is escalating.

He doesn't want to disappoint Hanna, and deep down he knows she's right. He needs to deal with his reaction to the journalist. This investigation has taken a greater toll on him than he realized.

The fact that another woman has been killed is nothing less than a nightmare.

Espen lets out a groan and buries his face in his hands. He appears to be on the verge of collapse.

"This is horrendous. We're going to have to close the hotel, there's nothing else for it." With a pleading note in his voice he goes on. "Are you sure it was murder? It couldn't have been an accident?"

"I'm sorry," Hanna informs him. "There is absolutely no indication that it was an accident. We have to wait for the pathologist's report, of course, but it looks as if the victim was strangled."

Espen seems to shrink before their eyes as the scope of the catastrophe sinks in. His phone is constantly bleeping, but he doesn't bother to switch it to silent. Or maybe he's so shocked that he hasn't even noticed.

Daniel feels for him, he is in a terrible situation, but they have no choice. The most important thing right now is to get as much information as possible about the latest victim so that they can make progress.

"What happens now?" Espen asks in a small voice.

For a moment Daniel isn't sure whether he's talking about the investigation or the hotel.

"What do I do? Should I send everyone home, all the guests and the staff, to be on the safe side?"

Daniel notices a burst blood vessel on his left cheek, tiny red threads spreading in all directions like a spider's web.

"It's probably best to wait a while," Hanna advises. "We need the opportunity to interview everyone who lives in the staff-accommodation block, to find out if anyone saw or heard anything."

"And we need all the information you have about the victim. Everything."

Apart from the woman's name, Aada Kuus, they have learned that she was twenty-one years old and came from Maardu, a small town in Estonia. Aada had worked as a cleaner for six months and was popular with her colleagues, although she was regarded as shy and reserved and didn't speak Swedish particularly well.

No one in the hotel can understand what has happened.

Why would anyone want to murder Aada?

Her clothes were undisturbed, so there is no indication of a sexual motive. However, it is hard to ignore the stabbing that took place just a few days ago.

"We can't help feeling that Aada's death might be connected to Charlotte Wretlind's murder," Hanna says. "Are you aware of any links between the two women? Did they have any kind of contact?"

"I can't answer that off the top of my head."

"Okay. Did Aada clean the Silver Suite when Charlotte was staying there?"

Espen looks confused, as if his brain were scrambled.

"Can you access her work roster?" Hanna clarifies. "It would be a start."

Espen focuses on the iPad on the table in front of him and searches the system.

"Aada was working on the night Charlotte was murdered," he says after a little while. "Not in the Silver Suite, but on the same floor."

"Can you see what time she was in each room?" Daniel asks. "I'm guessing it should be possible to see when she swiped her key card."

"I'll have to check that out with IT."

His voice is steadier now, maybe it's easier to function when there is a concrete task to carry out. This isn't the first time Daniel has dealt with a shocked individual, and he knows that everyone reacts differently.

There is no right or wrong.

Espen picks up his phone, and after a brief conversation, they have their answer.

"Someone is bringing the log," he says.

Within a couple of minutes, there is a knock on the door, and a tall man in hotel uniform appears. Daniel recognizes him—he's the guy who told Hanna about the argument at reception.

"Excuse me," he says to Espen. "IT told me to give you this."

He hands over a printout. Espen gives him an appreciative smile and receives a brief nod in return.

When he has gone Espen spreads out the documents on the table and pushes the relevant sheet of paper across to Hanna and Daniel.

"Okay, so this shows that Aada cleaned several rooms on the sixth floor late on Sunday evening. We can see which rooms she went into but not how long she stayed, because the card doesn't register when you leave. According to this log, she was in rooms 650, 642, and 633, all of which were due to receive new guests the following morning. Then she moved down to the fifth floor."

"Which of those rooms is closest to the Silver Suite?" Hanna asks.

"Room 633—it's next door." There is a little more color in Espen's face now. "It looks as if Aada went back to 633 late at night—six minutes after midnight. The late shift finishes at midnight, so I'm not sure why she would have done that—maybe she forgot something."

Daniel considers this information. The time of Aada's return to room 633 more or less matches the pathologist's estimate of Charlotte's time of death.

Admittedly an autopsy can't pinpoint the exact moment when a person stopped breathing—that requires some kind of supporting evidence or additional factors. However, in this instance there is a witness—the father in the room below who heard a noise at that time.

"So Aada would have been in the neighboring room when we believe Charlotte was murdered," Daniel says slowly.

Hanna nods in agreement. "That could be our explanation. If Aada happened to be in the wrong place at the wrong time, and actually saw the killer when he fled from the Silver Suite on Sunday night . . ."

It was just hours after the argument at reception, Daniel thinks.

"Do you know if Aada has anything to do with Paul Lehto?" he asks. "Would Lehto have had access to her work schedule?"

The last time they spoke to Espen Lund, they asked a whole series of questions about Lehto. He hadn't been aware of the quarrel between Lehto and Charlotte, and had reacted strongly to the information.

Now he reacts even more strongly, his eyes full of doubt.

"Do you really think Lehto could be involved in Aada's death?"

"I can't answer that," Hanna says. "But it's unfortunate if Aada witnessed the killer leaving the scene of the crime. He might have decided he needed to get rid of her."

Daniel thinks she could well be right. The consequences of this conclusion are terrifying. He closes his eyes for a second. It says a great deal about the perpetrator's character.

They are dealing with someone who not only kills in a burst of rage, but someone who is sufficiently cold blooded to take other lives if necessary.

He is prepared to kill in order to save his own skin.

62

A knock on the door makes Bengt Hedin glance up from his computer screen. He has been hiding in his office all day, canceling all his meetings and pretending to be busy.

He would have preferred to stay home, but doesn't want to do anything that could be perceived as suspicious. He forced himself to come into work this morning, tried to act like nothing had happened. After that detective showed up yesterday, Bengt feels as if everyone is wondering, even though he did his best to play down the visit over afternoon coffee.

As soon as the cop left, Bengt started googling their powers, checking to see whether they had the right to go through his assets without his knowledge. The legal language was complex and hard to understand, and in the end he gave up, told himself he'd been careful. He hasn't received a Swish transfer, or money paid directly into his personal account. Everything has gone into the family foundation, which Bengt alone administers. The police will never be able to track down that account—they're not that smart.

He still feels uneasy.

He has already done so much to hide his tracks, crossed boundaries in a way that he would never have thought possible.

The adrenaline is coursing through his body, and he is worried about the mass media. They are always on the lookout. The second murder at Copperhill is big news, and the reporters seem to know far more than they should.

Bengt has read every word, breaking out into a cold sweat. How come they have access to so much information? What will he do if they find him?

He runs a sweaty hand through his hair. With every passing day he becomes more and more entangled. It feels like trudging through a bog, with his feet sinking deeper and deeper.

Another knock, and the door opens to reveal his fellow party member Gunilla Nymark.

"Do you have a moment?" she wonders, leaning on the edge of his desk.

Saying no is not an option. Gunilla is vice chair of the party on the council. She has held the post for a long time—he can't afford to arouse her suspicions.

Her watery blue eyes are troubled in her narrow, slightly gaunt face.

"There's a lot of talk about Charlotte Wretlind's Storlien project," she says in a challenging tone of voice. "Some people are saying things might not have been aboveboard. Now that the plans might be put on hold because of the murder, we'd like to revisit the process, make sure everything was done correctly."

Bile surges up from Bengt's stomach as soon as he hears Charlotte's name. The hatred he feels toward her burns his throat.

If she hadn't sought him out, he would never have finished up in this mess. It was her suggestion of "financial compensation" that landed him here. The way she tempted him with more money than he earned in an entire year, if he could just see his way to smoothing the procedure so she could buy the land and secure planning permission.

Bengt, who had served the public sector all his life, deserved his reward—that was how she put it. Why should he say no when everyone else was feathering their nest?

There was absolutely no risk, she assured him. Wasn't it time for him to cash in too?

Charlotte ensnared him with her seductive talk. He felt seen, encouraged. And she was right—he had given up so many evenings and weekends to politics without anyone ever thanking him.

Then everything changed.

There were too many awkward questions, various officials started objecting, and he began to worry about the press conference. What if the truth came out?

He told her he wanted nothing more to do with it. And she had the nerve to threaten him with her fucking text messages. He was devastated.

Now she has gotten what she deserved.

It was her own fault, no one else's.

Gunilla coughs discreetly, and Bengt realizes he was lost in his bitter thoughts.

"The land transfer and the building permission you pushed through don't look good," Gunilla says. "We're going to have to make some kind of comment, possibly issue a press release. Damage control, if you understand what I mean."

Bengt leans back in his chair in an effort to gain a few more seconds of thinking time. This is an absolute disaster; his political career is hanging by a thread.

He needs Gunilla on his side if he is going to survive.

His stomach is churning with anxiety.

His mouth is dry when he speaks.

"What do you want us to do?"

One of the basic rules of politics is deny, deny, deny, but if you grovel enough, you are usually forgiven. Provided you can lay all your cards on the table.

He can't do that. Not even close.

"You need to come up with something," Gunilla says, heading for the door. "By the way, I've read all the documentation—just so you know. It doesn't look good, Bengt. You have to deal with this—do I make myself clear?"

She walks out and closes the door behind her. Bengt stares blankly into space.

How the hell is he going to get out of this?

63

Daniel and Hanna are waiting in the conference room. Espen Lund has gone to fetch Paul Lehto so they can question him at last.

Hanna is getting restless. She can't sit still, and keeps fiddling with her phone.

"We need to press Lehto as hard as we can," she says, pushing back her chair. She goes over to the window, rests her forehead on the glass, and closes her eyes, as if she is trying to gather her strength. Daniel knows exactly how she feels. He is also finding it hard to shake off the oppressive atmosphere after the conversation with Espen.

The more they found out about poor Aada Kuus, the more tragic her death appeared.

"We have no forensic evidence linking Lehto to either of the crime scenes," Daniel points out. "Just information about an argument at reception."

"He's a huntsman, so no doubt he can handle a hunting knife," Hanna counters. "Plus he owns a snow scooter and works at the hotel. We know there was a confrontation between him and Charlotte on Sunday—that's confirmed by two witnesses."

Everything she says is correct, but without concrete evidence it's irrelevant.

"That doesn't necessarily mean he's a murderer," Daniel says.

Hanna sighs loudly, then sits back down again.

"I know, I'm just so frustrated. I can't bear it that another woman is dead. It feels as if it happened right under our noses. What aren't we seeing?"

Daniel wishes he had an answer for her.

The big question is whether the quarrel at reception triggered the first murder. Is it likely that the incident made Paul Lehto so angry that he spontaneously, without any preparations, crept up to the Silver Suite and took the life of the troublesome guest? Then strangled Aada Kuus with her own scarf?

It doesn't sound reasonable, but he has seen other cases where an apparently minor event has led to a disproportionately violent reaction.

Deep human impulses such as anger, hatred, and desire are not always logical.

They can't rule out the possibility that Paul was so incensed that his emotions took over that night. There doesn't seem to have been any previous contact between him and Charlotte, except that she was staying in the hotel where he worked.

There is a knock on the door.

"Come in!"

Daniel recognizes Paul from his passport photo. He is slightly overweight and has dark stubble on his chin, as if he needs to shave twice a day.

"Espen said you wanted to talk to me?"

"We do have a few questions—take a seat."

Hanna fixes him with her gaze. "Why haven't you been at work for the past few days?"

Daniel has no objection to her direct approach. There is no point in pussyfooting around at this stage.

"I was sick." Paul's tone is defensive. "Surely Espen told you that?"

"We've been trying to contact you, but you didn't answer your phone."

Paul shrugs, which irritates Hanna.

"We sent a patrol car to your home, but no one answered the door. How do you explain that?"

"I must have been asleep."

Daniel isn't convinced, but they need more than this to regard him as a suspect.

"We heard that there was a confrontation between you and Charlotte Wretlind on Sunday," he says. "Did you stay home because you were afraid you might be a murder suspect?"

"We have eyewitnesses who were there at the time of the argument," Hanna adds. "What was it about?"

Paul sucks in his lower lip so far that it almost disappears. "Who told you that?"

"That's irrelevant," Daniel replies calmly. "We just want to hear your version of what happened."

"Was it Iris? Is she the one who gossiped?"

"It would be better if you answered the question. This is not about your colleague."

Paul looks furious, but Daniel isn't sure whether his anger is directed at Iris or the two police officers. There is an uncomfortable silence; then Paul inhales audibly through his nose.

"Okay, so Sunday was chaotic. All forms of transport were delayed because of the blizzard in central Sweden, which meant that a large number of guests arrived at the same time. I got them checked in as fast as I could, but it was impossible to please some of them. They took out their frustration on us, as if the bad weather was our fault."

He sounds surprisingly bitter, and Daniel wonders why he works at a hotel if he dislikes the guests so much.

"These rich bastards from Stockholm . . . They don't give a damn. They think they have a right to everything, and they treat the staff however they like just because they can afford to stay in an expensive hotel. As if we're not people too."

Daniel listens to the accent. It sounds as if Paul grew up in the far north of Sweden, maybe in Tornedalen on the border with Finland?

Could that be the explanation behind his contempt for the big city, for the unmistakable anger?

"In the middle of all the chaos that woman showed up and started acting up. She literally tried to push her way to the front of the line. She was complaining about the cleaning and the lack of toilet tissue. I did my best to calm her down, but at the same time it was my job to take care of those who were ahead of her. When I asked her to wait, she got even madder. And then . . ."

"What happened then?" Hanna prompts him.

"A tall vase crashed to the floor. I hadn't put it there, but I got the blame."

He shakes his head, clearly upset by the recollection. He obviously believes he was treated unfairly.

"It was such a mess, and Charlotte Wretlind just kept on. She criticized everything I did, and threatened to speak to my boss. She was crazy, if you ask me."

"So what did you do?"

"Again, I tried to calm her down as best I could. I don't think I actually shouted at her. I might have raised my voice a little, but it was no more than that. It wasn't a 'confrontation' as you put it." He spreads his hands wide. "Iris must have exaggerated. She does that sometimes. I'm afraid she's the kind of person who likes to gossip about her colleagues."

Paul doesn't seem to have any idea that Iris wasn't the only one to report the incident. The original tip-off came from the man in the concierge department. Nor does he appear to be aware of the irony in criticizing Iris for going behind his back while he's busy bad-mouthing her during this interview.

Daniel decides not to bring this up at the moment, but he can see from the skeptical look on Hanna's face that she is thinking along the same lines.

"So what happened after that?"

"The woman became hysterical. It wouldn't surprise me if she was menopausal, the way she behaved. She said I'd regret it and a load of other crap before she stormed off."

His insistence on blaming the argument on Charlotte and his comment on her hormonal cycle doesn't exactly inspire confidence in his account.

"At the time I didn't give it any more thought because I was so busy. It wasn't until the following day when I realized she was the one who'd been murdered during the night that it felt kind of . . . awkward."

"What did you do after the quarrel?" Daniel asks.

"I carried on working."

"So that was the last time you saw Charlotte Wretlind alive?" Hanna clarifies.

"It was, yes."

Hanna chews the end of her pen. "Did you ever enter the Silver Suite while Charlotte was staying there?"

"No, I didn't."

"Are you sure about that?"

"Absolutely."

Paul is sitting with his fists clenched. Is it because he is finding the conversation stressful?

Or is he lying?

"What did you do for the rest of the evening?"

"I finished my shift, got changed, and fetched the car from the parking garage to drive home."

"And what time was that?"

"Let me think . . . I finished around eleven."

"Is there anyone who can confirm what time you arrived home?"

"My wife. You're welcome to speak to her if you like."

"Was she really awake when you got home so late?" Hanna wonders.

Paul doesn't answer. Hanna waits patiently. Eventually he says reluctantly, "Come to think of it, she was asleep."

"So there's no one who can confirm the time you actually arrived back home," Daniel pushes him.

The sun is shining in through the window, water is dripping from the gutter outside, and thousands of snow crystals sparkle in the early spring light. The icicles hanging from the roof are shimmering.

The contrast makes the indoor environment feel even darker and more oppressive.

Hanna changes tack.

"You have a gun license and you hunt. Do you own a hunting knife?"

Daniel thinks of the bloodstained knife they found buried in the snow the previous day. The forensic examination has yet to be completed. If they manage to find just one fingerprint, it will be an enormous step forward.

And if they find any trace of Paul Lehto, that would be the end of the matter.

"I do." The question seems to bother him. "Why?"

"We'll need to see it," Hanna replies.

Paul opens his mouth as if to protest, then closes it again. Hanna makes a note before looking up at him.

"How well did you know Aada Kuus?"

"Who?"

"The cleaner who was found murdered this morning outside the staff-accommodation block."

"There's been another murder?" Paul exclaims.

Daniel tries to read his expression. He seems surprised, but it's hard to tell whether it's genuine, or whether he's simply a talented actor. Daniel has conducted countless interviews, but this guy is unusually difficult to read.

"You don't know who she is?"

Paul shakes his head. The sound of someone vacuuming the corridor can be heard outside the door. "No idea."

"Are you sure?"

"I swear."

His tone is eager, as if he wants to convince everyone in the room, himself included, that he is telling the truth.

"Where were you yesterday evening?" Daniel asks.

"I was at home. In Krok."

"With your wife?"

"Yes—ask her if you don't believe me."

"You were there all evening? You didn't go out at all?"

"I took the dog for a walk—I was gone for maybe half an hour."

Paul brushes away what might be a bead of sweat from his forehead. Daniel would have liked to hand him a napkin, then keep it in order to compare his DNA with the fragmentary traces Carina has collected.

"Do you suspect me of something?" he says hoarsely.

Daniel glances at Hanna. They are reaching the limit of how far they can push him. There is a risk that Paul will call a halt to the interview and demand a lawyer.

"We'd like to take a DNA sample if that's okay." Daniel is careful to keep his tone neutral.

"Why?"

"It's just routine," Hanna explains. "It will help us to rule out your presence in the Silver Suite, where Charlotte Wretlind was found on Monday morning."

Or at the place where Aada's body was discovered today, Daniel thinks.

There is a sudden flash of steel in Paul's eyes. He might be stressed, but he is no fool. He gets to his feet.

"No. I want to speak to a lawyer before I agree to anything."

THEN

December 28, 1973

It is late in the afternoon when Monica is asked to fetch some extra linen tablecloths from the storeroom. She hurries toward the basement, where the laundry is situated, suppressing a little shudder when she sets off down the narrow staircase. It is said that a young girl broke her neck here in the 1950s when someone pushed her down the stairs. Rumor has it that her unhappy spirit still haunts the corridors.

Suddenly a quiet voice calls Monica's name, then the door of the staff bar opens and Sean is standing there. Her eyes widen. What is he doing here?

Before she can ask, he steps forward and draws her to him, pulls her into the room where staff gatherings are held once a week.

Today it is empty and in darkness, with not a soul in sight.

Sean quickly closes the door behind them and turns the key in the lock. Then he pushes Monica up against the grand piano. His mouth seeks hers, his tongue forces its way between her lips, and he kisses her so hard that she can't breathe.

It feels unfamiliar, strange, forbidden. But also . . . wonderful.

"Oh . . ." she murmurs, letting herself be swept along.

Sean tastes of cigarette smoke and tobacco. It is like a dream as he presses himself against her. The kisses stop, and he takes a step back, breathing heavily.

"You drive me crazy," he groans. "I can't bear it, I have to have you."

Monica isn't quite sure what he means, but she doesn't want this moment to end. It's just like in the books she's read. She still can't believe she is capable of evoking such strong desire in such a handsome man.

"What are you doing to me, little girl?" Sean says hoarsely. He cups his hands around her cheeks, studies her face as if he wants to imprint it on his memory forever. "You've cast a spell on me, you know that?"

Then he kisses her roughly. One hand finds its way under her blouse, inside her bra. Monica stiffens, but Sean doesn't notice.

There is a sound from the corridor. She pushes him away. She absolutely must not be caught with a guest—she would lose her job.

"I have to go," she whispers. "Someone might come."

Sean looks so upset that her heart melts with love. This has all happened so fast, but now she understands the situation.

She loves him.

They love each other.

Fate has brought them together. They are meant to be a couple, even though he is married with children.

"I have to see you again," he says quietly. "Soon. I'll come up with something."

Monica nods, adjusts her clothing, and slips out of the room with her heart in her mouth.

64

It is almost three thirty by the time they gather for a briefing at the station.

For once Birgitta Grip is in the conference room when Hanna arrives. The other investigators in Östersund will be participating by video link, but Grip had a meeting with the municipal executive in Järpen about the case, and decided to come to Åre afterward. She is sitting at the top of the table, unbuttoning her thick jacket.

Hanna takes a seat opposite her while they wait for the rest of the team. Daniel is making a quick phone call, Anton has gone to the bathroom, and Raffe is on his way.

"How are you doing?" Grip asks as she removes her jacket.

Hanna has no intention of pretending that everything is fine. She carries with her the sight of Aada's lifeless and abandoned body in the snow. It brings back memories of eighteen-year-old Amanda, who went missing in December just over a year ago.

Seeing a young person die is especially painful.

"Not great," she answers honestly. "It's been a tough day. The fact that another person has been killed feels like a failure. We should have been able to prevent it somehow."

"I understand how you feel," Grip assures her. "You never get used to that kind of crime scene."

Many years of experience are reflected in her deep-set eyes. Hanna sees both sorrow and cynicism, but not a trace of defeatism.

Grip is the kind of police officer who never gives up, even though she has few illusions. She is due to retire in a few years. She is in the age group who really ought to go at sixty-five, but Hanna is hoping her boss will stay on for a few extra years as she is entitled to do.

"I want you to know that you are very much appreciated in the unit," Grip adds unexpectedly, giving Hanna one of her rare smiles. "Your background means you've brought a fresh perspective, which is valuable even for a faithful old servant like me. You're doing a good job, and we're so pleased you came to join us."

Hanna feels her cheeks flush with pleasure.

She isn't used to praise, and has no idea how to handle it—especially when it comes from someone who is known for keeping her distance and focusing on practical matters.

Just as the silence is becoming uncomfortable, Raffe walks in with a big Easter egg filled with candy. The bright colors are slightly jarring in view of the situation, but it's the thought that counts.

"Nilla dropped by with this," he explains, sitting down next to Hanna. At that moment she loves his partner—her body is crying out for something to boost its energy level.

The door opens and Anton comes in, followed by Daniel. The link with Östersund is activated, and Grip puts down her phone.

"It's been a tragic Easter week so far," she begins. "Another murder connected with the hotel. Have the relatives been informed?"

"We've spoken to the police in Estonia," Anton replies. "They haven't been able to find any contact details for family members. It seems as if Aada's father has never been present in her life, and her mother is in a nursing home."

"That's very sad." Grip looks around the table. "Who would like to begin?" She nods to Carina, who has just joined them.

Hanna takes the opportunity to help herself to a handful of candies.

"We've completed our examination of the location where the body was discovered," Carina says. "Unfortunately there wasn't much to go on as it's outdoors. Nor did we find any bodily fluids."

She points to the wall, where photos of the new crime scene have been put up next to the images of Charlotte Wretlind.

"There were no concrete traces of the perpetrator. The snow around the body had already been trampled by the time we got there, and since the road is only about a hundred yards from the location, it seems likely that the killer took that route. In the opposite direction, into the forest, the snow cover was untouched."

Hanna listens and chews. She sees her own disappointment at Carina's sparse information reflected in Daniel's eyes.

"The body is on its way to Umeå for the autopsy," Carina concludes.

"Is it possible to establish where the murder actually took place?" Daniel asks. "There didn't appear to be any signs of a struggle."

"Correct—but you have to bear in mind that Aada Kuus was small and slender, only around five foot four. If we're thinking it's the same perpetrator who murdered Charlotte, and that he is relatively strong, given the ferocity of the stab wounds, then Aada wouldn't have stood a chance. It seems likely that she was killed where she was found—I didn't see anything to suggest that is not the case."

"What about the witness who discovered the body?" Raffe wonders. "It was a dog owner, wasn't it?"

"We spoke to her when we were there," Daniel replies, "but all she'd done was raise the alarm. The dog reacted when they were out for a morning walk, and when they got closer, the owner realized what had happened."

Grip looks thoughtful. "What does it mean that the body was simply left out in the open? The killer made no attempt to hide what he'd done."

There is a logical answer to that question, Hanna thinks.

"Doesn't that indicate that she was a problem for the perpetrator?" she suggests. "Once he'd solved the problem, it didn't matter whether she was found or not."

"It's very bold," Anton says. "Not even hiding his victim."

Paul Lehto's bitter face comes into Hanna's mind. Could he be the one who left Aada Kuus in the snow?

Or is Bengt Hedin involved?

She reports on their conversation with Paul Lehto and their new theory that Aada Kuus might have witnessed Charlotte's murder.

"If we assume she happened to bump into the perpetrator when he was running away from the Silver Suite, then we have a rock-solid motive for wanting her out of the way. And once it was done, presumably the killer was desperate to get away as fast as possible, before anyone saw him."

"What did Aada Kuus say when she was interviewed?" Grip asks. "Didn't she mention seeing something?"

Anton consults a list. "No one spoke to her. It looks as if the officers who are interviewing the hotel staff tried to get a hold of her, but didn't succeed. I don't know why."

"Are there more employees who haven't been questioned yet?" Hanna asks.

Anton nods. "A few."

"We need to make that a priority," Grip says firmly.

Hanna glances at her boss. It feels strange to have her here in Åre instead of on the screen. She has a strong presence even in a remote context, but today she dominates the room. She turns her attention to Hanna and Daniel.

"Do we know when she was last seen alive?"

"It was last night. She worked an extra late shift and finished at midnight. According to the hotel's IT system, her card was used in room

343 at 23:50." Hanna glances at her notes. "The card was used only inside the hotel during Wednesday evening, which means that she never arrived home after work, but was murdered on the way."

"You mean the killer was lying in wait for her outside the staff-accommodation block?" Raffe says.

"Something like that."

"It's not very far," Daniel says. "Only a few hundred yards. If we're dealing with someone who knew what time Aada was due to finish, and where she lived, he could easily have waited for her in the darkness."

Hanna pictures the scene. The girl sets off from the hotel in the middle of the night. She leaves the changing room, walks through the parking garage, and opens the side door, heading for the staff accommodation. Presumably her attention is elsewhere—it's been a long day. She might not even notice her killer until he attacks her.

By then it's too late.

Hanna looks at Daniel, wondering if he feels as frustrated as she does.

"Who would be familiar with Aada's schedule?" Anton asks.

Hanna consults her notes again. "The manager told us there are three cleaning shifts. Anyone who was aware of that would know that she finished at midnight." A scraping noise from outside makes her glance up—it sounds like a snow-clearing machine.

"Let's talk about the MO," Grip says. "A knife was used on the first victim, but Aada was strangled. Could that indicate that we're dealing with two different perpetrators?"

Hanna has also considered this. From a purely hypothetical point of view, two different methods could suggest two different killers, but she finds it difficult to accept this theory. The odds on two murders being committed within such a small geographical area, only a few days apart, are just too long.

There are also similarities. Both murders involved close contact between the killer and the victim, which is less common than you might think. Most people instinctively shy away from killing at close quarters. For example, it is easier to use a gun than your bare hands.

Someone who is capable of stabbing a sleeping woman, not once but over and over again, is probably also capable of strangling a young girl. They have also established that Aada was probably in the room next door when Charlotte was murdered.

"My feeling is that it's the same person," Daniel says before Hanna has time to speak. This isn't the first time they have thought exactly the same, and she gives him an appreciative smile. It's one of the things she likes most about him—the fact that they often reach the same conclusion, even though they might argue passionately along the way.

He shares his thoughts with the group, reflecting exactly what Hanna was thinking. When he has finished, Grip folds her arms and takes a moment to consider.

"I think you're right," she says eventually, making a note on her pad. "Where are we with other aspects of the case? Any more on that Facebook group?"

Hanna briefly reports on what Nadim in IT has found. So far he hasn't gotten back to her on the mysterious IP address based in the council offices in Järpen—she must remember to email him about that.

"If the IP address turns out to belong to Bengt Hedin, that would strengthen our suspicions against him," Anton comments. He gives Hanna a meaningful look, and she nods.

"Our colleagues in Stockholm have checked out the alibi for Charlotte's alleged lover, Stefan Forsberg," Grip reports. "He's spending the week in Skåne with his family, so we can rule him out."

Hanna jots this down. At least that's one less strand to investigate. They can focus all their energy on Paul Lehto and Bengt Hedin.

It sounds as if both men had equally strong motives to want to rid themselves of Charlotte, while poor Aada seems to have lost her life mainly because she got in the way. Although if Hedin was the main perpetrator, he must have had help to get inside the hotel—or maybe he paid someone to carry out both murders?

Everything that has emerged so far, especially the need for a key card, indicates that an employee was responsible.

Could that man be Paul Lehto?

For once Hanna's intuition remains silent.

"What about the financial links between Charlotte Wretlind and the council?" Grip asks. "By the way, I've asked the prosecutor to make a decision on tapping Bengt Hedin's phone, so that should be happening soon."

Raffe looks up. "A couple of interesting things have emerged. If we examine the various transactions in which Charlotte was involved, we can see that substantial sums were transferred to accounts that appear suspect and have no natural link to the Storlien project."

"We could be looking at bribery," Anton adds, "but we'll need to dig deeper in order to connect Hedin to the transfers."

Grip gathers up her papers.

"So let's focus on Hedin and Lehto for the next couple of days, even though it's almost Easter. Keep digging, see if there's any connection between the two men and the victims."

"What about the background checks on the rest of the hotel staff?" Nisse Sundbom pipes up from Östersund. "Are they still urgent, given what you just said about Lehto?"

Needless to say he's nowhere near finished, Hanna thinks.

"Absolutely," Grip snaps. "We need to keep our options open."

"Okay," Nisse replies, his reluctance unmistakable. He doesn't sound as if he intends to work any faster, even though several days have passed already.

Hanna feels her irritation rising. They risk missing important details because of Nisse's laziness. There could be other employees they need to take a closer look at.

They definitely can't ease off at this stage. Quite the reverse.

Because another woman has been murdered.

65

The corridors in the council offices are beginning to fall silent. Bengt Hedin is still sitting at his desk. The sun is setting, and shades of pink and red are reflected in the windows of the building opposite. However, Bengt can feel the black shadows reaching for him.

He rests his chin in his hands as his thoughts go around and around. Everyone is hassling him, even his own party comrades.

What the fuck is he going to do?

His colleagues have gone home to celebrate Easter, but Bengt is still here with his door firmly closed. Tomorrow is a public holiday, as is Monday, so that means four free days in a row. Maybe that will give him some breathing space.

The conversation with Gunilla Nymark was alarming.

If he acts, he knows she will take no further action. However, the party is insisting that he distance himself from the background story of the Storlien project. He needs to come up with a solid and credible explanation for the way Charlotte Wretlind was handled, and why she was given preferential treatment in the planning process.

So that Gunilla will be satisfied and drop the issue.

He has to clean up after himself, erase anything that can link him to Charlotte and her fucking project.

No one should be able to trace the money, but what about the rest? The text messages he was stupid enough to send, the electronic trail we all leave behind us these days.

The police investigation into the murdered women at the hotel . . .

His stomach hurts, a sharp pain that makes his guts contract and sends bile surging up into his throat. He closes his eyes, longs for something that will get him drunk. An anesthetic to make him forget reality for a while.

He has no alcohol at hand, but there are other ways. With a few clicks he is on one of the porn sites he visits regularly.

This time he chooses one of the most hardcore clips, where men do things to women that make them howl with pain.

Bengt's gaze falls on the photograph on his desk, where his wife is smiling back at him. He ought to text, explain that he's working late, but he can't bring himself to do it. She is standing on the cross-country ski track, the sun is shining. It's more than ten years ago, before her hair went gray and she put on thirty pounds.

The last thing he wants is to go home to her constant whining.

Frustration makes him slam his fist down on the armrest. He wishes he had never met Charlotte Wretlind. She deserved to die, no doubt about it. Even though she's finally gone, she is still managing to destroy his life.

Bengt turns up the volume on his computer, he doesn't care if anyone is still around and might hear. The sound of the muscular man whipping the bound woman eases his thoughts.

He enjoys every single blow that lands on her bare skin.

66

The investigation is so intense right now that Daniel shouldn't be setting aside time to see Jovanka, but Hanna's words are ringing in his ears. He wouldn't be able to look her in the eye if he turned down the opportunity to speak to his therapist now she's found a slot for him.

His reaction earlier in the day frightens him. He didn't think that stress would affect him so strongly. Somewhere deep down he was convinced that he had finally learned to control his temper, but that persistent reporter had almost made him lose it completely.

He can't go on like this.

He doesn't want to.

Jovanka smiles warmly at Daniel when he walks into her consulting room at six o'clock in the evening. She is already seated in a gray wing-back armchair, looking relaxed. Opposite her there is an identical chair upholstered in blue, which is where Daniel usually sits.

There is a box of paper tissues on the small table between them. Daniel hopes he won't need them during the next hour.

"How are you feeling today?"

Daniel has learned that this is her standard opening phrase. Progress is always slow at the beginning of each session; it takes a few minutes for the conversation to start flowing.

The first time he came here he said virtually nothing for half an hour.

"Thanks for seeing me at such short notice," he mumbles, then takes a deep breath. "I'm working on the hotel homicide—I'm sure you've read about it. It's very intense. Today another murdered woman was found at Copperhill. My colleague and I had just visited the crime scene when . . ."

He pauses, gathering strength before he gets to the tricky part.

"Something happened. Something I should have handled much better, but it really got to me, and I'd slept very badly. I lay awake for far too long, brooding over childhood memories."

"So what happened?" Jovanka asks in her normal gentle tone.

It goes against the grain to put the incident into words, but eventually he manages to explain how the aggressive journalist, who reminded him so strongly of his father, triggered a wave of rage. How he reached a point where he was on the verge of resorting to violence, even though such a reaction goes against everything he stands for.

He dare not even think what it would have done to his career if he'd crossed the line.

"I understand. How did you feel?"

"It was tough. If my colleague hadn't stepped in, I don't know what I would have done. She was the one who insisted I should contact you."

He can't meet Jovanka's gaze. "I was so ashamed afterward."

There is a brief silence, but it feels okay, as if Jovanka is giving him the chance to come to terms with what he has just told her.

"On Monday we talked about your anger toward your father," she says after a moment. "Your perception that he chose his new family over you. You said he didn't take care of you properly when you went to visit him in Umeå, that you were often mad but didn't dare say anything. You had to hold back your anger."

Daniel doesn't remember exactly what he said, just that it was a challenging hour and that he felt exhausted when he drove away.

"Is there a particular memory you can tell me about, something that's stayed with you?"

Daniel can barely sit still. He feels increasingly ill at ease, he doesn't want to stir up those emotions, it's too painful, too hard to talk about.

The bitterness wakes up, like a writhing snake in the pit of his stomach.

"Try to tell me," Jovanka prompts him. "I think it will help."

He closes his eyes, remembers how unwelcome he felt in Umeå. How relieved he always was when it was time to return home to his mom in Sundsvall, a place where he was secure and loved.

He still has a problem when people talk in glowing terms about stepparents, as if it's a positive.

He has never regarded his stepmother as anything other than his father's wife.

The stepmother from hell.

Jovanka is looking encouragingly at him, and he searches for something concrete to talk about. He really wants to get up and walk out, but that's not an option.

"When my half sister was born," he begins tentatively, "they took my room."

"Your room?"

He pictures his old bedroom in Umeå. It was light and sunny, right next door to the bedroom his father shared with his new wife. But when he came to visit after his half sister's birth, everything had changed. The room had been painted pink, and his bed was gone. It had been replaced by a crib, and there was a white changing table by the window.

All of his toys had disappeared.

"They'd turned my room into a nursery."

"So where were you supposed to sleep?"

"In the attic."

Jovanka raises her eyebrows.

Daniel realizes that the memory still hurts. He will be thirty-eight in September, almost thirty years have passed, but it still hurts. He can't work out if he is embarrassed at his own reaction, or whether this is about his father letting down the little boy he was back then.

"Dad told me to follow him; then he opened the door to the stairs leading up to the attic."

He remembers how steep the staircase was, and how cold, as if the heat in the rest of the house simply couldn't reach that far.

"There were two rooms in the attic. The first was my father's study, but if you went along a narrow corridor, you came to another room, and that was where they'd put my things."

He closes his eyes again, recalling the detail. His father had explained that he was old enough to sleep up here all by himself—as if it were something fun and exciting. Daniel had noticed the dirty window—it was so high up that he couldn't see out.

After a while his father had fallen silent, but he had kept his gaze fixed on his son as if he was waiting for a reaction. A thank-you, perhaps, or a cry of joy over the new furniture from IKEA.

Even though Daniel was so young, he realized that his father was expecting praise.

His heart contracts with the pain. He was only eight years old.

He stood there in front of his father, wanting to ask what he should do if he woke up in the middle of the night and wanted to pee. The corridor leading to the stairs was dark and scary.

But the words stuck in his throat.

He didn't dare to complain.

It was impossible to tell his father that he was afraid to sleep on his own up in the attic. He was angry and upset, but too frightened to explain.

He wet himself on the first night.

"Tell me how you felt at that moment," Jovanka says, bringing him back to the present.

He looks down at his lap. A hard lump has formed in his throat. He glances at the box of tissues, he doesn't want to reach out and take one.

"It's fine, Daniel. This is a safe place. You can say whatever you want when you're with me."

When Daniel opens his mouth he can almost hear the high voice of a little boy.

"I hated him. And her. Both of them. I wished they would die."

"And how do you feel now, after so many years?"

He tries to analyze his emotions. They are complicated and messy, hard to put into words. It feels like a sharp stone deep in his chest.

"What does grown-up Daniel think today?"

"How can someone do that to a child? It was so obvious that they'd chosen their family over me. It was cruel and unfeeling."

Daniel's greatest fear is that he will repeat his father's mistake.

"What if I do something like that to Alice?"

"I don't think you need to worry about that. That's why you're here, to work through your problems, the issues that still affect you today, both personally and at work." Jovanka tilts her head to one side, her expression is warm and understanding. "It's completely natural that you've carried so much rage over what happened, and that you feel deep frustration. You were only a little boy—it's hardly surprising that you didn't dare to show your anger."

She pauses, as if she wants to give him a chance to take a tissue before she goes on.

"Today you are a grown man. No one can do that to you again. You have every right to get mad, but you can decide if and when to do so."

His eyes fill with tears. He manages a wan smile, reaches for a Kleenex.

Something inside him has eased.

He actually feels better.

67

There aren't many people in the grocery store in Duved when Anton rushes in two minutes before they close. He grabs a packet of chicken fillets and root vegetables to make a gratin, along with two cartons of milk.

As he heads for the checkout, he stops dead. It looks as if Carl is standing there paying. He is with another guy who is almost as handsome. In fact they look really good together, both with finely chiseled features and thick fair hair.

It must be his new boyfriend.

Given how good the guy looks, Anton is definitely out of the game. Why would Carl want to be with him when he can have someone like that?

He instinctively moves back behind the display of chips and soda. He absolutely does not want to speak to Carl. They might live in the same small village, but over the past year Anton has managed to avoid him. And yet here he is in the store, only a day after they bumped into each other at the council offices in Järpen.

What cruel game is fate playing with him?

Seconds pass as Anton considers the alternatives. He could put down his basket and sneak out—although that would mean he doesn't get any dinner. Or he can stand here and hide until Carl and his companion have left.

Both options suck.

Cautiously he peeps around the display. To his relief he sees Carl leaving through the glass doors. He doesn't seem to have noticed Anton.

Which is . . . good?

He waits a few seconds before venturing forward. When he has paid and is back on the street, he can't help looking around for Carl.

Needless to say there is no sign of him or his boyfriend. They are probably halfway home by now. Anton feels a stab of disappointment, although he ought to be relieved.

He makes his way to his apartment. His stomach was crying out for food a few minutes ago, but when he walks into the dark hallway, his appetite has disappeared. He goes into the kitchen and puts his purchases on the counter, then simply stands there.

Is this how the rest of his life is going to be?

Shuttling between work and home like a robot with his emotions shut down, because he lacks the courage to be open about what he really feels?

Or for whom?

Suddenly he hates himself for being such a coward. For not taking hold of his life.

He glances toward one of the cupboards, which contains a half-full bottle of vodka. Anton doesn't usually resort to booze to solve his problems, in fact he probably drinks less than most people his age, but this evening it's tempting.

However, he is well aware that he needs to be at the station early tomorrow morning. He can't afford to have a hangover.

After a brief hesitation he goes into the living room and over to the corner where he keeps his saxophones. Music is his true consolation, as it has been ever since he started playing at the community music school as a young boy. That's where he turns when there is nowhere else to go.

How often has he sat here in the semidarkness and lost himself in the melancholy of jazz?

He missed a session with the band on Tuesday because of work. They usually meet up regularly to play together. It is often the highlight of the week, but this time the investigation had to come first; it couldn't be helped.

He picks up the alto sax and slips the strap around his neck, then lets his fingers glide over the shining brass keys. This is his place, the only place he can release all the longing hidden in his heart.

As the melody of "If I Should Lose You" fills the room, he sees Carl's beautiful face before him.

The dream of a different life filters through those muted notes. They paint a picture of what he is longing for, a relationship that seems unattainable.

It's not for him, although he would love to be with someone.

He is so tired of being alone.

68

When Bengt Hedin wakes up, it is dark outside the window. He stretched out on the sofa after spending hours online; he must have fallen asleep. The sound of a text message woke him. From his wife, wondering where he is.

Why doesn't he answer when she calls?

Bengt can barely bring himself to read what she has written. *Stupid bitch*. He is in the middle of the worst crisis of his life, and she wants everything to be as normal.

He puts his phone in his pocket. Why can't she stop nagging? He can't cope with going home. She'll only start asking what's going on, insisting he tell her what's wrong, beg him to talk things through.

She's even suggested he should see a therapist. Ridiculous.

He'd rather sleep at the office, or head for the hunting lodge in Ullådalen. He'll be left in peace there. It's the only place where he can think clearly.

Maybe that's where he should go over Easter in order to formulate a plan?

With a grunt he sits up. The back of his neck cracks; he is sore and stiff, but he is no longer sleepy. He goes over to the desk and opens up the computer.

He brings up the home pages of the evening papers and is immediately confronted with photographs of both Charlotte and that stupid cleaner who got in the way. The more he reads, the angrier he gets. A sob story about Charlotte's son is the final straw. The guy is standing outside Åregården with tears in his eyes, as if he's begging for people's sympathy.

As if he's the one they should feel sorry for.

Bengt wants to tell him to grow up. If there's any justice, he ought to pay for what his fucking mother has done.

He shuts down the page, considers his next move. He's done with the porn sites for today. Instead he opts for Facebook and the Preserve Storlien group. There haven't been many posts over the past few days. He's had neither the time nor the energy to write anything, but suddenly the desire is back.

His fingers fly across the keyboard. He gives vent to his rage and uses cruder and more inflammatory language than ever before.

He empties out his hatred, like a mental bloodletting process.

It is almost intoxicating. And with every vile word, he feels better.

FRIDAY, APRIL 2 GOOD FRIDAY

69

When Hanna logs in on her work computer at seven o'clock on Good Friday morning, she has decided to go through the list of hotel employees who passed through the staff entrance on Sunday. Meticulous care is the name of the game.

Today she is the first to arrive. It's nice to have the place to herself after the intense tempo of the last few days. Tomorrow she is going to Lydia's for Easter lunch—if the case allows, of course.

A tickling sensation in her nose makes her sneeze loudly. Her sweater is covered in cat hairs. Morris, of course. He has continued to sleep in her bed, and she has already gotten used to the comforting feeling of cuddling up with him after a challenging day at work.

No one has come forward yet to say that he belongs to them.

She studies the list. Paul Lehto is there, as is the manager, Espen Lund, and the second victim, Aada Kuus.

Lehto swiped his card at one forty-five on Sunday afternoon. Espen came in at about four, and Aada's arrival was registered at ten to six.

Hanna sips her hot drink from the machine, which consists of milk and coffee in almost equal parts. She has never liked black coffee.

She thinks about the background checks that Nisse in Östersund was supposed to take care of. She doesn't trust him to be thorough, and would really like to check out the employees for herself. However, first of all she needs to go through the forensic reports on yesterday's homicide.

Her phone rings, but she doesn't recognize the number.

"Hi, it's Henry," says the voice in her ear.

Hanna frowns. Why is he calling her at this hour?

"I just want to thank you for your text about the newspaper article yesterday," he goes on. "It's kind of you to think about Filip."

Hanna feels embarrassed. With hindsight it seems over the top to have messaged Henry about the interview—it was done on impulse. Although Filip looks so lost; he needs an adult by his side to support him.

She knows she should keep her distance. As a police officer she isn't supposed to get involved on a personal level, but it's difficult when she sees what a hard time Filip is having.

This isn't the first time she has felt too strongly for the victim of a crime. She does her best to hold back, but the situation often touches her deeply.

"How is he?" she asks.

"Not great. We're all going back to Stockholm together on Sunday."

"I understand."

Hanna's thoughts turn to Aada Kuus. It must have been painful for Filip to hear about another murder at Copperhill so soon after his mother's death.

"It's probably best for Filip to get away from here, from all the reminders of what's happened," she says. "I imagine the latest death must have been hugely upsetting for him."

"It was." There is a pause, then Henry continues. "I'm so grateful for your concern. Not many police officers care so much."

"I'm just trying to do my job."

Hanna glances at the list of reports. She needs to get on with her work.

"How's the investigation going? Do you have a suspect yet?"

Henry should know better than to ask. She can't comment on an ongoing inquiry.

"We're making progress. Thanks for calling. Take care of your godson, and give him my best wishes."

"I will."

Hanna is about to end the call when she changes her mind. "By the way, if you think of anything, any small detail that could be relevant, please contact me."

A couple of hours later her back is aching, and she pushes the mouse away. It is almost ten o'clock, when the team is due to meet for another briefing.

As if by magic Daniel appears in the doorway.

"Ready?" His hair is standing on end as if he has just pulled off his woolen hat. A few snowflakes shimmer in his beard. He is surrounded by an aura of far more energy than the previous day.

Hanna is pleased that he told her about seeing a therapist, that he trusted her with such a sensitive matter.

"I saw my psychologist yesterday," he says without her having to ask. "You were right—I needed to prioritize a visit. Sometimes this pressure is hard to handle. It seems to bring out the worst in me." His smile is both grateful and embarrassed. "I feel so much better now—and that's down to you."

Hanna feels much better too.

70

The hill leading down to the village is so steep that Ida has to hang on tightly to the stroller to stop it careering off, out of control.

It's only a cup of coffee, she tells herself. Nothing else. She isn't doing anything wrong by meeting up with Gustav for half an hour in a café.

Plus Alice needed some fresh air. If she just happens to sit down with a former workmate, there is no harm done.

Daniel isn't home, he left early this morning and probably won't be back until late this evening. The hotel murder is taking up all his time. It was a terrible thing, and Ida sympathizes with the relatives. However, she recognizes the pattern. When Daniel is drawn into a major investigation, nothing else exists. Oddly enough, she doesn't feel remotely irritated this time—in fact it's almost a relief that they are seeing so little of each other.

Especially when her head is full of forbidden thoughts about Gustav.

Ida takes the subway under the E14 and emerges in the square. She turns left past Åregården and the old church. They have decided to meet at the bakery, which is a couple of hundred yards away.

She is there in minutes, but Alice manages to fall asleep in her stroller. Ida is pleased—it somehow feels easier to meet Gustav if she isn't awake.

She manages to get the stroller in through the door and looks around. There are chocolate Easter bunnies lined up on the counter by the till, along with Easter eggs of different sizes. Gustav is already waiting at a corner table by the big windows.

His curly hair is hanging loose over his shoulders. He's so cool. And so attractive.

He is wearing his ski gear, as if he is heading for the slopes afterward—probably with a group of tourists on an Easter break, Ida guesses. She feels a sharp pang of longing. Imagine being so free that you can just take off without having to think about anything else.

Gustav's face lights up when he sees her. He gets to his feet and comes over to help with the stroller as Ida attempts to maneuver her way between the tables.

"Is this your daughter?" he says, bending over Alice. "She's gorgeous!"

Ida is bursting with maternal pride. Alice looks like a little doll, lying there with her rosy cheeks and long eyelashes. She is wearing a cute onesie that Grandma Elisabeth gave her for Christmas.

"She is," Ida agrees, tucking the stroller out of the way so that Alice can go on snuffling happily in her sleep.

They each order a latte, and Ida also goes for a cheese sandwich. She didn't have much breakfast; she was too nervous.

It's only coffee, she tells herself for the hundredth time.

"Are you going out?" she asks with a nod to Gustav's attire.

"Yes. I've got a group doing the peaks in an hour. I'm meeting them at the VM8." He winks at her. "Want to come along?"

Ida spreads her hands apologetically. "It would be tricky with Alice."

"I was just kidding." Gustav laughs, showing his white teeth, then grows serious. "Those hotel murders are a terrible thing—is your partner working on the case?"

The fact that he has asked feels wrong; Ida doesn't want to talk about that.

Or about Daniel.

"Do they have a suspect yet?" Gustav continues.

"It looks as if it's the same killer," Ida murmurs, hoping he will drop it.

Gustav has pushed back the sleeves of his moss-green undershirt revealing a tattoo on one forearm—strange letters that she doesn't recognize.

"What does that say?" she asks, changing the subject.

"It's Nepalese and it means snow. I had it done in a little place in Katmandu."

"Wow—you've been to Nepal?"

"Just before the pandemic hit. Sometimes you have to get away. A group of us went traveling around Asia in the fall of 2019. We also went to Bhutan. It's fantastic—you should go."

Ida nods, although she knows it's never going to happen. Gustav's enthusiasm is infectious, and she is impressed both by his visit to the Himalayas and his tattoo.

She can't imagine Daniel having anything written on his body. He is way too wholesome for that.

"I had to choose between that and 'addicted to snow,'" Gustav explains. "But this feels more authentic."

"It's really cool," Ida says, resisting the urge to reach out and stroke his skin.

"Great minds think alike," he replies with a grin.

They both burst out laughing, and Ida remembers how much fun they used to have. He is almost always in a good mood, doesn't take life too seriously. She was the same when they worked together.

He is the direct opposite of Daniel.

She pushes away thoughts of her partner, ashamed at comparing Gustav to him.

"Fantastic skiing the other day," Gustav adds. "Amazing snow—and you're an amazing skier."

"Seriously—with your skills?"

Ida tries to keep her tone light, even though the tension between them is so strong she can almost touch it. She can't help wondering what it would be like to kiss him. It would be so easy, it would only take a second. They've already done it, long before she met Daniel— back when she could be a little bit drunk, a little bit crazy, and life was a game.

Gustav might have been interested in something more all those years ago, but Ida didn't have time for a relationship.

What would her life look like now if she'd taken that chance?

Alice wouldn't exist.

The thought is almost physically painful. Ida can't imagine life without her. She takes a bite of her sandwich to hide her confusion. They're just chatting over a coffee, she tells herself yet again. Gustav will be leaving in half an hour, and she will go back to the apartment and give Alice her lunch.

This evening Daniel will come home and they will have dinner together.

Then everything will be back to normal.

71

The core team has gathered in the conference room: Daniel, Hanna, Raffe, and Anton. Daniel only just managed to grab a coffee this morning, but for the first time in an eternity he didn't have any bad dreams.

Thanks to Jovanka, no doubt.

The first topic of the day is Paul Lehto. Hanna has just passed on the information about when he used the staff entrance on Sunday.

"Okay, so let's start with checking his alibi," Daniel says. "Then dig into his background to give us a clearer picture. I've nothing against questioning him again—he can bring the lawyer he insisted on."

Hanna nods. "We also need to speak to his wife. I tried to call her both yesterday and this morning, but she didn't pick up."

"Have we heard anything about the autopsy on Aada Kuus?" Raffe asks.

"It's Good Friday," Anton points out.

"I don't think they'll get around to it until next week at the earliest—the Easter break is slowing everything down," Daniel agrees.

Hanna is clearly frustrated. "I don't get why everybody else can have time off while we're sitting here working."

Daniel sighs. "You know how it is."

He shares her view, but it is what it is. Most of their colleagues, those who are not part of the investigating team or are on call, work office hours or a strictly laid-out roster. It's difficult to demand overtime from other units, even when it feels as if the four of them are working round the clock.

Anton raps his knuckles on the desk. "Moving on . . . I've gone through the interviews with the employees who have rooms in the staff-accommodation block."

"Anything interesting?"

"There's a girl from Ljungbyhed who works as a waitress at the hotel. She says she heard the sound of a snow scooter outside the block shortly after midnight on Wednesday."

"A snow scooter," Daniel repeats, rubbing a hand over his beard. He remembers the tracks they found on Wednesday when they were searching with Molly the dog for the weapon that killed Charlotte Wretlind. The clear impressions in the snow, indicating that a scooter had been parked on the edge of the forest.

Now it seems as if the same type of vehicle was also involved in the second killing.

"Aada Kuus should have been on her way home after her late shift at that time," Raffe says.

"That's right," Anton confirms. "And we have evidence to suggest that Charlotte's murderer made his escape by scooter on Sunday. It could be a coincidence . . ."

"Or not," Daniel says dryly.

Paul Lehto could easily have driven home in his car on Wednesday, exactly as he said, then come back on his scooter to strangle an eyewitness who constituted a threat to him.

Hanna's phone buzzes.

"Look what Nadim has found," she says, holding up the screen. "Guess whose IP address is the source of the aggressive comments on Facebook?"

She pauses for effect.

"Bengt Hedin's work computer."

"Why am I not surprised?" Anton says. "There was something very unpleasant about that guy—online hate posts are just about his level."

"A search warrant would be useful so we can access his computer," Raffe suggests.

"It's too soon," Anton objects.

Hanna begins to gather up her papers. "Can you guys take care of that? Daniel—we need to leave now if we're going to get to Storlien on time."

Daniel realizes she is right. They've arranged to visit the mountain hotel, and are meeting the site supervisor. In view of Charlotte's commitment to the project and the hate-filled outpourings on the Facebook page, they want to see the place for themselves.

Hanna has never been there, and Daniel isn't particularly familiar with the location.

"Look out for the evil spirits," Raffe says, half joking and half serious. "They say the old hotel is haunted."

Daniel is taken aback. "What do you mean by that?"

"Surely you know about all the old stories?"

Daniel shakes his head. He doesn't have time for this kind of nonsense.

But Anton, who grew up in Åre, has a wary expression on his face. "It's true. That place gives me the creeps."

72

It's a lovely drive, Hanna thinks as she gazes at the snow-covered forest lining the road to Storlien. It takes about forty-five minutes to travel from the police station along the E14, which continues to the Norwegian border just a few hundred yards farther on.

But Hanna has bad memories from this place.

They recently passed Lake Gev and Tångböle, where the murdered skier Johan Andersson was found by the roadside just over a year ago. The investigation was difficult and upsetting, and ended in tragedy. Hanna still finds it difficult to sleep sometimes because of the outcome, when the fatal shot was fired right in front of her before she could intervene.

It was that incident that made her realize how she felt about Daniel. In the midst of her despair he became her rock. He was there and he didn't let go, in spite of all her tears.

Her phone rings, interrupting her melancholy train of thought. When she checks the display, she sees that Filip Wretlind is calling.

"Hi, Filip—how's it going?"

"Not so good."

She hears him inhale sharply, as if he is suppressing a sob. His voice is shaky.

"Have you seen the article about Mom?"

Hanna doesn't know whether to deny or admit that she has read the wretched piece. She would prefer to say no in order to spare his feelings, but at the same time she doesn't want to lie.

"I have, yes."

"Are they allowed to do that?" He is clearly on the verge of tears. "That woman, the journalist, she twisted everything I said. I didn't put it like that at all, but she's made it sound as if Mom and I fought about my studies all the time—as if Mom didn't care about me. She absolutely did, I know she loved me. It was just that she had too much to do, because she was always working."

Hanna hears a car start up in the background. Filip must be outdoors, maybe he's in the square outside Åregården?

"I wish I'd never agreed to the interview. And I'm not a spoiled brat, as she puts it. I've never been given everything I asked for. I just wanted to tell people how generous Mom was, so they wouldn't think she was only interested in making money." He breaks off with another sob.

"I understand, Filip."

Hanna doesn't know what to say. Daniel is driving fast, the landscape is whizzing by. They have just passed Enafors. The turning for Handöl and Snasahögarna is coming up on the left. They will reach their destination in fifteen minutes.

"I wish there was something I could do," she continues; she can hear how pathetic it sounds. "Unfortunately it's not illegal to write an article like that, even if it is pure crap."

Filip has just lost his mother, and now this.

She tries to think of something that might make him feel better. There is no point in saying that he could report the newspaper to the press ombudsman; at best he would receive a judgment in six to twelve months.

She makes an attempt to console him. "I'm sure not that many people have seen it. Hardly anyone reads the evening papers these days."

"Yes, they do." There is anger in his voice now; he seems less crushed. "Everyone here at Åregården has read it. Lots of people recognize me and come over to comment on the article. Or they're curious and want me to talk about the murder, tell them how I'm feeling."

Hanna has no idea how she can help him. She mumbles a few meaningless phrases, promises to see if there are any measures that can be taken.

"You can always call me if you need to talk," she reminds him before they end the call.

It's been a long time since she felt so inadequate.

73

Shortly afterward Daniel leaves the E14 and negotiates the first roundabout. They have reached Storlien.

To the left lies the huge shopping center that the Norwegians love. They come over to make the most of the exchange rate and differing taxation, spending thousands of kronor on cheap food and drink. There is also a gigantic candy store where the customers use buckets as bags.

"That must be the mountain hotel," Hanna says, pointing to a dark-red building part way up the slope.

Daniel drives toward it. He has never been inside, although he has been here with Ida a few times to go cross-country skiing. He parks outside the entrance, which is in a whitewashed annex.

The whole place looks undeniably dead and abandoned.

Haunted, just like Raffe said.

"Isn't it strange that so many dreams and turbulent emotions are linked to this hotel?" Hanna says from the passenger seat.

Daniel contemplates the building in front of them. It exudes an unexpected air of melancholy, with an unmistakable aura of its long-gone glory days. It doesn't look as if it is waiting to be woken from its slumbers like Sleeping Beauty, but more as if it will never come back to life.

"It's hard to believe this was a renowned establishment back in the day," he says. "It's not even particularly impressive."

"I guess it used to sparkle and shine." Hanna undoes her seatbelt. "But now it's kind of depressing."

She has put Daniel's feelings into words. "Not much glamour left," he says.

"And yet people are furious at the idea that it might disappear. Charlotte definitely stirred up a hornets' nest when she decided she wanted to pull it down."

"Mmm."

Daniel screws up his eyes against the sun. All he can see is a barricaded structure of steel and wood. But two women are dead, and there is a great deal to suggest that this place lies at the heart of the investigation.

How could it mean so much that it led to . . . murder?

74

Anton has spent the morning continuing to go through the interviews with employees who lived in the same block as Aada Kuus.

The matter has top priority.

At the same time, he wants to keep digging into Bengt Hedin's activities. The information that his IP address is behind the abusive posts on Facebook is damning. However, they need a lot more if they are going to be able to prove that Hedin and Paul Lehto, or another member of the hotel staff, are responsible for the two murders.

After some discussion Raffe and Anton have decided not to confront Hedin yet. The text messages and Facebook posts are serious, but insufficient evidence.

It is better to wait and keep an eye on developments, then go in hard.

Hedin has given his wife as his alibi for Sunday night, but Anton doesn't set much store by that. He has spoken to her on the phone, and although she confirmed that her husband had come home, she admitted in the same sentence that she was "probably" asleep by then. Then she said the same again with regard to Wednesday evening.

It sounds exactly like Paul Lehto's statement. He also claimed he was home and that his wife could back him up . . . although she was asleep.

Anton tries to focus on the screen, but his concentration is poor. Forbidden thoughts come creeping in.

Thoughts of Carl.

An idea has begun to take shape.

Maybe he could contact Carl to find out more about Hedin? After all, they work for the same employer, in the same building. With a bit of luck, Carl might have heard or seen something that would help Anton to move forward.

It would be perfectly reasonable for him to contact Carl and ask that question; it wouldn't be awkward at all.

On some level Anton knows that he is grasping at straws, searching for a reason to call Carl, but it doesn't matter. As long as he is doing it in the line of duty, no one can say anything. Least of all Carl, who knows that Anton is working on a case that involves the council, since they bumped into each other in Järpen.

Even though Anton suspects that Carl has a boyfriend, he longs for him.

He can allow himself a brief phone call. As long as he doesn't get his hopes up.

He picks up his phone and scrolls down to Carl's number. Weighs the phone in his hand, with butterflies in his tummy.

Then he takes a deep breath and makes the call.

75

Hanna opens her car door. "Shall we go in?"

A man in dungarees waves to them as they get out. This must be Leffe, the site supervisor who is going to show them around. He looks as if he's close to retirement age; gray hair is peeping out from beneath his dark-blue cap, which is pulled well down over his ears.

"Are you from the police?" he calls out.

Hanna nods and Leffe points to a side door with a frosted pane of glass, about fifteen yards from what they had assumed was the entrance.

"We can go in this way. The main door isn't used anymore, to keep the heat in."

Leffe leads them into what was once the foyer, and presses a button to switch on the lights. They are standing in front of a wooden staircase with skillfully carved banisters and a dark-red carpet held in place by brass stair rods.

Hanna can almost see the guests from bygone days sweeping past in their beautiful clothes, delicate cocktail glasses in their hands.

"At least it looks better on the inside," Daniel says quietly in her ear.

Leffe leads them into the dining room on the first floor, then up another staircase to what is known as the Loft. He explains that dances were held here, to live music. There is a podium at one end for the band. In the opposite direction, up a few more steps, is the famous bar with its elegant black counter and tall cane-backed stools. Small groups of chairs made of dark wood with distressed gilding are arranged to make the most of the fantastic view.

"This is where the guests would have their coffee and cognac after dinner," Leffe tells them nostalgically.

Hanna stops dead in front of the window.

Unlike Åre, which is located on the side of a mountain, giving almost every building a view of the lake, this hotel has the sweeping panorama of the mountains as its focus. The landscape is less steep, with sparse vegetation; it is the white mountain birch that catch the eye, extending all the way to the Norwegian border, which can just be seen to the west.

This is just on the tree line; only a short distance away, the bare mountains await.

"It's very peaceful," Daniel says, gesturing toward the view before them.

Hanna agrees. It is easy to let your eyes rest on the gentle slopes, to lose yourself in all the whiteness.

"Are these the old ceiling paintings that everyone seems to be so upset about?" Daniel asks. Like Hanna he has seen the Facebook posts where members express their anger at the fact that the fine works of art will not be preserved if the building is demolished.

Hanna takes a closer look. They really are striking, colorful and imaginative. The ceiling is covered with various animals—reindeer, moose, and dogs. There are also Viking longboats, and native Inuit and Sámi figures in traditional dress.

"They are," Leffe confirms. "The whole lot will disappear if the plans go through."

"Don't you think some of the comments from the Facebook group have been unnecessarily aggressive?" Hanna wonders.

Leffe looks uncomfortable. He adjusts a barstool that isn't quite straight and pushes it a couple of inches farther in.

"They exaggerate," he says eventually. "But the hotel has stood for such a long time. It was built in the 1930s. The paintings have been here for generations."

He looks up to where a vivid sunset adorns the ceiling above the bar. "Just because something is new, that doesn't necessarily mean it's good," he murmurs.

"Do you know anyone in the group?" Hanna asks. "I've read some of the comments, and they're pretty graphic. The kind of thing that could be classed as making illegal threats."

Her question makes Leffe shift his weight from one foot to the other. He pushes his hands deep in his pockets and refuses to meet her gaze.

"I might know the odd person who could be a member, but . . ."

"Are you a member?" Daniel asks.

Leffe shakes his head in a way that makes Hanna suspect he might well be responsible for some of the posts.

She looks up again. The works of art really do have a unique charm, embodying times gone by and Scandinavian history.

But that is not a reason to resort to violence and murder.

THEN

DECEMBER 30, 1973

Monica has locked herself in the toilet for a few minutes' peace. A shiver runs through her whole body when she thinks about the note she received at breakfast time today.

Sean discreetly slipped it into her hand. Her heart pounds as she reads it again.

MEET ME TOMORROW AT 2 PM. ROOM 505

She has been walking on air ever since their encounter the other day; she can't think about anything but him.

He loves her and she loves him.

It is snowing outside the window, featherlight flakes dancing in the air. It is almost two o'clock, the temperature is still below freezing, but almost all the guests have gone skiing today.

Monica presses the note to her lips. She thinks she can just pick up a faint, lingering trace of Sean's aftershave.

She lay awake all night, imagining their future together.

She thinks she knows why he wants to meet her alone—he is going to tell her that she is the one he wants to be with, that he has spoken to his wife and is going to divorce her for Monica's sake.

She ought to be ashamed of wrecking their marriage, but her blood is fizzing with excitement.

At last she is going to start her new life, get away from this place, and discover the world.

Sean will give her a different existence, he will buy her jewelry and fine clothes. She will live in Stockholm, and never again will her parents be able to tell her what to do or say.

Time is flying by. Monica unlocks the door and leaves the staff toilet. She washes her hands meticulously and hurries out with her head full of dreams.

All of her deepest wishes are going to come true.

She is the happiest woman on earth.

The farther they go into the empty hotel, the more desolate it feels.

Hanna's footsteps make the floorboards creak. The four annexes are connected to the main building by dimly lit corridors that seem endless. Without Leffe as her guide, she would have gotten lost long ago.

She plods along after him. Daniel has excused himself to take a phone call, and is still in the main building.

Leffe opens a door to something that was once a family room. Hanna sees a green table, two green armchairs, and two single beds with green valances. The beds are at an angle, and above them are two rectangular cupboards in the same alarming shade of green. When Leffe tugs at one of them, another bed flips out from the wall.

It reminds Hanna of old-fashioned sleeping cars on overnight trains, where the bunks can be folded away when not in use. It feels simple, not especially exclusive, but then again things were probably different back then.

"This is the bathroom," Leffe says, opening another door to reveal a mustard-yellow bath and black-tiled walls. The handbasin is cracked, and Leffe advises Hanna not to lift the toilet lid.

He sighs. "It needs a major renovation. I think there's asbestos in the walls too, but I still don't know if it's necessary to tear the whole lot down."

They leave the family room and make their way up a couple of steps and into another corridor. Leffe stops and points to a room with the number 712 on the doorframe.

"The cleaners never dared to go in here alone."

Hanna can't work out if he's joking or not, but his tone suggests the latter.

"They always insisted on having company. One of them used to take her husband along when it was her turn. He would sit on a chair in the room while she did the cleaning."

"You mean it's haunted?"

Hanna wants to shrug off the story, but nothing in Leffe's voice suggests that he is kidding.

It feels a little uncomfortable, especially when she remembers what Raffe said before they left the station.

"Like I said—no one would go into room 712 alone."

They continue along another corridor and stop at a metal door. Leffe opens it a fraction and points to a worn stone staircase where the white paint is flaking badly.

"This leads to what used to be the staff bar, down in the cellar." He pauses, glances into the darkness.

"They say that a young girl was pushed down these stairs after the war. She broke her neck in the fall."

This new tale makes the hairs on Hanna's arms stand on end. What kind of place is this?

"So she died?"

"I'm afraid so." Leffe hesitates. "But it seems as if she stayed around somehow. I've been down there and felt that . . . it wasn't a good idea to go in."

Hanna doesn't know what to think. She has never been particularly superstitious; she doesn't believe in ghosts or angels. But looking at Leffe's lined face, his chin and cheeks covered in stubble, he seems totally serious.

He tugs at the straps of his blue dungarees. "I had the dog with me once, and he refused to go in with me. In the end I left."

He lets go of the door, and it closes with a protracted squeak.

"Do you know the name of the girl who died?"

Leffe shakes his head. "It was long before my time—I was born in 1958."

"How long have you worked here?"

"Since the seventies." He smiles, looking slightly embarrassed. "That's practically my whole life. I'm due to retire soon. I started out changing light bulbs, that was all I did at first."

Hanna runs her finger down the wall. The surface is a little rough, and there is a patch of damp in the corner. She can hear the sound of a dripping tap nearby. Leffe's stories have made her both curious and ill at ease.

"Has anything else of note happened at the hotel? Any kind of crime?"

"Why?"

"I just wondered."

Leffe has turned and set off back the way they came. Shadows dance over the scruffy walls.

"There was something in the early seventies," he says over his shoulder. "A young waitress was assaulted. I think it was Christmas '73, shortly after I came to work here."

"So what happened?"

"People said she'd been flirting too much with one of the guests, sending out the wrong signals, if you know what I mean. Then . . . well, you can imagine."

Leffe falls silent. When he speaks again, his voice is so quiet that Hanna can barely make out the words. "I guess the general view was that she had only herself to blame."

It's not surprising. In those days rape investigations rarely focused on the perpetrator or his behavior; instead all the blame was put on the victim. Police interviews were mainly about what the woman had been wearing, whether it was provocative or too daring. The police fixated on the victim's demeanor, and whether she had a history of multiple sexual encounters.

Had that young woman really said no in a way that made the rapist understand that she didn't want to have sex with him?

"If you know what I mean?" Leffe adds again, over his shoulder.

Hanna knows exactly what he means, and then some. She herself was raped many years ago, and didn't report her attacker. She couldn't face going to the police and being questioned. Or having her reputation trashed in court.

With hindsight, she thinks that was the wrong decision. She should have reported him, stood up for herself. However, she was young, only twenty-one, and the man was her middle-aged boss at the bar where she worked in Barcelona. It was Lydia who flew down and brought her home, made sure she got help to deal with the shock and trauma.

It was after that incident that she decided to train as a police officer.

"Did the case go to court?" she asks. "What happened in the end?"

Leffe stops with one hand on the banister.

"I can't remember. I think she got fired. The whole story was hushed up."

"Was it someone you knew?"

"Not directly. I was just a spotty kid changing light bulbs and so on, like I said. I went around in dungarees all day, and she was really cute, small and dainty, with kohl round her eyes and beautiful long hair with a center parting. That was the fashion in those days." He gives a melancholy little laugh. "She never even looked in my direction."

They have reached another staircase. The carpet is badly worn and frayed. Leffe takes a few steps, then stops again and turns around. His voice is full of sorrow when he adds, "I think it ruined her life."

77

Anton is in the men's toilets staring at his own reflection in the mirror. He feels so stupid for having contacted Carl. First of all it took him forever to gather the strength even to make the call. Then . . . nothing. It went straight to voicemail, and instead of leaving a message, he hung up.

His courage failed when it came to the crunch. He's going to have to look elsewhere for information on Bengt Hedin.

It is so frustrating. He splashes his face with cold water and shakes his head. There is no point in daring to dream. He ought to know better.

He switches off the light and closes the door. The corridor is silent and deserted. Raffe went home to Nilla a while ago, and Hanna and Daniel aren't back from Storlien yet.

As he walks into his office, his phone rings. The name on the display makes his heart flutter.

Carl.

He's not sure if he can manage to press the symbol to accept the call. He had just come to terms with the decision not to make any further attempts to establish contact. Just hearing Carl's voice on the answering service had made him go weak at the knees.

And at the same time, the feelings of shame came flooding back, the realization that he had thrown away their burgeoning relationship last year.

He has to answer.

"Anton."

"Hi, it's Carl—I think you called me?"

At first Anton is confused, he didn't leave a message. Then he realizes that of course Carl can see he's had a missed call.

And from whom.

He could blame it on a butt-dial. Or mumble something noncommittal and hang up.

Carl has moved on; Anton has seen it with his own eyes. He doesn't need to torture himself like this.

"Was there something you wanted?" Carl wonders.

The warm voice unlocks something within Anton. Carl sounds exactly like he did when they were together, when they lay chatting in the double bed before they fell asleep.

All thoughts of ending the conversation disappear, as does the original excuse of wanting to ask about Bengt Hedin and his work for the council.

The truth is perfectly simple.

He wants to be with Carl.

"I was wondering if we could meet," he says, his voice rough with emotion. "There's something I need to talk to you about."

78

It is five o'clock by the time Hanna gets back to the station. She is sitting at her desk with a pile of candy, and has just gotten hold of Paul Lehto's wife on the phone to double-check his alibi when he was "sick." The wife confirmed the information her husband had given—he didn't feel well after the weekend and had to stay home for a few days. She also repeated what she said earlier: that he was at home on both Sunday and Wednesday night at the times when the two women were attacked.

Hanna made notes and thanked her before ending the call.

The problem is that she doesn't know how much she can rely on Lehto's alibi. Many women would lie to protect their partner, especially in a case like this.

She has already gone through his background and checked all the databases to see if he has a record. Apart from the drunk-driving fine, there is nothing of note, nothing to suggest that he could be a killer.

She suddenly has an idea. She could try the K-archive in Östersund, where all crime investigations and police reports in the county are stored, everything that has ever come in to the police about an individual. The law decrees that information must be deleted from the databases after a fixed period—but it remains in the K-archive forever.

It is late on Good Friday, so it's unlikely that anyone will be there, but it's worth a shot.

She keys in the number and crosses her fingers. She is in luck—an administrator by the name of Cilla is still working. Hanna quickly gives her Paul Lehto's ID number and asks Cilla to see if there is anything in the archive.

Ten minutes later the phone rings.

"Hi," Cilla says. "I have actually found something that probably isn't in the system any longer."

She gives Hanna a quick summary and sends the information over. When the email arrives, Hanna has to read it twice. Nisse should have tracked this down days ago, but of course he couldn't be bothered. This is exactly what she was afraid of.

She prints out the document and goes along to Daniel's office. He is totally absorbed in something on his screen and doesn't even notice that she is standing in the doorway until she knocks on the frame.

"Have you seen this?" She hands over the sheet of paper and he quickly glances through it.

"Interesting."

Hanna sits down in the visitor's chair and stretches her legs in front of her.

"You could say that. So now we know that Paul Lehto is in the habit of coming into conflict with women."

She takes back the sheet of paper. Sixteen years ago, Paul Lehto harassed his ex-wife to such an extent that he became the subject of a so-called extended no-contact order. In other words, he was banned from visiting or even being in the vicinity of her home, workplace, or a series of other locations where she spent time.

Such an order is not granted without good reason.

Lehto must have behaved very badly toward his ex.

Needless to say, he has failed to mention this to the police. He probably hasn't told his employer either. It's not exactly something you would want to include on your résumé.

"Did he have to wear an electronic tag?" Daniel asks.

Hanna skims the text. If a previous no-contact order has been breached, then the law allows monitoring in the form of an ankle tag. Admittedly this doesn't stop the perpetrator from sending hundreds of messages or otherwise hassling the victim through social media, which often happens. However, it does constitute a physical deterrent from hanging around near the person who needs protection.

"Doesn't look like it."

Hanna thinks she knows why. The law on no contact has been tightened on several occasions. Sixteen years ago, it was relatively toothless. Electronic tags were much less common back then.

She glances toward the conference room across the corridor, where the pictures of the two murder victims are up on the wall.

A man who can harass his ex-wife to such an extent could easily turn on other women.

This new information indicates misogyny, a history of treating women badly.

So what is the situation with his current wife? Has he abused her, physically or mentally?

Statistics show that violent behavior is repeated; it's not that easy to break the pattern. The value of Lehto's alibi has been undermined. It is not impossible that his current wife didn't dare to say anything other than what he had told her to say.

Daniel spins around on his chair, which squeaks as usual. "No reports of abuse filed against Lehto?"

"Nothing like that, just the no-contact order."

This doesn't necessarily mean that Lehto didn't resort to violence during his first marriage. It could well be that his ex didn't have the courage to report him.

Hanna tries to avoid jumping to conclusions about violent men, but she has seen so many similar cases. She knows far too many exhausted women who have given up the battle to have their abuser brought to justice. Simply securing a no-contact order requires a great deal of strength from a woman in a destructive relationship. Going on to take part in a court case, with all that involves in terms of witness statements, cross-examination, and a defense attorney who questions every detail can be a superhuman task, even with the support of a complainant's counsel.

She knows this herself from bitter experience.

"So what do we do with this? Should we confront him?"

Daniel gives himself time to think. Hanna is very familiar with his expression—slightly turned in on himself, absentmindedly scratching one thumb.

"We wait," he says eventually. "We still haven't managed to establish a clear link between him and Charlotte Wretlind—something that could explain exactly what happened on Sunday. We also need evidence of a connection between Lehto and Hedin if we're going with the theory on some kind of collaboration."

"Anton and Raffe are working on that," Hanna replies, just as she is overwhelmed by a yawn. It has been yet another long day. She is starting to feel tired, even though she has no intention of giving up just yet.

Daniel glances up at the clock on the wall. "I have to go. I promised Ida I'd be home early today. She won't be happy if I'm late for dinner."

He pulls on his jacket. "You ought to go home too. We haven't stopped all day."

"I'm fine."

He gives her an apologetic smile.

"It's not easy for Ida—she has no idea what it's like to be a police officer. How a case kind of swallows you up."

Hanna focuses on her papers. "It's fine," she says without looking at him. "It is Good Friday after all."

Then she tries to muster up an understanding smile, even though she hates the fact that he is leaving, going home because of Ida and Alice. She hates it when he blames his family and complains to her.

It would be better if he simply said it was time to finish for the day. She doesn't want to be treated like a sympathetic colleague.

It makes her feel so lonely.

A failed singleton who has nothing better to do than work over a holiday.

79

When Filip emerges from Åregården, a man in a gray jacket is standing across the street, smoking.

The sight makes Filip want a cigarette, even though he has promised Emily that he will cut down.

They are on their way to Supper for dinner. She has booked a table in an attempt to distract him from that awful article on his mom. He has spent all day holed up in his room, driving himself crazy with rage and shame.

That journalist certainly had him fooled. He has made a fool of himself, and is thoroughly embarrassed. Worst of all, people are going to believe terrible things about his mom. And he is the one who helped paint that picture. He is finding it hard to forgive himself. He has been so naive, there is no excuse.

"Wait!" Emily calls out from the main entrance as she tries to catch up with him on the slippery street. "Don't go so fast!"

He slows down and puts his arm around her, kisses her forehead. They have been together since high school, and he loves her so much. Her family is like his family now; he has stayed over at her house countless times.

Her parents are still married, and no one talks about money or business at the dinner table. Her mother is a math teacher, and her father works in vocational training.

"I don't know how you put up with me," he says, kissing her again.

Emily smiles, and for a moment everything seems the same as usual. The world goes away. He stops and kisses her in the middle of the street; he just wants to hide in her arms and forget what has happened over the past few days.

A car sounds its horn, and they jump up onto the sidewalk, hand in hand.

When they turn into Mörviksvägen, he sees a dark figure out of the corner of his eye, doing the same. He looks a bit like the guy who was smoking outside Åregården just now.

It's almost as if he is following them.

Filip glances over his shoulder, but the man is gone. It's probably a journalist, wanting to ask more intrusive questions.

"Let's go," he says to Emily, increasing his speed.

He has no intention of letting some other bastard get a hold of him.

80

Morris hurls himself at Hanna as soon as she walks through the door, yowling so reproachfully that she feels guilty, even though she knows that Lydia and the kids stopped by earlier in the day to feed him. The children have no objection to playing with Aunt Hanna's new cat—they love visiting Morris.

She picks him up, whispering apologies. Her head is full of thoughts of the investigation, a snake pit of speculation about Hedin, Lehto, and the murdered women. It's all connected, but she can't see a clear pattern.

She carries Morris into the living room and sinks down onto the sofa so that he can settle on her chest, his favorite spot. He really does weigh a ton, but he can stay there for ten minutes before she fixes something to eat.

For some reason the trip to Storlien comes into her mind. Something feels wrong, but she can't work out why.

Just before they got in the car to leave, Leffe showed them some old photos from the sixties and seventies. It looked like a completely different world, with women in long gowns and men in dark smoking jackets.

However, judging by his stories, things weren't quite as charming beneath the surface. One woman with a broken neck; another who was raped and had her life ruined.

The treatment of the waitress sounded very familiar to Hanna.

But how can rape ever be the woman's fault?

She scratches Morris under his chin, gray and white cat hairs flying in all directions. There is no point in getting angry over an assault that took place fifty years ago. She needs to put all her energy into the current case, nothing else.

The cat stretches his neck so that she can get at him properly; he is loving the attention.

"Good boy," she murmurs.

Tiredness and the warmth of Morris's body almost make her fall asleep. When her phone rings in her back pocket, she would love to ignore it. She's exhausted, and it's almost eight o'clock.

Then again, it could be someone from work. Her sense of duty takes over.

"Hello?"

"Hi, Hanna."

The familiarity makes her unsure. At first she doesn't recognize the voice; then she realizes who it must be.

Henry Sylvester.

Is there a problem with Filip?

"Is Filip okay? Has something happened?"

"He's fine—that's not why I'm calling."

"Oh?"

Hanna doesn't understand. She tries to move Morris so she can sit up. In return she gets a pained look and a sharp claw in her stomach.

"It feels as if we have more to talk about," Henry says. "I'm wondering if you have time to meet?"

She is even more confused about what Henry wants. When she and Daniel went to see him earlier in the week, the conversation came to an abrupt end. He shut down with no warning. Hanna assumed it was because he was grieving for Charlotte, but now he seems to have changed his mind.

"What do you want to talk about?"

"If you come over to the Villa, I'll explain."

"Now?"

"Are you busy?"

Hanna glances at her watch. Admittedly she has no plans; all she had intended to do this evening was have something to eat, then go to bed. She has to be back at the station early tomorrow morning. The Easter lunch with Lydia is still up in the air.

"I think it's best if we do this face-to-face," Henry adds. He pauses, as if he is deliberately trying to arouse her curiosity.

Maybe he knows something about the rape at the mountain hotel? It sounded as if it might have happened during the years when his and Charlotte's families celebrated Christmas there.

She would really like to ask him a few questions about that.

"If you're interested in finding out more about Charlotte's business affairs, that is. Otherwise, we can leave it," Henry goes on slowly. "It's up to you."

81

Tiina is curled up on the sofa in the living room, trying not to cry. Ogge has disappeared; he isn't answering his phone, and she has no idea where he is.

Zelda comes over and lays her head on Tiina's knee—she is a clever dog, and knows that something is wrong. Tiina buries her face in Zelda's soft fur and lets the tears come.

After a long time she gets up and fetches some paper towels to blow her nose. She catches a glimpse of her tearstained face reflected in the refrigerator door. She looks terrible; her eyes are red and swollen.

It's hardly surprising that Ogge has found someone else.

She stares at the pot of daffodils on the table. Today is Good Friday, the day Jesus died on the cross to redeem the sins of man. Where she grew up it was a day of sorrow; you went to church, spent the time in quiet contemplation. It is many years since she did any of that. Ogge thinks it is nonsense, but Tiina remembers the kindly priest from her home village.

An idea sparks in her mind. She takes out her phone, googles "duty priest," and discovers that you can call 112 to make contact.

Dare she do it?

Who else is she going to talk to?

She looks around the kitchen, where Ogge's plate lies unused. He hasn't even sent her a text.

With trembling fingers she keys in the number and explains why she is calling. A man with a west coast accent answers after a few rings. He introduces himself as Roger, and tells her that he is a priest in Gothenburg.

Tiina bites the inside of her cheek in order to keep control.

"I'm happy to listen if you want to share whatever is troubling you," Roger says.

He sounds nice. Tiina takes courage and tells him about Ogge, how strangely he has been behaving recently. How his difficult background seems to be making him feel worse and worse, yet he refuses to seek help even though she has begged him to talk to someone.

It's hardly surprising that he feels bad. His mother took her own life in a long-drawn-out way, drinking herself to death before he turned twelve. He was placed in foster care, and life became sheer hell. On his eighteenth birthday, his foster parents threw him out on the street and told him to make his own way in life.

On many occasions when Tiina has been disappointed and has despaired of their relationship, she has thought about how wretched that must have been.

A young boy, left all alone in the world.

The priest listens, now and again he tentatively asks a brief question. Soon an hour has passed. Everything Tiina has been carrying inside her comes pouring out. The fact that Ogge came home long after midnight two days ago. She thinks he is cheating on her with another woman; he is bitter and nasty all the time. She talks about the way his drinking is escalating, how aggressive he becomes when he drinks.

It is as if he can't get over what happened to him during his childhood, as if all those horrible memories are coming to the surface again. He sits in front of the TV, making scornful comments on anything to do with father-and-son relationships. Shows about adopted children seeking their birth parents make him snort with derision.

"What can I do to make him feel better?" Tiina asks the priest.

She has seen the scars on his back from the worst beatings; she understands that this is a lifelong trauma. He also carries a huge burden of guilt over his mother's death, as if that were his fault too.

It has made him hard.

It also made him reach a decision: never to become a father himself.

Tiina would have loved to have a child with him; she often dreamed of it at the beginning, but Ogge made it very clear early on that he was never going to change his mind.

With hindsight she has often thought that she should have insisted. If Ogge had had a child of his own, then maybe he would have been able to leave his damaged upbringing behind. It would have been a fresh start, a chance to focus on the future instead of being trapped in the past.

Old mistakes don't have to be repeated.

Tiina lets out a sob; it's all so hopeless. She loves him, but she can't get through to him. And now it's too late. Ogge is in the process of leaving her for someone else.

"He's had such a difficult life," she tells Roger.

Of course Ogge is unpleasant sometimes, she thinks. He has had so many terrible experiences. Maybe that's why he's started seeing another woman—the angst has to come out somehow.

"This might be difficult to accept, Tiina, but I wonder if you're familiar with the term *codependency*?"

"What do you mean?"

She has heard the term, but doesn't really understand it.

"If you live with a person who abuses drugs or alcohol, it's easy to become codependent," Roger explains. "Some typical consequences are low self-esteem and a negative self-image. You get used to constantly fitting in with the other person's behavior. It's hard to set boundaries within the relationship." He pauses, as if to let the words sink in. "Does any of that sound familiar?"

Tiina stares into space. What is he trying to say? She has confided all her deepest secrets, and now Roger thinks it's her fault that Ogge feels bad.

"Tiina?"

She feels so let down. The tears begin to flow.

No one is on her side.

"I have to go," she mumbles, ending the call.

82

Daniel is tidying up after Alice in the living room, well aware that he should have stayed at the station and carried on working on the investigation. Instead he is picking up one brightly colored toy after another and placing them in a red plastic box.

Ida is sitting on the sofa, chatting to a friend on her iPad while the evening news is on TV.

"And now to the murders in Åre, where another woman was found dead yesterday," the news anchor announces.

Daniel looks up and sees images of Copperhill and the gray staff-accommodation block. The camera pans over the police cars, the cordon, and the curious onlookers. At least there is no sign of that idiotic reporter he almost punched.

Ida has put down her tablet and is listening to the item.

A male voice informs viewers that the latest victim was strangled, and that the police have not yet released the name of the woman. However, it is clear that this second murder is linked to what happened a few days ago.

Daniel frowns. How can they know that? As far as he is aware, the police have neither confirmed nor denied the connection.

"Who was murdered this time?" Ida wants to know.

"I can't tell you."

They have been through this discussion many times. Ida often asks about his work, and Daniel always has to say that he can't share information about an ongoing investigation. He has already said too much—yesterday he happened to mention that they are probably looking for the same killer.

"Sorry."

Ida gives a strained smile, and Daniel feels guilty for knocking her back. He gets up and goes to sit beside her on the sofa.

"You know how it is with a case like this . . ."

"Yeah, yeah. Confidentiality."

He puts his arm around her, gently nuzzles her cheek where the scent of her moisturizer lingers. A strand of hair has fallen over her forehead, and he pushes it back with his index finger.

Even though it has been a long and stressful day, he feels the excitement beginning to spread through his body. It seems like forever since they made love. There is always so much that gets in the way; they are both tired after work, and of course Alice takes up so much of their time and energy. She often ends up sleeping in their bed when she wakes up and cries during the night.

He once heard a colleague say that children are an excellent contraceptive, and he was right.

He glances cautiously at Ida to see if she is interested. She is hard to read today; she is barely reacting to his advances. She remains motionless, neither pushing him away nor responding positively.

Only when he tries to kiss her does he realize it's not happening.

"I'm on my period," she mumbles, sliding out of his embrace. She disappears into the bathroom, and Daniel hears her lock the door.

The sense of rejection is physically painful.

She doesn't want him.

83

Filip's desire for a cigarette comes rushing back when the waiter at Supper removes their plates after the meal.

He and Emily are sitting at a corner table, Filip with his back to the other diners. It feels like everyone knows who he is after that disgusting article. He avoids eye contact as much as possible, tries to concentrate on Emily so that the persecution mania won't take over.

"That was delicious, wasn't it?" she says, placing her hand over his. "Especially the sweet potato fries and the chili chocolate."

Filip gives her a grateful smile. He hasn't had much of an appetite over the past few days. Every bite of food seemed to grow in his mouth; it all tasted of mud. But Emily has made an effort for his sake, tried to ensure that he had a pleasant evening. She wants him to feel better, to think about something other than his mother's terrible death just for a little while.

The intense longing for a cigarette is growing stronger. He touches the pocket of his jeans where he has half a pack hidden away.

"Do you mind if I go out for a breath of fresh air?" he says.

It's better not to come out and say he's going for a cigarette. Emily doesn't like him smoking.

She sighs loudly, but doesn't object. "Okay, I'll order coffee. Do you want another drink?"

He has had only one beer all evening; he doesn't really want any more booze.

"No, I'm fine," he says, getting to his feet.

Twilight is falling when he steps onto the veranda outside the restaurant. In fact it is almost dark as he positions himself around the corner, out of the way, so that the smoke won't disturb anyone else. There is a notice asking guests not to smoke by the doors.

He lights up and takes a deep drag. It tastes good. At that moment he hears footsteps behind him, but he doesn't look up. He doesn't want to risk encountering yet another prying journalist asking stupid questions.

Henry called to console him, said the article is irrelevant. Today's news is tomorrow's trash; it's nothing to worry about. They are going home to Stockholm on Sunday.

Filip appreciates the fact that his godfather wants to help, but Henry doesn't understand how small and stupid he feels.

It was pathetic, trying to put things right by talking to a reporter about Mom. He was so gullible. Mom would never have done that. If she were still alive, she would have laughed at the very idea and told him to forget it.

The thought brings tears to his eyes.

Why did they fight all the time? He can't understand it now; how could he have acted so childishly? Mom only ever wanted what was best for him, and now she's gone.

He would do anything to be able to tell her how grateful he is for everything she did for him. To tell her he loves her, just once more. And that she was the best mom in the whole world.

He takes another drag, blinks back the tears. He is overwhelmed by guilt. It doesn't make things better in any way, but he can't help it. He wakes up every morning ashamed of his behavior and his ingratitude.

So many things he took for granted.

The tip of his cigarette glows in the dark; the lump in his throat grows bigger.

He suddenly has a sense that someone is standing behind him.

Way too close.

He turns to look, feels a sharp pain in his neck.

And the world disappears.

84

The exterior lighting at the Villa creates a welcoming and almost festive atmosphere as Hanna drives up the incline to Copperhill. The snowy landscape enhances the effect of the lights, and the huge windows glow invitingly.

She isn't really in the mood for this kind of excess. All she wants is to get information from Henry that will move them forward in the hunt for the murderer. She has no intention of spending any more than thirty minutes here; then she will go home, have something to eat, and curl up in bed with Morris pressed close by her side.

She parks next to what she assumes is Henry's rental car, an ordinary Kia. To be honest she had expected something else, maybe a Porsche or Mercedes SUV. More in keeping with his image.

Although by now she ought to know better than to allow her prejudices to take over.

She undoes her seatbelt. Wonders whether to send a quick text to Daniel so that someone knows where she is, but it feels over the top. Henry hardly constitutes a threat, even if they have considered the possibility that he might be involved in the murders.

That theory is seeming more and more unlikely. He has an alibi, and it has been established that there were other ways for him to withdraw from the Storlien project if he wanted to. In addition, his combined resources are such that the project constitutes only a small part of his portfolio.

He is also Filip's godfather, and genuinely seems to care about the boy.

She decides to trust him.

Henry opens the door almost as soon as she rings the bell. He is wearing a simple black polo shirt with black jeans; he reminds her a little of Steve Jobs, but with silver-gray hair.

He smiles warmly. "Good to see you—welcome!"

His tone makes it sound as if she has shown up for a date.

Hanna tries to shake off the feeling that there is something more in the air. She is suddenly conscious of her own clothing—scruffy jeans and a thick blue sweater. Her hair is tied back in a messy ponytail.

Doesn't matter, she tells herself. Her appearance is totally irrelevant in the context.

"How's Filip?" she asks over her shoulder as she takes off her boots in the hallway. "That article was terrible."

"It was." Henry leans against the wall with his arms folded. "I called the editor and demanded that they take it down from the net, but I doubt it will happen."

Hanna doubts it too—the newspapers know their rights. She notices how Henry's voice is filled with sympathy when he talks about Filip. He seems a lot nicer this evening than during the interview the other day. She's glad she messaged him about the article.

"Come on in," he says, leading the way into the living room, where the main lighting is subdued and lots of candles in different holders are arranged in the corners.

An inviting open fire is crackling away, and blues music is playing softly in the background. Hanna thinks she recognizes Dorothy Moore's melodic voice. Over the past year she has gone along to listen to Anton's band in local venues. To her surprise she has discovered that she enjoys jazz and blues, even though in the past she was skeptical about those genres.

"I was just about to open a bottle of champagne," Henry adds, pointing to the coffee table, where an ice bucket is waiting with the neck of the bottle sticking out. "May I offer you a glass?"

Hanna shakes her head. "Not when I'm on duty, I'm afraid."

"That's a shame. It's a particularly fine year."

He picks up the bottle and shows her the label with its golden lettering. Hanna knows it is one of the best producers in the world.

And one of the most expensive.

"How about this?" Henry proposes. "I'll pour two glasses; then you can decide what you want to do."

He sits down on the sofa and fills the tall glasses two-thirds of the way. Hanna can see right away that the vintage wine is perfect. The bubbles are tiny, the color pale yellow and tempting.

She can almost smell the aroma of apples and nougat, bread and a hint of lemon. During her years as a bartender, she developed an interest in wine, and went on several courses. She knows that a bottle of champagne contains forty-nine million bubbles, while a bottle of prosecco has only around five million.

Champagne is in fact her favorite drink, but Henry couldn't possibly know that.

He picks up his glass, holds it in the air to toast her, then takes a sip. It is clear that he is a connoisseur; he rolls the drink around on his tongue, allowing the flavors to bloom on his palate.

"Are you sure I can't tempt you?" His tone is teasing.

He is looking at her the way he did toward the end of the interview, when she thought she was on the brink of getting him to reveal something big. They are in desperate need of help to move forward in the investigation, and she really hopes this visit will pay dividends.

His expression is enigmatic. The atmosphere has changed; there is a tension between them. He pushes the second glass toward her. Hanna hesitates; surely a sip or two wouldn't do any harm? Then she shakes her head again.

"You said you had something to tell me about Charlotte and her business affairs?"

Her tone is demonstratively clear—she doesn't want Henry to forget that she is here because of work.

He leans back, stretches out his left arm so that it rests on the decorative velvet cushions. Once again Hanna gets the feeling that he isn't taking this particularly seriously.

"I said that mainly to get you here." He gives her a disarming smile. "You're an attractive woman. Single, I believe. Just like me."

Hanna frowns. Has he lured her here under false pretenses? And had the nerve to check out her marital status?

She slams her notebook shut. There is no point in staying—this is a waste of time. He is toying with her, even though he knows she is in the middle of a case involving horrific crimes.

What a jerk.

And so is she, falling for the sentimental crap about taking care of his godson.

But something holds her back.

She really does want to hear more about Charlotte's background. Henry is their best source, and she trusts her intuition—she believes he has valuable information. So instead of getting up to leave, she gives him a casual smile. He isn't the only one who can play this game.

"You can think what you like. I'm here to work. And given that I've come all the way here, the least you can do is offer some information about your business partner."

"I wanted to offer you champagne," he says, elegantly turning her words back on her. His tone is amused, almost intimate. All his attention is focused on her. Hanna shuffles uncomfortably—it's been a long time since anyone looked at her like that.

Henry's gaze is kind of hypnotic.

"Maybe you can do both." She attempts to sound worldly wise. "Let's talk about Charlotte; then we'll see."

"Ask away. I am at your disposal."

Henry winks at her. She ought to be annoyed, but his indisputable charm is winning her over. She forces herself not to smile as she opens her notebook at a clean page and picks up her pen.

"Why do you think Charlotte was murdered?"

Henry's face closes down. "Trust me, I really wish I knew the answer. What's your theory?"

He has no idea that he has touched a sore point. The problem is that they don't have a credible hypothesis at the moment, just a whole lot of loose strands leading in different directions.

Hanna is pretty sure that Charlotte overstepped the mark in her determination to push through the Storlien project. The question is whether that was the reason for her death.

Bengt Hedin seems to have had a motive to get rid of her, but the circumstances suggest that two people were involved—one instigator and one killer.

Hanna thinks Hedin might have been the brains behind the crime, perhaps in collaboration with Paul Lehto. But they can't exclude the possibility that Lehto acted alone, that Charlotte's murder was an impulsive act that had nothing to do with Hedin.

Lehto also has a history of harassing his ex-wife, which means he has a past that indicates violent tendencies.

On the other hand, the threatening text message exchange between Hedin and Charlotte is incriminating.

She can't make the pieces fit together.

"Hanna?"

She realizes she was lost in her own thoughts. Henry is waiting for an answer.

"I'm afraid I don't have a clear idea," she admits. "That's why I'm asking."

Henry puts down his glass. She notices that he has beautiful hands. One is resting on his right thigh; he has long fingers with well-manicured nails.

Christian, her ex, had short, stubby fingers. She never learned to like them in the five years she and Christian lived together.

"Charlotte was a complicated person," Henry begins. "As I'm sure you've realized. She didn't always make herself popular; she often came across as extremely goal oriented when she wanted something."

This matches the impression Hanna has formed of the dead woman. Charlotte wasn't especially likable. Then again, driven women who work in the top echelons of the business world are often painted as ice-cold bitches. It is no secret that women are judged more harshly than men in public contexts. Hanna isn't surprised that Charlotte has been described as someone who would stick at nothing to achieve her goals.

That doesn't mean she deserved to die.

And she was struck by the fact that Filip defended her; he insisted that his mother loved him deeply. He is devastated by her death.

Which is important to bear in mind.

"I've lain awake going over and over it all for the past few nights," Henry continues. "And I do believe the murder is connected to business."

The nonchalant attitude is gone. He is serious now, with sorrow and melancholy in his eyes. But there is something else too.

Fear?

"The level of violence . . . It makes me think of the Russian Mafia, if you know what I mean? Charlotte was prepared to push through the hotel project at any price. I hope she wasn't so desperate that she turned to organized crime . . . but what if she did?"

Hanna looks up. Is he suggesting that Charlotte sought help from criminal networks to bring the project to fruition?

"And now she's dead," Henry adds. "In such a terrible way."

There is no mistaking his sincerity. He and Charlotte had known each other for over fifty years, since they were children. Her business depended on him. It's not surprising that her death has made him think about his own fate—is he worried that he too could be a target?

No one is immortal. The gods take whoever they want.

Her sympathy begins to return.

Henry empties his glass and clears his throat. His voice is quiet and sad when he speaks.

"I'm pretty sure that Charlotte paid out large sums of money in bribes, to smooth the passage of her application for planning permission. I'd decided to bring the matter up with her when I arrived here. That's why I'm wondering if the Mafia could be involved, or similar players. If she got into bed with criminals, metaphorically speaking, and something went wrong, could she have been subjected to blackmail? I should have mentioned this the first time we spoke, but it felt . . . awkward. I've been afraid to follow the idea through."

Hanna is thinking feverishly. A couple of pieces of the puzzle are falling into place. Henry is worried that the money Charlotte has paid out is linked to organized crime, but this also shines a light on something the police already suspect: that illegal money has been used to bribe Bengt Hedin.

Henry's information strengthens the hypothesis about Hedin's involvement. And his motive for homicide.

Hanna gives him a grateful smile. It was worth her coming here—her intuition was correct.

Henry did have something important to tell her.

85

The only sound in the bedroom is Daniel's regular breathing. He is deeply asleep; it is only Ida who can't settle.

She crept off to bed before him, pretended to be asleep when he came in.

It's all so confusing. She doesn't know what's going on, just that it felt wrong when he tried to come on to her in the living room.

She didn't want him to touch her.

Now she's lying here in the darkness, wondering if it's because she feels guilty about meeting up with Gustav today, and the fact that she even toyed with the idea of kissing him. Or is it worse than that?

Something deeper and more frightening?

She is no longer attracted to Daniel.

Nothing happened between her and Gustav, she tells herself yet again. The fantasy about kissing him was only in her head. In reality they chatted over coffee for less than an hour, then he had to go off and meet the group doing the peaks.

Okay, so he asked if they could see each other again, but that's a perfectly reasonable question when you're friends.

At the same time she can't deny that something happens to her body when she thinks of him.

If only she could feel that way about Daniel.

Ida turns onto her back and stares up at the ceiling. If she is no longer in love with her partner, what is going to happen?

Nothing is straightforward. They're a family; they have a daughter together. She can't simply walk away with Alice, especially given how much family life means to Daniel. He is so fixated on being a better parent than his own father was.

She doesn't know if she can do that to him, take his daughter away from him for half of her childhood.

Can she do that to Alice?

But what are they going to build their future on if the attraction has gone? Is she supposed to go on living with a man she doesn't want to have sex with?

Can she do that to herself?

Last winter, when Daniel was completely taken up with two major investigations, first the case of the missing teenage girl, then the murdered skier, something happened to their relationship. She felt alone, abandoned. The fact that he prioritized his work over her and Alice hurt her deeply.

It made her loathe his job.

With hindsight it was hardly surprising. Alice was only three months old when Amanda disappeared. Ida was a new mom, very anxious, and everything seemed so difficult. It was tough to be alone with a tiny baby when she was constantly afraid of doing something wrong. She was also worried that Daniel might get hurt, even killed. She imagined all kinds of scenarios, was terrified at the thought of being left alone as a single mom, worked herself up to a breaking point.

They had two serious crises during that investigation.

The first time Daniel got so stressed that he had an outburst of rage in the kitchen. In the end he hurled a plate at the wall and stormed out. His temper has improved, and he is seeing a therapist, but Ida can't erase the memory of that evening.

The second time, during the next case, Ida became so desperate that she took Alice and moved back in with her mom. It felt like the only way out, although she was ashamed of behaving like a spoiled teenager.

She hears the sound of a car passing by outside the window. It is late, she must try to get some sleep.

Ida remembers how bad she felt last winter. The situation with Daniel's job changed her; she became insecure and whined all the time—a person she didn't recognize.

She doesn't want to be that kind of partner. She misses her old self, the girl who stood on her own two feet and walked away when something didn't suit her.

A new realization comes creeping in.

This time, when Daniel is away from home most of the time, she doesn't feel the same anxiousness. Quite the reverse—it's almost a relief when he isn't here. She can do what she wants, and things are easier with Alice when Ida makes the decisions without having to compromise.

Facing the truth frightens her even more.

She is happier on her own than with Daniel.

86

The music coming from the discreet speakers at the Villa has moved on to a new playlist. Dorothy Moore has been replaced by the saxophonist John Coltrane. Hanna thinks she recognizes "My One and Only Love."

Anton has taught her more about jazz than she realized. She must remember to thank him some time.

She and Henry are sitting quietly, but the atmosphere is relaxed and not at all awkward. Hanna is enjoying the lovely melody in the background as she considers what Henry has told her. She ought to go home, but while she's here she wants to take the opportunity to ask about the assault at the mountain hotel in the seventies.

"On a completely different matter—I'd like to hear more about your winter vacations in Storlien. You said that your family and Charlotte's used to celebrate Christmas and New Year's together there."

"We did." He winks at her. "If it will make you stay a while longer, I'm happy to talk about those days."

It seems as if Henry is flirting again. Hanna ought to find this irritating, but somehow it feels fine—possibly because he is being quite open about it. Or because he appears to be genuinely interested in her. He is nothing like the men she has met in the bar in Åre. Admittedly he is considerably older—twenty years or so—but he is still handsome and in good shape.

"So who was there?" she asks, ignoring the invitation.

"Let's see . . . This would be in the late sixties and early seventies. I think I was seven the last time we went there, which means Charlotte was eight."

Hanna does a quick calculation in her head. If Henry was seven, that must have been the same year the assault took place, according to Leffe. It sounds too good to be a coincidence.

"Do you remember if anything unusual happened that Christmas?"

"What do you mean?"

"I heard about an assault that allegedly took place over Christmas 1973. A young waitress was raped."

Henry looks surprised. "How did you find out about that?"

"So you remember the incident?" she counters.

"No . . . yes. I wasn't aware of it at the time."

Hanna doesn't understand why he is speaking in riddles. Fifty years have passed—it surely can't be a sensitive issue now.

"So you heard about it later—how come?"

She sounds more challenging than she had intended, but Henry doesn't take offense. He thinks for a moment, gazing at the candles on the table.

"That summer—so six months after Christmas '73—I overheard my parents arguing about it when we were staying in the country. It seemed"—he pauses—"as if Charlotte's father was involved."

Hanna can't hide her surprise. Charlotte's father was mixed up in the tragic story? She vaguely remembers that he died a few years ago.

"In what way was Curt Wretlind involved?"

"Unfortunately I believe he was the one who was hanging out with the poor girl."

"Hanging out?" Hanna raises her eyebrows at the choice of words. "As I understand it, she was the victim of a serious assault. She was forced to have sex against her will. That's not what I would call 'hanging out.'"

Henry holds up his hands. "You're right, of course. But the expression I heard back then, and you must remember that I was just a child, was exactly that—they were 'hanging out.'"

Once again he reaches for his glass and takes a sip before continuing.

"My mom was very upset. She and my dad were in their bedroom at our place in the country. They probably thought I was asleep, but their voices were so loud that I couldn't help hearing through the wall. Mom was saying that she would never celebrate Christmas with Charlotte's family again."

"She took the girl's side?"

Something flickers across Henry's face, but Hanna finds it difficult to interpret.

"I guess she was seeing it more from Charlotte's mother's point of view. She didn't like the fact that Curt had cheated on his wife during a family vacation. It didn't look good."

Hanna is taken aback. Such a cynical response! And yet she recognizes it—she grew up with the same attitude. The importance of constantly keeping up appearances, whatever happens.

Her own mother would presumably have reacted the same way.

"My perception was that my father was trying to persuade my mother not to make a big thing of what had gone on. He wanted to plan our next trip to Storlien, but Mom refused to have anything to do with Curt. Dad had to meet up with Curt on his own, and after that we never holidayed together again. It wasn't until years later that Charlotte and I renewed our friendship, because we went to the same high school."

"Do you remember anything else?"

Henry twirls his glass between his fingers, and his expression grows sad.

"From what my mom said, it sounded as if the poor girl got pregnant."

"She had a baby?"

"I think so, but I don't know for sure."

Hanna gazes out of the huge window, but the darkness is too dense to see anything. Even Åreskutan is not visible against the sky. There is no full moon shining tonight.

It's hardly surprising that Leffe said the girl's life was ruined. As if the rape wasn't bad enough, she ended up pregnant as well.

At least Hanna didn't have to go through that.

It must have been a terrible situation.

87

It is much later, and Henry has told her everything he remembers, both about the assault and their Christmas celebrations in Storlien. At first Hanna felt uncomfortable, but then she forced herself to focus on the information Henry was providing.

Then they moved on to chatting about old traditions. Henry's childhood memories are familiar to Hanna, even though he is considerably older. She has also spent Christmas in Jämtland, trudging through the snow to the early morning service by the glow of burning torches.

She is beginning to relax now, even though it is very late. First thing tomorrow she will dig deeper into what she has learned. She needs to let Daniel know about the mysterious payments Charlotte made, and she is looking forward to hearing his take on the matter.

Henry smiles. "So what do you say, Hanna? Have you finished work for this evening?"

He reaches for the champagne bottle, and to her surprise Hanna sees that the glass in front of her is empty. She must have drunk it while they were talking, although she has no recollection of doing so.

That means she can't drive for several hours. What a stupid thing to do.

Her body already feels heavy, tiredness is catching up with her—or maybe it's the alcohol. The living room is so beautiful and cozy; she could easily lean back on the sofa and fall asleep.

She focuses on the two candles on the coffee table. They are burning with a tall, bright flame, moving slightly in the draft. It feels good to give in, forget all the difficult thoughts. She is a little tipsy, but decides that it doesn't matter. She will just have to call a cab. In any case, all her colleagues are at home with their families right now—why should she be the only one who's always working?

But something else is coming to life. Henry's obvious interest is making her body tingle.

It's been almost a year since she's had sex.

Christian's behavior had made her self-esteem plummet. Once she had started to recover from that, her feelings for Daniel had gotten in the way.

She has gone to the local bar a few times in recent months, determined to find someone to spend the night with. If nothing else, it might stop her thinking about Daniel. On every occasion she has changed her mind at the last minute. Picking up a guy for a one-night stand felt too cheap, too depressing.

She doesn't want to be that desperate.

Instead she has ended up going home alone, feeling sorry for herself.

Henry gets up and comes to sit beside her.

Their faces are only inches apart. She is aware of his fragrance, an expensive blend of sandalwood, jasmine, and pepper. It smells of success and self-confidence. Sophisticated elegance.

There is no doubt that he is attractive.

Or that he knows it.

He also seems to have enough self-possession not to be bothered by the fact that she is a police officer.

Maybe it turns him on?

Mom would like Henry, Hanna thinks idly, sinking deeper into the soft cushions. She still insists on spending time with Christian and his new girlfriend, Valérie, even though he dumped Hanna without a second thought. Ironically, she still blames her daughter for the breakup, which never ceases to astonish Hanna.

And it still hurts.

Henry gently caresses her cheek. She can't remember the last time a man touched her in that way, so warmly and affectionately.

She has longed for Daniel to do exactly that.

"You're very beautiful for a cop," Henry says softly.

She can't remember the last time someone said she was beautiful either. And although she knows it's not true, she still likes hearing it.

She yearns for intimacy.

That warm tingling feeling is egging her on, while a faint voice in the back of her mind whispers that this is madness. She cannot let Henry seduce her. It would constitute gross misconduct in the line of duty, and then some. She has just managed to build herself a platform in Åre; it would be insanity to risk that.

Another voice tells her that it is wonderful to be here with him. It is so long since she felt wanted and desired. She has almost forgotten what it's like.

At work she puts all her energy into hiding her feelings for Daniel. He must never know what she really wants, but it is exhausting, listening to him talk about Ida and Alice every day. She often wants to tell him to shut up when he confides in her that there are problems in his relationship.

It is painful to be regarded as a friend.

Daniel has no idea what she is thinking, but sometimes she wants to yell at him, tell him he could be with her if he is so frustrated at home.

It is unthinkable, of course.

After Christian's betrayal, she could never do the same to another woman, especially not when there is a child to consider.

She would rather leave her job in Åre than come between Daniel and Ida.

"Isn't it time you finished for the day?" Henry whispers, moving a little closer. "Don't you deserve a break?"

It doesn't matter if Henry is interested in her for one night only. At least he wants her.

Unlike Daniel.

88

Their lips are almost touching when Hanna's phone rings in her back pocket.

She is so surprised by the sound that she bangs her forehead on Henry's chin. The blow makes him cry out; he bounces back against the sofa cushion, and his hand flies to his face. As Hanna mumbles an apology, she takes out her phone and answers.

"It's Emily," says a young, agitated voice.

Hanna is confused—who's Emily? She searches her memory and realizes this must be Filip's girlfriend—she was with him on Tuesday.

"Hi, Emily." Back to reality.

It is almost midnight, way too late to call unless something is wrong.

"Filip is gone!" Emily almost shouts.

Hanna makes an effort to pull herself together.

"What do you mean Filip is gone?" She sits up straight and meets Henry's worried gaze.

"We had dinner at Supper." Emily's voice is shrill with anxiety. "Filip went outside for a smoke, but he didn't come back. I waited at the restaurant for nearly an hour; then I went back to Åregården to see if he was in our hotel room, but he wasn't there." She is crying now. "I don't know where he is, and I can't get a hold of Henry. I've been trying and trying!"

Hanna glances at Henry; he must have switched his phone to silent. "Have you tried calling Filip?"

"Of course I have! I've texted and called at least a dozen times, but there's no answer, not on Snapchat either. You don't understand—he's gone!"

Henry is listening closely. He can tell from Hanna's questions that something isn't right, and mouths *Speaker* so that he can hear what Emily is saying.

Hanna ignores him. She doesn't want anyone to know that she is with Henry at this time of night.

"Listen to me, Emily. Are you sure he hasn't just gone for a long walk around the village?"

Emily is still crying.

"Emily?"

"He's been gone for such a long time. He would never do this without telling me."

Hanna swears silently over the situation in which she has put herself. How could she be so stupid as to sit here drinking champagne? Now she can't drive.

"Could he have gone to see a friend?"

"He doesn't know anyone here, apart from Henry."

Hanna can confirm that Filip isn't here.

"And the two of you hadn't had a fight?"

"No! He's disappeared!"

Hanna looks out of the window again. It is pitch black; the temperature is well below freezing. The circumstances are not ideal for a young man from Stockholm wearing sneakers to set off on a spontaneous long walk.

"Okay, so this is what we're going to do," Hanna says, sounding much calmer than she actually feels. "You stay in your hotel room in case Filip shows up. I will speak to my colleagues and check if anyone has seen him in the village."

She adds a few words of consolation and makes Emily promise to let her know immediately if Filip returns. Then she ends the call.

Henry's face has lost all its color. He takes out his phone; Hanna can see that he has several missed calls from Emily.

"Do you think the two of them might have quarreled?" Hanna asks. "You know Filip much better than I do—would he take off if he was mad at Emily?"

Henry shakes his head. "It's not like him to disappear without a word. He cares about her way too much. I've met up with them a few times this week, and everything seemed fine between them."

Hanna tries to think clearly.

Filip has been gone for only a few hours, which isn't much at his age. Under normal circumstances it wouldn't be a police matter until he had been missing for at least twenty-four hours. Plus he is grieving, which can have an impact on "normal" behavior.

For all they know he could be sitting by himself somewhere with his phone switched off, drowning his sorrows in booze.

But Emily sounded hysterical. And Henry is clearly worried.

A shiver runs down Hanna's spine.

Would Charlotte's murderer be so cruel as to go after her son too?

89

Less than an hour later, all police patrols in the area have been informed that Filip Wretlind is missing, and they have been asked to keep a lookout for him. Hanna has provided a description: He is six feet tall, has wavy fair hair, blue eyes, and rounded cheeks that make him look younger than he is.

Henry added that he is probably wearing a dark-blue padded Moncler jacket.

Hanna is still at the Villa. She feels stone-cold sober, but she dare not get behind the wheel yet. They are sitting at one end of the huge dining table, and Henry has made them both a strong espresso.

Hanna has also spoken to the regional operations center and explained the situation. Then she called the maître d' at Supper and asked her to find out whether anyone on the staff had noticed Filip going outside to smoke.

If anyone remembers the smallest detail, they must speak up.

She did the same with the Åregården hotel. If anyone has seen Filip, they must contact the police immediately.

Henry's eyes are dark with worry. He too has tried Filip's number many times, without success. It rings and rings, but no one answers. This means his phone isn't switched off; Hanna can't decide whether this is good or bad.

"I should have insisted that he stay here with me," Henry says. "There are enough bedrooms. But he didn't want to be in the hotel where his mother was murdered—that's why I booked a room at Åregården for them."

"It's not your fault that he's missing."

"It feels that way." Henry buries his face in his hands. "I've watched Filip grow up ever since he was born, and now he has no one else, apart from Emily. His father checked out a long time ago. I should have taken better care of him. I have sons of my own—I know how important a father figure is."

He sounds devastated. He raises his head and looks Hanna in the eye.

"Oh my God—what if he's been kidnapped?"

Hanna would like to put her arm around his shoulders and reassure him. Tell him that Filip will probably be back soon, that everything will be fine. But she is just as worried as he is.

After two murders in a week, her nerves are jangling with anxiety. She hesitates, then reaches out and squeezes his hand. It feels neither strange nor inappropriate.

It feels right.

He returns the pressure gratefully. His skin is warm and dry beneath her fingertips; she maintains the contact for a few seconds longer. Earlier in the evening she hadn't given much thought to the age difference, but now the fact that Henry is twenty years older is all too evident.

"Help me go through this," she says, both to distract him and to clarify her own thoughts. "Those payments you mentioned, could they have been bribes?"

Henry takes a deep breath and exhales through his mouth. "I wish I knew."

Hanna nods. There is a crackling sound from the hearth. The fire has burned down, but the logs in the middle are still glowing. She gets

up and goes over to the coffee machine. Without asking she makes them both another cup and fetches milk from the refrigerator. She finds a dish of chocolates on the counter and brings it with her.

It's going to be a long night.

In the best case scenario, Filip will be found within a few hours—at least that's what she is trying to tell herself. There doesn't have to be any kind of criminal activity behind his disappearance, it's not necessary to believe the worst.

At the same time, it's very worrying. All bars and restaurants have to close at the same time because of the restrictions. There is nowhere for Filip to go.

It is almost two o'clock in the morning—nearly six hours since Emily last saw him.

Filip is still missing.

With every hour that passes, the likelihood that he has been abducted increases.

And Hanna has no idea where they should start searching.

90

Filip's head is spinning when he regains consciousness.

At first he can't work out where he is. Everything is black; it is so dark that he wonders if his eyes are actually closed.

Is this a nightmare? Is he still asleep? Is he in bed in the hotel room, with Emily beside him?

Then he realizes that isn't the case. His eyes are open, but however much he blinks it is impossible to see anything in front of him.

He can't even make out faint contours.

Where is Emily?

Where is he?

Slowly he becomes aware that he can't move. His arms and legs are bound. He has virtually no feeling in his hands, which are tied behind his back. Something is pressing against his hip, but when he tries to wriggle to find a more comfortable position, it proves impossible. The space is too small.

He can barely turn, can't even stretch his legs without his feet coming up against something solid.

There is also a strange smell, unpleasant and acrid, like diesel. It is making him feel sick. It's as if he is lying in the trunk of a car.

He tries to breathe in through his mouth, but he can't do that either. A gag cuts into his skin.

Filip is panicking now, he wants to stay calm but how can he? Instead he breathes faster and faster without taking in enough air. The fear spills over and explodes, makes him tug at the ropes until his wrists ache.

He screams for help, but only a muffled sound comes out.

But he can't stop.

He desperately continues to shout, until all that remains are rasping sobs. His nose is blocked with mucus and tears, his body is shaking so uncontrollably that he bangs his forehead on the roof. His head starts pounding, and somehow the concrete pain steadies him a little.

He manages to gain control of his breathing, makes an effort to think.

What actually happened?

The last thing he remembers is going outside for a cigarette. Someone tapped him on the shoulder.

Then everything went black.

The panic comes flooding back with such force that he feels dizzy.

He must have been kidnapped.

But why?

91

They have been waiting for news for hours now, and Hanna has dozed off on Henry's sofa. When her phone wakes her, it is almost five o'clock in the morning. She is dizzy with the lack of sleep, and there is a dull ache at the back of her head.

Henry is fast asleep on the other sofa, opposite her. His cheek is resting on a cushion, his ear on the armrest.

"Hello?" Hanna says breathlessly.

A colleague on patrol is on the other end of the line.

"Have you found Filip Wretlind?"

The wind crackles in the microphone as the officer explains why he is calling.

"No, but we just picked up a guy who was staggering along the E14 and we drove him home. He was still drunk. He'd had a nap at a friend's house, then woke up and decided he had to get home to Björnen. He told us he'd seen another guy outside Supper who was in an even worse state than him, so drunk that his companion was practically carrying him. I think our guy wanted to show himself in a better light, but the thing is that the young man he saw matches Filip Wretlind's description."

Hanna tightens her grip on the phone.

"So what time was this? When he saw him?"

"Around eight in the evening, apparently. Our witness said he was wearing a dark-blue Moncler jacket."

The time fits with what Emily told her.

And the clothing.

"Did he see where Filip went?"

"He said the two of them were heading toward the parking lot at the train station. The person we think was Filip was barely capable of walking. He was being dragged along."

Hanna frantically tries to process this new information.

If Filip had been drugged, or suffered a blow to the head, that could explain why he appeared to be so drunk. According to Emily he hadn't been drunk at all—in fact he'd had only one beer during the course of the evening.

"Did your informant notice anything about the person he was with? Was it a man or a woman?"

"It was a tall man, but our guy has no idea what he looked like. He doesn't recall much, just that he was wearing a dark hat pulled well down over his forehead."

"Age?"

"Again, no idea."

"Did he see if they drove away?"

"No. It's possible that he might remember more tomorrow when he sobers up. We've got his contact details."

All of Hanna's forebodings are coming true. It doesn't sound as if Filip left the restaurant of his own free will.

Henry has woken and is sitting up, listening to every word with his fists clenched on his knees.

Hanna immediately calls Daniel. It's the middle of the night but it can't be helped—she has to wake him now.

He answers after five rings.

She hates saying the words out loud.

"It's about Filip Wretlind. I think he's been kidnapped."

92

Filip tries to force his eyes open, but it's no good; there is a strange weight pressing on his face; he can't see. It's as if he is wearing a hood.

Someone is carrying him in their arms.

Is it Mom?

He remembers the feeling of safety when he was little and afraid of the dark. When he cried and she would fetch him from his nursery and carry him into her room. He would be allowed to snuggle down beside her in the double bed and fall asleep while she lay reading.

Mom always smelled so good, of bergamot, gardenia, and something else. That was the smell of *her*.

Filip is semiconscious, but this is different—a mixture of sweat and stale booze, unfamiliar and unpleasant body odors.

Mom is dead.

The grief when the memory suddenly returns hits him with full force. She doesn't exist anymore; she has been murdered.

He will never see her again.

And now he has been abducted.

He becomes aware of the cold penetrating his clothes. He must be outside; he is no longer shut in the narrow, claustrophobic space from before.

Whoever is carrying him is breathing hard with exertion. Gasping and puffing with damp breaths that smell of beer. A vague thought stirs in Filip's mind. He ought to break free, try to escape.

But he can't do it; his muscles won't cooperate; his body is unresponsive. Plus both his arms and his legs are still bound.

He hears a creaking noise, as if a door is being closed. Then it gets warmer; they must be indoors now.

Filip slips into unconsciousness again.

He wishes Mom were here.

SATURDAY, APRIL 3 EASTER SATURDAY

93

Tiina feels like a robot when she arrives home on Saturday morning after an early long walk with Zelda. She couldn't sleep, so shortly before six o'clock she gave up, got dressed, and took the dog to the forest. It is usually Ogge who takes Zelda out before breakfast, it's their special time, but Tiina still has no idea where he might be.

It is Easter Saturday.

Three days have passed since Ogge came home in the middle of the night and she began to suspect that he was seeing someone else. The following morning he took off, and she doesn't know where he is. People ask after him, and she has nothing to say. He isn't answering his phone and is ignoring her text messages; she has lost count of how many she has sent.

The house is empty when she opens the door. The scooter is there, but Ogge's car is missing. Zelda dances around while Tiina fills her food bowl and gives her clean water. Then she goes down to the cellar to put on a wash. Everyday tasks are all she can cope with right now. If she sits at the kitchen table brooding, she will go crazy.

The tears begin to flow as she makes her way down the stairs. She switches on the light and starts loading the dirty clothes into the machine. Her shoulder aches when she bends forward. It is so stiff that she can't reach properly, in the end she has to kneel down to push things into the drum.

When she gets up she notices something white in the gap between the tumble dryer and the washing machine. She grabs hold of it and out comes a white sports sock. It is Ogge's; it must have been the one that was missing when she did his laundry the other day.

As she brings it into the light she stiffens. It is covered in dried patches of something red. If she didn't know better she would think it was . . . blood.

She sniffs cautiously. It smells unpleasant, and it frightens her.

Tiina stares at the sock. There is no doubt that it is the one that she couldn't find on Sunday night.

She drops it as if it is red hot. Then she goes over to the drying cupboard where she had hung everything up. Nothing is left. That can mean only one thing.

Ogge has fetched the washing himself.

This is another thing he never does, and Tiina leaves the cellar and rushes up to the bedroom. She yanks open the door of his closet and checks the drawer where he keeps his T-shirts. The freshly washed top is lying there. He hasn't bothered to fold it properly as she does, just bundled it in with everything else.

She picks it up and holds it in front of her. Goes over to the window to see better. It has been washed, but it isn't as clean as it might be. In the bright daylight she can see faint shadows of something that appears to have splattered all across the chest.

She sinks down on the bed.

Her head is spinning.

If there was blood on the sock, there could have been blood on the T-shirt too. There could have been blood on all his clothes, which was why he washed them right away. But he has got bloodstains on him before. She doesn't know how many times he has come back from the moose hunt with clothes that needed several washes before they were clean.

If he had put everything in the laundry basket on Sunday night she would have found it the following day, and she would have thought nothing of it.

Or would she?

The hunting season has been over for a long time.

Last night she was convinced that Ogge was having an affair. It would explain so much—his irritability, the mysterious scooter trips in the middle of the night, the increased alcohol consumption over the past year, the growing bitterness.

She had thought that the worst that could happen would be him wanting a divorce.

Now there could be another explanation, one that is far more terrifying.

One that she hardly dares think about.

94

In the pale morning light, Daniel can see that Hanna is almost transparent with exhaustion. Her hair is more tousled than ever, and she has dark circles under her eyes. Apparently she has been up all night, and he is equally concerned about Filip's disappearance.

He can't help reproaching himself.

Shouldn't they have realized that Charlotte's son could be in danger, after the murders of his mother and Aada Kuus?

He hears his inner critical voice asking how he could allow the boy to be kidnapped before their very eyes.

The whole team is gathered around the table in the conference room. It is seven o'clock in the morning, and Anton and Raffe are sitting next to Daniel and Hanna. So is Birgitta Grip, who stayed over in Åre. Everyone has been called in at short notice.

It is Easter Saturday, but that is the last thing on their minds.

A call has gone out for Filip Wretlind, and all patrols in the region have been informed. Given the circumstances, the case is being treated as an abduction. Filip has probably been taken away, presumably by the same person who is behind the two murders.

A patrol is on the way to Supper to see if there are any traces of Filip or the kidnapper. The parking lot at the train station will also be searched.

The hypothesis is that the kidnapper left his car there and dragged Filip across the road. They have no idea where he went after that, but they have posted information on the police home page and on local Facebook groups. They have also contacted Missing People to ask for assistance.

Daniel has a sudden flashback to the case involving Amanda eighteen months ago, when Missing People helped with the search.

Patrols have also been sent to Hedin's and Lehto's homes to check where they are—and whether they have an alibi for the time when Filip was taken.

"We should have fucking realized he was in danger," Hanna says. Her tone is strained, she is finding it difficult to sit still, and she is swearing more than usual. "I don't understand how I could be so blind. I shouldn't be a fucking cop."

"None of us knew," Daniel says gently.

He can't help looking over at the wall where the pictures of the murder victims are on display. The last thing he wants is to see a photograph of Filip next to his dead mother.

Mother and son together in the worst possible scenario.

"It must have been that article in the paper," Hanna continues, as if she hasn't heard his comment.

"I saw it too," Anton says, halfway through a cheese sandwich. "What a pile of crap."

"Filip was standing in front of Åregården in the picture they used," Hanna exclaims. "They even wrote that he was staying there because he didn't want to go to the hotel where his mother was killed." She sighs deeply. "We might just as well have messaged the perpetrator and told him where to find Filip."

Grip glances up from her phone and looks at Hanna.

"There's no point in self-reproach. We have to find out who took Filip—that's all that matters at the moment. So where are we?"

Daniel can see that Hanna is trying to compose herself. She goes over to the whiteboard, picks up a blue marker pen and writes down *Bengt Hedin* and *Paul Lehto*. She gives a brief summary of the previous day's discussions, and the new information about Lehto's past.

"I've also been given more details strengthening our suspicions that Charlotte's financial dealings weren't entirely up front. It seems likely that she was bribing Bengt Hedin."

"Where has this come from?" Anton wants to know.

Daniel is wondering the same thing—Hanna seems slightly uncomfortable.

"I had a conversation with Henry Sylvester, Filip's godfather. When it became apparent that Filip had gone missing. He told me."

This annoys Daniel—why hadn't Sylvester mentioned it earlier? He should have shared that kind of suspicion with the police from the get-go.

"Why didn't he tell us?"

"He thought organized crime might be involved," Hanna replies quickly. "He was scared."

Grip coughs into the crook of her elbow before she speaks. "If we think this is the same perpetrator as in the two homicides, and that he has abducted Filip, then this is probably not about a kidnapping to be followed by a ransom demand. I don't think money is the motive behind the abduction."

The import of her comments is devastating.

Daniel feels his heart rate spike. They are dealing with someone who has already displayed a staggering degree of ruthlessness. Charlotte

Wretlind was stabbed to death. Aada Kuus was strangled with her own scarf.

Filip is only twenty-three years old, and a total innocent in this context.

That doesn't matter. If it is the same perpetrator, there is only one reason why Filip has been taken.

He is going to die, just like his mother.

After the briefing Hanna accompanies Daniel to his office.

"So what do we do now?" she asks hoarsely, sinking down on the visitor's chair. She lands heavily on the base of her spine, the same body part that suffered from an uneasy doze on Henry's sofa.

"We wait for more information."

That's not enough for Hanna. Time is running out. Her whole body is screaming at her to do something. Right now.

The adrenaline is making her ears buzz. If only she had advised Filip against doing the newspaper interview—then maybe the killer wouldn't have realized the boy was in Åre.

Or worked out where he was staying.

She pictures the perpetrator following Filip and Emily when they went out to eat yesterday evening. He wouldn't have dared to attack at that point, because Filip had company. However, if he was waiting outside the restaurant when Filip came out for a smoke, he would have seen his chance.

"There's one thing that doesn't fit with the other murders," Daniel says. "If we assume we're dealing with the same perpetrator—why was Filip abducted rather than killed on the spot?"

That hadn't occurred to Hanna. Daniel is right, it deviates from the pattern. Both Charlotte and Aada were killed in the place where they encountered the murderer. This time he has made the effort to take his victim, which is more complicated.

The question makes her feel marginally less guilty. In a way the fact that Filip has disappeared rather than been killed gives a glimmer of hope.

It might mean that he is still alive.

"Maybe there were too many people around," Daniel continues. "The risk of being seen was too great, so he decided to take Filip's life somewhere else."

Hanna understands what he means. The entrance to Supper is clearly visible from Sankt Olavs väg, which runs past the train station and through the village. There would have been plenty of people around at eight o'clock on Friday evening. After all, their eyewitness, the guy the patrol car picked up, had noticed Filip.

What happened next?

Hanna hates the thought that Filip could be lying dead somewhere because they failed to find him.

If that is the case, then everything they are doing now is too late.

"There must be other motives," she says, mainly because she can't bear the idea that the boy is beyond help.

"Like what?"

Hanna searches for an explanation.

"Maybe he's sorry for what he's done, and wants the chance to explain himself to Filip face-to-face, with no witnesses?"

The look on Daniel's face is skeptical to say the least. "Like some kind of confession, you mean?"

To be honest, Hanna doesn't know what she means. Her brain feels like porridge.

"When are we expecting to hear from the phone company?" she asks, her heart sinking.

"Soon, hopefully."

They are trying to trace Filip through his phone, and have contacted the service provider to ask for a location. Under normal circumstances this shouldn't take long, but today things are moving slowly. The fact that it is early morning and Easter Saturday doesn't help.

They have also checked with Emily to find out if Filip has activated the find function on his phone, but she doesn't know.

Hanna isn't feeling very well. She sways on the chair, and Daniel gives her a searching look. "When did you last eat?"

She can't remember; she definitely didn't have dinner yesterday. She is faint from tiredness and the lack of food.

"I'm not sure," she admits.

"Wait here." He disappears to the kitchen and returns with a cup of tea and a cinnamon bun from the bag Raffe brought in earlier in the week. It has gone pretty dry, but Hanna gratefully nibbles the sweet dough, which gives her a small energy boost. Enough to remember what Henry said about the waitress who became pregnant in the 1970s, and the fact that Charlotte could have a half sibling.

She realizes they have to look into this. If the killer has gone so far as to kidnap her son, then a half brother or sister could be in danger.

She quickly shares Henry's revelation with Daniel, who frowns at her when she has finished.

"Why didn't you mention this at the briefing?"

Hanna stares down into her cup. The truth is that she had forgotten, but also she was embarrassed about the hours she had spent at the Villa. She is finding it difficult to look Daniel in the eye after what almost happened between her and Henry. If Emily hadn't called, they would probably have slept together.

Not that it's any of Daniel's business.

I can do what I want, she thinks. *I don't have to inform my colleague about my love life.* However, the very fact that she had been alone with

Henry late at night, in the middle of an investigation in which he is involved, is a sign of poor judgment.

She can't imagine any of the team being so reckless, especially not Daniel.

Or Anton.

"I'm sorry," she says wearily. "Of course I should have brought this up earlier. It's all been . . . a bit much."

Daniel looks unconvinced.

"Why don't I try calling Leffe, the site supervisor at the Storlien mountain hotel?" she offers in an attempt to shift focus. "He might be able to help us dig out more information—maybe he knows the name of the woman Charlotte's father assaulted?"

She takes out her phone, finds the number. Sends up a little prayer that Leffe will answer and have something useful to contribute.

If there is another person who is related to Charlotte, they can't let him or her fall victim to the unknown perpetrator.

Suddenly Anton appears in the doorway.

"Bengt Hedin is missing."

Hanna looks up. "What do you mean?"

"I just spoke to the patrol who went over to his house. According to his wife, he hasn't been home for the last few nights. He's not answering his phone when she calls or texts. She is out of her mind with worry."

Hanna catches Daniel's eye.

Filip has been kidnapped. Bengt Hedin is gone, impossible to reach.

It can't be a coincidence.

THEN

NEW YEAR'S EVE 1973

Monica glances over her shoulder before knocking on room 505. She can't risk being seen when she is meeting a guest for a romantic encounter.

The thought makes her smile as Sean opens the door and pulls her close.

After a long embrace, she gazes around with delight. The décor is enchanting, a million miles from anything she has experienced until now, especially her own home. The suite is divided into two sections, an outer area with a mustard-yellow sofa and armchairs, then an archway leading to the bedroom with its double bed.

Sean wraps both arms around her and clasps her to him.

"Oh," he moans. "You are completely irresistible, little girl. You drive me crazy."

He kisses her, thrusting his hard tongue into her mouth. It takes up all the space. His hand finds its way inside her blouse, as urgent as the other day in the staff bar. In no time he is touching her breast, determinedly kneading one nipple between his thumb and forefinger.

He is so rough that it hurts.

Monica tries to push him away, but Sean doesn't seem to notice.

"Wait," she mumbles, but he won't stop.

Instead he pushes her skirt up above her hips, revealing her tights and knickers before yanking them down to her knees. Monica is embarrassed; it feels weird standing in front of him with the lower half of her body naked. Exposed.

"Wait," she says again, louder this time.

This wasn't how she had imagined their date. She had pictured something more romantic. He would tell her he had fallen madly in love with her, whisper sweet nothings in her ear. Tell her she was the one he wanted to be with for the rest of his life.

A deep, intimate kiss as a sign of their new bond.

Sean ignores her objections. He shoves her toward the bed, and when the backs of her knees meet the edge she ends up underneath him. Somehow he has bunched up her blouse so that now one breast is protruding from her bra.

Monica feels a rising panic.

She doesn't want this. She can't do this.

She is a virgin, she has hardly even kissed a boy.

"You're so fantastic," he groans in her ear. "Your body is amazing!"

"No," Monica whispers. "Stop."

He doesn't even notice; he simply bends down and takes her breast in his mouth. While he is fumbling with his belt and lowering his pants, he sucks so hard that it brings tears to her eyes.

It hurts. She is frightened, but dare not protest. In the end the words slip out anyway.

"I don't want to do this. Stop!"

Finally Sean reacts. He props himself up on his elbows, stares at her in total confusion. Their faces are only inches apart.

His gaze is different now; his eyes are hard and cold.

"What do you mean?"

"I don't want to do this. Not like this."

Then he slaps her. Right across the face. The blow is so hard that she can taste blood in her mouth.

"You little slut," he practically spits at her. "Do you think you can treat me like a fool? You've been throwing yourself at me all week—it's too late to change your mind now!"

Monica is so terrified that she begins to shake. Not a sound comes from her mouth, even though she wants to explain that she wasn't flirting with him, that she isn't teasing him now.

She thought he loved her. That they were going to be together for the rest of their lives.

His face is bright red. The handsome features are totally distorted.

"Sean," she whimpers without thinking.

"My name isn't fucking Sean, it's Curt."

Monica dare not move, she freezes, she is incapable of crying out or resisting. She simply lies mute and motionless on her back as he thrusts into her.

The pain is the worst thing she has ever known. It feels as if she is being split in two, all the way up into her belly.

It goes on and on.

Somehow she tunes out. Fixes her gaze on a point on the pale-green wall, imagines that she is far, far away, not here.

Someone else is lying on the bed, offering no resistance.

Eventually he is done, and slides out of her.

She sees that there is blood on his penis when he stands and zips his pants.

"Get dressed and get the hell out of here," he snaps on his way to the bathroom. "My wife will be back from the slopes soon—you can't be around then."

Her lip is split, and the area between her legs is throbbing. But it is the contempt in his eyes that hurts Monica the most.

To him she is nothing more than a cheap slut.

That is when she begins to hate herself.

96

Hanna calls Leffe while Daniel organizes the search for Bengt Hedin. She still feels nauseous with tiredness and anxiety over Filip, but at the same time, she is determined to press on with the new information.

No reply. It is early for a Saturday morning, but surely he ought to be up? She is fizzing with impatience as she tries again, drumming her fingers on the table as the signal rings out.

"Hello?" a sleepy voice mumbles eventually.

At last.

Hanna introduces herself and outlines the situation without going into detail. "I was wondering if you know whether a child was born as a result of the assault you told me about the other day?"

Leffe is breathing heavily. "Yes. That fucker destroyed her life, and he refused to take any responsibility for what he'd done."

"We need to contact the woman who was raped—it's a matter of urgency. If you don't recall her name, maybe you can think of someone who would remember her?"

Silence.

"Hello?"

Hanna can't shake off the feeling that Leffe knows a great deal about the incident—otherwise surely he wouldn't care so much after all these years. If he doesn't answer her questions, she is going to get in the car and drive over to Storlien. It is quite a distance, but it might be worth it if she can get him to talk by standing face-to-face.

Maybe Leffe thinks he is protecting the victim and her now grown-up child, but he couldn't be more wrong.

"This is a matter of life and death," she says, trying to get across the importance of his cooperation. "If you know the woman's name, you have to tell us. We need to speak to her right away." Hanna stands up and starts pacing back and forth. "Please," she begs.

"Her name was Monica," Leffe replies with sorrow in his voice. "Monica Mogren. She was so beautiful back then . . ."

Thank God.

"And the child?"

"She had a little boy. He must be nearly fifty now."

It was exactly as Hanna thought—Leffe knew the story, and the identity of the woman who had been so shamefully treated.

"Do you have an address for them?" She can't hide her impatience.

"Monica left Storlien. I don't know where she and her son went—I never saw them again."

97

It doesn't take Hanna long to find the now-deceased Monica Mogren and her son in the public registry. She grabs her jacket and shouts to Daniel, telling him she has an address. They hurry to the car, and Daniel reverses out of the parking lot.

"Do you really think Mogren could be in danger too?" he asks as he heads for the E14. "A half brother that no one knew about?"

He sounds dubious, as if he is worried that they are devoting their time to the wrong thing.

Hanna agrees that Filip's disappearance is their number one priority, but she can't cope with the idea that yet another person might come to harm right in front of them.

"If Hedin and Lehto are capable of abducting Charlotte's son, then they could easily go for her half brother. We must at least warn him."

She has already tried calling him several times, but there is no reply. This might simply mean that his phone is switched off because of work, or because the battery needs charging. However, there is a risk that he is in acute danger if the blood tie to Charlotte is key.

If Charlotte knew she had a sibling and had already made contact with him, then Hedin and Lehto might have been aware of his existence.

"Can you go any faster?"

Daniel takes the next bend at such speed that Hanna has to grab a hold of the door handle on the passenger side.

She realizes he isn't convinced, but she trusts her intuition. They have to find the half brother before anyone else does. According to their colleagues on patrol, Hedin is still missing, and there is no sign of Lehto either. His wife claimed he was out with the dog when the officers called, but he isn't answering his phone.

Suspicions against both men are piling up. Why would they be avoiding the police if they are not behind the two homicides?

Filip must be found.

They still haven't heard from the phone's service provider, and no new sightings have come in over the past hour.

Hanna shifts anxiously in her seat. The stress is rising with every minute. Her thoughts are all over the place, and the lack of sleep certainly isn't helping.

The landscape swishes by. The weather is overcast and very windy, buffeting the trees along the E14.

They are heading for Ängena, a collection of houses ten minutes from there on the road to Duved. That is where Erik Mogren lives—the child who was conceived in Storlien as a result of rape just under fifty years ago.

Today he is an adult. Charlotte's half brother, Filip's uncle.

Hanna silently goes over the details she found in the register. Married, no children. Father unknown, mother deceased.

Finally a sign appears, and Daniel takes a right. After one more turn, they arrive at a small single-story dwelling with blue wood paneling and white window frames.

As soon as the car stops, Hanna leaps out and runs to the door, with Daniel close behind. There is no bell, so she knocks loudly.

The sound of a dog barking comes from inside—this is encouraging, someone should be home.

She knocks again, and after a minute or so, a plump, middle-aged woman opens the door. Her hair is all over the place, and she has clearly been crying—her face is red and her eyes are swollen.

Hanna inhales sharply.

It is obvious that something is wrong.

Are they too late?

98

Tiina stares at the woman in the woolen hat. She seems agitated, her breathing is rapid, and her hand is raised as if she is about to knock again. Behind her is a man with a short beard, wearing a dark-blue padded jacket.

When they introduce themselves as police officers from Åre, Tiina can't cope anymore.

"Is he dead?" she asks, dropping to her knees in the hallway. She buries her face in her hands and whimpers. The woman, who says her name is Hanna, steps forward and helps Tiina up.

"We need to talk," she says. "Can we go and sit in the kitchen?"

Tiina nods. She sinks down at the kitchen table with images of Ogge swirling around in her head. A faint groan emerges from her lips, and Zelda reacts. She comes padding in from the living room and positions herself protectively beside Tiina's chair.

The man, who is called Daniel, pours her a glass of water. He sits down next to her, and Hanna takes the chair opposite.

"You asked if he was dead," she begins. "Who did you mean?"

"My husband," Tiina whispers.

"Erik Mogren?"

"Yes."

"What makes you think he's dead?"

Tiina is twisting her hands together in her lap, so tightly that the skin whitens over her knuckles. The emotional roller coaster of the last few days made her think the worst when the police appeared on her doorstep.

Nothing is as it seems.

"Why are you here?" she mumbles.

"We think your husband might be in grave danger," the man informs her calmly. "We need to contact him as a matter of urgency."

"He's not dead?"

"Not as far as we know."

He's alive.

The words release something within Tiina. If Ogge is in danger, then she must have gotten it wrong. That's why he is inaccessible, he is hiding.

The relief is so great that she has to grip the edge of the table to keep her balance. Then she remembers the other stuff, the bloodstained sock, the marks on the T-shirt that haven't gone away. The nocturnal outing on the scooter around the time when a woman was strangled outside the hotel.

Tiina weeps with exhaustion and confusion.

Everything is so chaotic.

"Do you know where your husband is?" the woman asks gently. "If so, it's really important that you tell us."

"He's been gone for several days," Tiina sobs. "His car isn't here, and I can't get a hold of him."

She feels the room begin to spin. Not even Zelda's damp nose on her knee can quell the rising panic that threatens to take over.

"What do you mean, you can't get a hold of him?" Daniel asks.

Tiina's breathing is shallow, and her eyes are darting from one officer to the other.

"I've called and texted over and over again, but he doesn't answer."

"And you have no idea where he might be?"

"No."

"Has anything unusual happened during the last week?" Hanna asks. "Has your husband received any threatening calls, or suspected someone could be following him? Has his behavior changed?"

Tiina sees the bloodstained sock in her mind's eye yet again. She doesn't know for sure if it means anything.

But something terrible must have happened.

"We just want to help." Hanna's voice is so kind and sympathetic that Tiina gets a lump in her throat.

"It started last week," she whispers. "It's been impossible to talk to him since then. And it's gotten worse and worse since that first woman was murdered where he works."

The walls are closing in.

Tiina tries to focus on the glass of water, but it seems to be moving farther away.

"Where does your husband work?" Daniel asks.

Hanna is leaning across the table. Tiina raises her head and looks into their worried faces.

"At Copperhill."

99

Not only is Erik Mogren employed at the hotel, he was also absent from home at the times when Charlotte and Aada were murdered. And he has a personal motive for Charlotte Wretlind's death.

The new information floors Daniel. Tiina has shown them the bloody sock and the T-shirt with its faint stains.

They came here because they thought Erik Mogren could be in danger. Now they are faced with a completely different scenario, one that changes everything.

In all likelihood Mogren is the killer they have been hunting.

The same person who told Hanna about the altercation between Paul Lehto and Charlotte Wretlind. Tiina has shown them a photo, and Daniel recognized him as the man from the concierge department.

It was nothing more than a red herring.

Mogren was smart enough to have used the argument at reception to cast suspicion on his colleague. His quiet tip-off had fooled both Daniel and Hanna, although her intuition had eventually led them to his home.

How could they have missed Mogren when they went through all the employees who had been on duty in the hotel on the Sunday when Charlotte was murdered?

Daniel reads the same shock and surprise on Hanna's face as he is feeling.

Tiina keeps talking. Daniel tries to concentrate while processing this new information. His brain is working double time.

The focus shifted from Paul Lehto the second they found out that Mogren is employed at Copperhill, but at the moment Daniel can't work out if there is a connection with Bengt Hedin. No one has managed to track him down yet.

"Do you really think Ogge could be behind the murders of those women?" Tiina's voice is barely holding. "Sorry, I mean Erik. He's been known as Ogge ever since he was a teenager."

Daniel would like to say something reassuring, place his hand on hers, but it's not looking good. Erik Mogren has both a hunting permit and a gun license, and he owns a snow scooter. It seems likely that the sock Tiina found will provide forensic evidence. She has also confirmed that his shoe size is forty-five, which matches the print from Charlotte's room.

Erik also appears to have a strong motive, albeit a deeply tragic one.

The facts speak for themselves.

Daniel clicks his ballpoint pen several times.

Erik Mogren has avenged his mother's misfortune on his father's daughter, his own half sister. And now he seems to have turned his attention to the rapist's grandson.

The most important thing right now is to find Filip. All available resources have been deployed, and a nationwide call has gone out.

Daniel glances at his watch. The chances of finding Charlotte's son alive are dwindling with every passing minute.

Through her tears, Tiina has told them everything she knows. She has described her husband's terrible childhood, talked about his mother who died of alcoholism. It is a tale of unimaginable tragedy. Monica Mogren was treated appallingly, both by her employer who hushed up the assault and gave her the sack, and by her parents who broke off all contact when they discovered she was pregnant. Then the community turned its back on her when she tried to raise her son alone. Alcohol was probably the only way to deal with the trauma and angst that followed the rape in the mountain hotel.

Daniel can't help thinking about his own mother, who also brought up her son alone. Francesca too was the victim of a devastating betrayal, but somehow she managed to put her son's well-being before her own pain. They had a close relationship, but now he feels a new admiration for her, and the fact that she found the strength to give him a secure childhood without allowing the bitterness to take over.

He would love to thank her for that.

Hanna looks up from her phone. She has been in touch with the service provider to request a location for Mogren's cell. This is their best chance of tracking down Filip. A little while ago they had been informed that his phone had been found in the snow at the parking lot by the train station, out of charge.

"Do you know if your husband's gun is still in the cupboard?" Daniel asks.

Tiina's expression changes to one of horror. Her face is red and puffy. She is constantly stroking her dog, as if the feel of Zelda's soft fur is her only way of clinging to reality.

"What do you mean?"

"We need to check if it's in the house."

He refrains from spelling out what he fears: that her husband is armed.

Tiina fetches the key to the gun cupboard and gives it to Daniel with shaking hands.

"It's in the cellar," she mumbles.

Hanna looks at him inquiringly when he returns to the kitchen. He shakes his head. Tiina lets out a sob when she understands the significance.

The gun is gone.

Daniel checks his watch; the CSIs should be here at any minute.

"Do you really have no idea where your husband might have taken Filip?"

"I don't know," Tiina whimpers. "I honestly don't know."

"You don't own a summer cottage or a hunting lodge?"

Each scenario passing through Daniel's mind is worse than the previous one. If Mogren is both armed and aggressive, and has already committed two murders, any hope of finding Filip alive is fading fast.

A man who has already crossed so many lines has nothing to lose.

"Please think carefully, Tiina. He must have gone somewhere."

She shakes her head.

"I swear I have no idea! We don't own another property. If I knew anything, I'd tell you, but it's impossible to work out how he thinks. He's been like a different person recently."

Hanna is standing by the sink, with an odd expression on her face.

"What is it?" Daniel asks.

They make eye contact for a few seconds.

"This might sound completely crazy . . ." She breaks off, as if she can hardly believe what she is about to say. "Is it possible that Mogren has taken Filip to Storlien? Gone back to the place where it all began?"

Hanna can't explain why, but her whole body is telling her that she is onto something. The spooky, abandoned mountain hotel could be the answer to the riddle.

She can't believe she stood face-to-face with the perpetrator and didn't realize who he was. Instead of seeing Erik Mogren as a cold-blooded killer, she accepted him as a conscientious and dutiful individual, an employee who was trying to do his job, but was uncomfortable at having to pass on his concerns about a colleague.

Mogren had deliberately led them in the wrong direction, and she had willingly followed.

How could she have been so gullible?

The pressure and the irritation with herself make her feel shaky when she calls Leffe again. She has gone into the hallway so that Tiina won't hear. Mogren's wife is still sitting at the table, clearly in shock. Her daughter is on the way from Östersund to be with her.

"Have you seen a man aged about fifty moving around the hotel area, either last night or this morning?" Hanna asks as soon as Leffe answers. "Possibly with a younger man in his twenties?"

She gives him the names and descriptions of both Mogren and Filip.

"Mogren drives a 2022 silver-gray Volvo V70, registration XZK 937," she adds.

"Do you want me to drive over and take a look?" Leffe offers. "It's only five minutes from my house."

"Please. As quickly as you can."

Does Leffe understand the gravity of the situation? Hanna doesn't want to scare him, but at the same time, it's important that he doesn't put himself in danger.

"If you do see him, you absolutely must not approach him or show yourself," she adds. "Keep out of the way and call me immediately."

"Okay. Will do."

Leffe sounds shaken as he ends the call. Through the window Hanna sees a patrol car pull onto the drive. Carina and her team will also be here before long; the whole place will be crawling with police officers.

Her phone buzzes—a text from Henry.

Have you found Filip?

When she left the Villa at dawn, Henry's face was gray. He made her promise to contact him as soon as there was fresh information.

Take care of Emily, Hanna had said before she got in the car. *Drive over there or bring her here. Neither of you should be alone under these circumstances.*

There was no other advice she could give.

Not yet, she messages quickly.

Daniel has joined her in the hallway. "Who are you texting?" he wonders, adjusting his gun belt.

"Lydia—I told her I can't talk."

Hanna doesn't want to lie, nor is she prepared to explain what happened with Henry overnight. It's too complicated, and they have other priorities.

In the cold light of day, she can't believe she was attracted to him. Or can she?

Daniel is standing so close that she could stroke his cheek. Her longing to do just that is no less powerful than yesterday. She is so tired of holding everything in all the time. Apart from Daniel, Henry is the first person who has aroused her interest in years, making her body tingle.

Her phone rings—Leffe.

"I'm standing outside at the back of the hotel. It looks as if there's been a break-in."

"Go on."

Hanna presses the phone to her ear.

"There's a smashed pane of glass in one of the doors. It has a cylinder lock, so all you have to do is reach in and turn the catch."

Hanna's head is spinning. The idea that Mogren might have gone to Storlien came out of nowhere—she can't really explain it.

Have they been lucky enough to find him?

"And the car? Have you seen Mogren's car?"

"It's here. There's a silver-gray Volvo parked at the side, with the number you gave me. No one inside."

Hanna closes her eyes, overcome with relief. They have located the murderer. The fact that the car is empty suggests that he is somewhere inside the former hotel building.

Which means Filip might be there too.

If he's still alive.

The brutality of the two previous murders doesn't fill her with confidence.

"Do not go inside the hotel," she says firmly. "You have to keep away. The person in there is very dangerous."

Daniel has opened the door to the other officers. He signals to her that it's time to go, but Hanna holds up her hand so that she can finish the call.

"We've got him!" she exclaims as soon as she has hung up. "Mogren is at the mountain hotel in Storlien."

101

Exactly twenty-seven minutes have passed as they approach the roundabout for Storlien. Daniel has never driven so fast.

Every minute feels like an eternity.

If Filip isn't already dead, they are facing a hostage situation. There is also a great deal to suggest that Mogren is mentally unstable, which makes him even more unpredictable.

The tires screech as Daniel turns into the hotel complex without slowing down.

Hanna has called the duty officer at regional dispatch and requested the immediate deployment of a SWAT team with an experienced negotiator. RapidReach text messages have gone out to all key personnel who are usually brought in during a hostage situation like this. Unfortunately the only police helicopter is being used elsewhere, so the team will have to drive up from Östersund. This means it will be three to four hours before they are on the scene—optimistically at around two thirty.

Daniel would like them here right now.

To be on the safe side, he parks some distance away from the entrance. Leffe is waiting for them behind one of the neighboring buildings.

"Do you think Filip is still alive?" Hanna asks Daniel as she unfastens her seatbelt.

"I hope so."

He knows he sounds terse. That isn't his intention, but the gravity of their position has pushed aside all superfluous words.

The hotel looms up a few hundred yards away. The sky is gray and overcast; the windows stare down, black and empty. Someone could hide absolutely anywhere in there.

Daniel's heart is pounding as he stares at the complex. He thinks of other critical incidents in which he has played a part. In Gothenburg, where he worked to bring down criminal gangs, he was at serious risk on more than one occasion. These were difficult challenges in particularly exposed areas.

This could be worse.

He wishes there was a handbook for dealing with a perpetrator of Mogren's caliber. Even if Filip is inside the hotel, and still alive, he is still at the killer's mercy. In which case they are facing the enormous task of persuading Mogren to give himself up, to hand over his prey unhurt. However, if he is in the throes of some kind of psychosis, it might not even be possible to establish contact.

Mogren has already killed twice. He has no reason to spare Charlotte's son.

Daniel gets out of the car with a heavy heart.

This is no ordinary hostage situation where the kidnapper wants something in exchange. This is what is known as a victim situation: Mogren has abducted Filip for emotional reasons.

He has picked out his victim in order to do him harm, not in order to effect some kind of exchange. He seems to be living entirely within his own world of bitterness and old injustices. Otherwise he wouldn't have taken his revenge on his own half sister and nephew.

How do you even reach a man like that?

102

Half an hour later the mountain hotel is completely surrounded and cordoned off. The police patrol cars are at the front, the snow scooters at the back.

A large group of onlookers has gathered and been moved away.

Hanna has just walked in a wide circle around the outside of the entire complex with Leffe to get an overview. There is no other damage apart from the broken pane of glass in the door, which suggests that Mogren got in that way. However, there is no way of knowing whether he is still in the main building itself.

He could be anywhere.

So could Filip.

Hanna's stress levels are making her pulse race, and all her senses are on full alert. Leffe is doing his best to help, but fear and confusion are written all over his lined face. This kind of intense mental pressure is hard to handle.

It is more than challenging for everyone involved.

As they head back to Daniel, who is talking on the phone, Hanna wonders how they are going to communicate with Mogren. Somehow they have to get him to talk to them. Trained negotiators are on their way from Östersund, but it will be hours before they arrive.

It could be too late.

By this stage Mogren must be aware that the police have tracked him down. He only has to glance out the window to see the cordons. At the same time, it is essential that he doesn't become so stressed that he does something stupid.

It is a very fine balancing act.

The most important thing is to help him to act rationally, to give up and hand himself over. Without anyone getting hurt.

The priority is to get Filip out, then to prevent Mogren from harming himself out of sheer desperation.

Another death must be avoided at all costs.

103

There are a thousand choices, Daniel thinks. But only one solution.

And he won't know if he has found the right solution until the drama is over.

Every decision they make from now on could be critical, and could cost lives.

He has just spoken to the duty officer at regional dispatch. Daniel has been made critical incident officer; his experience from Gothenburg makes him best suited to the role.

It isn't a responsibility he can refuse, but it feels like a heavy burden. As soon as the SWAT team arrives, he will have backup, and he must then decide whether or not they should go in.

There is no sign of movement behind the windows. The hotel appears to be empty and desolate, like a mausoleum to Charlotte's grandiose plans.

The wind whips up the snow around Daniel's feet. He is freezing; he is not properly dressed for spending so much time outdoors. He can smell a blizzard in the air, and dark clouds have moved in from the North Atlantic via Norway.

Hanna arrives back and passes on her observations.

"Mogren could be anywhere," she concludes. "But as he broke into the main building, I'd go for that initially."

"A UAS is on the way," Daniel informs her. "With a thermal imaging camera."

Hanna nods. During the past few years, the police have turned increasingly to the use of drones. They are known internally as UASs, short for unmanned aerial systems. When they are equipped with infrared cameras, they can be used to search for animals and people in the dark, or inside buildings. They can also detect very small differences in temperature and convert these to thermal images, which the system displays as colors.

This enables the human eye to interpret what the camera registers.

"How long before it gets here?" Hanna stamps her feet up and down. She isn't dressed for this kind of weather either.

"The pilot should arrive at any minute."

To be honest, Daniel wishes Grip were here. Having the boss on the spot would make him feel more secure, but during the morning her cough had worsened. She is now at home, waiting for the result of a COVID test. Meanwhile she must self-isolate.

It can't be helped. They have gone through the current state of play over the phone.

He turns his head as he hears the sound of a car engine. A blue Audi has been allowed through the cordon and pulls in beside them.

Petter, the UAS pilot, has arrived.

Daniel explains what is going on, and within a very short time, a quadcopter with four propellers is hovering above their heads. This model is often used in search operations in the mountains to locate people who have been buried in the snow. Now it is a case of pinning down Mogren and Filip so that the SWAT team will know where to go in.

In seconds it is high in the air, a black insect with artificial eyes.

The hum of its engine is barely audible.

"Start with the main building," Hanna says.

Her eyes are glued to the double screens showing what the system picks up. She is looking for a sign that someone is in there, a glimpse of Mogren or Filip, an arm or a face.

The mountain hotel is huge—they have thousands of square feet to search.

Daniel pushes that thought aside. He turns to Hanna; her expression is one of grim determination. This time it feels as if they have an almost impossible task before them.

"I think we have one or more individuals directly below the drone," the pilot says suddenly.

Daniel glances up at the drone, which is hovering motionless in the air.

"That must be the dining room," Hanna says breathlessly. "Or maybe the old Loft, where we were the other day. The room with the bar and the ceiling paintings."

She points to one of the short sides of the building and takes a step closer to Petter.

"Fly as close as you can to those windows."

The quadcopter changes direction and heads toward the section where the Loft is located. Daniel is staring so hard at the screens that his eyes are hurting. Hanna lets out a small cry as a shadow passes by.

"There! I'm sure I saw something!"

The drone has moved on, but Daniel also thought he saw a silhouette that didn't belong in the room.

"Fly back," he says quickly. "We need to take another look."

The pilot moves the joystick. Daniel and Hanna wait as the seconds crawl by. Then the quadcopter is in the correct position, hovering motionless once more.

It is dark inside the window, it is not easy to see through the dirty glass, but the image on the screen appears to show someone sitting on a chair.

"Is that Filip?" Hanna whispers. "Do you think it could be him?"

The figure is not moving, the head is lolling onto the chest.

Hanna inhales sharply. "Is he alive?"

104

When Filip wakes up he is sitting in the middle of a room with a dark carpet. There are large windows all around, with nothing but whiteness visible outside.

The bright light hurts his eyes so much that he closes them again.

The next time he opens them, he is even more bewildered. He is alone, there is no sign of his abductor, and he is in a place that resembles an old-fashioned bar. There is a long counter behind him, with small groups of chairs and tables dotted around. The ceiling is covered in highly stylized paintings of animals and people in pastel colors.

In his confused state it looks bizarre, like a weird version of Dante's *Inferno*.

Is he under the influence of drugs?

He still can't move. His arms and legs are tied to the chair; he has no feeling in his muscles. The gag has slipped down a little, making it easier to breathe, but the panic means he is shaking uncontrollably.

Was this how his mom felt in the moments before she died? Was she as afraid as he is now?

She had always represented the security in his life. When Dad didn't get in touch at Christmas, she would always wrap presents and pretend they came from him so that Filip wouldn't be upset.

There is a horrible musty, stale smell, and he is very thirsty. His lips are dry, and his tongue is sticking to the roof of his mouth. When he tries to swallow, there isn't enough saliva.

Is he going to die here—of thirst?

Filip tugs at the ropes, but his efforts are in vain. The pain makes him grimace; the skin around his wrists and ankles is already sore and red-raw. He cannot free himself.

He slips in and out of consciousness. When he comes around again, he can't work out how much time has passed. But something is different, there is a flashing light in the distance. The white landscape has changed.

Blue light.

It vanishes as quickly as it appeared, but it does allow a faint hope to stir in his breast.

Filip prays, silently and feverishly. Please let it mean that the police are here, that they have found him.

That someone is on the way to rescue him.

Here I am, he wants to shout. *Help me!*

But all that emerges is a muffled groan.

It doesn't matter how hard he tries, it is impossible to make himself heard.

105

The softly undulating mountain landscape acts mostly as a bitter reminder to Hanna of her own inadequacy. The pressure is too great. She doesn't want to contemplate the beauty of nature when the situation is so challenging.

She feels as if she has been leaning forward and staring at the images from the drone for an eternity. They are almost certain that it is Filip who is tied up in the bar on the top floor. However, they cannot determine what state he is in.

There has been no sign of Erik Mogren, but the thermal imaging camera indicates that there is another person in the building, not far away from Filip.

"We have to establish contact with Mogren," Hanna says. "We can't wait for the negotiators from Östersund."

Daniel pulls his hat down over his ears. "I suggest you start talking to him in the meantime. I'm sure you can get him to listen better than I can."

Hanna stares at her colleague. "I have no training in this kind of thing."

"At least you studied psychology at university."

True, but none of her textbooks have prepared her for this. There are 150 trained police negotiators in Sweden, and Hanna is not one of them.

"You can do it." Daniel sounds completely convinced.

"I'm not sure." Hanna can hear the tremble in her voice. The smallest misstep could have fatal consequences—it is a terrible responsibility to take on.

"You've got the necessary skills," Daniel assures her. "Believe me. You'll do a much better job than anyone else."

He puts his arm around her shoulders and draws her close. For a few seconds she allows herself to relax, leaning against him and feeling the warmth of his body.

"You're the best cop I know," he adds quietly. "You've got this, Hanna."

When he lets go she is calmer, more confident. He believes in her ability, so she must do the same.

She closes her eyes, tries to remember what she has read about negotiating in a hostage context. It is important to create trust by showing empathy and listening actively. This requires the ability to put yourself in the other person's position.

The goal is to ensure that no one gets hurt, which means you must assume you are approaching a person in crisis.

At the same time, Erik Mogren is acting rationally in his own eyes, so she will have to try to alter his behavior of his own volition. By building up trust it is possible to create an atmosphere in which he will be ready to listen to the suggestions of others.

Slowly she turns her head and looks up at the bar and the bank of shining windows.

Filip is in there, tied to a chair. She really wants to believe he is alive. She has to proceed from that assumption.

She takes out her phone.

Filip's life is in her hands.

106

The phone rings out, but Erik doesn't answer. Hanna tries again, and again.

"I need to be able to call out to him," she says to Daniel.

Within minutes a megaphone has been produced. Hanna positions herself behind a tree so that Mogren will be able to hear her, but she won't be exposed to danger. They have to assume he is armed—the gun cupboard in his home was empty.

She raises the megaphone to her mouth and shouts as loudly and clearly as she can.

"Erik Mogren, this is Hanna Ahlander from the Åre police. I'm trying to call you. Please answer your phone."

She gazes up at the windows. Daniel is standing a short distance away, and gives her an encouraging nod. After a moment she repeats her message; then she tries Mogren's number again.

The phone rings seven times—no answer. The line is a little erratic, the seconds tick by, and she is clutching her phone so tightly that her fingers are damp with perspiration.

There is no sign of movement behind the dark windows of the mountain hotel.

She hears the screech of brakes as a train slows down on its way to the station in Storlien.

The air goes out of Hanna. This isn't going to work.

She is about to end the call when a hoarse male voice says, "Hello?"

The relief is so overwhelming that she almost drops the phone. Then the adrenaline kicks in, sweeping aside any hesitation. She empties her head of all the opinions and feelings she has had about Mogren so far, deletes her own likes and dislikes.

All she can see in her mind's eye is his face.

A man in crisis.

This is probably the worst day of his life. He is agitated, and incapable of making a rational decision. They don't know each other; they have spoken only once for a couple of minutes. She doesn't know the circumstances that have led to this point. She has a very limited knowledge of his childhood and what is driving him now, or the burning hatred that seems to have led to the two brutal murders.

None of that matters anymore.

Right now Erik Mogren is simply a human being, and the last thing he needs is her contempt. She will treat him with dignity, show him respect and sympathy.

Above all, she is not here to judge him. That is the only way she can hope for a resolution that will not end in tragedy.

"Hi, Erik," she says in a clear, warm voice. "My name is Hanna Ahlander—we spoke in the foyer at Copperhill the other day. Thank you for answering your phone."

There is a long pause before he speaks. The air feels colder; Hanna is acutely aware of her frozen feet.

"What do you want?"

His tone is hostile, his voice hoarse. He sounds like a different man from the one she met at the hotel, when he quietly told her about the altercation between Paul Lehto and Charlotte Wretlind.

"I just want to talk to you, that's all."

Hanna makes an effort to sound interested, and realizes that she actually is. She genuinely wants to understand what has brought him here.

"How are you feeling?" she adds.

"None of your fucking business!"

He sounds unsettled, his breathing is rapid. This is not good—someone under pressure is unpredictable. The smallest sign of a lack of respect could trigger a violent response.

In his position it is all about keeping control.

"I understand," Hanna replies.

"No, you fucking don't!" he yells in her ear. "You have no idea what's going on in my head!"

Hanna takes a deep breath. No doubt Erik is facing utter desperation, knowing that the police are outside. This makes him dangerous. The more powerless he feels, the greater the risk that he will resort to violence again—it is his only tool when it comes to mastering his environment.

"I'm sorry," she replies in the same calm tone. "I just meant I understand that you're in a difficult situation." She waits for a few seconds before continuing, giving him space if he wants to say something.

"I'm not trying to pressure you, but I want you to know that no one has come here intending to harm you. We just want to help work out a solution. Together."

She glances up at the hotel again, thinks she glimpses movement on the floor below the bar. As if Mogren is standing by the window immediately below the location where they think Filip is being held captive.

Which means he must be in the dining room or the Loft, just as they suspected.

405

"We're not going to enter the building until both you and I are in agreement, okay?"

"How can I trust you?" Erik snaps. "Why should I believe you? All you want is to lock me up and throw away the key."

"I imagine this must be very hard for you." Hanna means every word.

Erik is breathing heavily now, and says something she can't make out. At least he isn't yelling anymore.

She thinks back to the day when they stood together in the foyer. His features were smooth, giving nothing away. Now his deep frustration is coming across very clearly, and she can imagine that his face is distorted.

"I'm here," she reassures him. "All I want is to help you. If you'll let me?"

The key thing is to keep the conversation going so that he doesn't hang up.

Hanna is prepared to do her utmost to gain Erik's trust, to make him feel he can turn to her for advice and support. This is the most critical moment in his life.

But the fear is pounding within her body just as much as his. As long as they are talking to each other, Erik can't hurt anyone.

Which means there is still a chance to find a way out.

107

In the end Filip slips into a kind of torpor, and the room disappears. He is slumped on the chair with his eyes closed. His thirst is increasing as the hope of rescue fades.

He is vaguely aware of an agitated voice speaking loudly in the background. He opens his eyes and looks up—has his kidnapper returned?

Is this when he is going to die, just like his mom?

Images of her dead body drift through his mind. He didn't get to see her, but the little he has heard is enough. Her throat was cut, she choked on her own blood.

His heart is racing, and he fights to remain conscious. He wants to scream and shout, even though he knows it is pointless. Instead he forces himself to listen to whoever is talking on the phone.

Filip can hear the answers, but not the questions.

The man sounds angry and bitter, switching between feeling sorry for himself and cursing the people who have done him harm. He makes excuses for his actions and blames others, says he was forced to do what he did.

Slowly Filip begins to make sense of it all. The truth is horrific and more terrifying than he could have imagined.

It makes him tug at the ropes binding his arms and legs. Nothing happens this time either, however hard he tries. He is in significant pain from the wounds caused by the chafing.

Then his strength runs out and he gives up.

I haven't done anything, he wants to yell to the lunatic behind him.

The man seems to have moved farther away, his voice is fainter now. Then it disappears completely, and Filip is alone again.

"I haven't done anything," he whispers into the emptiness.

108

Daniel has never seen Hanna so focused.

They have brought in the motor home that is often used as a mobile police station; today it is operating as the command center. Hanna is sitting at the far end so that she can continue talking to Mogren in peace and quiet. She is linked to a group that allows others to listen in, which means that Daniel is able to participate, but Mogren won't hear any comments he might make.

The conversation between Hanna and the killer is volatile to say the least. One minute he is yelling at her; the next he is weeping with fury. It is as if he has no filter; he is so wound up that he can barely express himself coherently.

Daniel finds what Mogren is saying deeply unpleasant. The way he rationalizes what he has done.

A sane person doesn't say that kind of thing.

How is Hanna going to get to a point where it is possible to reason with him, when he is so hysterical and unpredictable? Daniel has no idea.

But Hanna keeps her composure. She asks brief questions and listens to the responses, with measured pauses. She acknowledges whatever Mogren says with a well-judged reply or comment. Daniel notices how skillfully she uses Mogren's own words; instead of simply saying that she understands or agrees, she repeats what he has just said. This is a way of providing affirmation, while at the same time building trust between them.

Daniel would never be able to do this. He is far too quick to judge; he doesn't have the patience necessary to assure a violent killer that everything is going to be all right.

Not when he knows what the man has done.

The SWAT team has just arrived from Östersund.

If it weren't for Filip, Daniel would give the order to storm the building. Their black bus is parked by the general muster point. A sniper in a snowsuit is in position in case it becomes possible to take a shot at Mogren, while the rest of the team are covering what is known as the "white side"—the main entrance. The remaining facades have also been given color-coded designations to avoid any confusion over which section of the hotel they are talking about.

In his earbuds Daniel hears Hanna mention Filip's name.

"How's Filip?" she ventures. "How's he doing?"

Silence. Daniel breaks out in a sweat as they wait for an answer. Has Hanna gone too far? Was it too soon to ask the question?

Timing is key, saying the right thing at the right time. Otherwise the fragile relationship she has worked so hard to achieve could come crashing down. Daniel tries to make eye contact with her, but she is concentrating so hard that she doesn't even notice.

"I don't want to talk about Filip."

"It sounds as if you're very angry with him," Hanna says.

"Too fucking right."

She ignores his aggressive tone. "Can you tell me more about that? What has he done to you?"

Mogren's breathing is ragged and shallow.

"You know perfectly well what his grandfather did to my mother!" he bellows. "I don't want that rapist's genes passed on!"

"Tell me what's upsetting you so much."

Mogren talks about blood vengeance going back through the generations.

He is insane.

If Daniel were on the other end of the phone, he would be telling Mogren what a sick bastard he is, having ruthlessly murdered two innocent women. Or he might sarcastically point out that Mogren carries the same DNA profile as his first victim.

"I can't bear the thought of him getting away with it," Mogren says more quietly.

He is talking about his father, Curt Wretlind, as if he were still alive.

As far as Daniel is concerned, this is yet another sign of his distorted perspective, but he can't help feeling contempt when the man refuses to accept responsibility for his actions. There has to be a limit on the extent to which you can blame your own misfortune on your parents.

The last year's therapy sessions have made Daniel realize that.

There is no such thing as original sin.

In the middle of this tragedy, he feels a fresh insight begin to form.

Each person creates their own life.

In the end we always have a choice.

"I understand how you might feel that way, but Curt has been dead for many years," Hanna says gently.

"Someone has to pay for what he did! None of this is my fault."

Once again Daniel feels sheer contempt, but Hanna's tone is sympathetic.

"It's perfectly natural for you to be so angry, given what happened. But have you thought about where you are directing your anger?"

Mogren continues to spew out fury and hatred.

Daniel checks the time; it is almost four o'clock. They still have no confirmation that Filip is alive.

He scribbles *How's Filip?* on a Post-it and pushes it across to Hanna. There is already a pile of notes with different questions in front of her. It's Daniel's way of helping without speaking—he doesn't want to distract her.

She takes it without reacting, and Daniel is so proud of her. She is so strong; she is managing to sound both empathetic and engaged without asserting her authority.

Other negotiators are on the way, but there has been a delay. Colleagues from Sundsvall have had to be brought in because some staff in Östersund are on Easter leave.

"Are you near Filip? How is he doing?"

"He's upstairs."

"Where?"

"In the bar. I can't stand looking at him."

Daniel leans forward. It definitely sounds as if Filip is alive.

"Of course. In that case it's probably wise not to be in the same place." Hanna's voice carries just the right amount of sympathy. "Young men can be hard work sometimes. And he's only twenty-three, much younger than you. In fact you're old enough to be his dad."

She keeps chatting, sneaking in references to Filip from time to time.

Daniel knows what she is doing. She is trying to get Mogren to regard Charlotte's son as flesh and blood. A real person, not a symbol of old injustices.

This will increase the chances of persuading him not to harm Filip.

"I've got an idea," Hanna says a few minutes later. "If you find it too difficult to speak to Filip, maybe I could do it instead?"

Daniel notices that her knee is jiggling up and down, even though her tone remains calm and steady.

"Not now," Mogren says unexpectedly. "My battery is about to die."

Hanna gives Daniel an agonized look. They have to keep the conversation going, or there is no hope.

"What do we do?" she whispers.

"Burner phone," he whispers back.

They can send in a new phone to keep the lines of communication open.

"Okay, this is what we're going to do," she says, without a trace of anxiety in her voice. "If you just wait a little while, we'll get you another phone."

Mogren says nothing. There is a scraping noise in the background.

"Tell him where we're going to put it," Daniel whispers.

"How about if we open the door to the left of the main entrance, and leave a box containing a new phone? Then you can call me when you've got it. How does that sound?"

There is no response for some time. Hanna's shoulders are hunched. Daniel can hardly breathe.

Eventually Mogren grunts.

"If you're lying to me, then it's Filip who will pay."

"I promise we're not going to try anything," Hanna assures him quickly.

And then, before he can reply, the connection is broken.

109

Hanna is waiting for a new phone to arrive. Someone has given her a chocolate cookie, which she is munching in order to give herself some energy. Every muscle aches from the tension of the last few hours.

Filip's life is in her hands.

She must not fail.

The door opens, and in comes Jonas Höglid, the leader of the SWAT team. He is well over six feet tall, and his heavy uniform and sturdy body armor make him appear even bigger. He looks at Hanna as if she were an object to be assessed.

"The best thing would be to separate the perpetrator from the hostage," he says in a matter-of-fact tone. "If you could persuade Mogren to come down to the entrance, my team can go in the back way with tear gas."

The suggestion stresses Hanna out. If Mogren realizes he is under attack, anything could happen.

Daniel is also skeptical. "That carries a significant risk. If he works out what we're doing, then . . ."

Jonas runs a hand over his shaven head. "The other alternative is to lure him to a window so we can get a clear shot."

"We need to carry on negotiating," Hanna says firmly. "However long it takes."

A few more hours won't matter if it saves a human life.

"We need to prioritize measures that will reduce violence," she continues. "I think we should keep talking to him."

She looks to Daniel for support, but Jonas is hard to convince. "It's well below freezing out there. My team's combat-readiness is dropping with every hour that passes. We can't wait around indefinitely."

A colleague comes into the motor home to inform them that a fully charged phone has been sent into the hotel. He gives Hanna the new number on a piece of paper. She holds it in her hand. It is as light as a feather, but it feels like a ton weight.

This could be the key to a peaceful resolution.

Or a catastrophe.

"I trust you, Hanna," Daniel says. "You can do this."

He gives her an encouraging nod, and she manages a wan smile in return. She is both exhausted and full of adrenaline.

It isn't over yet.

It won't be over for a long time.

"Okay, we go again," she says, calling the number.

110

The shuffling footsteps on the stairs terrify Filip.

As long as he was alone in the bar, at least he was unharmed. He has waited and waited, hoping that the police will rescue him. Instead his kidnapper seems to be on the way back.

Filip still has no idea who he might be, but those approaching footsteps fill him with fear.

A middle-aged man appears in the doorway. He has dark hair and narrow eyes, with a big belly beneath a thick, scruffy sweater.

He looks big and strong.

Hard.

His expression is full of such venom that Filip instinctively presses himself against the back of the chair. He has never encountered anyone who radiates so much hatred.

And they have never even met before.

He stares as the man moves closer. He is sure he's never seen him before, and yet there is something familiar about his face.

The man says nothing, and now Filip sees that he is carrying a green plastic container in each hand. He puts them down on one of the round tables and unscrews the caps, one after the other.

The smell makes Filip recoil in horror.

It is gasoline.

The man ignores Filip. It is as if he is invisible, as if he doesn't exist.

The man begins to splash the gasoline around the chair where Filip is sitting. Pools of liquid are immediately absorbed by the dark carpet. The acrid fumes fill the air, making Filip cough.

Fear explodes in his chest.

"Mom," he whimpers helplessly into the gag. "Emily."

The man continues to ignore him as he splashes the gasoline in a long trail behind him, then disappears down the stairs.

The fumes are nauseating. Soon Filip feels so ill that he has to fight not to be sick.

He tries not to think about what would happen if he threw up into the gag. The fear of choking on his own vomit makes him swallow frenetically, over and over again.

Then the tears come, dripping from his nose onto the gag. All the snot and mucus make it hard to breathe, but he can't stop.

He doesn't want to burn to death.

He doesn't want to die.

"Mom," he groans quietly.

Save me.

111

It is almost six thirty in the evening, and Hanna can feel that she has been on the phone for many, many hours. Her back is protesting and her glutes are stiff. There is an ache just below one ear, even though she is using a headset.

"You just don't get it!" Mogren yells.

"I'm sorry," Hanna says, backing off immediately.

They have started to talk about how badly his mother was treated after the brutal rape.

"She had to carry all the blame, and she lost her job even though she was the victim. Her parents kicked her out, she had nowhere to go."

"It sounds terrible. I can't begin to imagine what it must have been like."

Mogren has been repeating the same thing for the last hour. It really is a dark and tragic story, and Hanna's heart bleeds for the young woman.

"That fucking hotel only wanted to protect its own reputation." He lowers his voice, as if the rage triggered by his memories is threatening to choke him. "They didn't care what happened to my mom. Or me. They can burn in hell. Just like the vile creature who is supposed to be my father!"

"What do you mean?" Hanna rests her chin on her hand to ease the tension in the back of her neck.

"He got away scot-free. No one held him accountable; it was only my mom who had to pay. He carried on with his life as if nothing had happened, while she worked her fingers to the bone to bring me up alone. And then *she* came back."

"She" is Charlotte.

Little by little Hanna has teased out the motive behind the first murder. What happened when Charlotte began to stay at Copperhill on a regular basis, and Mogren realized whose daughter she was. How the sight of her made him increasingly frustrated. Her snobbish big-city attitude brought back everything his mother had told him.

Terrible childhood memories came swirling to the surface.

Charlotte's plans to restore the Storlien mountain hotel to its former glory infuriated him. He couldn't bear the thought of the place coming back to life.

It would be a constant reminder of what his mother had been forced to go through.

Ever since he was a little boy, she had imprinted his father's name, Curt Wretlind, in the child's mind. He grew up with the story of the man who had behaved with such ruthless cruelty, he was reminded over and over again that Curt refused to accept responsibility for his son.

During all those years Erik attempted to make contact only once, and Curt refused to have anything to do with him. He denied paternity, told him never to contact him again. If Erik made the slightest attempt to contact Curt's wife or other children, he would regret it.

In the end the dam broke.

It was the evening when he witnessed the altercation at reception, when he saw how badly Charlotte behaved toward Paul Lehto.

It proved once and for all that she was exactly like her father. She simply took what she wanted and treated everyone else like shit. Curt

Wretlind's egotistical, self-obsessed bloodline had continued, and it was unbearable. Okay, so the original perpetrator was dead, but Charlotte was very much alive.

That was when Erik made his decision.

He had dreamed of punishing her. That was why he took her key card in an unguarded moment. Now it was clear what he had to do. It was as if fate was directing his actions.

Deep down it was all about penance and atonement. Someone had to pay for what Curt had done.

That was why Filip had to be removed too, according to Erik's twisted logic.

Daniel hands Hanna a bottle of Coca-Cola. She drinks gratefully. She isn't hungry, but is beginning to feel dehydrated. The slight pressure over her temples is a sure sign.

Erik Mogren and poor Filip must also be suffering from the lack of food and drink.

However, it does feel as if they are making some progress. Over the past hour Erik hasn't sounded quite as aggressive. His mood swings have become less frequent, and a few times he has even asked for Hanna's opinion.

She hopes this means that she is getting through to him.

"What can I do for you?" she says when a natural pause arises.

"I'm hungry."

This is the first time during the entire conversation that he has diverted from his main theme—bitterness because of the assault almost fifty years ago, and its consequences.

"I'm sure you must be—we've been talking for a long time. I'd be hungry too if I were you."

"I want a pizza from Flamman."

Hanna recognizes the name of the nearby restaurant. "I'm sure we can arrange that. Shall I order one for Filip too?"

"Fuck him."

Hanna wonders if the time is right to make another attempt to speak to Charlotte's son.

It's make or break.

"I'd really like to hear him say he doesn't want anything, if that's okay with you?"

Silence.

When Hanna looks down she realizes she has her fingers crossed. It's childish, but she really hopes she will be able to speak to Filip.

"Wait a minute."

She hears Erik's footsteps moving across the floor. Then comes another voice, weak and strained, but she recognizes it.

Filip. He sounds terrified.

"Hello?"

"Hi, Filip," she says, as gently as she can. "It's Hanna from the police in Åre. How are you doing?"

"Help me," he whispers.

"He'll be fine as long as no one tries to get in here," Erik says.

"I promise we won't come in without your agreement," Hanna assures him, just as she has done several times already. It is a huge relief to hear Filip's voice.

He's alive.

"Tell her about the gasoline," Erik says in the background.

"He's splashed gasoline all over me," Filip sobs, on the verge of hysteria. "It's everywhere." He is wheezing, and suddenly he yells, "He's going to kill me! You have to break in!"

"Shut the fuck up!"

The sound of several blows makes Hanna recoil. Then there is a faint whimpering that seems to come from Filip.

It is horrible to hear him being mistreated and knowing she cannot intervene. She could scream with frustration.

Seconds pass. She hears muffled sobs in the background, then Erik is back on the line.

"I want a moose meat pizza and a Coca-Cola."

His voice is ice cold. It is as if the meaningful conversations of the past few hours never happened.

The sight of Filip seems to have fanned the flames of his rage.

"If you make the slightest attempt to get in when you leave the food, I will set fire to the gasoline. The whole place will be razed to the ground."

Hanna swallows hard. Daniel, who has positioned himself beside her, is ashen-faced.

This is much worse than they could have imagined. One wrong step and Filip will die.

"I hear what you're saying. You've got nothing to worry about."

She has to get through to Mogren, she can't lose him now.

Her mouth is dry as she pleads with him.

"Please, Erik. Don't do anything stupid that you're going to regret."

The floor is cold beneath Erik's feet as he stands in the doorway of the small kitchen.

He is wearing his pajamas; it is the middle of the night, and he has just woken from a horrible nightmare. That was when he discovered that Mom wasn't in bed next to him. His cheeks were wet with tears after the bad dream, but Mom didn't come when he called. After a while he plucked up the courage to get out of bed and went looking for her in the little cottage.

Now he sees that she is lying on her stomach in the middle of the kitchen floor. One cheek is resting on the plastic mat, her eyes are closed, but her mouth is half open.

A trail of white spittle has trickled down her chin.

"Mom?" he says tentatively. "What are you doing?"

She doesn't react. It looks as if she's asleep, but he doesn't understand why she is lying here in the kitchen instead of in bed.

Why didn't she lie down beside him as usual?

Hesitantly he moves closer. There is a horrible smell, and he instinctively backs away. It seems as if Mom has been sick right in front of the sink; he sees a pool of reddish vomit.

The ends of her long black hair have ended up in the disgusting mess. Several empty wine bottles are on the floor next to a white pill bottle.

"Mom," he says again, louder this time. "Wake up!"

She still doesn't react, and fear squeezes his heart. Without her he has nobody. He is the only one in his class without a dad, and he has never met his maternal or paternal grandparents.

Something wet runs down his cheeks. He is crying, although he shouldn't. Mom often tells him that he must be brave. He has turned eleven and is a big boy now.

He edges closer, despite the stench. Tries to work out if Mom is still breathing.

She is completely motionless. When he cautiously reaches out and touches her, she is unnaturally cold. Her chest isn't moving either.

Slowly the truth begins to sink in.

Mom is never going to wake up again.

Now he really is alone.

112

Dusk has begun to fall in Storlien, and the mountain birch trees are casting long shadows on the snow. Daniel has gone outside to get some fresh air. Hanna is still in the motor home, having something to eat. When they sent in the pizza, the conversation was interrupted. Erik hung up, and they haven't yet made contact again.

Daniel hopes the food will make the guy feel better, or at least more capable of reaching a rational decision.

One that involves giving himself up.

Or at least letting Filip go.

While Hanna was on the phone, the cloud cover has blown away. It is now after eight o'clock, and the mountain hotel is bathed in a warm evening glow. The pink clouds are reflected in the windows of the bar where Filip is being held captive. For a moment it looks as if the place is on fire, and Daniel gives a start. Then he realizes it is only the reflection of the burning sunset.

Everyone's nerves are on full alert since they found out that Mogren has drenched his hostage and part of the hotel with gasoline. The consequences if he fulfills his threat don't bear thinking about. So that was why he kidnapped Filip instead of killing him outside the restaurant.

He intends to burn the whole place down, and let Curt Wretlind's last living relative die in the flames.

It is a revenge so horrific that it's hard to take in.

The sound of an engine catches Daniel's attention. A police car approaches and stops at the cordon. Tiina is sitting in the back seat.

Under normal circumstances it is best to avoid having a close relative present in challenging hostage situations, but they are desperate. The decision was made to ask Tiina to come here, in the hope of finding other ways to reach Mogren.

Tiina gets out of the Volvo, and Daniel sees that she has brought the dog with her.

"Thanks for coming," he says, making a huge effort to sound calm.

The police cars and cordons would frighten anybody.

"Have you been informed of what's going on? That your husband is holding a young man hostage inside the hotel?"

Tiina looks as if she is at the breaking point. Her eyes are red-rimmed, as before.

"Yes," she whispers.

"Why did you bring the dog?"

"Erik loves Zelda more than anything—probably more than me." She blinks nervously. "I thought it might be good to have her here."

Daniel bends down and pats the dog's head. Erik hasn't mentioned Zelda during his conversation with Hanna, but according to Tiina she is the apple of his eye.

Interesting.

Could it be possible to divert Mogren's thirst for vengeance through his beloved pet? He seems to be totally indifferent to Filip's fate, but what if the dog might make him relent?

In hostage negotiations there is sometimes talk of a *black swan*, something that can influence the adversary and dramatically alter the whole scenario.

Could Zelda be their black swan?

They can't afford to dismiss the idea. Everyone cares about something or someone.

By this stage Daniel is prepared to clutch at the smallest straw.

"Sounds like a good idea," he says to Tiina. "Come with me and we'll tell Hanna."

113

Hanna feels the tiniest spark of hope when Erik calls her back just over an hour later.

This is the first time he has been the one to make contact. She prays with all her heart that this means he is reconsidering his actions.

Daniel is sitting beside her and has just told her that Tiina has brought the dog.

Hanna begins by chatting about the pizza, then says, "Erik, how long are you going to keep Filip there without food or water?"

"Don't talk to me about Filip!" he yells. "He doesn't deserve to live."

So far Hanna hasn't argued against Erik's various tirades, but now she decides to make an attempt.

"Is it really Filip's fault that his grandfather did such terrible things to your mother?" Her heart is in her mouth. "He wasn't even born back then."

And then it happens.

Erik's mood changes; his tone goes from aggressive to emotional. Suddenly he breaks down, sobbing piteously.

"I ought to die as well. It's too late, it's all too late!"

Daniel inhales so sharply that Hanna has to shush him.

This is good, she mouths. *It's a way in.*

For the first time since she started talking to Erik, she feels that there is a real connection. He is opening up, seeking support, revealing the depths of his despair.

However, this means they are faced with a different scenario. The balance has shifted. It's no longer only about rescuing the hostage—now there is also a very real suicide risk.

"No one deserves to die," she says. "Especially not you."

"I've done such terrible things. I've murdered two women. How am I going to be able to live with that?"

"I promise we can talk about this," Hanna assures him.

"You don't understand. I carry his bloodline too."

Once again he is talking about Curt Wretlind, the man behind this dreadful tragedy. Hanna can feel his pain, it is raw and genuine.

The space between them is filled with powerlessness and frustration.

"I'm just as dirty as the rest of them," Erik whispers. "None of us deserves to go on living."

114

"We have to go in now," Jonas Höglid says to Daniel. "We can't wait any longer."

He is standing in the snow with his legs apart, hands on his hips, looking Daniel in the eye. He nods toward the motor home, where Hanna is still on the phone.

"She's been at it all day and she's gotten precisely nowhere. For all we know the hostage might already be dead. This is a complete waste of time. We've waited far too long, and there's a limit to what my boys can cope with. They've been on standby for over five hours."

Jonas is about ten years older than Daniel, and comes from Östersund. A muscular man who talks louder than necessary. He spreads his hands wide.

"If we don't intervene soon, it could be too late."

Daniel flexes his fingers inside his gloves as he weighs up the alternatives. They are faced with a choice where every decision could mean the loss of human life.

Hanna has made significant progress. She has established an effective channel of communication with Mogren. He has gone from bitterness and aggression to admitting what he has done and acknowledging his guilt. At the same time, he still seems convinced that death is the only way out. He is agitated and trapped, very close to the breaking point.

An unpredictable man driven by immense self-loathing.

They have no idea how Filip is doing, plus Mogren is barricaded in a building that could go up in flames in minutes. All it would take is a few matches or a lighter for the disaster to become a fact.

With each passing hour, the pressure increases.

"I think we should go in with three men," Höglid states firmly.

Daniel has met his type before. He himself behaved that way at the beginning of his career, he was the kind of police officer who preferred action to discussion. Sometimes it is unbearable to remain passive when lives are at risk, but that is not enough to justify a critical decision like the one facing them now.

"My boys are trained for situations like this," Höglid continues. "They can take Mogren out before he has the chance to harm the hostage."

"But what if he's in the bar with Filip? Can they really make it all the way up there without Mogren realizing what's happening?"

Daniel chooses his words with care. It is not a good idea to create an internal conflict.

"All it would take is for someone to step on a creaky stair, and the game is up," he adds.

"They know what they're doing."

Daniel doesn't like the way Höglid dismisses him before he has finished speaking. In the end Daniel is the one who will make the decision—he is the senior officer at the scene.

The question is whether they should wait and give Hanna more time, or go for what might be the safer option and send in specially trained armed officers?

Two lives are hanging by a thread. Maybe more, if something were to go wrong during the operation. It would take so little to fail—the margins are desperately slim.

It is an inhumanly difficult decision.

"I think we should give Hanna another hour," he says.

Höglid considers the suggestion for a few seconds.

"Okay—but no more. At exactly nine thirty I'm sending the boys in."

115

It is like being inside an hourglass with the sand trickling through way too fast.

Hanna is trying to ignore thoughts of the incursion which will soon begin. She wishes Daniel hadn't told her about the limited time available; then she would have been able to concentrate fully on Erik.

As it is, the clock is ticking in the back of her mind, and the pressure is unbearable. Cold sweat is running down her spine; her heart is pounding so hard that her chest is hurting.

They are talking about Erik's childhood; she has asked him to tell her about his foster home.

At this precise moment it doesn't matter that he is a double murderer—Hanna sees nothing but the child in him. The six-year-old who witnessed his only parent's gradual decline. The eleven-year-old who found his dead mother's body in the kitchen. The young boy who first ended up in a violent foster home, then had to fend for himself as soon as he turned eighteen and society no longer had any obligation toward him.

"I'd really like to help you," she says. "If you'll let me."

"You can't. No one can help me. I have nothing to live for. It's over, don't you understand?"

"There are people who love you," Hanna counters. "You have to believe that. Your wife Tiina is sitting in a car parked outside the hotel. You can see it from the window. She came here for your sake."

Erik gives a weary sigh. The hopelessness coming down the line is almost worse than his previous aggression.

"It's too late for me and Tiina."

"That's not true. Would you like to talk to her?"

"There's no point." His voice breaks. "I don't want to see her."

"But she's here, whatever you say." Hanna hears the shrillness in her own voice and forces herself to tone it down. "Tiina has come because she cares about you. She doesn't want you to die. No one does, including me."

The back of the chair is hard against the base of her spine. She can smell plastic.

Erik takes a deep breath, as if he is about to say something. Hanna hopes—prays to a higher power—that he is going to come to his senses. She has been waiting for the right moment to reveal that his dog is here. Her instincts tell her it's time.

"By the way, Tiina has brought Zelda with her."

Silence. The only sound is the faint murmur of conversation outside the motor home.

"Zelda's here?"

There is an almost imperceptible spark of hope in Erik's voice. It is so unexpected that it gives Hanna goosebumps.

"Zelda is waiting for you—she's desperate to be with her daddy. Don't you want to come out and see her?"

"I can't do that."

"Why not?"

"Because you'll shoot me."

The fear in Erik's voice pushes everything else aside. It vibrates in the air; it is almost tangible.

Hanna puts as much conviction as she can summon up into her response: "Erik, I promise you. We are not going to harm you. You have my word—no one is going to hurt you."

She turns her head, looking for Tiina and Zelda. They are sitting in a patrol car about twenty yards away.

"Wait a minute," she says. She leaves the motor home and hurries over to the car. She opens the back door and speaks softly to the dog. When Zelda shows an interest, Hanna holds out the phone.

"Say hello to your daddy," she says encouragingly, while giving Tiina a sympathetic look.

"Hi, Zelda," Erik says shakily.

The dog pricks up her ears at the familiar sound. Then she barks and sniffs the phone.

"Did you hear that?" Hanna says, adjusting her headset. "She agrees with me—she really wants you to come out and give her a hug."

Another, longer silence.

"I daren't," Erik says eventually.

Without thinking Hanna makes another suggestion.

"What if we do the opposite—Zelda and I will come in and get you. Would you come with us then?"

Erik says nothing. She can hear his shallow breathing.

She looks up at the dark-blue night sky. She sees the white moon, almost full, over in the east. The headlights of the patrol cars cast a harsh light over the white landscape. The hotel complex looms in the shadows like a gigantic eagle's aerie.

There are fifteen minutes to go before the SWAT team goes in.

Time is running out.

She thinks about Filip, held captive inside. About Erik, who doesn't know where to turn.

If she is going to save a life, it has to happen now.

What she is planning to do goes against all the rules, but there is no other way. She quickly disconnects the link to her colleagues so that no one else will hear what she says to Erik.

"Stay where you are. I'm coming to you."

Then she grabs Zelda's leash and walks quickly and resolutely toward the hotel, even though no one is allowed to get closer than one hundred yards.

Through her headset she hears the sniper from the SWAT team reporting on her movements: "Negotiator with dog on the way to the white side. I repeat, negotiator with dog on the way to the *white* side."

She increases her speed, breaks into a run so that no one can stop her, and heads for the side door next to the main entrance.

"Hanna?" Daniel shouts from behind her. "What the hell are you doing?"

Without slowing down she turns her head, gives a dismissive wave, and disappears into the hotel before Daniel or anyone else can intervene.

116

The darkness that envelops Hanna when she slips inside is so compact that she feels as if she is wearing a blindfold. She takes out her flashlight and chases the shadows away.

She is in the foyer. To her left is the reception desk, covered in brown-and-white cowskin, and straight ahead lies the wide staircase that she remembers from her previous visit.

The main entrance is to the right.

The air is cold and musty. The only sound is her own ragged breathing.

Where is Erik?

Zelda whimpers softly by her side.

"It's okay, sweetheart," Hanna whispers, clutching the leash tightly. "Let's find your daddy."

Her phone vibrates in her pocket. Daniel is trying to reach her, but Hanna rejects the call. He immediately tries again, but Hanna rejects that one too.

She is going to get into so much trouble for this afterward.

If there is an afterward.

She makes her way cautiously toward the staircase with its dark carpet. Her heart is pounding so loudly that Erik ought to be able to hear every beat. She peers up at the ceiling; the red-painted stairwell forms a square atrium, all the way up to the top floor.

That's where the bar is.

The room where Filip is being held.

Silently she heads to the dining room and slowly sweeps the beam of her flashlight all around. No sign of anyone. Chairs and tables are set out as if dinner were about to be served. There are even cloths on the tables.

All that is missing are the guests and the staff.

It's creepy.

As Hanna continues up the stairs, the faint smell of gasoline reaches her nostrils, and a shudder runs down her spine. To be on the safe side, she feels for her gun. It is exactly where it should be, and gives her a sense of security.

One more flight of stairs up to the Loft, where the dances used to be held back in the day.

Erik should be here somewhere.

And Filip.

She ties Zelda to the banister so that the dog won't get in the way.

"Hello?" she calls out tentatively, drawing her gun. "Erik, are you here? Filip?"

117

Filip no longer believes he will be rescued. He has been sitting here for hours and hours, and nothing has happened. When the sun went down and darkness fell, the last faint hope disappeared.

The police are not coming in.

He can't free himself and get away.

He is drenched in gasoline; his nose is bloody and swollen from the blows his kidnapper delivered. He is going to die here, all alone, only days after his mom.

Perhaps it's for the best—without her he is lost.

He hears the odd ticking sound from the walls; otherwise there is silence.

There has been no sign of the man for a long time—he might even have left the building. He's probably gone, and no one dare come in to save Filip in case the hotel goes up in flames.

The thought makes him whimper; nothing is more terrifying than the idea of being burned to death. The fumes around his chair have faded slightly, but they are still a reminder of the fate that awaits him.

Images come and go in his befuddled brain.

He sees Emily, and feels a pang in his heart. He doesn't want her to remember him as someone who let her down, someone who simply walked away and left her.

He loves her so much.

Why hasn't he told her that more often? She has always been there for him, comforting him and loving him. But he will never see her again.

He lets his head droop toward his chest. He just wants to give up. Exhaustion is making his brain work so slowly; he closes his eyes and tries to fall asleep. Then at least he won't feel the thirst; that is the worst thing at the moment. His tongue is swollen; he cannot produce any saliva.

The thin skin on his lips has cracked due to the lack of moisture.

A sound from the floor below makes Filip react. He can hardly summon up the strength to raise his head, but he manages to crane his neck a fraction in order to hear better.

Surely it was a voice, calling out a name?

Or was it merely a hallucination?

His eyelids are almost stuck down with blood and tears as he peers into the darkness for a sign that someone is there.

Someone who might be able to help him at long last.

He really does want to live.

118

Hanna is gripping her gun so tightly that her hand hurts as she makes her way up the last few stairs.

She is moving in a crouched position with her flashlight switched off. It feels safer—with it on she would be a clear target if Erik has changed his mind.

He is afraid and upset, she tells herself. *He isn't going to hurt me.*

She tries to cling to those thoughts as she heads for the bar. One stair creaks when she treads on it, and the sound makes her freeze. It seems unnaturally loud in the silence, revealing exactly where she is.

She dare not move in case Erik is hiding in the gloom. Maybe he is lying in wait for her. Maybe she has misjudged his state of mind.

After all, he is a double murderer.

She waits for quite a while, then sets off again.

The smell of gasoline grows increasingly strong the higher up she goes. She stops when she reaches the top step. She can't see Erik, but she has a strong feeling that she is no longer alone. She senses the presence of another person in the wide loft stretching out before her.

He is there in the darkness, she is sure of it.

Where is he?

Is he going to attack her?

Suddenly a table lamp is switched on in the far corner. Hanna blinks as the light takes her by surprise—then she sees Erik.

He is sitting waiting for her, his shotgun lying across his knees.

The shock now that he is actually right there in front of her is almost overwhelming. And he is armed.

Is he going to shoot her?

But he looks tired, lost. He seems to have aged ten years since their conversation in the foyer at Copperhill a few days ago.

"Hi," she says slowly. "How are you doing?"

She hides her own gun behind her back so as not to spook him.

He is slumped in a dark-green leather armchair. His eyes are dull; he doesn't seem aggressive, just resigned, as if the spark within him has died.

Hanna can see that he is holding something in his hand, something small, rectangular, and yellow.

It looks like a lighter.

The sight makes her stomach turn over.

"Don't come any closer," Erik says. "Or I'll set the place on fire."

His voice is dull, but there is no doubt that he means what he says. He holds up the object so that she can see more clearly. It is indeed an ordinary cheap cigarette lighter. Then she notices the green plastic containers with the caps off at his feet.

The smell of gasoline fills the entire room.

"Get out of here," Erik says.

Hanna takes a step forward. "Surely we can talk first?"

"There's nothing to talk about."

She doesn't know how to interpret his words. Does he mean that Filip is dead, or is he referring to himself?

The adrenaline coursing through her body is making her feel dizzy.

Please don't let it be too late.

"Where's Filip?"

Erik waves in the direction of the bar. She can just make out a half staircase, and she thinks she can see a figure slumped on a chair, but she isn't sure.

"Is he still alive?"

"I think so."

Erik seems apathetic more than anything, but he is holding the lighter in a firm grip. The yellow plastic reflects the glow of the lamp, shining ominously at her.

So little separates them from disaster.

She can't tear her gaze away from the lighter. She is breathing too fast, but is finding it difficult to control her body. She is beginning to wheeze; she can't get enough oxygen into her lungs.

She coughs, playing for time.

What the hell was she thinking? Why did she come running into the hotel on her own instead of letting the SWAT team do their job?

"Let me talk to Filip," she pleads. "No one needs to die today."

Erik looks at her sadly.

"Zelda is here," Hanna says. The dog is her last hope. "She's waiting for you outside the dining room."

A glimmer of interest flares in Erik's eyes. He raises his chin a little, looks at Hanna suspiciously. "You brought Zelda with you?"

At that moment the sound of barking comes from downstairs. She must have heard Erik say her name. She barks loudly and insistently at her master, and when nothing happens she begins to howl.

Hanna realizes that she has to make a choice.

Either she focuses on freeing Filip, or she tries to persuade Erik to come downstairs to see his dog. That means she will be separating him from his victim, which might lead to Filip being saved.

If she makes the wrong decision and Erik becomes so desperate that he uses the lighter, all three of them will die.

She is still holding her gun, but she dare not shoot in the poorly lit room. If she misses, and he gets away with the lighter, everything is lost.

Zelda barks again, and Hanna is counting on the fact that Erik will not start a fire as long as the dog is in the building. He cares more about Zelda than anything else.

He will not sacrifice his dog to the flames.

Hanna prays to God that she is right.

119

Daniel is standing by a grove of small mountain birch. He has already called Hanna five times, but she has obviously decided to ignore him. Her phone rings out, but she doesn't answer.

He could wring her neck right now. What she is trying to do isn't in the least heroic, just utterly idiotic.

He has never been so angry with her as he is right now.

He has never been so terrified either.

Hanna is in a life-threatening position, and there is nothing he can do to help her.

Jonas Höglid comes stomping around the corner of the hotel.

"What the fuck is your colleague doing?" he yells from ten yards away. "This is completely unprofessional!"

"You can't go in now," Daniel says firmly, even though the SWAT team is waiting by the side door, ready for action. "It's too dangerous. You'd be risking Hanna's life."

Höglid looks as if he is trying to swallow a whole series of swear words; his jaws are so stiff that Daniel can see the muscles working beneath the skin.

"There will be consequences when this is over," Höglid snaps. "I hope you realize that."

Daniel doesn't give a damn about him and his fury. All he can think about is the fact that Hanna is in the same building as Erik Mogren, a man who has committed two brutal murders and is holding a young man hostage.

A man who has threatened to burn down the entire hotel with his victim inside.

He is just about to tell Höglid to shut the fuck up when the other man signals to his team to move away from the side door. To Daniel's relief they immediately comply.

Höglid has obeyed Daniel's order. For the moment the operation is on hold.

Hanna has been given some form of respite.

But will it be enough?

120

Zelda is barking loudly. Hanna is on the landing, and notices that Erik's attention is focused on the direction from which the sound is coming.

He is reacting to her barking.

He still cares.

Could she shoot him now, while he's distracted?

At that moment Erik turns his head and looks straight at her.

The risk is too great. Her hand drops to her side, and she decides to make one last attempt to persuade him.

"Put down the lighter, Erik. Let's go and say hi to Zelda. She's desperate to see her daddy."

Erik doesn't move. He is sitting there in the semidarkness with the lighter in one hand, the other resting on his knee. Hanna can just see that he is sweating profusely, perspiration is trickling down both temples.

Is he crying too?

It's hard to tell if it is tears or sweat dripping from his chin.

She wonders whether she dare go over to him. Is that what it will take for him to make up his mind? Can she trust her gut feeling—that he doesn't intend to harm her?

"Are they going to take Zelda away from me?" he says quietly.

Hanna understands that he is talking about the aftermath, what will happen if he decides to give up.

Bearing in mind what he has done, the legal process will take many months. Erik will probably be given a long jail sentence, unless the psychiatric assessment determines that he is suffering from a severe mental illness.

"All I can say is that your dog is really looking forward to seeing you. Can't you put down the lighter and come downstairs with me?"

Erik's fingers open and close around the small plastic object. He weighs it in his hand, gazes at it sadly.

Hanna doesn't take her eyes off him.

Then he gets to his feet and walks toward her.

121

Daniel sees the side door open slowly. He prepares himself for the worst; he can't let himself hope for a better outcome.

Just as he catches a glimpse of Hanna inside, he sees the SWAT team instantly prepare to fire. Their weapons flash in the moonlight as they assume their positions with lightning speed and well-practiced movements.

He begins to run toward the hotel. He is shouting, but can barely hear his own voice.

"Don't shoot! Do *not* shoot!"

The door opens wide, and Hanna is standing there. Behind her is a tall man in a black jacket, with a dog in his arms. It seems as if Hanna tells him to put down the animal and raise both his hands, because he nods and obeys clumsily.

"Don't shoot!" Daniel yells once again as Hanna takes a few steps forward with Mogren.

Then chaos breaks out.

Two members of the SWAT team push Hanna aside and hurl themselves at Mogren. They force him down onto the snow with his hands behind his back. Meanwhile the dog is running around, trying to bite them, attacking fiercely in order to protect her master. Someone grabs a hold of her leash, and as she is dragged away from Mogren, she begins to howl hysterically.

Hanna scrambles to her feet, blinking in confusion at the melee around her. She seems totally disorientated.

"The hostage is on the top floor," she calls out. "He's alive, but there's gasoline everywhere."

Then she sways, and Daniel reaches her just before her legs give way. She droops in his arms like a limp rag doll, and he clutches her to his chest. He doesn't know whether to tell her off or console her. In the end he does both.

He is so relieved that she is okay. That it all went well in the end.

What would he have done if she had died in there? The thought is unbearable.

"Never do anything like that again," he whispers as he strokes her hair. "Never ever."

Hanna is crying so hard that her whole body is shaking.

"You have to get Filip out."

Daniel turns his head and sees that police officers and firefighters are hurrying into the building.

"They're on their way," he assures her. "You don't have to worry."

He holds her even more tightly.

"It's over."

122

Lake Åre shimmers in the moonlight as Daniel drives toward Solbringen, where Hanna lives.

There is no one else on the road, it is almost midnight, and a myriad of distant stars sparkle in the dark sky.

Hanna is sitting beside him, curled up and in a world of her own. Her forehead is resting on the side window; she has hardly said a word since they left the police station. After the resolution of the hostage drama, everyone gathered for a debrief. It is an established rule: No one is allowed to go home after an incident like this without talking it through first.

Filip has been taken to the hospital in Östersund, and all suspicions against Paul Lehto have been dismissed. Bengt Hedin, however, is still missing—he has a lot of explaining to do, but that can wait. Right now Daniel is enormously relieved that the murderer was arrested without anyone else being hurt.

He glances at Hanna—her eyes are closed. She didn't say much during the debrief. It is clear that the long hours of negotiation have taken their toll.

He turns into her street.

"Would you like me to come in?" he asks when he pulls up outside her house.

She gives him a wan smile.

"It's okay. It's probably best if you go home to your family. It's late."

Daniel feels a sudden pang in his chest.

His family.

Ida and Alice are waiting for him.

That is where he belongs.

But Hanna looks so small in the passenger seat. He doesn't want her to be alone after what she has been through. Her input today was huge—she saved not one but two lives. It's hardly surprising that she is completely drained; she gave so much of herself that there is nothing left.

"What you did today . . ." He places a hand on her arm. "It was incredible."

If he could, he would hold her close and never let her go.

"Thanks."

She sounds utterly exhausted.

"Are you sure you don't want me to come in for a little while? We could have a cup of tea and talk."

He doesn't want to be parted from her, every minute together suddenly feels precious.

Hanna shakes her head. "I'll be fine. And I've got Morris."

"Morris?"

"My new cat." She is about to explain, then changes her mind. "I'll tell you about him some other time." She gets out of the car. "Thanks for tonight."

Just before she goes into the house, Daniel glimpses a gray-and-white cat in the doorway. She picks the animal up before disappearing from view.

He really wants to jump out of the car and go after her. Spend the night talking, promising Hanna that nothing bad will ever happen to her again.

He has never been so scared as when she went into the hotel.

The world stopped turning, time stood still.

What would he do if she didn't exist?

MONDAY, APRIL 5 **EASTER MONDAY**

123

There aren't many people in Mrs Maggie's restaurant in Duved when Anton walks in.

He looks around the cozy room, where dark wooden tables combine with a wonderful mixture of mismatched chairs and secondhand finds. There are vases of yellow flowers everywhere, and an enormous Easter egg on the bar.

Anton has deliberately arrived early; he isn't meeting Carl until seven thirty. That's twenty minutes from now, but he needs to gather his thoughts for a while. The last few days have been hectic—the aftermath of the hostage drama in Storlien has kept everyone busy.

Erik Mogren has been remanded in custody, where he will remain until his trial. Filip Wretlind is still in the hospital under observation. Bengt Hedin was finally discovered in his hunting cabin, where he had spent the last few days, keeping a low profile. They are hoping to gather enough evidence to charge him with bribery and corruption.

Anton has worked nonstop since the "major event," as the case is designated internally.

A waitress comes over, and he orders a glass of red wine—then changes his mind and goes for a beer instead. He doesn't want Carl to think he's showing off.

When the door opens again, he stiffens, but it is only a family collecting pizzas. Anton peers through the window. The restaurant is on Karolinervägen, the street where Carl lives just a few hundred yards away. It will take him only a couple of minutes to get here.

But there is no sign of Carl. Anton takes out his phone and begins to surf the net as he sips his beer. For once the press has praised the Åre police for their resourceful effort that saved the hostage from a terrible death.

The online editions of the evening papers are full of positive comments, in spite of all the criticism they published earlier in the week.

"Hi," says a voice behind him.

Carl has arrived without Anton noticing. He is so handsome that Anton can hardly breathe. He stands up to greet him, but does it so clumsily that he knocks his glass of beer onto the floor. The waitress hurries over with a cloth as Anton grabs a few paper napkins and tries to help.

Eventually the mess is cleared up, and all the broken glass has been removed.

Anton's self-confidence is also shattered.

"Can I get you another beer?" the waitress asks.

Carl speaks up first. "I'd like a glass of Chianti, please."

"No problem."

"I'll have the same," Anton says quickly, wiping the last drops of beer from the table.

They sit down and look at each other. Neither of them says anything for a few seconds.

"So," Carl begins. "That was an interesting welcome."

Anton laughs and blushes. He feels stupid; he would almost like to stand up and leave.

What a fool he was to believe they could start over.

The waitress arrives with their wine, and without looking at Carl, Anton picks up his glass and takes several sips before realizing he should have been polite and toasted his companion first.

He has messed up again.

The awkward silence seems to go on and on.

"By the way, did you hear about Bengt Hedin?" Carl asks, as if he is attempting to rescue the situation. "He was the one you came to see at the council offices last week, wasn't he?"

Anton nods. "What about him?"

"He just issued a press release—it came through on my phone on the way here."

"Oh?"

"Apparently Charlotte Wretlind had made a generous donation to the community via the council." Carl leans back on his chair. "The plan is to build up a youth facility in Storlien so that the village can grow by encouraging families with children to move there. Charlotte transferred a large sum to Hedin just before she died, so now he's going to set up a foundation in her name. To honor her memory."

Anton simply shakes his head. If Hedin imagines he can avoid being charged with bribery and corruption by using the money in this way, he is wrong.

Although right now work is the last thing he wants to think about. He reaches for his glass and realizes it is empty.

Carl changes the subject. "You said you wanted to talk to me about something. When you called."

Anton isn't ready. He looks around in a panic, desperate to order more wine and avoid meeting Carl's searching gaze. He starts to fumble with the menu in front of him.

Carl simply waits. Smiles. "I was so pleased to hear from you. I thought I saw you the other day when I was in the grocery store."

Anton's cheeks are burning. He had hoped that Carl hadn't noticed him lurking behind the shelves.

"You mean when you were shopping with your boyfriend?" he mumbles. He knows he has no right to an opinion on Carl's love life, yet the question sounds somehow reproachful.

Carl bursts out laughing. "You mean Fredde? He's my younger brother."

"Your brother?"

Anton stares at him in confusion. Thank God the waitress has brought another glass of wine, and he drinks more than half in a single gulp.

Actually they did look very much alike, come to think of it.

Carl brushes aside his uncertainty. "I've thought about you a lot. I hoped you'd get in touch eventually. When you'd finished thinking things over. It was crystal clear that you needed to work out who you are and who you want to be." He places his hand on Anton's. His touch makes Anton's entire body tingle. "And if you want to be with me."

Anton is drowning in Carl's warm gaze. He wants that hand to remain there forever.

What people will think of his sexual orientation has never seemed so unimportant.

Without hesitation he leans across the table and kisses Carl.

For a long time.

124

Alice is asleep in Daniel's arms as he carries her from the car to their apartment. They have been at Ida's mom's for a belated Easter dinner.

"Would you like a cup of tea?" Ida asks once Alice is settled in her cot.

She gives him a sad look which is impossible to interpret. She has been quiet ever since he arrived home on Saturday, not at all her usual energetic self. She is probably as exhausted as he is. He still has a great deal to process following the events in Storlien, and dinner with Elisabeth was an effort, however well meaning his mother-in-law might be.

The emotions from Saturday, the feeling of sheer despair as the hostage drama neared its conclusion, wash over him again. Those moments when he didn't know whether Hanna would survive inside the gloomy hotel.

Ida is already on her way to the kitchen to make tea. Daniel would really like to go to bed, but if she wants them to sit up for a while, then he ought to do it for her sake. They hardly saw each other during Easter week, and he knows how that kind of thing can damage their relationship.

"Sure," he says, following her.

Ida places two mugs on the table, then lights the candles while he fetches milk from the refrigerator.

"We need to talk," she says when they are sitting down and she has poured the tea.

Daniel feels an overwhelming sense of weariness. He knows what this is about. Ida has never liked his job. Or rather, the way he allows himself to be swallowed up by his work when the situation is critical. He has almost been waiting for her to kick off. They have had this discussion frequently in the past; they have talked about her anxiety and her perception that she comes second.

Each time he has done his best to reassure her that she and Alice mean everything to him, whatever happens.

He is doing his best.

What more does she want from him?

Ida blows on her tea, both hands wrapped around her mug. She looks as if she is building up to something.

Daniel is beginning to wonder whether he has read her correctly when she comes out with it.

"I don't know if I'm still in love with you."

He stares at her, utterly confused. This was the last thing he'd expected. Okay, so it's been a struggle since Alice was born, and he is well aware that a large part of the problem is down to him. But he has taken responsibility, he has started to see a therapist, made an effort not to bring his work home.

Ida's eyes are shining with unshed tears. She looks desperately unhappy.

"I think we need to be apart for a while," she continues. "To work out what we want."

She touches the long braid hanging over her shoulder, stares into her mug as if the answers might be there. Then she dashes away a tear with her index finger.

"Sorry," she whispers.

Daniel can't take it in. He hears the words, but he doesn't understand what they mean.

Nothing in his life has prepared him for this.

Ida is looking at him as if she is expecting a response, but Daniel has no idea what he is supposed to say. All he knows is that a debilitating exhaustion is taking over his body.

He feels groggy, dizzy, even though he is stone-cold sober.

When he gets to his feet, he is so disorientated that he can hardly stand, let alone react to what Ida has just said.

"I'm going to bed," he mumbles, staggering out of the kitchen.

"Shouldn't we talk about this?" she calls after him.

"Later."

Daniel can barely keep his eyes open; it is as if the shock is shutting down his system. It is all so bewildering, and he is totally worn out after the past week.

He dare not even consider what Ida's announcement will mean for Alice.

All he wants is to lie down. Fall into a deep slumber that will obliterate reality.

Tomorrow he will try to sort out his life.

Right now he has to sleep.

125

Hanna has spent most of the last two days resting.

She is lying in bed with the covers drawn up to her chin and Morris contentedly curled up on her shoulder. This is a compromise; he would prefer to lie on her chest, but it becomes so hard to breathe that she has shuffled him up a little way.

The bedside lamp is on, the rest of the room is in darkness. It's nice, restful for her eyes.

She has just eaten. She hasn't had the energy to cook a proper meal since she got back from Storlien, but this afternoon Lydia came by with the leftovers from the Easter Saturday lunch that Hanna should have been at. The week certainly didn't turn out the way the sisters had hoped—they hardly saw each other. But today they were able to talk in peace and quiet, Lydia gave Hanna a big hug and listened without interrupting. Tomorrow they are going skiing in Ullådalen; they will sit down on a west-facing slope and have coffee and cake in the afternoon sun.

Enjoy the temperature, which is slightly above freezing, and the feeling of the snow beneath their skis.

Early spring is the best time of the year in Åre.

The experiences from the mountain hotel still linger in the back of her mind, but Hanna hasn't had any difficulty sleeping. Quite the reverse; she wants to sleep all the time. It is as if she used up all her energy on Saturday.

Daniel has been in touch, and Birgitta Grip has reminded Hanna that she has a counseling session booked for later this week. She has assured both of them that she is doing fine, under the circumstances.

Hanna strokes Morris's soft fur. There is a tangled knot by one of his hind legs, and she is trying to tease it out with her fingers when her phone lights up with an incoming call.

It's Henry.

Hanna hesitates, then answers.

"Hello?"

"How are you?"

The warmth in his voice makes her happy. He sounds genuinely concerned.

"I'm really, really tired," she tells him truthfully.

"What you did for Filip . . . I don't know how I'll ever be able to thank you."

"It's my job." She is embarrassed and holds up a dismissive hand, even though he can't see her. "How's he doing?" she asks.

"Improving. I'm picking him up from the hospital in Östersund tomorrow. He was very dehydrated when he was brought in, and apparently he'd also been drugged—that was how Mogren got him into the car. Physically he's okay now, but mentally . . . that's another matter. He's going to need a lot of support—and therapy."

Poor, poor Filip, Hanna thinks. No twenty-three-year-old should have to go through a trauma like that.

"I'm going to ask him to move in with me for a while," Henry goes on. "I think he needs a stable home environment, even if he does have Emily."

"Sounds like a sensible idea."

Hanna is glad that Henry is taking care of his godson. If Erik Mogren had had an adult by his side when his mother died, then maybe things would have turned out differently. Broken people can do terrible things in order to ease their own pain.

The events of the past week provide tragic proof.

"Hanna," Henry says, lowering his voice, "I'm taking Filip to Stockholm, but I'm coming up again in a few weeks. There's a lot to sort out with the Storlien project now Charlotte is gone."

Hanna sinks back against the pillow. The only sound in her bedroom is Morris's contented purring. Tiredness is creeping up on her again, and she closes her eyes for a few seconds.

"I was wondering if we could meet up when I'm back? I'd like to invite you to dinner, to say thank you for everything you did." Henry falls silent, then laughs as if he is embarrassed by his own words. "Actually . . . that's just an excuse. I was really thinking of it as more of . . . a date."

Hanna's tummy tingles. She props herself up on one elbow, disturbing Morris, and waits for Henry to go on.

"I've never met anyone like you," he says. "I think you're . . . fantastic."

A smile spreads across her face. There is something about Henry; he makes her feel safe.

And desirable.

It's been many months—no, years—since she experienced that sensation.

"Do you?" she replies, making no attempt to hide the pleasure his words have given her.

"Yes," he says slowly. "Absolutely. I would love to see you again."

His voice is warm, his words sincere.

They find their way deep inside Hanna, melt something that has been cold and frozen for far too long.

"If that's okay?" he adds. "If you want to?"

ACKNOWLEDGMENTS

From day one it has been a pure pleasure to write *Hidden in Memories*, and I have been fortunate enough to receive help from many people both in Åre and elsewhere.

I have taken certain liberties in dramatizing the hostage negotiation and the actions taken by the police in Storlien, but they are largely true to real life. However, for the sake of the plot, I have made the local council a landowner in Storlien, although in fact the area is privately owned. I must stress that both the political committee and the corrupt politician in Åre are entirely fictional, as is the angry Facebook group and all the employees at Copperhill Mountain Lodge (which, by the way, has no concierge department).

Mrs Maggie's restaurant in Duved features in the novel, even though it didn't actually open until September 2021.

I take full responsibility for any possible errors in the narrative.

Warm thanks to Eva Ottosson Rask, director of Copperhill Mountain Lodge, and to Detective Inspector Andreas Zehlander, group chief Åre/Krokom, who generously answered countless questions during the course of the journey.

I am also deeply grateful to the following people who have given freely of their time and knowledge:

- Sanna Matsson, police commissioner, head of violent crimes, Östersund
- Lars-Göran Berglund, group chief for the regional SWAT team, Östersund
- Mikael Johansson, property supervisor, Storlien mountain hotel
- Janne Werkelin, partner, Åregården
- Daniel Danielsson, chair of Åre council
- Inspector Erik Norlander, Åre, dog handler
- Sergeant Lars Olsson, Åre, former dog handler

I have gained much pleasure and useful information from listening to the Umeå police podcast and the Öst/Eastern police podcast, which have provided a real insight into police work.

Thanks as always to Detective Inspector Rolf Hansson, who has helped me with various manuscripts for many years, and to my dear friends Anette Brifalk, Helen Duphorn, Madeleine Lyrvall, and Gunilla Petersson, who all read and commented on the manuscript during the writing process. Thanks also to Ulrika Bauman Edblad in Åre for her wise observations.

An author is nothing without her publisher. I would therefore like to thank my wonderful publisher Ebba Östberg and my good friend and development editor John Häggblom. My fantastically committed editor Lisa Jonasdotter Nilsson battled with the text to the bitter end. Thank you, Lisa—you made this book immeasurably better.

As always it has been a privilege to work with the super professional Sofia Heurlin and everyone else at Bokförlaget Forum, and to the amazing PR gang at Micael Bindefeld AB.

Anna Frankl, you are a super-agent and wonderful to work with! Thanks also to Joakim Hansson and everyone else at Nordin Agency, as well as my terrific assistant, Madeleine Jonsson.

My beloved daughter and colleague Camilla Sten has contributed invaluable opinions for which I am very grateful.

Finally—thank you, my darling Lennart. Because you are always there for me.

Åre, September 1, 2022
Viveca Sten

ABOUT THE AUTHOR

Photo © 2023 Peter Knutson

Viveca Sten is the author of *Hidden in Snow, Hidden in Shadows,* and *Hidden in Memories* in the Åre Murders series—which has been adapted into a runaway #1 hit series on Netflix—and *Buried in Secret, In Bad Company, In the Name of Truth, In the Shadow of Power, In Harm's Way, In the Heat of the Moment, Tonight You're Dead, Guiltless, Closed Circles,* and *Still Waters* in the #1 internationally bestselling Sandhamn Murders series. Since 2008, her books have sold more than ten million copies, and the Sandhamn Murders series has been adapted into a Swedish-language TV series shot on location and seen by an estimated one hundred million viewers around the world, in close to a hundred countries. Today, Viveca divides her time between Stockholm, Sandhamn, and Åre. For more information, visit www.vivecasten.com.

ABOUT THE TRANSLATOR

Marlaine Delargy lives in Shropshire in the United Kingdom. She studied Swedish and German at the University of Wales, Aberystwyth, and she taught German for almost twenty years. She has translated novels by many authors, including Kristina Ohlsson, Helene Tursten, John Ajvide Lindqvist, Therese Bohman, Theodor Kallifatides, Johan Theorin, with whom she won the Crime Writers' Association International Dagger in 2010, and Henning Mankell, with whom she won the Crime Writers' Association International Dagger in 2018. Marlaine has also translated nine books in Viveca Sten's Sandhamn Murders series, and *Hidden in Snow*, *Hidden in Shadows*, and *Hidden in Memories* in Sten's Åre Murders series.

Printed in Dunstable, United Kingdom